An award-winning social communications and brand adviser by profession and a musician at heart, **Victor Ghoshe** is an explorer and a social researcher.

Ghoshe writes in the historical thriller and paranormal genres. Deeply researched, his historical thriller *The Job Charnock Riddle* topped the charts as an Amazon bestseller of 2016. TIMES described the book as 'Our own Da Vinci Code version'.

Former senior adviser to BBC Media Action, Ghoshe's literary works have been translated into several languages.

Ghoshe lives in New Delhi, India with his wife Juthika and two sons, Shivaank and Hrishaant.

TOMB OF GOD

VICTOR GHOSHE

RUPA

Published by
Rupa Publications India Pvt. Ltd 2021
7/16, Ansari Road, Daryaganj
New Delhi 110002

Sales centres:
Allahabad Bengaluru Chennai
Hyderabad Jaipur Kathmandu
Kolkata Mumbai

Copyright © Victor Ghoshe 2021

All rights reserved.

No part of this publication may be reproduced, transmitted,
or stored in a retrieval system, in any form or by any means,
electronic, mechanical, photocopying, recording or otherwise,
without the prior permission of the publisher.

This is a work of fiction. Names, characters, places and incidents are either the
product of the author's imagination or are used fictitiously and any resemblance
to any actual person, living or dead, events or locales is entirely coincidental.

ISBN: 978-93-89967-70-8

First impression 2021

10 9 8 7 6 5 4 3 2 1

The moral right of the author has been asserted.

Printed at Thomson Press India Ltd., Faridabad

This book is sold subject to the condition that it shall not,
by way of trade or otherwise, be lent, resold, hired out, or otherwise circulated,
without the publisher's prior consent, in any form of
binding or cover other than that in which it is published.

To my sons
Shivank & Hrishaant

In the limitless space and infinite time,
it's bliss to be able to create something for you.
I hope you discover the romance and dangers of adventure
and fall in love with it.

*The most beautiful thing we can experience is the mysterious.
It is the source of all art and science. He to whom this emotion is a
stranger, who can no longer pause to wonder and stand rapt in awe,
is as good as dead; his eyes are closed.*

—*Albert Einstein*

And a river went out of Eden to water the garden. And from thence it was parted and became into four heads. The name of the first is Pison, and the name of the second river is Gihon, and the name of the third river is Tigris; it flows east of Assyria. And the fourth river is Euphrates. And the Lord God took the man and put him into the Garden of Eden to dress it and keep it.

—Excerpt from *Genesis 2:10–15, The Bible*

Na nuunam daivatam kincit kaalena balavattaram
(There is no God more powerful than time)

—*Valmiki Ramayana*, 2-88-11

Dedication generates knowledge,
and the Vedas say—knowledge is freedom.

—Tulsidas in *A Garden of Deeds: Ramcharitmanas,
A Message of Human Ethics,* p. 37

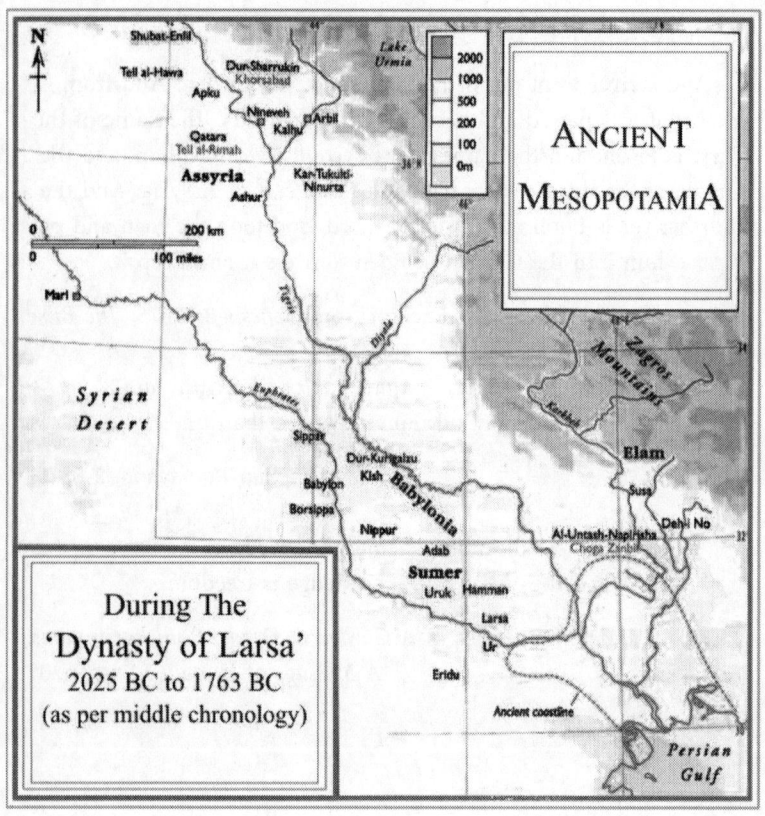

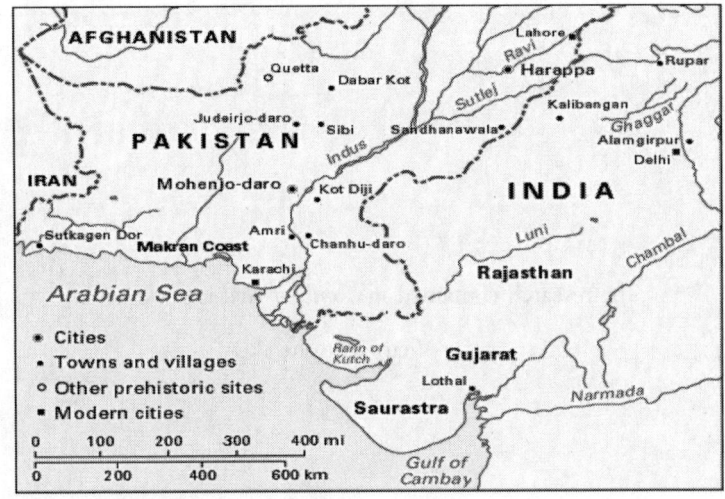

Ancient Harappan Civilisation

Note: Maps are not to scale

The research contained in *Tomb of God* is accurate.

—Victor Ghoshe

PROLOGUE

The Mesopotamian City of Nimrud, 730 BC

The after-world chamber for Queen Yaba was built a few days ago. And it was now ready for her earthly body.

Leaning on an outer wall of the chamber, Ninki stood all by herself. She rubbed her palm across the fresh white surface and felt the dampness from the last coat of plaster. Her body shivered, her heart hammered loud enough that she could hear it, yet she knew she had to finish the job before she was dead. She wrote faster on the damp surface of the wall.

Ninki knew her brother was far away, finishing a secret task. A task that involved using a skill their family had nurtured for generations. She believed he would eventually come back for her. But she would not survive long enough to meet him. So she had to leave a message for him—a message that would take him on the trail of the secret she had been harbouring. But she had to be quick about it, for it was almost time for the queen's funeral.

She hoped her brother would appreciate her idea. Maybe he would smile and call her smart; maybe he would shed a tear for her. She used the skill her grandfather had taught her—writing coded cuneiform; she etched on the soft plaster of the outer wall of the tomb. Drops of sweat formed on her forehead and trickled down to her eyelashes but she didn't care. She had to leave clues for her brother—and she had to make sure no one but he understood the message that would lead him to her body, to the tablet she clutched and then to the place where a centuries-old secret was hidden, for they were the last of its keepers.

Finishing her work, she stood up and looked at it for the last time. She blinked, drawing herself fully back to the moment at hand. She clutched the round-shaped tablet her grandfather had helped her make before dying…that would be her last earthly connection to her brother. She wiped hot tears and took stock of the situation. She had done her part; now it was time for her to go. The prospect dismayed her, but she hurried along towards the entrance of the chamber, where other serving men and women had, in all likelihood, gathered already.

Ninki joined the other men and women walking down to the great death pit—a name they had given the newly built after-world chamber for Queen Yaba. All of them had already tied the gold and silver ribbons on their arms. Ninki stumbled along with the group, clasping in her palm the tablet which was much more precious to her than her own life, for it held the secret of a hidden place of immense value. She tried to coil one of the ribbons around her arm with only one thought in her mind—would the message that she held in her hand survive? It had to. It was the only remaining clue to a secret that had the power to change the world in the time to come.

Ninki was yet to finish tying the ribbon when the lead server handed her the potion, which she gulped down before going back to fastening the ribbon. But the potion took hold of her body before she could finish. And with that started the painless process of her being carried away to the afterworld, leaving behind her earthly body and a message hidden in her earthly hand. She fell to her knees on the dusty ground and her whole body shuddered. Tears streamed down her cheeks; she began to pray to her God—Nanna, the Moon God. Her muscles gave up and she dropped to the ground, lifeless. Her right arm continued to clutch the tablet. Half-tied to her left hand, the silver ribbon swayed for eternity, and the entrance to the chamber was slowly sealed from outside.

ONE

Thar Desert, Rajasthan, north-western part of India
Present day, early October

There are bad days. And then there are really bad days.

The sun, like a ball of fire up in the sky, scorched everything beneath at forty degrees Celsius.

With no viable escape from the heat, things seemed to be getting a little too much for Haban Sangma. The gamocha—Assamese cotton towel—he had tied loosely around his head struggled in the dusty hot wind that blew from the West. Wherever he looked, there was an endless ocean of sand. Only, the dunes were not the usual shifting piles of sand—there were many high sand hillocks rising here and there from beneath the surface.

Haban mumbled a profanity in his native tongue. Hailing from Meghalaya in north-eastern India, he had never, in his twenty-eight years of life, experienced such a hot wind. It had only been a couple of hours since he had left his tent after lunch and the October sun was already making the water almost boil even inside his well-insulated water bottle. This was not the first time he was cursing himself for agreeing to join this natural gas exploration project for a multinational oil company, the one that had brought him to this terrible place.

Haban pushed his sunglasses a little higher up his nose and pulled out the water bottle from a sling across his left shoulder. *Before the goddamn sun vaporizes my water into steam, I might as well take a few sips*—he finished the thought with the same cuss word he had mumbled moments ago, albeit aloud this time, and gulped down some water, wincing because of its temperature.

He placed his hand on the flaming, sunburnt skin of his face and felt the two-day-old stubble. This was not how he had planned to spend his late twenties when he had joined Assam Petrochemicals two years back. He'd thought he would not have to go far from his home state, or at the very least not step outside the north-east. But then his company sent him for a two-year-long training to Nobel Oil Company, United Kingdom (UK), and eventually got him to join this exploration project in Rajasthan.

Haban looked around him again. The tents and the transmitter mast of the camp stood in the distance on his right, barely visible through the blistering heatwaves. To his left was a mound of sand. 'That one would give me a better view of the place,' he mumbled.

The IT guys had already marked out ten satellite-selected locations on his mobile application. Now all he really had to do was identify those ten pre-selected spots on the ground and insert four-feet-long metal sticks with special microphones installed in them inside the sand—all of which would then be connected with the newly developed application in his cell phone. The application would do the rest of the work by sending different sonic frequencies through the earth's surface and analysing their feedback signals. Nobel Oil Company claimed that when their new application would be launched, the orthodox oil surveys that involved massive preparation and thousands of man-hours would become a thing of the past.

He started walking in the direction of the mound. After a good fifteen minutes he reached the bottom and started to climb. The mound was by no means tall, but seemed to be the tallest of the bunch of sand hillocks nearby. It stood like a watchtower in the vast desert wasteland of Thar. As he climbed, his walkie-talkie came to life with a message from the camp. Jabbar had been sending him a message every two hours, a practice mandated by the company protocols. Haban reached the top and uttered a short 'back in an hour' into the walkie-talkie before returning it to its position on a metal hook on his belt. He reached for the bottle once again and drank some more water, then poured some on his handkerchief and rubbed it on the back of his neck.

Haban casually looked down at his surroundings from the top

of the mound and something next to his feet caught his attention. He immediately sat on his haunches to get a better look. It was small in size and looked unfamiliar. He decided to pick it up for closer inspection. But as he reached out with his right hand, the ground beneath his feet moved with a sudden jerk.

Before Haban could react or find his balance, the sand receded from under his feet and he began sliding down a crack on the side of the mound created by the tremor. His throat was choked with sand before he could let out a cry, and he continued his descent downhill, banging into stones and inhaling unfathomable amounts of dust on the way. All he could think of was to try to protect his face with his hands as he bounced off the newly exposed rocks, but his forehead hit something hard and he blacked out.

◆

The first thing Haban felt when he came to his senses was a weird tasteless substance in his mouth. It was stuck around his tongue. He coughed and spat out a mouthful of coagulated sand. His head throbbed where the stone had hit him. He tried to sit up, but his back resisted, and he thought better of it. He barely managed to lift his left hand and rub his eyes free of sand so that he could see. He then checked his belt for the walkie-talkie, only to feel nothing in its place.

Haban looked up to figure out where he was. He realized that he had tumbled down the mound. As his eyes adjusted to the light, he looked around and discovered that the shape of the mound had changed. From over his left shoulder, he noticed an opening in the side of the mound—a deep cavern exposed by the sunlight. He thanked his stars that he hadn't fallen straight down into it. The sharp stony insides of the cave would have killed him instantly.

As he tried to stand up, he gasped in pain. But pushing the thoughts of pain aside, he stretched his legs and instantly felt something roll away from beneath his left foot.

It was a round object, about four inches in diameter. 'This is what I found up there. Could it possibly be a clay tablet?' Haban muttered. 'Perhaps a hard-burnt one.' He took the object in his hand for inspection and winced from the pain in his lower back, as also from what could be a pulled muscle in his left leg. The seven-or-eight-millimetre-thick tablet had a hole in the middle and some familiar inscriptions on one side. It didn't seem to be made of clay though. It felt rather metallic to the touch. Haban pushed his sunglasses to the top of his head to see the tablet in better light. 'Not clay for sure—the fine concentric circles on both sides are etched too perfectly for that. It looks like the work of a machine. Could this be metal?' he wondered. 'I will have a better look later and shall keep it as a memento,' he told himself as he stowed away the tiny object in his pocket.

Haban then set about in search of his walkie-talkie. He walked, dragging along his injured leg, towards the entrance of the cavern. He was still struggling with the thought of how the look of the entire place had changed in a moment. 'Was it a quake? That's too large a gorge to have just opened out of nowhere!' he mumbled. *Unless it was always here, only hidden beneath layers of sand brought in by the desert winds over several hundred years*—his chain of thoughts was interrupted as his eyes spotted the walkie-talkie a little way inside the entrance to the cavern, lying lifeless along with a few more round tablet-like objects akin to the one he had pocketed. 'Good God!' he limped towards the walkie-talkie, lying battered and full of sand. He hoped it would still be in working condition. It wasn't a Chinese handset, after all.

He stood in the shadow of the cavern and switched on the device. Yes, it was alive. Adjusting his eyes to the low light inside, he carefully bent over to glance deeper into the cavern.

What he saw surprised him so much that he almost dropped the walkie-talkie again.

'What is this!' he exclaimed, his eyes widening with surprise. 'Could this be an ancient treasure trove?' he wondered. 'But this is the Thar Desert, for God's sake!'

Still recovering from his amazement, Haban looked closely to assess what lay deeper inside the cavern. He took out his cell phone from his pocket and pressed a button. 'It's working!' he cried in disbelief and quickly took some pictures as proof of his incredible discovery before coming out of the cavern.

As he limped back towards his camp, Haban couldn't help thinking that things were happening rather too fast for his comfort. He wiped the sweat off his face with the long sleeve of his shirt. He stopped in his tracks and stood still, silently debating with himself. He had three options: he could either keep the discovery to himself, tell his bosses about the find or inform the local authorities. His mind tried calculating the possible consequences of each decision. If he kept it to himself, there was no way he could take home the bounty without first making a huge investment, which seemed impossible. If he told his bosses, he might still make something out of the bounty, since they were powerful people with a global presence and influence. And if he informed the local authorities, it was likely that they would promise him something in exchange for the location and then have him killed and dumped beneath the sand somewhere in this desert without leaving behind any trace.

He looked back, committed the site to his memory and took some more perspective snaps on his cell phone to be sure of the location. He had zeroed in on his next step by then. He would contact his employer as soon as he reached camp, send them the photographs he had taken and wait for their instructions.

'I can't believe it—this is huge!' Unaware of what lay in store for him in the near future, he exclaimed, 'I am going to be rich! Bloody rich!'

◆

'Almost there,' Haban mumbled as he spotted the dish and the transmitter pole of his camp in the distance. He stopped to catch his breath while his leg and lower back continued to throb and his forehead bled. He took out his cell phone and started keying in a message. It was long, and Haban had to delete and rewrite it several times to set the tone right. He added some of the pictures he had clicked and pushed the 'send' button with a smile playing on his lips. He tried to imagine the facial expression of his boss when he read the message.

The message did not transmit in the first go. Haban walked closer to the camp and tried again, this time succeeding in sending it. He reached the tent soon after, where he washed up. He then took out some antiseptic lotion from the first aid box they carried and applied it on his wounds.

Then he called out to Jabbar to make a strong cup of coffee for him. As Jabbar got busy with the kerosene stove in the corner, Haban changed into comfortable pyjamas and a t-shirt and hung up the day's clothes on a hanger. He flipped through all the photographs he had clicked a little while ago. 'This is the best thing that has ever happened to me in my life,' he smiled as he slid the phone into his shirt's pocket.

◆

Early next morning Haban woke up to an unusual buzzing sound coming from a distance. He sat up on his bed roll and asked Jabbar to check what was happening. Jabbar was making breakfast. He walked out of the tent, only to come back in for the binoculars. 'Looks like a chopper,' he exclaimed from outside, 'but...' his incomplete sentence hung in the desert air as a deafening sound overpowered it. The powerful sound hit Haban standing inside the tent, shaking the ground with it.

'It's a big noise!' Haban rushed outside, and he didn't have to look far to be shocked. The mound he had climbed yesterday—the hillock with the unimaginable treasure inside—had been wiped out. Dark clouds of smoke emerged from the very place, covering a large part of the early morning sky.

Soon after the explosive reverberation, Haban heard the buzz again. A moment later, from behind the clouds of black smoke, appeared a single-seat attack helicopter.

It came straight towards their camp. 'My God...' As Haban uttered these words, a long, dark object was dropped from the belly of the helicopter. The last thing Haban saw was the ominous-looking object coming straight at him.

The next moment the camp, along with its occupants, was blown to smithereens in a violent storm of fire and metal fragments. All that remained of its existence were mutilated human body parts, scraps of cloth and metal in the middle of the Thar Desert.

TWO

Kolkata, India
Present day, 12.30 p.m.

'Except for one UN mission to Iraq, scorching Middle East isn't really my thing,' said Eric. 'I am more of a professor teaching history in different universities of the world—especially those sweeping European universities with landscaped campuses, surrounded by nature and well-mannered people.'

'But this one is different,' said Eric's long-time friend and senior colleague in archaeology, Dr Huntley. They were sitting in the Departures lounge of Kolkata Airport. An exceptionally tall waiter brought their meal. Eric raised the bowl to his nose to take in the smell of his steaming hot almond chicken with honey.

'Oh, how much I miss Aurin whenever I get to eat good food!' he exclaimed.

'How is Auri boy anyway? Is he still in England finishing his studies, or has he returned?' Dr Huntley inquired after Eric's brother.

'He is fine. Last week when I checked, he was in the UK, planning a trip to India for a cross-country bike rally,' Eric said, rolling his eyes.

'I'll call him in the evening for updates.'

'That's good,' said Dr Huntley, 'this is the right age for adventure!'

'Well, you and I are exceptions to the rule then!' Eric smiled, his thumbs gently rubbing his temples in a circular motion. His eyes were visibly bleary from lack of sleep.

'Eric, I can see you are tired, and I also know why.'

'Why?' Eric raised one brow.

'You are tired of urban life, Eric. You need your dope.'

'And what do you think my "dope" is?' Eric asked.

'Adventure! Pure adventure, my friend!' Dr Huntley grinned.

Eric was about to respond, but a waiter interrupted. 'Your lamb kung pao will be served in two minutes, sir,' the waiter bowed and informed Dr Huntley, forcing the grin on his lips to give way to a benign smile.

◆

At forty-one, all Eric wanted was a quiet life with lots of aesthetics. He had begun to hate violence, for wherever he went, people were either killed or died for the wrong reasons. While he had given up the position of Additional Director at the Archaeological Survey of India (ASI) a few years back, the field life of his earlier days had already taken a toll on his health. A part of many prestigious excavations in India and abroad, Eric had had a very busy career as a seasoned archaeologist. Eric's senior colleague and friend Dr Peter Huntley was over seventy; he was stout and had a stark white beard. He was a British archaeologist who had retired from his regular archaeology work and now headed a museum-cum-historical-research facility in Trongsa, Bhutan.

Eric looked at least seven or eight years younger than his age. His face appeared to be chiselled out of granite, with sharp lines, thick cheekbones, dark eyes, short black hair with a hint of grey around the temples and the tanned, rough features of a man who had spent a great deal of time outdoors. Anyone with even a little experience in the sun could tell the weathering of this man's face was equatorial and harsh. The thin crinkling around his child-like eyes told stories of his excavations and gunfights—especially stories of squinting down the barrels of guns with a finger on the trigger while taking a call on whether to pull it or not. His belly looked flat and hard and there were thick cords of muscle in his neck and arms. His scarred hands looked like they could crack jawbones at the drop of an eyelid.

Starting out as a hands-on archaeologist with ASI, Eric's academic mind had helped him bag a bureaucratic position at a very young age. Recently, however, he had quit his high-profile government job and embarked on a career in academics as a history lecturer in Presidency College, Kolkata. Barring a couple of people, no one in his circle of family and friends knew that under the façade of an academic job, he was secretly involved with India's intelligence agency, Research and Analysis Wing (RAW), and heading a special wing. Even his cousin Aurin had been unaware of this until one of their recent adventures together.

Eric's aunt's son, Aurin, was around seventeen years his junior and doing his doctoral research in Art History at the University of Oxford in the UK. Just eight months earlier, they had been part of a rescue mission that had ended up being a treasure hunt based on a three-hundred-year-old riddle—the Job Charnock Riddle.

◆

'All right,' said Eric, 'let me tell you something, Dr Huntley. You are my senior in the field of archaeology and have always been there for me. But that can't be enough reason for me to tag along with you to Iraq for an excavation based on bits of half-cooked information!' He then changed his tone. 'I understand it's a very interesting lead for you, and you don't want to miss the chance of unearthing an ancient secret in the Sumerian ruins. But what possible reason could there be for me to give up six months of my life to burn in northern Iraq, digging desert sand with you, when I have a perfectly good job at a world-class university with ten promised lectures in five other European universities and an offer to write a book on our recent adventure that led us to the Job Charnock treasure?'

Dr Huntley looked into Eric's eyes. 'Because the last thing anyone needs is another adventure book,' he smirked. 'Don't you see, Eric, kids do not read books any more; they are hooked to their gadgets, 3D video games and online chats. Grow up, boy… I have nothing against your teaching career, but the world is moving much faster than you think.'

'Okay, so what are you offering me besides heatstroke, blisters and ruthless desert robbers?'

'Well, I haven't yet shared everything with you, Eric.' Dr Huntley took a deep breath and continued, 'It's quite a story!'

◆

Dr Huntley closed his eyes and stroked his forehead with his thumb and index finger for a few seconds to clear his thoughts. Then he spoke. 'Nimrud is one of the great ancient cities of the Assyrians, who dominated Mesopotamia from the tenth century BC up to 612 BC, before the Persians destroyed them. In 1988, my friend Dr Muzahem Hussein, an Iraqi archaeologist, was digging under the royal palace in Nimrud and sensed he was standing on a hidden chamber. He eventually engaged more people and uncovered a tomb which was later identified as belonging to the eighth century BC.

'Inside the tomb rested two women, perhaps queens. They were placed in the same sarcophagus, one on top of the other, and covered in embroidered linen and ornate gold jewellery. One of the women had been dried and smoked at high temperatures, giving us the first evidence of mummification-like practices in ancient Mesopotamia.'

'Although I have heard about this excavation in parts, I remain, as ever, a huge fan of your storytelling abilities,' Eric interrupted Dr Huntley. 'Your narrative about Dr Hussein's discovery is getting more interesting by the minute; please carry on.' Eric eased his body into the soft backrest of his chair with more than just a hint of seriousness in his voice.

Dr Huntley shrugged. 'Apparently the tomb contained a curse,' he said, 'meant to descend upon the person who opened the grave of Queen Yaba, the queen of Tiglath-Pileser III—the king who reigned from 745 to 727 BC. The first woman was Queen Yaba, and the second, Atilia, the queen of Sargon II—the king who ruled Assyria from 722 to 705 BC. Their identities were inscribed in cuneiforms inside a gold bowl found inside the sarcophagus.'

The lamb kung pao arrived, and Dr Huntley got busy serving himself a sizeable portion.

He continued, 'Several male and female corpses were also found inside the tomb, though none of them had a sarcophagus. Hussein noted them to be slaves who might have been buried along with their mistress. One of the female corpses was found clutching a small, round tablet in her hand. It particularly caught Hussein's attention since the woman, unlike all other slaves, seemed to have still been coiling her arm band when she died. Hussein found it abnormal for a girl who knew she was about to die to keep holding on to a tablet. He instinctively knew the tablet was of immense importance.

'Hussein retained the tablet for later inspection. He also discovered cuneiform scripts on an outer wall of the chamber. The writing, apart from a few similarities, was different from the regular Sumerian script. The little part of the message that he could decipher from his knowledge of the Sumerian script mentioned a girl and a tablet that had directions to 'the secret tomb of the Moon God'. He couldn't decipher the entire message and took pictures to check it later. Hussein inferred that the tablet mentioned in the cuneiform message was the one he had found on the female corpse. On pure instinct, he neither enlisted the tablet as a find nor talked about it with his team.'

Dr Huntley stopped. He cut a small piece of the juicy lamb on his plate and popped it in his mouth. He took his time to chew his food and finally said, 'A year later, Hussein had managed to decipher a little more of the coded message he had photographed on the wall and went back to the site with a new excavation permit, in search of the secret tomb.'

'Was this in 1989?' Eric interrupted.

'Yes.' Dr Huntley replied. 'Now, here is the most interesting part, Eric...'

'Yes, I am with you,' Eric prompted.

'This time he found a second tomb, some six hundred metres away from the first site, which was hundreds of years older than the previous one. But this one had been looted by tomb robbers thousands of years ago. After months of excavation, Hussein made a brilliant discovery. He found an antechamber full of priceless artefacts and gold ornaments that the looters had somehow missed. This antechamber also contained a large bronze coffin with the body of a middle-aged man, a vessel that held a ten-inch gold replica of a ship within and a round tablet that looked absolutely similar to the one he had found earlier. The chamber was filled with gold jewellery and a pile of gold figurines and furniture. The middle-aged man appeared to be a powerful naval general and Hussein was intrigued to study everything in the tomb thoroughly. He decided to keep the ship and the tablet for his own discreet collection.

'The mummy and the rest of the treasures were on display for a few months before the Persian Gulf War broke out in 1991. The display was packed away in haste and stored in a vault beneath Baghdad's central bank for protection. The bank was bombed, burned and flooded during the 2003 invasion of Iraq, and the treasure was never found.'

'The point...?' Eric interrupted, wiping his mouth with a napkin.

Dr Huntley seemed to jolt out of his reverie and return to the present moment and place. 'The point...the point...' he repeated Eric's words a couple of times until he remembered what he had been talking about. 'The point—yes! Actually, there is a twist in the tale, and it occurred very recently.' Dr Huntley tented his fingers on the table and looked up at the ceiling to compose his thoughts before finally speaking up.

'After his discovery of the antechamber and the hidden treasures, Hussein had a health issue and decided to take some years off from fieldwork. He took up a lecturer's position at a university in British Columbia, Canada and settled there. Now, as recently as a few weeks ago, while he was cleaning his study, he found both the tablets neatly stored in a box. Once again intrigued by the mystery that surrounded them, he dug up the old photographs he had clicked of the tomb's outer wall and started working on the cuneiforms with renewed energy.

'This time, he was able to decipher some additional part of the wall writing and read that inside the secret tomb of the Moon God that is mentioned in the inscription, there is supposed to be a divine secret, and the trail that leads to it lies in the writing itself.' Dr Huntley stopped to eat another chunk of meat topped with kimchi salad and then continued, 'After a series of discussions, we figured out this place could be Nineveh, which is very close to Nimrud, the place where Hussein found the two tombs and the antechamber.'

'Yes, three is kind of a comfortable number, I have seen,' blurted Eric. 'People generally stop looking for things after finding three!'

'That's a wonderful insight!' Dr Huntley smiled in approval. 'But Hussein didn't stop there. He ran some calculations and identified a few spots at Nineveh that could be excavated. Right now, even as we speak, he must be narrowing down the options to one or two sites. He has got new excavation orders for Nineveh and Nimrud from the General Directorate of Antiquities of Kurdistan, and I am joining his team in Baghdad tomorrow. We will reach Nineveh by late evening and start the excavation work in a day or two.'

'When does Dr Hussein join you?' Eric asked.

'That's the point,' Dr Huntley banged his hand on the table. 'Hussein is at his university campus in Vancouver, as he has fractured his leg. He thinks he will be able to join us in another two weeks. That is really why I was requesting you to join me.'

'So you need an interim guy?' Eric grimaced.

'Not an interim guy, Eric!' Dr Huntley rolled his eyes, visibly agitated. 'You know how I love to talk and discuss! And you know how very important these discussions are to an excavation like this!'

A smile replaced his agitated expression as he tried to figure out if he had already convinced Eric or needed to say more.

'Forget it!' he sighed, for Eric didn't appear convinced. 'You are still the stubborn lamb you've always been,' he banged his hand on the table again. 'Can I at least list down your number as an emergency contact?' he asked.

'Of course,' Eric smiled back. 'After all, how many stubborn lambs do you have in your phone book that you can count on?'

THREE

Kolkata,
Next day, 6.30 a.m.

In less than forty-two hours of his last visit to see Dr Huntley, Eric was back at Netaji Subhas Chandra Bose International Airport. Only this time, he was the one flying. The previous night, sometime between dinner and midnight, he had received a call from his senior, Dr Naidu. The conversation was rather short, but serious enough for him to embark on a journey early that morning.

The previous morning, RAW's Satellite Information Analytics Division (SIAD) had tracked down information of a missile attack in the Thar Desert, not very far from Bikaner in Rajasthan. Though the Rajasthan police didn't report the incident—they probably didn't even know about it—the SIAD had reported it to the higher authorities, and the authorities had sought the assistance of the Special Intelligence Bureau (SIB) in the case, mostly because of two reasons. First, the area was really close to the India–Pakistan border, and second, the

SIAD had reported that more than one military-grade guided missile had been used in the attack.

◆

Eric Roy secretly ran the newly formed SIB at the RAW. Working closely with Dr Naidu—a retired officer of the Indian Armed Forces—and partially reporting to the Ministry of Home Affairs, this side of Eric's life was full of action, unlike the academic one.

RAW is the largest intelligence wing of the Republic of India, which meant Eric's job involved dealing with death and other rough things happening within and outside the country. One of the biggest misconceptions about RAW is their role in stopping crime. They rarely send out agents to investigate a case. Instead, they have state-level offices called Regional Bureaus that are monitored by the SIB. From there, all facts are entered into a central database that can be accessed via RAW's network. Fingerprints, DNA information, terrorist updates, high-priced smuggled artefacts, updates on other investigations—all of it is available twenty-four hours a day, three hundred and sixty five days a year.

But then again, it isn't always enough. Sometimes a head of a small division is forced to hop on a plane and take control of a case—possibly to cut through red tape or handle a border-related issue or to deal with the media. Eric hated doing most of these things. He believed that in this line of work, the only things that mattered were fair play and justice. Correcting a wrong in the fairest way possible was the philosophy he lived by. His grandfather had always told him, 'If you can work on this, boy, then all the other shit will take care of themselves.'

◆

Police inspector Hukum Singh had the pathologist of the state government-run hospital morgue remove the flap of the blue tarpaulin sheet to reveal the fragments of the two bodies the police had recovered from the desert.

'Any cell phone found?' Eric asked in a low voice, looking at the horrible scene laid out on the table before him.

'Nahi—no cell phones were found', came the prompt and sharp reply from Hukum Singh.

'Who found them?' Eric asked, this time with more command in his voice.

'A team of our desert patrol found them.'

'You really have desert patrols? I have my doubts,' Eric grimaced.

'Apparently, yes,' Hukum Singh said sourly. 'And you can't insult me like that just because you are from the Special Bureau!' he added.

'I am not insulting you!' Eric smiled, without taking his eyes off Hukum Singh's face. 'I am only surprised why this incident was not reported and why the Bureau had to be informed by the SIAD team. Do you understand what we are dealing with here? Do you have any clue what type of weapons can cause this kind of damage? Do you understand your responsibilities as the officer-in-charge of a border station that falls inside a well-defined conflict corridor? And do you understand the consequences of not cooperating with a senior agent?'

The tall policeman lowered his eyes, his teeth biting down on his lower lip.

Eric tried not to smile. He had just busted the huge balloon of Hukum Singh's feudal arrogance, and had loved doing it. In his mind, he knew he would continue to do so until Singh learned to take orders from a senior agent. At times when he was furious, Eric let people know who he was and how much authority he held. It always helped him get his job done without being asked stupid questions and without any delay.

'Make sure I get a detailed report by 7 p.m. at my hotel,' he growled, looking at the corpses. 'Now arrange a taxi to take me to the site of the incident. And I do not want any of your men to be around while I am investigating.'

Hukum Singh's arrogance had disappeared by now. He mumbled a quiet 'Ji, sir-ji' and darted towards the morgue door to follow Eric's orders.

FOUR

Bikaner,
2.15 p.m.

Eric stood on the sand dunes under the blistering midday sun, about twenty-five kilometres outside Bikaner city. The sky was solid blue without a single wisp of cloud in sight. There was a faint smell of explosives in the air. The heat came down on Eric particularly brutally after the air-conditioned tourist car Hukum Singh had arranged for him. The car was parked a few kilometres away, on a narrow strip of asphalt, along with its driver. Eric could feel the sweat trickling down his body under his shirt. An uncomfortable sensation ran down his spine...he didn't want to be out there any longer than was absolutely necessary.

Far below the sand dune he stood on, the site of the explosion was obvious. A smattering of tarpaulin scraps, bits and pieces of cloth, twisted shards of utensils and remnants of a ruined communication system lay about inside a huge circle of discoloured sand. A sad reminder of a moment that took away two lives forever.

Eric distracted his mind from sliding into a swamp of emotion. He walked down to the site and focused on the scattered remains of the massacred camp, and on everything his eyes could see and his mind could read. Everything looked obvious and quite easy to explain, yet something about this incident didn't quite add up for him. He bent down and looked at the torn pieces of clothing that still clung to a metal hanger made of thin wire. He pulled out those sand-covered remnants of a shirt and a pair of trousers and searched the pockets.

And there it was—a congealed piece of metal scrap still in the shirt pocket. 'Cell phone,' he whispered as he carefully put the metal object along with the cloth bits in a plastic bag as evidence, and slipped it in the pocket of his cargo pants. The next thing he discovered was unfamiliar to him. One of the pockets of the pair of trousers held a small tablet-like object. Round in shape with a hole at the centre, it had an ancient look about it. Eric was sure it was not one of those regular clay seals found from the ancient Kalibangan excavation sites in this region—this one had a different feel to it.

As an archaeologist, Eric had seen a number of pre-Harappan seals found in this region, the most noteworthy among them being the square-shaped seal depicting a bull. The seal-like object that he held in his palm now carried an inscription similar to that on one of the most popular bull seals of Mohenjodaro. Most of the seals from those times, however, were square or rectangular in shape and made of terracotta. He pushed aside all thoughts, slid the tablet in another pocket and went back to concentrating on the job at hand.

Eric had been briefed about the probable type of missile used and the kind of flying machine that had brought the weapon to the site. He knew exactly the kind of particles and fragments he needed to look for and collect to help the forensic team confirm the make of the missile and, if possible, the carrier. As he stood up to stretch his limbs after finishing his job, he looked around and could see nothing but sand. The terrain was not entirely plain; several mounds of sand rose up here and there. But something didn't seem right.

About a kilometre and a half to the left of where he stood, Eric spotted another large circle of discoloured sand. It looked like someone had chopped off a huge sand cliff from its base using a gigantic knife. The major part of the hillock had indeed been chopped, but the blow seemed to also have caused a good part of the hillock to collapse into a cave beneath it. A thin opening still remained on the surface; a crack—a little darker in colour, almost camouflaged by its surroundings.

'What the hell!' Eric exclaimed, already walking in the direction of the circle. 'And here I thought if there was more than one missile, they were targeted at the camp only. Now it looks like they had two totally separate targets. God, don't give me any more surprises please! Not today!'

◆

Twenty minutes and an exhausting walk later, Eric squatted next to a wreck that had been a huge mound in the middle of the desert until a day or two ago, though almost nothing remained of it any more.

'This place looks like an archaeological site...' Eric mumbled to himself as he held his head in his hands. 'Huh! It could be an undiscovered Kalibangan mound like those that were found in this region in the 1960s. But there's no way to confirm that... There is absolutely nothing to collect apart from the dust particles of history!'

Soon Eric found the place to be full of tiny fragments of early Kalibangan pottery, which bore close resemblance to the pottery of the Indus Valley Civilisation. But the bigger pieces that mattered were gone. He felt pangs of sadness hitting him hard. A huge piece of 3,700–4,500-year-old history had just evaporated from the face of the earth. The voice of one of his mentors echoed in his ears, 'You would be surprised to know how much history lies hidden in a single piece of household pottery. It's not just pottery. It's a slice of human life from a lost time.'

Eric had seen old photographs of excavations in this region. He was familiar with the chessboard-like town plan of Kalibangan. Each house had a courtyard and a series of rooms running around it on three sides. Some houses had a well and a flight of stairs to the roof. *Houses have always been about human aspirations,* he thought. *Just like today, people in the third millennium BC would also have dreamt of nice houses...but time consumes everything. What remains is the dust we call history.* An old photograph flashed in Eric's mind. A photograph of an extraordinary-looking house that his team had excavated somewhere in this region, with floors made of burnt tiles that had fascinating geometric designs. The lady of the house must have insisted to her man to beautify the house of her dreams. Eric smiled. 'We only discover how insignificant we are when we come face to face with time,' he sighed.

Eric scratched his chin and tried to push history and his own emotions aside to focus on the task. 'It was a thousand-pound explosive, at the very least,' he muttered. The heat, the questions plaguing his mind, everything seemed to annoy Eric. He wanted to pack up and move his butt out of that place. But he knew he had to find answers first. The most important questions that needed answering were: Who all were behind this? What was the motive?

Minutes before, with the finding of the cell phone remnants, Eric had thought he was at least a little closer to some clues, even if not to the answers he was looking for. But with the discovery of the second explosion site, he was suddenly exasperated over how such a large piece of history was lost now because of some vandals.

The discovery of the cell phone remains came as a bonus for him. He'd never expected to find a clue like that—at least after such a confident 'no' from Hukum Singh. He only hoped the forensic guys would manage to retrieve some data from the chip. Of course, there was at least one more thing to be happy about—the SIAD had proved to be active and alert. Even an air attack in the middle of a remote desert as tiny as this had been tracked with precision by them.

Eric walked back towards the car, lost in thought. Taking out the tablet from his pocket, he looked at it for some time, weighing it in his palm. The object looked ancient, but it was not made of clay—a clay tablet like this would have made a much more convincing case, for many of the pre-Harappan and Harappan mounds had been found in the close vicinity. But the newness of the substance created quite a disparity. What was it made of? And how did they etch these perfectly concentric grooves?

We could get the material tested, he thought. *We might learn something new. Something I have no idea about.* He smiled, put the tablet inside a zip-pouch, and slipped it back into his pocket.

The universe has its own way of connecting things and people. Little did Eric know that the zip-pouch in his pocket contained one of the most well-protected secrets of all time—a secret that would change his life, and a large part of world history, forever.

FIVE

Excavation site, Outskirts of Mosul district, Northern Iraq,
5.10 p.m. (local time)

Two days had passed since the excavation team had arrived at the Nineveh desert. One of the greatest cities during ancient times, Nineveh was settled as early as 6000 BC, during the late Neolithic Age. Here archaeologists had uncovered layers dating back to early Hassuna culture period, which was during early sixth millennium BC, and by 3000 BC, the area had become an important religious centre of Mesopotamia.

Dr Huntley thought of talking to Dr Hussein. He called the latter's residence number from his satellite phone and walked out of the camp into the desert. He knew there was a small settlement of a few houses to the south, but he wanted to keep this phone conversation to himself and also needed a stroll to think for a while and to find some answers. So he walked north. Connectivity was no issue since they had installed their own telecom tower near the campsite, and as his call went through, he knew it was working perfectly.

'What are you saying, Hussein?' Dr Huntley cried into his cell phone as he walked on the sand dunes. 'The tomb is not in Nineveh?'

'No,' Hussein replied from his university apartment in Vancouver, 'you heard right.' He cleared his voice after finishing his sentence.

'What makes you think so?'

'I've deciphered yet another line from the wall writing, and it clearly states that the trail of this secret tomb is in a tablet. The description of the tablet matches with the one I had found inside the tomb. This newly deciphered line also mentions that the tomb is in between a mountain range and a water body, far from this place—which means far from Nimrud.'

'Is there a chance of a misinterpretation?'

'No, I don't think so!' Hussein said confidently. 'Because we read the phrase "tomb of the Moon God" and then we were misled by the fact that Nineveh was the centre of the Moon God, Nanna. Moreover, I feel this makes more sense because Sennacherib, in the later part of the sixth century BC, moved the capital of the empire to Nineveh from Nimrud. It remained a major city and the royal residence until it was destroyed during the fall of the Assyrian Empire between 616 BC and 599 BC. But what we are looking for is far older—probably by a thousand years. There is no way that our site can be in Nineveh.'

'All right! So which mountain range do you think the line could be referring to?' Dr Huntley couldn't hold back his curiosity.

'It should be the Zagros Mountains,' said Dr Hussein. 'I need to look up the ancient water bodies that existed around that region though.'

'Good, check the Great Zab river as well. It flows along the western side of Zagros. Perhaps we may still be talking Iraq,' Dr Huntley smirked. 'See if you can give me something in a day or two; that'll be good. We can wait for two more days while you work on deciphering the entire writing and come up with the name of a place for us to start with.'

'I don't know how much I will be able to do with this blessed leg. I needed to go down to a couple of museums to work the puzzle out; nevertheless, I will try my best!' said Hussein.

'Let us do it, Hussein; my sixth sense says we are very close to something big. And I am sure the wall writing you had photographed twenty-seven years back is going to help us. We'll also get help from the round tablet you had borrowed from that attendant girl at the tomb,' Dr Huntley laughed, making sure Hussein heard it. He knew Hussein, despite being highly adventurous, was running low on motivation as he battled his fracture. Humour had always been Dr Huntley's way of motivating people, and he hoped he could help Hussein with it too.

'Inshallah! I wish I was on my feet and able to work with you guys at the site,' Hussein smiled on the other side. 'But I am taking a little extra care now so that I can be fit enough for the tougher part of the excavation.'

'Don't worry, Hussein, I will keep you informed about every little development here. Just remember that the "go ahead" comes from you! So you better get well soon, my friend! I know you, and I know your lineage!' he added before hanging up.

◆

Dr Huntley looked at the satellite phone in his palm, thought about the discussion he'd just had with Hussein, then slowly pushed the phone into the back pocket of his jeans. As he looked further to his left, he could see the sun setting over the horizon, the cloudless sky beginning to look dull.

It was an old habit—Dr Huntley always walked when he needed answers. Many years ago, one of his teachers had told him about the benefits of walking, and he had been practising it since then. It didn't just calm down his mind; it also helped settle things into different folders of the brain.

Dr Huntley glanced at his wristwatch. *It's only been an hour!* he thought. He knew he was not far from the camp, but he also knew that losing track in a desert was not just about how far you were from your base—especially when you were strolling after sunset. He felt a sudden chill run up his spine. He cursed under his breath, knowing too well that sudden drops in temperature could be followed by drastic changes in weather. Out in the open desert, such changes could be deadly. He walked faster.

The closer he got to his camp, the more quickly the temperature fell. To add to this, a cold breeze picked up strength. The desert wind whistled past his ears as he climbed a dune and spotted the communication mast of his camp. He was glad his journey was almost over.

Unfortunately, he didn't know his nightmare had only just begun.

◆

After ten more minutes of walking, the entire camp was visible. Dr Huntley climbed up the last sand dune, but the very next moment he froze in his path and shrieked.

He couldn't believe the ghastly sight that lay in front of him. Was this the same camp he had left an hour ago? Almost everyone from the team lay dead on a bed of blood-soaked sand surrounding the camp. Who could have carried out such a massacre? Why would someone butcher innocent archaeologists and excavation workers so ruthlessly?

Dr Huntley had heard stories of secret brotherhoods and other groups of people who guarded these deserts, especially the ancient ruins, but he had never paid attention to any of those tales. People had been dying or disappearing in the deserts since the early ages of human history, but he could never believe they had all died at the hands of bloodthirsty murderers.

He wanted to go to the camp and see for one last time the people he had convinced to join him on this mission. He wanted to cry over their bodies and give them proper burials. But there was also the danger of someone waiting there for him. Without any weapon or training, walking into the camp could be like walking to his death. He was also slowly beginning to understand the whole new responsibility he now had on his shoulder: someone needed to tell the world what had happened there. Someone needed to stay alive to warn others about the threat that lay hidden in these deserts.

SIX

New Delhi,
Next day, 12 p.m.

Aurin walked along the outer circle of Connaught Place, making his way to Saravana Bhavan, the famous restaurant that offers South Indian delicacies. He was accompanied by his Facebook friend, Alex Pradhan. The sky was rather blue for a mid-October afternoon. The temperature was below thirty, with low humidity and a gentle breeze.

Alex was a bike fanatic from Darjeeling and the moderator of a bikers' group on Facebook called 'Gods on Wheels'. Aurin had joined the group a few years ago and was all set to take part in the group's first cross-country bike trip the next day. Stretching over 3,055 kilometres from Chandigarh to Baghdad, the organizers called it the 'Across the Hindukush' rally. Over the Hindukush Mountains and through the treacherous trails of Pakistan, Afghanistan, Iran and Iraq, it was a dream trip for any serious biker. Even until a month back, Aurin had not been very keen on joining the trip. But Alex had convinced him to be his co-rider, and so he had flown in from the UK to join Alex in New Delhi. Today they were going to get all the papers signed and stamped from the Ministry of External Affairs, and tomorrow they would embark on the adventure with the group. Even the thought of the route they were going to take made Aurin's heart beat faster. This trip was going to be big!

As they turned onto Janpath Road, Aurin's phone buzzed inside his pocket. He pulled out the handset, only to fumble and drop it on the ground. It hit the concrete sideways and broke into four–five parts.

'Who called?' Alex asked. 'Was it the agent we got to collect our papers from?'

'I don't know,' Aurin winced. 'I couldn't even look at the number before I dropped the phone.'

'No worries, I'll fix it for you,' said Alex, 'once we find a table at the restaurant.'

'I was hoping you would fix it,' Aurin smiled, 'as you know, I am technologically challenged.'

The duo climbed up a flight of stairs to the first floor of Saravana Bhavan. Aurin caught the first waiter they met and quickly placed their order. The elderly waiter smiled and pointed at an empty table. Alex wanted a ghee roasted masala dosai and Aurin fancied gorging on a maharaja thali. They grabbed the table that was next to a large window overlooking Janpath Road, which was teeming with afternoon office traffic. Unending streams of commuters passed on both sides of the road. Within a few minutes, water was poured into clean glasses for them and masala papads were served. Alex wasted no time in breaking off a crispy corner of a papad and popping it into his mouth.

Aurin smiled, 'Hungry?'

'Very!' responded Alex.

'Well, before the food arrives, you have a job to do, my friend.' Aurin reached into his pocket and pulled out his phone—all its pieces.

Alex put down the rest of his papad and studied the device. He had majored in computer applications and was good with electronics.

'Something is jamming the battery slot!' Alex grimaced. He grabbed a fork and went to work. In the next three minutes, the phone was fixed. He pressed the power button to check whether it was working and kept it on the table. And there it was—the start-up tone, with soft light spreading all over the screen.

'Here you go, boy!'

'Thanks, you just saved me a hundred and fifty bucks. I hear that's what they charge just to open the backlid of your phone, let alone fix it.'

'Good, you pay for my dessert then!' Alex smiled wickedly.

The waiter came over with the thali Aurin had ordered. The large plate had several small bowls lined along its edge, the contents of which included traditional South Indian vegetable preparations, along with sambhar and rasam. At the centre of the plate lay a generous serving of rice and pooris. Another waiter served Alex his masala dosai. One glance at the piles of food before them, and both friends knew they would need filter coffee to wash it all down in the end.

They got engrossed in eating without a second thought as to who could have called Aurin, even as precious time ticked away.

◆

Aurin's phone started ringing. As it lay too close to an empty bowl, the vibrating noise was further exacerbated to the point where people from other tables began turning around and staring at them. Aurin picked up the phone and answered the call.

'Hello.'

Static filled the line for a few seconds.

'Is this Aurin?' A male voice—deep, elderly and oddly familiar—boomed from the other end.

'Yes,' Aurin replied. 'May I know who's speaking, please?'

'Aurin, my boy, where were you! People have been trying to reach you for over an hour. This is Father Smit, in case you haven't recognized my voice yet.'

'Father Smit! It's so great to hear from you! My phone was not functional for a little while. I am sorry I didn't recognize your voice. Is everything fine?'

'Where is your big brother Eric? I cannot reach his mobile phone either!' Father Smit asked without answering Aurin's question.

'Ric da is away from Kolkata for some work, I believe.'

'Do you know anything about Dr Huntley?'

'Umm, yes, Ric da had met him a couple of days back. Later, on one of our phone calls, he had also mentioned that Dr Huntley was gearing up for some excavation…that's all I know about him.'

'There is some disturbance in the connection, Aurin, let me call you again.' Father Smit hung up.

'Who was it?' Alex asked.

'Father Gebrand Smit. He's a Dutchman, a senior archaeologist and an art historian who has left everything to become a community worker. He taught my elder brother Eric history and physics in school. The three of us got involved in an adventure some months ago.'

'The one that had something to do with Job Charnock?' Alex asked, but before Aurin could respond, he got another call. As he pressed the green icon on his phone screen, he nodded a 'yes' to Alex.

'Yes, Father Smit...' said Aurin.

'There is a situation, Aurin.' Father Smit's voice was much clearer this time, though it seemed to have taken on a grave tone. 'Apparently Dr Huntley's site was subjected to a massacre. People were killed. And then I got this strange call from probably the only survivor of the massacre, a girl named Marina.'

'What! Oh my...' Aurin could barely whisper. 'How did she reach you?'

'She said Dr Huntley had given three emergency numbers to all his team members: Eric's, yours and mine. Looking for help, she tried reaching Eric and you before me. She found all her team members dead at the campsite when she returned from a nearby village market, but she didn't find Dr Huntley or his body. He could have survived the attack, but she has no clue about his whereabouts.' Father Smit paused for breath.

'Where is she? Where is the excavation site?'

'Marina is hiding in a motel room in Mosul and is too shaken to come out. She has texted me the details of her motel. I think I will have to go there, talk to her, and find Dr Huntley if he is alive... that's why I needed to consult Eric so badly!' Father Smit sounded exasperated.

'Where is Mosul?' Aurin asked.

'It's a district in Iraq.'

'Did you just say Iraq?'

'Yes...Mosul is in Iraq. Northern Iraq to be precise...some kilometres from Baghdad.'

'No! It can't be!' Aurin exclaimed.

'Yes, it is, Aurin, I know!'

'No, not the Mosul thing,' Aurin managed a laugh. 'I am flabbergasted because it is too much of a coincidence!' he cleared the confusion.

'What do you mean?'

'I mean to say, I am leaving for Baghdad tomorrow.'

'You must be kidding! I don't believe this.'

'I am not kidding, Father Smit, I am going on a Chandigarh–Baghdad bike trip. We are a group of nine people.'

'On nine bikes?'

'Five bikes—one biker and one navigator per bike.'

'You are one man short then.'

'Yes, Father Smit, one of us broke his arm two days ago.'

'Is it too late to apply for the vacant position? I mean, it's going to be rather difficult for me to reach Mosul on a travel visa when time is the only key.'

'Could you borrow the look of a man in his late forties?'

'Oh, you know it—I pretty well can. I might just have to dye my grey hair.'

'And get a cut after that,' Aurin added.

'Well, I am not going to cut my hair, for sure.'

'That should be okay, I guess. Great then! Can I call you back in ten?'

'Yes, sure. I admit I still can't believe this coincidence!' Father Smit smirked as Aurin disconnected the call.

SEVEN

Jodhpur
Same day, 1.00 p.m.

When Eric boarded the aircraft from Jodhpur Airport after a peaceful two-hundred-and-fifty-kilometre ride from Bikaner, a fellow passenger's cell phone buzzed loudly. The man took the call and Eric instantly remembered he had switched off his cell phone before boarding the Kolkata–Delhi flight the day before and had never switched it back on. He hadn't had to, for he had used his laptop's satellite connection to contact his office the previous evening. He quickly dug through his leather carry-on case, found the phone and switched it on.

As the phone took its time coming back to life, Eric pushed his hand luggage into the overhead bunk and took the aisle seat he had booked. Once seated, he glanced at his cell phone: twenty-one missed calls. One text message.

What the hell! What's wrong?

There was no one in his family who could be missing him that badly. No such friend either. So many calls to his phone, that too in one day, was a rather big deal.

Anxious, Eric scrolled through the numbers on the list of missed calls to figure out the caller, but the same message appeared against each entry: private number.

'Shit!' he mumbled. *Was it some government agency?*

He was attached with the Indian intelligence and some branches of the armed services at the moment and he had also done consultancy work in the past for several other secret agencies of the Government of India. Not that all the people he worked with were friends. But if any of those agencies was trying to reach him, it wouldn't call twenty-one times. It'd track him down, follow him, grab him and throw him into the back of a van.

'Sir, will you please switch off your mobile phone? We are about to take off,' Eric heard the airhostess tell him.

'Oh, sure!' Eric looked directly at her with his best smile on. 'Give me one second please; this is urgent.'

He quickly scrolled down the screen to find out when the calls had started coming in. The first call that he had missed was made at 7.40 p.m. the previous evening. 'Maybe there's something of interest in the message?' he wondered as he fumbled through the various options in his phone to finally open the message that had lain unread in his inbox since 7.55 p.m. the previous night. The airhostess returned and touched his shoulder, requesting more firmly this time, 'Sir, please!' Eric hurriedly read the one-line text message no one would ever want to find in their inbox: *This is serious. Please call—it's a life or death situation for me.*

EIGHT

Two and a half hours later, seated on a plush sofa at the New Delhi Airport lounge, sipping on his black coffee, Eric once again checked his cell phone. *Who could have needed to connect with me so badly? I must find out who this is.* As if on cue, his phone started to ring in his hand and he saw the words 'private number' flashing on the screen.

'Think of the devil...'

Four rings went by, then five. Eric took a deep breath and answered it: 'Hello?'

Static filled the line.

'Hello?' Eric repeated.

There was a three-second pause before he heard a response.

'Hello,' said the voice. It was meek and feminine.

'Who is this?'

The woman ignored his question. After another pause, she asked, 'Is this Eric?'

'Yes, this is Eric Roy. Who is this?'

Again, static filled the line for a few seconds, followed by a gasp and faint weeping sounds.

'Are you all right?' Eric inquired, keeping his voice as comforting as possible.

'You are Eric, a friend of Dr Huntley's, right?'

'Yes, I am. What happened to him? And who are you?'

There was a pause. 'I am Marina Martinez,' she then said.

Eric's eyeballs moved round and round as he racked his brains for any connection. No, he did not know who she was.

'Marina, where are you calling from?'

'I am in Mosul, Iraq.'

'Are you with Dr Huntley?'

She didn't speak for a few moments and then burst out crying. Eric feared the worst, but kept up the conversation.

'Marina, where is Dr Huntley?'

A pause—and then a thunderbolt: 'They have killed everyone! I don't know what happened to him. I couldn't find his body among the others.'

'What?' Eric was astounded. 'What do you mean?'

'Yes, they killed everyone. I am alive because I wasn't at the camp when they came. But I am sure they are looking for me and will kill me too!'

'Who is "they"?'

'I don't know.'

Eric paused, not sure what to ask next. Then he said, 'Marina, were you a member of the excavation team Dr Huntley was leading in Iraq?'

'Yes, I was…but there's no one left now…' she wailed.

'How did you get my number?'

'Dr Huntley had shared three emergency contact numbers with all of us. The first one was yours. He said if there was any kind of emergency, or if anything bad happened here, we should call you.'

'That was good thinking, I must say. Did you call anyone else?'

'Yes. Since I couldn't get through to you in the first attempt, I called the other two numbers too. One was Aurin's, but I couldn't connect with him either. I finally managed to get through to Father Smit, the third emergency contact, and told him about my situation.'

'Okay, that's great, I'll talk to him. But this moment onwards, you only talk to me and no one else. Is that clear?'

'Yes...' Eric heard her faint reply.

'Now tell me Marina, where exactly are you?'

'I am staying in The Mosul Inn, a small motel near Nineveh. I haven't even opened the window ever since I checked in here yesterday.'

'You are Spanish, if I am not wrong. Correct?'

'Yes.'

Eric swore under his breath, not sure what to do. Dr Huntley was missing. Marina was freaking out. The only functioning Spanish embassy in Iraq was in Baghdad, which was nothing less than a good five hundred kilometres from where Marina was. If there was one closer to Nineveh, it could have been a safe place for her to go and hide in. Back in his archaeology days, he used to know people around the world who could help him out in an emergency like this. But he had been out of that business for years. There was no way for him to know if his old contacts were still in the game—or even alive, for that matter.

'Did you guys find something at the site? I mean a tomb or a mummy or something of value?'

'No, we had hardly started our work.'

'That's weird...' Eric mumbled. 'Marina, listen to me. I assure you, everything is going to be fine. You just need to be a little stronger,' he added in a firm voice.

'They killed everyone; now they are coming for me!'

'I understand, Marina, that it is tough for you. But let me share something with you. Do you know why Dr Huntley told you to call me? It's because he knew if you needed my help, I'd be there. So trust me when I say this.'

The line was filled with static for a while.

'Marina, are you there?'

There was another pause. Then she asked, 'How will you help me?'

'It's simple…I am coming to find you and Dr Huntley, and to get you guys out of there.'

NINE

One of the most important skills for an operative is the ability to adapt. Whether it is hand-to-hand combat or planning a mission, a soldier of a special force has to make the best of a bad situation, or he won't survive very long. Knowing how fucked-up a situation he was in, Eric decided to contact one of the very few people he could count on.

'IT support,' answered the guy at the other end of the line.

'Hey Sid, how are you doing, boy?'

Sid Patel, Eric's team member and IT support, straightened up in his chair next to a desk cluttered with empty chips packets, countless coffee cups and a high-end computer.

'Much better now, Chief. I'd been waiting for this call since you left for this assignment!'

'What? You didn't go home? What the hell!'

'How could I, Chief? I was the only one who knew you were on this. And I am supposed to be your eyes and ears, right?'

'That's right,' Eric softened his voice. 'Sid, I am sorry. I always pull your leg when I call you, and you are still good to me. I am glad that I am working with you.'

'That's a good point, Chief, for I am consulting a psychiatrist because of you.'

'What!'

'Just kidding, Chief!' Sid smiled on the other side of the line. *It is good to bust your senior's balls sometimes*, he thought. 'Tell me, Chief, how I can help you.'

'Sid, I need a favour.'

'Shoot, Chief.'

'I need you to check up on a massacred excavation site at Nineveh in Iraq's Mosul district, and I need you to tell me what exactly happened there.'

'Do you give me permission to hack foreign satellite feeds, especially the Middle Eastern and Russian ones?' Sid asked as he tied his long unruly hair into a ponytail.

'Ummm… Okay, do what you have to!'

'All right, Chief, I have recorded your response as "yes" just in case I need to save my ass for this later,' Sid muttered. 'Now, please tell me the coordinates. And the time.'

'Umm…' Eric fumbled for a moment and said, 'Sorry, I don't have the coordinates. Nineveh is a very small place in northern Iraq, and this site is on the outskirts. I am sure you'll figure it out. It could have happened any time since 12 o' clock yesterday—local time.'

'Okay, well, it sounds tough to get feeds for that long a time interval, but it is not impossible. Let me check my database to see if I can hack multiple satellite servers and get multiple feeds.'

'One more thing, Sid, I need background information on a Spanish woman named Marina Martinez, hometown unknown. Current employer could be Dr Peter Huntley or Dr Muzahem Hussein.'

'Give me a moment, Chief, that would be in a different database.'

'Just out of curiosity, how many databases do you keep, Sid?'

'Let me phrase it this way, Chief: I have to keep multiple databases just to keep track of my databases.'

'Impressive, though I don't know how you do it.'

'I am a smart-ass college dropout, sir,' Sid quipped as he typed away like a storm using all ten fingers on his keyboard.

Eric smiled, 'That's right, how could I forget! Best of luck, kid!'

'Hold on, Chief, I got her. Here you go. Marina Martinez, born in Rome in 1983, citizen of Italy by birth and citizen of Spain by choice… Graduated from Simon Fraser University, Vancouver… Grad school ID, valid driving licence, entered Iraq on 8 October, red hair…and quite a bombshell if I may add. I have never seen anybody look this good on an ID... Shit, I am extremely sorry for my choice of words, Chief!'

Eric smiled again. 'Thank you, Sid, and best of luck with the Nineveh feed. Call me when you find something. Hang on, one more thing,' Eric said as he remembered something. He pulled out the transparent evidence bag from the side pocket of his laptop case and said, 'Listen, Sid, I am sending you a packet in two hours with the remains of a cell phone I found at the bombing site, and another thing that looks like a seal or a tablet from the pre-Harappan era, but is made of something weird—I haven't been able to figure out what. I want all possible data and information to be retrieved from the phone, and the round object to be analysed. Could you arrange that for me, please?'

'Anything for you, Chief, and I have just sent Marina's photograph to your clean sim.' With that, Sid signed off.

◆

The thought of having to ask her father for help was enough to keep Marina awake. No matter how she tried to rationalise it, she just couldn't get past his basic ideology: women were weak; men were strong. God, even the thought enraged her. How could someone still think along such lines in this century? To make matters worse, she knew if she went to him for help, he would smile and say, 'I told you...women are weak and will always turn to men for help at the end of the day!'

She couldn't bear the thought of that madman saying this to her face. And why would she even think of going to the man who had abandoned her as a little girl and turned his back on her when she had needed him the most? It was her uncle—her father's elder cousin— who had helped her mother and her survive, and her maternal uncles had then helped them resettle. She'd shifted with her Spanish mother to Barcelona at the age of twelve. She had adapted her mother's maiden last name and studied in Spain but kept in touch with her uncle. He was the one who had encouraged her to study archaeology and had gotten her this Sumerian assignment. Since the time she had shifted to Barcelona, she had refused to ever turn to her father. And today, once again, she told herself, 'No way in hell!' She thought of calling her uncle for help, but then rejected the idea. She could fend for herself, and she would.

TEN

It was a little before midnight, and it was pouring.

Eric tried calling Father Smit and Aurin, but he was informed by both their networks that their cell phones were out of coverage area. Eric typed a text message to both of them: *Have talked to Marina in Iraq, starting immediately to find her and Dr Huntley. Pls don't contact her, could be risky. Don't call me. I'll call you when I call you. Bye now.*

Eric finished packing for Baghdad and made himself a cup of coffee. As he settled in his grandfather's chair with the coffee mug, his mobile screen came alive and the device started vibrating on the dark chestnut desk in front of him.

'Sid, give me some good news!' he blurted out as he answered the call.

'Where are you, Chief? Are you anywhere close to your laptop?'

'Yes, I am in my study, packing for Baghdad. I'm leaving for the airport in an hour to catch a flight to Delhi. Okay, I have my laptop open right here on my desk.'

'Great, I am mailing you a link. Please use the code I have texted you to gain access to this Comm. Channel. It is protected by a modified version of the CCEP type-1 encryption algorithm developed for us by an Israeli agency. There are some video feeds on it; check them out.'

'What's CCEP?'

'Commercial COMSEC Evaluation Program.'

'I am sure it is. Thanks anyway,' Eric smiled to himself.

A few minutes later, when he opened the secure link and found three video clips, Eric understood what Sid had been talking about. It looked like Sid had hacked into a Russian surveillance company's secure site. The company apparently surveyed the entire world with three satellites, constantly capturing what was happening anywhere on earth. Sid must have sifted through several terabytes of content and then downloaded those three clips. With the help of technology, Eric was now about to come face to face with actual footage of what had happened at the excavation site where Dr Huntley was supposed to dig.

In one quick glance, Eric could ascertain that Sid had numbered the clips chronologically. He had also included local time tags along with the names of the files. Without a moment of hesitation, Eric clicked on the clip tagged 'one'. Its time tag showed *Day X_17.10 hrs local time*. It was a satellite feed and was absolutely unclear. Sid must have enlarged the view and saved the file. Eric could make out nothing initially, but then his eyes started reading through the blurry images and he spotted the camp with about twenty-five tents out in the desert. At the centre of the camp, people were relaxing in small groups. Then he saw a man come out of one of the tents and walk lazily into the desert. The satellite camera hovered in the sky above for about twenty minutes and by the end of the clip the person walking out was no longer visible, and neither was the camp.

Clip number two was likely filmed by a drone and not a satellite, easy to make out by the size of the file—it was ten times larger than either of the other two. It must have been shot from a height of 3,000–4,000 feet. The angle was wide and, unlike the dull grainy footage of the previous clip, this one reproduced colours more rationally. The clip was tagged *Day X_18.05 hrs*. This was what Eric was actually looking for, because this clip showed the carnage, or at least a part of it. Some seven-eight people could be seen running away from the camp in a state of panic. They yelled for help, tripping over the dead bodies of their teammates.

On a closer look, Eric found out why. Their screams were caused by men dressed in black thawbs, their faces wrapped in long headscarves, holding open swords in their hands. They were everywhere in the camp, mercilessly killing people. Archaeologists—men and women—enjoying their evening tea were meticulously slaughtered by these black-robed men.

Eric replayed the clip. It was more than an attack or even a massacre. It was a neatly planned operation. The finesse with which it was executed clearly showed the involvement of a trained group. It was the type of work that was taught by washouts of Mossad and other top agencies around the world. At least that was what Eric thought.

The third video clip was tagged *Day X_18.55 hrs*. At three minutes, this one was the shortest among the three. It was again a satellite feed and hence unclear, but it was clear enough for Eric to spot a woman walking towards the camp from the west. As she neared the camp, she saw the dead bodies, ran towards them and wept, holding a few of them to her bosom, and then suddenly straightened up. She seemed to have figured out that she could also be in danger. She got up and ran back in the direction she had come from, disappearing quickly from the field of the camera's vision.

ELEVEN

Enfield India was organising the Across the Hindukush rally to announce the launch of their new Thunderbird 500. Developed for adventure enthusiasts and designed for comfortable long rides, this bike would be best launched at a long-distance rally, it was thought. Twenty-four active bikers' groups from the central and southern parts of Asia were shortlisted and the Gods on Wheels group was finally selected for the rally.

The Gods on Wheels members were all in New Delhi and had been gearing up for the long journey. Every one of them was dying to ride the two hundred kilogram beast that the makers proudly claimed was just like riding a 125cc bike.

Most of the arrangements were in place. The papers they had been waiting for included clearances from the external affairs ministries of five countries—India, Pakistan, Afghanistan, Iran and Iraq. The papers arrived in New Delhi on the eve of their journey and so did Father Smit.

By nine that evening, everything was ready as per the organising agency's plan, and a new member had secretly replaced an injured biker of the team following a final nod from Alex Pradhan, the leader of the group.

◆

The Asian Highway project was initiated by the United Nations (UN) in 1959 with the aim of strengthening trade and social interaction between Asian countries.

Interestingly, the first car to cross the entire length of the new Asian Highway from east to west was an Aston Martin driven by Richard Meredith and Phil Colley in 2007. Following the AH1 and AH5 from Tokyo to Istanbul, Meredith and Phil drove over fifteen thousand kilometres and the journey took a total of forty-nine days and they crossed eighteen countries.

Richard Meredith was a travel author and had written a book named *Driven Together*. Rob from the bikers' group was a huge fan of his writings and often mentioned that they had not only inspired him to be a travel blogger but also an adventurer. For Alex, Aurin, Father Smit and the gang, the rally was exciting, but for Rob, it was to be the most poetic milestone of his writing career.

Starting out from Delhi, the bikers were to reach Chandigarh by air, from where they would hit the road. Crossing the border at Wagah, they would ride through Lahore, Islamabad and Peshawar in Pakistan. Across the mountainous Afghan border at Torkham, their route would snake through the breathtaking landscapes of Kabul, Jalalabad and Islam Qala in Afghanistan. Entering Iran at the Islam Qala border, the bikers would reach Tehran via Torbat-e Jam, Neyshabur, Damghan and Semnan. From Tehran, crossing the Iran–Iraq border near Khosravi, the bikers would only be left with a final 694 kilometres to cover for Baghdad.

TWELVE

Eric flew out of Delhi on a 5.40 a.m. Gulf Air flight and reached Baghdad by 1.00 p.m. He booked a taxi from the rental booth at the airport for Samarra, an Iraqi town on the Baghdad–Mosul highway. As per his travel guidebook, Samarra was one of the four Islamic holy cities of Iraq and was about 124 kilometres north of Baghdad. It was considered the largest known ancient city in the entire world, with its majestic ruins extending along the eastern bank of the Tigris river. Present-day Samarra is a fairly well-populated town run by the Saladin Governorate.

Samarra, to Eric's mind, was also a strategic location for someone who had a secret mission to accomplish in Mosul. Only a little over four hours by road from Mosul, Samarra was the best landing spot for any operative to analyse the situation on ground and get an idea about the field and the players.

Eric pulled his only piece of luggage to the parking lot specified for taxis and spotted the licence plate of the old yellow Lada that was assigned to him by the booking clerk at the booth. The driver, a young man in his early thirties, was dozing in the driver's seat, a newspaper spread over his chest. Eric woke him up and showed him his booking slip. The driver folded his newspaper, kept it on the passenger seat next to him, rubbed his eyes sleepily and took the slip from Eric.

'Samarra?' he asked.

'Yes, what's your name?'

'Abu Hassan,' the young man smiled.

'What's your real name?' Eric asked dryly.

'I thought you take it—like other travellers. Everyone believe we all are Abu Hassan here.' He smiled broadly, showing off teeth that could do better with some cleaning. 'Abdul Baseer.'

'You speak English, I see.'

'Sure. Very excellent. Kate Winslet.'

'Kate Winslet?' Eric raised a brow.

'Sure, Cameron Diaz,' Abdul Baseer nodded vigorously, '*Vanilla Sky*. Surely excellent.' Then he began to sing 'I fall apart', a track from the movie *Vanilla Sky*, swaying his shoulders in a slow dance move. He sure had a good voice.

'Enough,' said Eric, raising both his hands in a manner of surrender. 'I have already paid a hundred dollars for this ride,' he opened the rear door of the Lada, threw his bag in and took his seat. 'Now tell me how much time you will take to reach Samarra and drop me off at a decent hotel.'

'Three hours, sir,' replied Abdul Baseer. 'Two and half, if lucky!' He switched the engine on. Putting the car into gear, he rolled it smoothly out of the parking lot. Eric found the sidewalks busy with pedestrians walking in both directions. The air was thick with dust and heady with the scent of seekh-kebab masala.

Lunchtime in Baghdad.

♦

Hitting a broad avenue, Abdul Baseer's driving style abruptly changed. He raced through the traffic, with pedestrians leaping out of his way, cart drivers hurling curses at him and several drivers honking.

'I think three hours will be better!' Eric screamed from the back seat.

'Certainly, excellent!' Baseer grinned.

But Eric couldn't see him make any move to slow down the car.

Seconds later, Eric screamed again, louder this time. 'Slow down the damn car!'

Baseer turned around in his seat, completely ignoring the traffic ahead. 'I take you to Grand Festivities Square for the Arc of Triumph; we call it the Swords of Qādisīyah...only twenty minutes, you see Saddam Hussein's work of art—two big hands coming out from ground, holding two 141-foot swords—the swords make big arch—excellent!'

'Please, for Allah's sake, turn around!' Eric leaned forward and physically turned the young man's head towards the road. 'Drive safe, and don't talk, Baseer!'

Baseer obeyed. He drove, keeping his eyes on the road from then on, but he kept talking with the same enthusiasm, 'You no believe, the artist use Saddam's hands as model for design—in fact, use real print of Saddam's thumb.' He went on proudly, 'Certainly excellent!'

'My dear friend, I have seen the Swords of Qādisīyah and the Hands of Victory.'

'Excellent!' Baseer said, turning around in his seat and flashing his perpetual smile.

Eric clasped his shoulder and said, 'Don't get excited, Baseer, drive carefully!'

'Yes, certainly. Excellent!' Baseer grinned back at Eric and then he began to sing 'I fall apart' once again.

'Straight to Samarra,' Eric tapped Baseer on the shoulder.

Baseer nodded, still singing, lost in his own euphoria.

THIRTEEN

A satellite town of Baghdad, Samarra had old Iraqi-style buildings making space for the few modern hotels cropping up here and there. The Tigris lay masked by a line of new hotels and resorts. The original town that lay behind this façade was cramped with old buildings, dusty roads and bundles of overhead cables criss-crossing to form a canopy of sorts over the town streets.

The settlement was built by Caliph Al-Mu'tasim in AD 836 to replace Baghdad as the capital of the Abbasid Caliphate and later abandoned in AD 892. Despite the rather short term of honour, Samarra remained a legend in Arab history with its artistic, literary and scientific splendours.

Baseer guided the taxi on to an exit lane off the highway for Samarra, and the first thing that caught Eric's eye was the golden dome of a mosque. Like a jewel in the centre of a crown, the dome and the pair of minarets on its two sides rose high above the buildings around them. Eric was astounded to see such classical architecture in this rather out-of-the-way location.

'What's that?' Eric asked Baseer. 'And you don't have to look at me to answer this.'

'That one? Yes, excellent,' Baseer quickly returned to his trademarked expression, 'That is Al-Askareyya Shrine. It has tombs of last imams. It is also memorial to imam who will return and bring peace. This one excellent shrine. The old gold dome more beautiful than this, but all gone in 2006 bombing. The beautiful minarets also bombed later.'

'That's sad,' Eric said. 'Yes, they bring back the mosque and now it open for all,' said the young taxi driver. 'I remember, 2006, I came here in Samarra with my uncle. No one heard sound that big. Dust everywhere. People choking—what chaos!' Baseer closed his eyes and took a deep breath. When he spoke, his voice seemed to come from far away. 'Danger everywhere. Militants with guns firing from vehicles... Government was helpless. But now things good—you want visit?'

'Thanks, Baseer, but no, I am not in the mood to visit a mosque right now. I will not be able to appreciate any work of art at this moment.'

Their taxi entered a narrow dusty lane where vendors stood in shaded corners selling vegetables and home-baked bread that were much bigger than the Indian bakarkhanis. Two-wheeled carriers attached to tractors transported piles of vegetables and other grocery items. The air was heavy with the fragrance of spices and, in some places, kebabs. People chatted lazily and vendors shouted at the top of their lungs.

Vehicles belonging to another time were parked everywhere, pulled haphazardly off the narrow streets. They crossed a large building with archways at the main level, which might once have been home to small businesses that had long since been shuttered and locked. Ornate wrought-iron balconies were half-covered in satellite TV dishes, poking their parabolic antennas into the blazing blue sky.

Baseer rolled up the windows and switched on the car air-conditioning. Then he resumed his guide talk, 'This excellent time, I take you to other tourist spots if you want.' He took yet another turn out of one of the many narrow alleyways, and all of a sudden they were on a wide road with pavements on both sides. 'This is good side of Samarra; that is Tigris. You find all good hotels this side.' Baseer slowed down the taxi and, with a quick neck-and-eye movement, suggested that Eric get down and check out the hotel on their left.

FOURTEEN

Aurin and Alex were the leanest and fittest of the group, and Father Smit, travelling as Rudy, the injured member, was the tallest. Surprisingly, he looked as fit as Aurin and Alex and quite neat in a pair of faded jeans and a brown leather jacket over a white t-shirt. His long grey hair—now dyed black—was swept back in a tight ponytail, and his regular pop-singer spectacles had been replaced with a pair of World War II bikers' goggles. In short, he looked the part, like one of a gang of bikers half his age. The rest of the guys were all aged between twenty-four and thirty-three and dressed like any typical Indian youth. Only Nitin, Akki and Pablo, all from Mumbai, had tattoos all over their arms and necks; Rob and Jojo did not. Ashu and Nick, the two most sober-looking bikers of the group, were technical experts from Enfield.

Two things had always stood out on Aurin's face—his movie star-like high cheekbones and a big chin. Alex, on the other hand, had a geeky appearance with a bespectacled, acne-ridden face. Among other members of the group, Rob, a short, stocky guy from Arunachal Pradesh, was the designated journalkeeper and blogger. There was another boy from Dehradun, Jojo, who had such a fair complexion that the others called him 'paleface'. Jojo was the second-in-command.

With a fine riding experience on a brilliant highway, the first stretch of the journey from Chandigarh to Wagah border was a piece of cake for the bikers. Entering Pakistan from Wagah and making way to Lahore also turned out much simpler than what Aurin had expected, since Enfield Pakistan had arranged for everything well in advance. That was all for the biker group on day one. They only got their first real feel of the cross-country rally when they got to the Lahore–Islamabad lap of the journey on the second day.

FIFTEEN

Baseer drove Eric in and out of small and mid-sized hotels around Samarra, and Eric chose what appeared to be the best of them—a moderately priced, two-storey lodge with three additional one-storey bungalows, all arranged in a circle in a beautifully landscaped compound lined with date and palm orchards.

After letting go of Baseer, Eric checked into one of the three one-storey bungalows. The room was newly painted, the floors polished and the windows sparkling clean. Eric took a quick shower and slipped into a white t-shirt and washed denims. He topped up the look with black aviators and a straw hat Father Smit had brought him from Goa on his last adventure. He then headed to the only restaurant on the lodge premises.

The sun was setting over the Tigris, and the palm leaves swayed in the breeze. Eric glanced over his shoulder at the tranquil scene and took a chair, along with a small round table, out to the balcony of the restaurant. For the first time since that morning, he felt hungry. He hailed a waiter and ordered two types of seekh kebab, stuffed paranthas and an apple pie with hot chocolate sauce.

He was just finishing up his meal and struggling to decide between tea and coffee when a man appeared at his table. Though he was less than five feet tall, the man had a surprisingly broad chest and a strong frame. He wore expensive denims and a khaki summer jacket over a black t-shirt. He sported a salt-and-pepper beard on a fair, oblong face. His hair, the same shade as his beard, was coming down to his shoulders. His thick eyebrows lent an intelligent depth to his black eyes. He could be anything between fifty and sixty years old.

'I am Suleiman,' said the man, pulling a chair to sit across from Eric. 'Looks like you need a guide.'

'And how do you figure that?' Eric asked, lapping up the last scoop of his pie. He glanced back and forth between the Tigris and Suleiman's face.

'Easy peasy,' Suleiman smiled, sitting down. 'You are no tourist for sure. You don't look like someone travelling for business either. And then you walk like a soldier and have a thinker's eyes. It looks like Samarra is not your real destination but rather a midway stop on a longer journey, if I am not wrong. You are probably trying to go somewhere you should not go or cannot go without risking your life… Am I close?' he added after a few seconds of heavy silence.

Eric ignored the question.

'And what would your background be, Mr Suleiman, if I may ask?'

'The same as yours, I believe,' replied the man, 'largely confined to this region, though.'

'I don't think so,' Eric said. 'A fighter for hire, maybe?'

'Soldier of fortune is how I like to put it,' Suleiman shrugged. 'I think we are the two sides of the same coin, Mr Eric Roy; what do you think?'

'Interesting that you know my name.'

'Being good to people always pays off. I am good to the people who do the small jobs. The clerk who works the desk here is one of them.'

'You are from Samarra?'

'Well, I winter here. I summer in Afghanistan.'

'Aah! Not a good choice for a summer retreat, I must say.'

'I know. That's one of the drawbacks of multiple citizenships. My father was a Canadian archaeologist, and my mother was Iraqi. I was born in Herat, Afghanistan, a little after World War II and raised in Canada and Iraq. So, Canada is my third home, where I spend some months each year to avail of the free medical care. Quite a tolerant country it is…all kinds of people from different ethnic backgrounds.'

He smiled.

'What exactly is your line of work?'

'This is Samarra, my friend. Every second person is a spy here—American, European, other Islamic country agents, you name it! Here you don't have a line of work. Either you come up with ways to survive, or you simply don't survive. Look at this place,' he gestured around him, 'this town was traditionally, and until very recently, dominated by Sunni Arabs. Tensions arose between the Sunnis and the Shias during the Iraq War. In 2006, the dome of the Al-Askari Mosque was bombed and smashed to pieces, setting off a period of rioting and reprisal attacks that claimed thousands of lives across the country. Men were killed, women disappeared, children starved to death.'

'I know people of Iraq have seen bad days.'

'Life is tough here, my friend,' Suleiman grimaced. 'The civil war ended in 2007, but violence continued. In 2014, the city was attacked by the Islamic State of Iraq and the Levant—the ISIL. That's Samarra—and it's Iraq too, if you look closely.' Suleiman continued after a pause, 'Now to answer your question, what is my line of work—my primary line of work is art,' the short man smiled.

'What kind of art?'

Suleiman smiled again. 'Well, I am a facilitator. I help people get or experience things they wish to. I fulfil dreams.'

'Poetic!' Eric blurted out. 'And enigmatic too…but where exactly does *art* fit in?'

'Haven't you heard what John Maeda says about an enigma?'

'Who is John Maeda?' Eric raised a brow. He was beginning to like this long-haired weirdo. He was charming in a satanic way, and undoubtedly intelligent.

'He is an American designer and a technologist,' Suleiman replied. 'His work explores the areas where design and technology merge.'

'Okay, and what's his thought on an enigma? If that helps our conversation get anywhere…'

'Maeda said that the artist needs to understand the truth that lies at the bottom of an enigma.'

'That's a nice thought. A little complicated though...but what are you getting at, Mr Suleiman?'

'What I mean to say is that I am an artist who deals with mystery and enigma for his livelihood every day. And yes, I know that sounds pretty complicated too.'

'But how does this discussion connect us to an enigma?'

'I presume you have a complicated mission on your shoulders, and you need help.'

'Why would you think that?'

'Mr Roy, let us finish this hide-and-seek game, for God's sake. Just tell me what you have to do or where you need to go! I shall help you. I mean, in exchange for money, of course. I have mentioned that's what I do. That's my business.'

'Why don't we cut the twaddle and get to the point, Mr Suleiman?' Eric said dryly. 'And you must know, you have cropped up in my life as I stand at a rather critical junction between a cup of coffee and a masala tea.'

'Masala chai, of course! It's not Paris, my dear friend, it is Samarra,' he smiled broadly. 'I might join you as well.'

On some invisible signal from Suleiman, the waiter suddenly turned up at their table. The short man placed an order in the local dialect. The waiter bowed and slipped away.

'By the way, have you heard the metaphor "having an appointment in Samarra"?'

'No, I am not much of a literature guy, you see!'

'You are a soldier, I know,' Suleiman smiled wickedly, 'but listen to this, for it is damn interesting. "Having an appointment in Samarra" signifies death. It is a literary reference to an ancient Babylonian legend, retold by Somerset Maugham, in which Death is both the narrator and a central character.'

Suleiman paused to breathe, and Eric remembered a dialogue from a 1990 Hindi film named *Agneepath* that supported a similar idea, '*Maut ke saath appointment...*'

Suleiman continued with a twinkle in his eyes, 'The story behind "the Appointment in Samarra" subsequently formed the inspiration behind a popular novel by John O' Hara. And you would be surprised to know that "The Six Thatchers", a 2017 episode of *Sherlock*, is also based on it.'

Their tea arrived, and Eric noticed a plate of an unfamiliar-looking food item along with the two cups of masala chai.

'Freshly baked brownie and vanilla ice cream topped with fried dates and ginger-flavoured honey. If you are in Samarra, you have to try this delicacy.' Suleiman smiled as though he was the host and Eric his guest.

Eric scooped up some of the dessert, including a thin slice of a fried date, and tried it. The ice cream and the brownie melted in his mouth, and the honey added a strong hint of ginger to the whole medley. Eric closed his eyes and chewed on the juicy flesh of the date, and in no time, everything around him ceased to exist, and he experienced bliss.

SIXTEEN

With the first sip of hot masala chai, Eric straightened up in his chair and said, 'But you could also be a policeman setting me up, isn't it?'

'Yes, but that would be unprofessional.'

'This is Iraq—it is the last place I would come looking for professionalism! And I understand I could end up in a nightmarish prison for ten years before the case even comes to court.'

'Yes, of course, this is Iraq, where you could be rotting away in a nightmarish prison for much more than ten years because you had this in your possession.' Suleiman reached into his jacket pocket and took something out. He held out his palm for Eric—the small object he held in his hand was a firearm.

'But that's not mine; I never possessed it!' Eric hissed with his eyes wide open.

'Yes, of course I know that, but you won't be able to convince the Iraqi police if they found it in your luggage tomorrow.' Suleiman slipped the pistol back into his pocket. 'The point is, I went through your luggage some thirty minutes back while you were down here enjoying your food, and I didn't turn you in. And believe me, I could have, and it would have brought me good money too. But I still think I can make a better deal with you on your yet-to-be-revealed mission.'

'...Okay,' Eric said after taking a long, hard look at Suleiman's face. 'Let's talk business.'

During the discussion that followed, Eric told Suleiman an abridged version of his story, keeping some parts to himself. He said one of his friends was part of an excavation team in Nineveh. Three days ago, someone had informed him that there was a problem at the site. He had called his friend several times since then, but none of his calls had got a response. He had tried contacting the local authorities, but couldn't connect with them either. Now he had come to check out the site for himself and find his friend. He told Suleiman he expected him to be around and help with the language, local intelligence and strategic support. He didn't reveal anything about Marina to Suleiman. All he said was that he believed something was majorly wrong at Nineveh.

◆

When Sid called, Eric was in deep sleep.

It was the dead of night—a time reserved for only two kinds of calls: emergencies and wrong numbers. Eric hoped it was the latter.

He rolled over in his bed and reached for the sideboard, knocking something over that went crashing to the floor in the dark. Groggy from the sudden wake-up call, he had no idea what had fallen, and he certainly wasn't curious enough to find out. All he wanted was to go back to sleep.

'Hello,' he mumbled into his mobile phone, expecting the worst.

A buzzing tone greeted him, and then he heard Sid's voice.

'I have news about the damaged cell phone, Chief.'

'Good or bad?'

'I am the labourer, you are the boss—I tell, you decide.'

'Shoot.'

'Looks like the oil man found something far more valuable than oil in the Bikaner desert. And someone wanted to erase it from the face of the earth.'

'Good. I'll investigate after I clean up this mess and come back to Delhi.'

SEVENTEEN

There is no computer in this world that can even come close to that thing called human intuition—especially the insight-driven intuition of a supertechie like Sid Patel.

It was three in the morning and Sid was still on his computer, scanning file after file, image after image, just to find something relevant, something connected to the massacre in Nimrud. After his fifth coffee, he did something weird. He opened a program he had developed a couple of years ago for a specific investigation, and he ran the coordinates of the Bikaner missile attack and the Nineveh massacre through it. He didn't know why he did it. He certainly did not expect to get anything relevant out of it. But that's the thing about intuition—you don't know why you're doing something, but you just can't resist the urge to do it. The program took some minutes to crawl through a series of search engines, and then his computer screen came up with something he wasn't familiar with.

A name.

Luigi Pio Tessitori—a scholar of languages from Italy who had come to India and scouted around in the deserts of Bikaner to explore the Kalibangan mounds. Tessitori found these mounds interesting because they were just like the ones archaeologists had found in Harappa. Today, only for Tessitori's relentless searching through the region, the mounds of Bikaner are recognised to contain remnants of Indus antiquity.

Born in December 1887 in Udine, a small town tucked away in the north-eastern corner of Italy, Luigi Pio Tessitori had nothing literary or Indian about him. Nor was there likely to have been anything 'oriental' in the general curriculum at the Liceo Classico Jacopo Stellini, the town school where he had studied before moving to university. Nevertheless, Luigi had gone ahead and studied Sanskrit and had come to India. The reason why his name appeared on Sid's search was a bit of a surprise. Luigi was the only man to have excavated at both the locations: the deserts of Bikaner and the ruins of Nineveh.

◆

The rich mosaic of information found in the accounts of travellers, traders and missionaries had whetted Tessitori's interest in India much before he moved to the University of Florence, where he was to take his degree with honours in the Humanities. Along with his degree papers, he also took up Sanskrit classes on his own. Surprisingly, in a couple of years, along with Sanskrit he also mastered Pali and Prakrit, so much so that his classmates started calling him Indian Louis.

Among the several Sanskrit scholars Tessitori studied under, there was one from Turin, a man of letters named Gaspare Gorresio, who held the first chair to be instituted in Sanskrit within Italy. Turin was the first capital of Italy, followed by Florence and Rome, and Turin's university, founded in 1404, was one of the oldest in Italy. Gorresio had studied in Paris under the Sanskrit luminary, Eugene Burnouf (1801–1852), whose student list included Max Müller. Burnouf gave

Gorresio the confidence to take up the onerous task of editing a complete edition of the Ramayana. Gorresio's edition and an Italian translation of the same text were published between 1846 and 1870.

It was the first time Valmiki's epic had appeared in Europe in the Bengali or 'Gauda' form, which made Gorresio an important point of reference for the Italian

Indologists who succeeded him and devoted themselves to the Ramayana.

Tessitori was to be among the first of many such Indologists.

EIGHTEEN

As a young man of twenty-three who had just completed his thesis on the *Ramcharitmanas*, a poetic version of the Valmiki Ramayana, Tessitori, in a letter to a learned Jain acharya named Vijaya Dharma Suri, said, '...it is since my childhood that I am fondly attached to India and I consider her the principal object of my life. I wish to come to India and to continue my search of the Ramayana. I request you to arrange a job for me so that I can come to India.'

And Tessitori came to India.

But the trail of his journey was labyrinthine, beginning in remote Italy. Falling in love with India through Sanskrit and the Ramayana, and then through unexpected twists and turns, he reached India. Three decades and many more turns later, he was digging at the Kalibangan mounds.

After a series of odd jobs in India, Tessitori was invited by the Asiatic Society of Bengal to join its Linguistic Survey of India, where Sir George Grierson engaged him to lead the bardic and historical survey of Rajputana. He reached Rajputana in 1914 and stayed there for five long years. During this time he translated and noted innumerable medieval chronicles and poems from Rajasthan.

Along with his linguistic work, Tessitori roamed around Jodhpur and Bikaner in search of archaeological sites on behalf of Sir John Marshall (1876–1958), the Director-General of the Archaeological Survey of India from 1902 to 1928. He retrieved Gupta and Kushan terracottas from mounds in Bikaner and Dulamani in Ganganagar as well as two enormous marble statues of Goddess Saraswati somewhere near Ganganagar. He also deciphered and published the inscriptions found on Goverdhan stone pillars and tablets in the Jodhpur–Bikaner region.

Tessitori noted the proto-historic ruins in the Bikaner–Ganganagar region, correctly pointing out that these pre-dated Mauryan culture. The finding later enabled the discovery and excavation of the Indus Valley Civilisation site of Kalibangan. It was his relentless efforts that brought Kalibangan to be considered as the most important Indus Valley site in Rajasthan today. Scholars say Tessitori dug up the Kalibangan mounds to discover secrets that would change history books in the years to come, to discover hidden layers of Indus connections that no one believed even existed, and to show the world how just pure love and passion for history can unearth an entire bygone civilisation.

After Tessitori's death in India, his books, journals and personal items were sorted. Some were sent to his father in Udine, and some were sold at an auction. Tessitori was buried at Bikaner. Even now, many scholars think that when Tessitori was buried, a great amount of knowledge about a lost civilisation and about the Kalibangan artefacts was buried with him.

◆

Continuing his search with the keywords 'notes and writings of Tessitori', the next thing Sid Patel stumbled upon was a short article on his journals, which were sent back to Udine with some of his belongings after his death.

Sid started looking up every museum in Italy with a possible connection to Udine. After an hour of methodical searching, he found one—the archaeological museum Civici Musei di Udine had a dedicated room for Luigi Pio Tessitori and his works. An online tour of the room also showcased photographs of the two journals of Tessitori.

Sid smiled and stretched his arms. 'I have earned myself a Bournville chocolate today,' he grinned.

NINETEEN

The M2 Motorway was well-maintained and for the most part easy to drive on. The bikers had heard so much about the mountainous region of Chakwal and the salt range they'd cross on the second day from the waiters of the hotel where they had stayed for the night, that they expected to enjoy their ride doubly. But what they found out was different.

Including Chakwal and its salt range on a list of 'scenic places to visit' was an insult to places with scenic views everywhere. Rocky brown turf stretched out for miles in every direction. Without the aid of GPS, they wouldn't have known they were crossing the region they had heard so much about. However, Rob still wanted a group photograph for the blog, and they all had to oblige.

They covered a total of 381 kilometres from Lahore to Islamabad. There was a fee to be paid to cross the M2 Motorway, but the riders didn't have to pay, since the organising agency had already cleared all such things up for them. It took five hours for the group to reach Islamabad. On the way, they stopped at a service area called Bhera to relieve the fatigue that had set in from constant riding. Bhera proved to be a good service joint, with a Gloria Jeans Coffee and a Subway alongside other basic facilities. The toilets were clean, but Aurin found something weird. The urinals were placed a little too high. 'Life is beautiful with a blessed B!' he mumbled as he raised his torso a couple of inches, transferring his weight onto the toes, to relieve himself.

The scenery around the joint was neither beautiful nor interesting. Even so, Aurin couldn't complain, as the joint was crowded with college girls on a group tour, and they were far more beautiful and interesting than any scenery. Ever the charming lad with a child-like smile, Aurin had a good time chatting up the girls and obliging them with group selfies.

The next 183 kilometres between Islamabad and Peshawar went by uneventfully. They preferred to take the Grand Trunk Road over the Motorway, since they had heard it offered more scenic views, and they didn't regret that decision.

Rebuilt by Sher Shah Suri in the sixteenth century, the Grand Trunk Road or GT Road served as an ancient Mauryan route during the reign of Chandragupta Maurya. Extending from the mouth of the Ganges in the east to the north-western frontier of the Mauryan Empire, the GT Road is one of Asia's oldest and longest major roads. It has acted as a link between the Indian subcontinent and Central Asia for more than two millennia. It runs from Chittagong in Bangladesh to Howrah in the state of West Bengal in India, and then across northern India through Delhi and Amritsar. The road connects Lahore and Peshawar in Pakistan and terminates in Kabul, Afghanistan. The road was considerably upgraded by the British in the mid-nineteenth century.

◆

From Peshawar, it took a little over an hour for the group to reach the Torkham border. The evening darkness had descended by the time they reached Torkham. Toying with the idea of crossing the border the next morning, they stopped at a tea stall. The owner, a turbaned man with a white beard who served them their tea, told them about the conflict that had been raging between Pakistan and Afghanistan at this border. Pakistani authorities claimed that the militants responsible for the 2014 attack on Peshawar's Army Public School had entered Pakistan through Torkham. He also told them that Pakistan had closed the border for some time. Eventually, the two countries had agreed to reopen the border crossing for the sake of the thousands of stranded travellers on both sides.

'How is it over here, running a business with all this political turmoil and everything else that goes on?' Alex asked the stall owner.

'My ancestors were Pashtuns from Herat in Afghanistan. We are common people; we have no problems with each other. Look at me; I built a life for myself in Pakistan, and I am almost a Pakistani today,' the bearded man said. 'There are friendly people on both sides of the border. As you see all around you, this is a mountainous region, and we have scarce—if any—sources of entertainment. So we often cross the border and visit the sheesha bars on the other side, just for fun. I have many friends and relatives on that side; many of them come to drink tea at my shop late at night.' He winked and flashed a contented smile.

'That's nice to know.' Aurin nodded and smiled back.

'You see, my friends, many have attempted to conquer this region. Alexander the Great and Genghis Khan are two of the biggest examples. But no one could take away this beautiful land from the proud Afghan tribes of those days.

'You must have read—in the seventies, the Soviets entered the arena as yet another conquering party. The Afghan people fought back hard. Leading the campaign were none other than the Mujahideen. It is estimated that over 1.5 million civilians were killed in that war. The Mujahideen used guerrilla warfare tactics when they fought within Afghanistan's borders, in cities and in the countryside alike. That provoked the Soviets to begin bombing and utilising landmines, leaving Afghanistan in tatters. Finally, the Mujahideen managed to exhaust the Soviets and force them to flee these lands.'

'Sorry, I didn't get your name.' Rob interjected.

'Why sorry, my friend...I never told you my name!' The man laughed, though all they could hear was a strange kh...kh...kh... sound. 'Azar,' he introduced himself, shaking hands with Rob once he had stopped laughing.

'What actually happened after the Soviets were gone?' Rob took out his journal and pen and began fishing for more information.

'Afghanistan was back in the news for the Taliban war!' He started laughing hysterically again. 'The Taliban had emerged as the political winners of Afghanistan after a series of civil wars post the Soviet invasion,' the man said. 'Today, with the Taliban having been removed from power, Afghanistan is once again under a new leadership. The current president, Ashraf Ghani, wants to change the future of this war-torn nation.'

Tired and battered after the last mountainous lap of their long ride, the group decided to stay the night at a small motel owned by Azar's brother. They planned to get a good night's sleep and some breakfast before they crossed the border the next morning.

◆

That night, sitting in a sheesha bar with some of the other bikers, Rob wrote in his journal, *Afghanistan has been seeded in my dreams since the beginning of my travel career, yet when the idea of travelling through the country came up, gruesome visuals of its gory history clouded my mind... Today, sitting in a smoky sheesha bar at the Pak–Afghan border, after several pegs of local liquor inside my belly and holding my Afghanistan visa in my hand...my thoughts run wild once again. Shall we get across? Is this madness? My mind is plagued with so many vivid scenarios of what might go wrong... Am I going mad? Before I go mad or fall asleep tonight,* he kept on writing, *I must write, at the end of this second scorching day of our long journey: Who am I? I am a traveller, I'm a wanderer and madman. I'm a scar of love... in my loneliness. But on a starry night—I am a Legend.*

◆

Afghanistan houses over fifteen hundred historical sites, and excavations have revealed evidence of architectural influences that are both Eastern and Western. Afghan cities were sites for the exchange of Chinese silks, Persian silver and gold all the way from Rome. Much before it arrived in China, Buddhism spread to Afghanistan, and the Bamiyan Buddhas are the evidence. The Kushan Dynasty rulers had encouraged the spread of Buddhism to China. The continuous cultural exchange on the Afghan lands also resulted in Chinese designs and patterns influencing Islamic architecture in the fourteenth century and Mongol administration ideas being adapted into Afghanistan's laws. Aspects of intangible cultural heritage that developed through Silk Route trades during various periods continue to be a part of Afghan culture, including the number of languages spoken, and their hospitality. Since Afghanistan had no access to the ocean, it saw a decline in trade, once naval technology began to develop in the fifteenth century and naval routes were gradually used to lower costs and shorten lead times.

Torkham was the busiest port of entry between Pakistan and Afghanistan, serving as a major transporting, shipping and receiving hub. Highway 7 connects Torkham to Kabul through Jalalabad—the route the bikers were to follow.

TWENTY

He had not eaten anything for the last seven hours, and he didn't know if it was day or night in the world outside. The only thing that mattered to Sid at the moment was solving the mystery that he knew must have its roots somewhere in an era long lost.

After a few failed attempts, Sid finally broke into the secured archive portal of the Civici Musei di Udine, where they stored the digital copies of their displays. After an hour-long systematic search, he found the two journals he was looking for amidst a huge number of documents relating to the early twentieth century alone.

Unfortunately for him, one of the two journals turned out to be incomplete. It was just a PDF compilation of sixty scanned pages out of the original two hundred-page-journal of Tessitori. Sid downloaded both files and hoped he had got the right parts, or else he would have to keep searching.

With a fresh cup of coffee, Sid started sifting through the journals that Tessitori had written some hundred years ago. It was clear that Tessitori was absolutely impressed by the artefacts he had excavated at Kalibangan. He was so fascinated by some of the inscribed seals that he not only set aside special sections in his journal to describe them in detail, but also sketched a few of them that he thought merited visualising.

'I have written about my discovery of the three objects from Kalibangan to Sir George Grierson of The Asiatic Society of Bengal during my brief stay in Italy in 1919,' Tessitori wrote. 'One of them is a very different kind of a seal. Unlike the Harappan and other Indus Valley seals, this one is probably made of some unknown metal. Both sides of the seal bear thin concentric circular lines while only one side bears Indus inscriptions in known scripts. I told Sir George that I have a feeling the inscriptions were made for a specific purpose, other than trading.' On another page, he wrote, 'I suspect the seal to be an extremely interesting find: the mound itself on which it was discovered was very interesting. I believe it is prehistorical or at least non-Aryan. I only wish the inscriptions could tell us more!' He added, 'Grierson has suggested to me to show the seal to John Marshall upon my return to India.' He added in the footnote, 'I think I have to personally meet him and request him for a more planned and a bigger excavation in the region…'

At the end of the PDF file, there was a one-page note from the curator, which read as follows:

But the universe had different plans, and Tessitori couldn't do what he thought of doing. Because on his way to India from Italy, he contracted Spanish influenza and died in Bikaner after suffering for a few days in November 1919. And the knowledge of the seals was buried with him...

John Marshall never got to know what this ill-starred Italian had found in Rajasthan. In fact, no one will ever know the possible direction that Tessitori's discoveries would have taken if they were not brought to a halt by his early and unfortunate death.

Sid opened the second PDF file. It had thirty pages from Tessitori's journal—all sketches of Harappan objects and seals he had found. He turned page after page but didn't find anything odd or anything that matched the descriptions by Tessitori—'concentric rings on one side and Indus inscriptions on the other'.

His spirit waning, he took a moment to survey his chances and flipped through the last few pages, hoping to find something that fitted. Instead, he found something better.

♦

The twenty-seventh page had sketches of both sides of a circular seal which appeared bigger than the others so far. The seal had concentric grooves on both sides.

Sid enlarged it on his screen and looked carefully.

Both sides of the seal were drawn in pen and ink with special care. The circles were so fine they seemed to be etched by a modern-day laser machine. One of the two sides had Indus inscriptions amidst the concentric circles, which were so common that even someone like Sid, whose history was as bad as his Greek, could almost recognise them.

Tessitori had repeated his observation at the bottom of the page.

> *This is a very different kind of seal, and much thinner. Unlike the Harappan and other Indus Valley seals, this was probably made of some alloy unknown to us.*

Sid picked up his cup from the desk to drain the last bit of coffee at the bottom, and then a light bulb flashed inside his mind. He read through the lines once again.

> *...different kind of seal... Unlike the Harappan and other Indus Valley seals...probably made of some unknown alloy...*

Where was it that he'd recently heard something similar? He racked his brain but couldn't remember anything.

And then, this little packet sitting on the corner of his desk came into his cone of vision.

'Eric,' he whispered.

Yes, of course, it was Eric Roy, his boss, who had used almost the same words to describe a seal he had found!

Sid threw his empty coffee cup into the bin and grabbed the packet, which bore his name on the top in Eric's handwriting.

◆

When the morning light pierced through their dusty motel window, an intense realisation of what lay ahead pierced through their minds. But an hour later they were busy devouring a delicious Afghani breakfast, which included eggs cooked with tomatoes and green onions, thick sweet breads called rohts and a savoury sambosa with ground beef and spinach filling, with a sweet dish on the side called alwa—a pudding made of roasted semolina and homemade cheese with raisins and thick cream. Araash, the innkeeper, made tea for the group and served it on a large wooden tray at the end of the meal. It was milk-brewed steaming chai, which Araash served with a smile fixed on his face. The food and the chai helped the bikers brush their worries and dark thoughts aside and they hit the road. The border was tight with security. Looks of concern flashed across the faces of the border guards when they saw a group of bikers crossing into their lands.

Pakistan's Frontier Corps and the Afghan Border Police are the two main agencies that control Torkham. They are backed by the Afghan and Pakistani militaries. There is also some presence of the NATO forces on the Afghan side of the crossing, mainly personnel of the US army. The bikers were told that the American Forward Operating Base was located a few miles from the crossing in Nangarhar province.

Upon first sighting Afghanistan after crossing the border, Aurin found the country different from any other place he had seen before. The run-down streets and dilapidated houses were brimming over with amputee war vets and burqa-clad women begging to the people entering their nation. It was a heart-breaking scene, which brought him face to face with the reality of a region that had suffered so much for so long.

They rolled along slowly on their bikes and surveyed their surroundings. Sitting on a broken slab of mortar on the side of the road, a blind old beggar played a battered rubab and sang along. For a moment, Aurin couldn't recall where he had seen someone playing that instrument before. Then he remembered he had seen it in the immensely popular song 'Mehbooba' from the legendary Hindi film *Sholay*.

The blind man's song echoed in the mountains all around.

Father Smit whispered in Aurin's ear from the pillion seat, 'Your journey through Afghanistan would have a different meaning, Auri boy, if you only knew what this old man is singing about!'

'I didn't know you understand Pashto as well!' Aurin said.

'I do, but this is not Pashto. He is singing in Dari, which is Persian in Afghanistan.' Father Smit placed his hand on Aurin's shoulder.

'Tell me, Father, what does his song say? I like the tune.' Aurin slowed down his bike.

Father Smit translated what the old man was singing:

If leadership rests inside the lion's jaw,
so be it. Go snatch it from his jaws.
Your lot shall be greatness, prestige, honour and glory.
If all fails, face death like a man
Go snatch it from your life...
Go snatch it from your life...

Aurin looked around him and whispered in his mind, 'Afghanistan, you have become a part of me forever!'

TWENTY-ONE

Highway A01, also known as the Ring Road, was developed on an ancient 2,200-kilometre road network that circulated within Afghanistan, connecting Kabul, Ghazni, Kandahar, Herat and Mazari Sharif. Well-documented by Greek and Buddhist sources in the fourth century BC, this part of the Asian Highway Network exposes a traveller to the most spectacular mountain landscapes.

The only public transport available on some sections of this route are the infamous Milli buses. Managed by the Afghan Ministry of Transport and Civil Aviation, Milli buses are the cheapest mode of transport available in Kabul and some other places including Kandahar, Panjshir Province and Parwan. These buses are often overcrowded and meet with fatal accidents.

The bikers travelled from Torkham towards Kabul through rugged and mostly barren terrain. The Jalalabad–Kabul section of Highway A01 followed the Kabul river gorge for sixty-four kilometres, taking them over treacherous mountain roads. They found several roadside signs warning drivers of the fatal traffic accidents that occurred in the area due to reckless driving, and they instinctively took extra care while riding through the region. In Alex's words, 'Beauty and danger go hand in hand!'

◆

They wanted to avoid the hustle-bustle of big cities like Jalalabad and Kabul, and so they bypassed both and headed for a place called Panjab, 477 kilometres from the Torkham border. It was the only place where standard lodging was available on the entire thousand-kilometre stretch between Torkham and the Afghanistan–Iran border.

Alex pulled over and killed his bike's engine. He and his navigator Jojo—the paleface—climbed down and stretched, as did the rest of the bikers. The group was about to reach the Afghan version of Panjab and had stopped at a roadside joint just short of their destination for a tea break.

An irrigation canal ran along the left side of the road. The tea stall stood on its lush green banks surrounded by grazing goats. The soft metallic jingle of their bells wafted over to them with the cold breeze that blew from the north.

'We are doing good miles,' Aurin announced. 'Let's have a cup or two of tea here—this place looks fantastic!'

'You and your tea!' Alex smiled. 'But that's a good proposition.' He pulled out a folded map from his cargo pants' side zipper and concentrated on it. A few seconds later, he mumbled, 'This canal is the only source of water for this whole area. As per the map, we are almost there.' He nodded cheerfully. 'We are doing better than our plan.'

Father Smit, who was riding pillion, climbed down from the bike and stretched. He then took out his mobile phone lazily and checked it. A quick gaze at the screen and he whispered, 'Auri boy, sometime between the last dinner and now, my phone has received this message from Eric. Finally he is on the trail and he has asked us to stay put till he calls.'

'Good,' said Aurin, 'that takes some of the pressure off our shoulders. Let us then enjoy the journey a little more.'

On reaching Panjab, they found a motel named Arkhanchi with

basic amenities and decided to settle there for the night. For dinner, they ordered yakhni palaw, a brown rice dish with meat and stock, lamb kebabs, some kind of dumplings called 'mantu' with a filling of onions and ground beef, and challow with korma. Aurin wondered aloud if the challow was indeed just well-cooked, good quality white rice. Seated across from him, Father Smit replied, 'Auri boy, don't be surprised. This is similar to our chawal and the Iranian chelow… And please, don't tell me you never knew the chelow kebabs you ate throughout your St Xavier's days at Peter Cat in Park Street had an Iranian connection!'

TWENTY-TWO

Marco Delfino, the twelfth Count of Udine, Italy, referred to as Count Udine of Friuli in the five hundred-page annual report of Delfino Antiquities International, stood in his private office and stared down at large-scale topographical maps laid out on a gigantic marble conference table.

Delfino was in his late fifties and had a broad forehead, thinning salt-and-pepper hair swept back, a long, clean-shaven face and the darkened lips of a long-time smoker. He had a frail structure and was around six feet tall. There was a hint of a Friuli accent when Delfino spoke, but that was where any hints to his Italian origin ended. Major Bill Robins, American by birth and a washout of the Armed Forces of the Italian Republic, and now Delfino's Director of Special Projects and Acquisitions, stood beside him. Bill had a square face, blue eyes and a well-built body with heavy forearms. He was over four inches taller than the Count.

'Do we have any coordinates for the other site at the given location, Bill?' Delfino asked in a cold voice.

'No, not yet, Count.'

'Do you know why we had to destroy that pre-Harappan site in India, which could easily be valued in billions of Euros?'

'It was a conflict zone, and we didn't have any options for transportation.' Bill remained calm.

'Yes, that's one reason, but not the only one.' Delfino's voice deepened as his eyes focused on Bill's face. 'We could have arranged some way to take the artefacts out, but the main reason was that we didn't want to have a living twin of the main site when we know the other site is much bigger and more accessible. The key to this business is simple—an ancient archaeological site, just like an artefact, becomes priceless when it is the only one on earth. We also have clients and their weird wishes along with other reasons, of course, which you don't need to know. So, do we have a location?'

'My teams are working on it, Count. One of the teams has a lead as well. Their intel has found a group of archaeologists connected with the 1989-90 Nimrud excavation who are back for the third time to dig in Nineveh, Iraq.'

'Find out what they are up to—fast,' Delfino snarled.

'I am on it.'

'You actually need to issue an order to all your teams searching for the site to keep a watch on all active excavation sites in the region this moment onwards,' Delfino instructed. 'And for every probable site, they need to have transportation plans. The treasure is worth nothing in the middle of the desert or a hostile territory if we don't have a sound transportation plan.'

'Roger that, Count.'

'One more thing. If we create a mess, we'll have to clean it up as quickly as possible.' Delfino kept staring down at the maps. 'What about Ivan, by the way?'

'He flew with a discarded missile carrier, did his job in the Thar Desert and flew back safely. The hidden site and witness have both been dealt with, but it looks like the SIAD has picked up his scent.'

'The witness?' Delfino furrowed his brows. 'You mean the oil kid who actually put us onto the whole thing with his email?'

'Yes,' Bill nodded. 'He's gone. But I am really curious to know how we intercepted his email.'

Delfino looked at Bill for a couple of seconds and then dug out a cigar case from his trouser pocket. He lit a cigar, took a hearty drag and said, 'You're lucky I have some spare time to enlighten you. At the Echelon monitoring station outside London near Chatham, most of the world's communications are recorded. This surveillance programme is operated by the US with the support of four other nations party to the UK–USA Security Agreement—Australia, Canada, New Zealand and the UK, together known as the Five Eyes. The Echelon programme was created in the late 1960s to monitor the military and diplomatic communications of the Soviet Union and its Eastern Bloc allies during the Cold War.' Delfino paused for another puff. 'By the end of the twentieth century, the system had allegedly been altered beyond its military and diplomatic roots to also act as a global interception system for commercial as well as private communications.' Delfino paused for another drag. 'It is actually a huge spying device, which snags worldwide communications and runs them through several review programmes. Predetermined keywords are identified and flagged, and after several rounds of scanning, the communications are either forwarded to a proper intelligence service or ignored as unimportant.'

Bill kept nodding through the entire monologue.

Delfino continued, 'Haban's email from Rajasthan was passed up to a satellite before being relayed back to earth. As it was relayed back, Echelon snatched the message and ran it through some programmes. Fortunately for us, there were one or two words in it that triggered a review. So, the email would have been sent on a journey from England to the National Security Agency in Maryland, then on to the Central Intelligence Agency in Langley, Virginia, except...' Delfino smiled, '... there is someone inside Echelon who happens to know us and so the review request came to us instead of its official destination.'

Bill kept nodding his head the same way, but this time a grin appeared on his face.

'Coming back to business,' Delfino said, 'if SIAD has picked up Ivan's scent, take him out immediately. We can't get tied up over small issues now; any witness is a threat.'

'Sure, Count.' Bill said meekly. He was still overwhelmed by the new piece of information he had just received from his boss.

'Do we plan to use the photographs taken by the oil kid for our next phase of explorations?'

'I think we should, sir.'

'Don't think; take action!' hissed Delfino. 'Share those photographs with all the team leads and brief them once again on what we are looking for. A visual lead is always better. Any other mess I need to know of?'

'Negative.'

'Find me someone who can deal with this whole thing in Iraq better.'

'Yes, Count.'

'And do it quickly. Too many people know about this already.'

◆

By the time the sun rose in the eastern sky, they were already riding.

They felt the crimson dawn creeping up their sides and over their left shoulders, promising to burn them through the day.

They headed for Islam Qala, a city in the western Herat province that lay on the Afghan–Iran border and one they had to cross on their way to Tehran. It was the official point of entry into Afghanistan from neighbouring Taybad, Iran. All trade between the two countries passed through this town. But before Islam Qala, they had to reach Herat.

Herat lay in the fertile valley of the river Hari, though it went by different names across the region. Some called it Hari Rud, some called it Harayu, and some marked it as the Saraju river from the

Ramayana. By the sixth century BC Herat was settled. Scholars noted a mound called Kuhandazh to the north of the Old City as the site of a fort that was built by Alexander in 330 BC following his conquest of the Achaemenid city of Artacoana. After Alexander's exit, Herat was ruled successively by the Seleucids, Parthians, Kushans, Sasanians, Hephthalites, Umayyads, Tahirids, Saffarids, Samanids, Seljuk, Ghaznavids and Ghurids. Herat thrived under the Silk Road trade between the Eastern Mediterranean, India and China, and became an important city of the Ghurid dynasty in AD 1175. The city was eventually destroyed by the Mongols in AD 1221.

The closer they got to the Afghan–Iran border, the more dreary and rocky the landscape of Herat turned out to be. The occasional patch of raw, dusty scrubs appeared on the scenery, desperate to survive in the arid environment. The highway ran like a single trail of a jet plane in the air and was the only marker of the twenty-first century in the midst of a region that had not changed much over several millennia. It was hard to believe they were within a few flying hours from the cosmopolitan cities that throb with high-end restaurants to temperature-controlled super luxury malls.

◆

'We are literally following in the footsteps of Marco Polo!' Alex exclaimed after splashing his face with some water from his flask. One of their bikes had developed technical problems and refused to run, which had caused the group an unexpected delay of four and a half hours. They were still about two hundred kilometres away from Islam Qala and some eighty kilometres from Herat, and the sun had almost gone down.

'You are right,' replied Rob. 'Afghanistan has seen tremendous changes over thousands of years, but the country's landscape is such that the major connecting routes have remained the same through all of these years.'

'If you observe the common people of the country, you will

find nothing much has changed for them either,' Father Smit added. 'Afghanistan has undergone major political changes, but for the vast majority of Afghans, daily life continues in much the same vein as it has for centuries.' He punctuated his sentence with a signal to Alex to pass the water bottle.

'That's true, but...' Aurin spoke, stretching out his arms and legs in the shape of an X, 'you need to travel through Afghanistan to learn that tourist infrastructure is almost non-existent here.' He looked around at everyone's faces and added, 'Days are long and hard, coupled with non-existent tourist services and toilets that you can't use.' Then he broke into a grin. 'I never knew there could be something like peeing bottoms up, but today I can write a thesis on the subject!'

'But then again, my friend,' opined Rob, 'don't let the trivial things put you off. In my opinion, Afghanistan is the most fascinating country in the world, in its own rugged way!'

♦

The whizzing wind turned chilly, hinting at a cold night ahead, and darkness enveloped them. They drove their bikes through flat and empty land, with nothing to see for miles, barring an occasional service station or a herd of wild camels.

'Do we camp here for the night? Or shall we drink some coffee and set out to kill some more miles?' asked Aurin.

'We are about one hour away from Herat,' said Alex. 'Let's take a coffee break and reach Herat tonight.'

They rolled their vehicles onto the endless dry land off the side of the highway and parked them in a circle next to a huge boulder. They washed their faces, rubbed wet towels on the backs of their necks and cleaned their earlobes. It was a routine Father Smit had demonstrated on the first day of their journey, and they had all liked it. Since then, it had turned into a group ritual. None of them could ever have imagined that such a simple thing could rejuvenate the body like magic.

After a short coffee break, the group was surprised to discover that they were not exhausted at all, not even after riding throughout the day in the scorching heat. They decided to ride on and cover some more miles before calling it a day. This section of the road was broken, and their challenge was a lethal combination of rugged terrain and complete darkness, but they all voted to have a taste of the dark side of adventure as well. And so they rode on into the night, eager for the next part of their journey, not knowing that what awaited them was a hell of an adventure.

TWENTY-THREE

The group geared up and the wheels began rolling, one bike after another, on the twisting dirt track that vanished behind a large boulder.

One of the major drawbacks of using coffee as an energy source is its debilitating effect on the human bladder. At least that was what Father Smit thought as Aurin went to relieve himself while the other seven members changed gears and rode off into the dark of the desert night.

A caffeine-induced pressure transported Aurin to a state of trance, and his mind took him places—in a vision, he travelled through the salty waters of the Sunderbans to the dampness of Chittagong to the Irish lands with its soft breeze. He could smell the Worcester snow and the Trongsa Mountains, and he almost smelled Iqbal Miya, their guide on the previous adventure, cooking fish on a slow fire.

He finished his business and thought, *This is so much better. I am starting to hate this concept of 'high urinal bowls' all over again!* He mumbled, 'You can use the urinals all right, but they are so damn high you start worrying that your pants or hands might touch them while you're at it!' Aurin shrugged, 'This is outright scary!' He unclipped a small bottle of hand sanitizer hanging from his knapsack, rubbed his hands with the liquid and breathed in the cold dryness of the terrain. 'Life is beautiful with a blessed B,' he whispered to himself as he walked towards the rear light of the bike that awaited him with a thumping engine.

♦

'It looks like the half moon is a little early tonight, Auri boy!' Father Smit exclaimed, looking up at the crystal-clear sky. 'She'll show us the way—we are in luck.' He laughed loudly and tapped down on the first gear with his toe as Aurin adjusted himself on the pillion seat. Father Smit rolled the bike and picked up speed.

As he twisted the handlebar and turned the bike around the large boulder, that very moment Aurin captured movement in his peripheral vision. Something was following them. A silhouette soon emerged against the fire they had just left behind—a man on horseback galloped towards them, and some more followed behind him.

TWENTY-FOUR

The road was bumpy, and Father Smit struggled to keep his balance on the one-ton beast. In the rear-view mirror, he saw the leading horseman closing in fast and pulling something out in the red glow of his bike's taillight—it appeared to be a long, dark metallic object. He was almost upon them—upon Aurin, to be precise, since he was on the back seat. The dark metallic object flashed in the rear light once again. This time Father Smit recognised the rifle barrel.

He tried balancing the bike through a narrow clearing between two boulders. Out of the corner of his eye, he saw the leader of the horsemen holding up his rifle by its barrel and swinging its wooden stock in the air like a cricket bat. The blow hit Aurin on his right shoulder, and he toppled from the bike. Luckily, even after the heavy blow, Aurin did not land on a rock but fell on his left arm on a dusty stretch of earth. Father Smit wasn't so lucky. He couldn't keep his balance, and the bike skidded down the road, hitting a large boulder and flinging his body over it.

Aurin recovered fast, coughing as he sat up. The horse rider pulled on the reins to slow down his horse and turn around for another attack, ready to crush Aurin to dust. And this wasn't the only pursuit Aurin had to worry about. He knew there would be more of his clan joining the attack any moment. He sat on the dirt track, hands sweeping back and forth in panic, finding nothing but pebbles.

Their bike lay on the ground some ten feet away, purring away with its lights still on. The horse rider charged straight at Aurin, the headlight of the bike dancing on his galloping frame, making him look even more demonic. He held his gun high over Aurin, brandishing it like a sword ready to slash Aurin's head in half.

Dust, pebbles…stone!

Aurin's hand had found what it needed. He snapped it up and threw it straight at the rider's face, using all the skills he had learnt playing cricket through his school and college years.

There was a 'thud', followed by a scream, and the rider fell off the horse. Supporting his body with one hand on the ground, Aurin saw the horse's hoofs towering over his head, all set to trample him. He threw himself sideways, rolling over as the horse thundered away. He rose up on his hands and knees and made a run for the fallen man's rifle.

Recovering from the blow, the bearded man also flapped about on the ground, looking for his gun. Pouncing on him, Aurin pinned him to the ground and punched him so hard in the face that his turban went flying.

But the next moment, he saw the nearest horseman coming dangerously close. Aurin picked up the gun, turned the barrel to face the rider and pulled the trigger. But he missed. The rider kept coming at him as he tried to shoot again, but the horse proved faster. The man landed a kick on his shoulder, flinging him face-first on the ground next to the first rider. The gun fell out of his hand. With his shoulder burning with pain, Aurin rose, supporting himself on his hands again. The horseman made a quick turn to come around for another attack.

Aurin looked around for the gun but couldn't find it. It couldn't have landed more than a few feet away. Two more men on horses arrived on the scene but stopped short, probably to enjoy the fight from a safe distance. The second rider turned his horse around and charged straight at Aurin, who crawled back and felt the barrel of the gun against his knee. He picked it up even as his shoulder ached. The horse looked like a silhouette of a thundering giant in the light from the fallen bike. Aurin gathered all his strength and fired just above the horse's head.

The rider fell backwards and the horse took a giant leap to jump over Aurin, its front legs sweeping the gun out of his hands in the process. At the last moment, Aurin ducked with his face down in the dust to avoid being crushed by the horse.

Bereft of the gun once again, Aurin was left with nothing to put up a fight. He looked up to find the other horsemen closing in. Lying in the dust, he counted the seconds until he would hear the sound of the firing that would end his life. But what he heard instead was the ignition of a 500cc engine followed by a heavy thump that came directly towards him.

◆

In the blaze of the Thunderbird's headlight, Father Smit could see three horsemen approaching Aurin. The man in the lead grabbed the barrel of the rifle that was slung over his back. He brought it forward and lowered it to hip level, readying to fire at Aurin.

Father Smit wasted no time and twisted the throttle. The engine revved. 'What do I do now…?' He racked his brains.

On an impulse, he cut straight across the stony terrain on his bike and intercepted the lead horseman. His guess was that the rider planned to get close enough and then stop and take a head-on shot at Aurin.

And he knew he wasn't going to let that happen. Not tonight.

He leaned forward on the tanker of his bike. The cold dusty wind hit him in his face, and he forced the throttle to its limit. He finally had a plan.

At the precise point of interception between Aurin and the lead horseman, Father Smit twisted the handlebar. Sweeping across dust and stones, the bike swerved towards the horse, while simultaneously, Father Smit threw himself on the other side, towards Aurin. Scared at the sight of the bike coming straight at him, the horse jumped, causing the rider to lose balance. The horse succeeded in dodging the bike and galloped away, whereas the rider lay rolling on the stony ground. The other two horses were also scared by the spectacle and ran off in different directions along with their riders.

Father Smit rolled on the ground to reach Aurin.

'The gun, the gun!' Aurin pointed Father Smit towards the gun he had lost some moments ago. Father Smit scrambled back to his feet and dived for the gun on his right. When he bounced back up, he had it in his hand. He pinned the fallen man—presumably the leader—on the ground with his boot and pressed the barrel of the gun to his temple. Just then, the earth rumbled with the sound of several engines.

Led by Pablo—the Mumbaikar—all of their fellow bikers had returned.

TWENTY-FIVE

The town of Islam Qala had a population of about sixteen thousand. The Afghan Border Police (ABP) secured the border, while the regular Afghan National Police were in charge of all other law enforcement activities. Islam Qala also had a small base of the Afghan military. The town was populated by Tajiks, Pashtuns and Hazaras, a mostly Sunni population, aside from a few Shia Muslims. The average low temperature of Islam Qala during October was around eight degrees Celsius, but that night was much colder.

After the attack, the group had decided to get as far as they could in the least time possible. So they rode to Islam Qala, bypassing Herat. They spent the night in a cheap motel and started off a little late the next morning. During breakfast, they discussed the incident near Herat city, and the innkeeper told them about a couple of notorious groups on horses who mugged unaccompanied travellers and looted them along that stretch.

The security situation and tourist infrastructure of Afghanistan were the two things so far that Aurin had a lot to complain about, but he was yet to learn that crossing the Afghanistan–Iran border was a simple process. The border was open for foreigners and the border officials were cooperative. They were much more professional than most of the group members had expected them to be. Thanks to the presence of several armed forces of both countries on either side of the border, the security system worked just fine.

The border at Islam Qala was connected to a newly built section of Highway 97 via Torbat-e Jam and Neyshabur. Islam Qala to Tehran was to be a little over a thousand kilometre journey for them. The road was new and good, so they all agreed to ride straightaway to Tehran, for they all wanted to spend at least one night in a decent hotel.

◆

As they entered Tehran, they found out the streets were wide and spacious. The old market areas were dusty, overcrowded and noisy; honking cars and trucks were everywhere. People walked or cycled about in the narrow lanes of the market and vendors hawked their wares on donkey carts. The group headed for the more upmarket part of the city and eventually booked themselves in Hotel Espinas Persian Gulf, a sophisticated hotel in downtown Tehran that several websites recommended. The exterior of the hotel seamlessly blended modern design elements with rich natural material, and the serene ambience of the hotel instantly calmed the tired bikers. The hotel had a large swimming pool and a wellness centre that to the men looked like a tranquil beach resort where they longed to relax, with their fingers nursing Long Island cocktails after the journey they'd had.

A warm and cozy coffee shop overlooking the beautiful city of Tehran offered special lattes and several other delicious brews along with freshly baked cakes. The hotel had two elegant restaurants—one Mediterranean and the other traditional Iranian. The concierge suggested to Aurin that they should dine at the Mediterranean restaurant, as the traditional Iranian chef was on leave. But that was for later.

The men went upstairs to their second floor twin-sharing rooms that were on the two sides of a single corridor. Aurin and Father Smit had a couple of lazy shots of vodka from the mini bar looking out at the lights of an unknown city. And then they all hit the swimming pool.

◆

The breakfast spread was lavish and some of the guys did not want to leave their tables the next morning. Finally, when they all did, Rob suggested that they visit a mystic place called Behistun or Bisotun in the Kermanshah Province of Iran on their way from Tehran. He promised that the detour time wouldn't exceed an hour. 'I really want pictures of this place to add colour and depth to our travelogue!' he pleaded with the group.

Rob didn't know much else about the place except that it was a UNESCO world heritage site. And none of their mobile phones had enough connectivity to allow them to look it up online. Not that anyone cared that much. They all agreed to go.

TWENTY-SIX

As the bikers reached closer to Mount Behistun, they found out it was a node of the ancient Silk Road and would fall on their way to Baghdad. Rob pointed out huge rock inscriptions some hundred metres up on the mountain wall. He said, 'In old Persian, the place was called Bagastana, which means "a place where gods dwell".'

There were four gigantic multilingual inscriptions engraved on the side of the cliff. Hundreds of square feet of rough rock surface had been cut and polished to give relief for the inscriptions. In the largest one, Darius had documented how the supreme god Ahuramazda had chosen him to dethrone a usurper, how he had set out to crush several revolts, and how he overpowered his foreign adversaries. On one of the inscriptions, the Imperial Coat of Arms or the symbol of Zoroastrianism—the Faravahar—was engraved beautifully.

'Mindblowing!' Rob exclaimed. 'Look at that! How could they reach all the way up there and etch something this fantastic?' He stood in awe.

'Zoroastrianism was spread via the Silk Road to the West,' Aurin said. 'I have read that like the Rosetta Stone, some of these multilingual inscriptions and rock reliefs were crucial to the decipherment of cuneiform script.'

'The more you travel on the Silk Route,' noted Father Smit, 'the more you believe in the power of human determination and ability. They were human beings with a vision, who thought of building roads through these mountain terrains; and they were human beings with hands made of flesh and bones, after all, who built these roads.'

◆

The Iraq–Iran border crossing near Khosravi was well-organised. It was much better than what Alex and his biker gang had expected it would be. It looked like the officers had already been informed of the group's visit. They had a piece of paper ready with the details of all the members. As this border was a high security and conflict zone, they were all a little worried, but it turned out to be nice and easy.

Aurin watched with his bike's engine thumping as a bored official came out of a concrete building on the left of the barricade. The officer walked up to the bike in the front and collected papers from Alex. He checked the papers, held out his hand for a bribe as though it was the most normal thing in the world and stared at Alex's bike. Aurin noticed Alex diligently avoiding the look and handing over five twenty-dollar notes after counting them twice. The officer returned their papers after tallying their names against his own copy and called someone from the cabin. A second officer walked out of the cabin and joined them. He was armed with an AK-47 assault rifle slung across his chest. The man pushed a switch to pull up the barricade and let the riders pass, staring longingly at the bikes as they zoomed past him one after another. Aurin didn't take his eyes off the man's trigger finger until they were well past the barricade.

'That was fun, Father Smit!' Aurin said with his eyes focused on the road ahead.

'I don't know if it was fun, but I sure as hell was worried about their hungry glances!' Father Smit laughed from the pillion seat.

TWENTY-SEVEN

It happened years ago. Much before security cameras were introduced in museums and libraries. Marco Delfino, a history student, had found something incredible at the Udine Museum in Italy while on a part-time restoration assignment. It was a copy of one of the most popular epics of India, the *Ramcharitmanas*, which, along with several other books, had been donated to the museum by a certain Tessitori family after the death of its owner. The incredible thing was not the book, but two pages in the book, on the corners of which were some things written in pencil. Things even the museum authorities didn't know the book had. Delfino had torn out the two pages and smoothly pocketed them when he found the scribblings.

Delfino tried deciphering the coded messages for many years after that, and with professional help he found partial success as well. He had come to know that the scribbled lines were the key to an ancient relic that was the source of unthinkable power.

He travelled to several places hinted at by the coded message. He even photographed and documented his journeys. By the age of thirty-eight, he had shortlisted four probable locations. He used future generation geological instruments prototyped by his friend, who was developing them for the German military. Being advanced technology that no one else had access to, the software and equipment allowed him to scan every inch of the ground, from the topsoil to over fifty feet deep, at those locations. It was a kind of study no one had conducted before.

Unfortunately, Delfino couldn't find success. He still hadn't found the big secret he was hoping to unearth.

TWENTY-EIGHT

They crossed Khanaqin and embarked on the last lap of their long journey. In five more hours they would reach Baghdad. They headed east for another one and a half hours, eventually driving up along the shores of Lake Hamrin. They were near the end of Route 5, which would transform into a bridge and take them to the other side of the lake.

The scorching sun was above their heads, and they all looked longingly at the shadows of palm trees on both sides of the road that snaked along the lake shore. The bike in the front glided to the right on a dirt path, scrambled under the shadow of a bunch of palm trees and stopped. Alex and Jojo climbed down from the bike and walked towards the rest of the group. Alex stretched out his hands and said in a theatrical voice, 'Gentlemen, I give you Lake Hamrin.' He took a deep breath, filled his lungs with the fresh air and continued, 'The town of Hamrin is on the western shore of the lake, and that, my friends,' he pointed in the north-western direction with his right hand, 'is the southern tip of the beautiful Hamrin Mountains.'

'You'll make a good tour guide, Alex,' Aurin muttered. 'Just take the theatrics out of it!'

Everyone laughed at the comment, including Alex.

Aurin added, 'Can we have a proper lunch, please? The clean air here is highly appetising, and canned food is simply no answer to it!'

Everyone in the group paused to appreciate the beauty of the waterfront. The asphalt of the Route 5 bridge gleamed in the midday sun like a thin line of ether in the middle of the water body that stretched out in front of them from left to right.

Father Smit said, 'I agree with Aurin…' Then he met Alex's eye and immediately added, 'Not on the tour guide part of his statement, but on the canned food part for sure.'

Everyone laughed again and agreed. Without a word, Alex took out the map from his cargo pants' pocket. He spread it open on the seat of his Enfield and pointed at some settlements on the other side of the lake. They decided to cross the lake and settle for lunch at a decent roadside food joint.

The ride along the side of Lake Hamrin was a wonderful experience. The road was as smooth as a runway, and the view on both sides was breathtaking. After all the dusty roads and desert landscapes they had crossed, the cobalt water of the lake soothed their eyes, and the smell of the fresh air drenched their souls. Above all, the thought of freshly cooked food instantly brought on pangs of hunger. Once on the other side of the lake, they drove eastward and reached the settlement they had found on the map. They looked around for a food joint and stopped at the first one they could find.

It was nothing fancy—a small roadside joint offering the regular meals of the region. They ordered döner kebab, which was parantha-wrapped grilled meat, and kubbah, minced meat ground with wheat and spices.

The owner was a bulky, ever-smiling man with a thick moustache and a white cloth wrapped around his head. He welcomed them with a broad smile. It seemed like the joint didn't get much business and the owner was happy to have people to talk to. The bikers settled into wrought iron chairs around a number of round tables crammed into the small space in front of the kitchen. The owner introduced himself as Khaled and joined them.

'Welcome to my humble food joint, my friends. I can assure you no one within a radius of 150 kilometres can serve you the authentic taste of the region that you will get here.' He paired his speech with a peculiar constant nodding and an equally unusual smile.

'Of that I am sure, Mr Khaled,' said Jojo. 'We are very hungry and need something quick and nice—that's why we have ordered döner kebab and kubbah. We have a long way to go, you see!'

'Please also try our rice dish—maqluba with freshwater fish; I promise you'll thank me later,' Khaled urged. 'And you know what?' he continued. 'Food should never be taken in haste, my friend.' He raised a hand. 'You respect your food today, and the Almighty will arrange for the next day.' Khaled kept nodding and smiling. 'People of this region have always respected food. You might not believe this,' he started yet again, 'but archaeologists have found a list compiling over eight hundred different items of food and drink in Iraq recorded in cuneiform tablets in 1900 BC. The list included twenty different kinds of cheese, a hundred varieties of soup and three hundred types of bread—each with different ingredients, fillings, shapes and sizes.' Khaled paused for breath.

'The man sure knows his food well!' Father Smit observed.

Everyone smiled in amazement at their host's knowledge of the traditional food of the region. Aurin made a mental note to study ancient recipes and find the time to document them in a blog.

'Let me tell you this,' Khaled continued, 'written in 1700 BC, a cuneiform tablet found in Babylon, near Baghdad, mentioned twenty-four recipes for meat and vegetable stew, enhanced and seasoned with onion, garlic and spices and herbs like cassia, cumin, coriander, mint and dill. Stew is a mainstay of this region's cuisine. Why don't you order some?' Khaled suddenly got excited. 'I assure you there is nothing ancient about them here—my kitchen makes all our stews fresh!' He laughed.

The group felt relaxed at the prospect of good food and an entertaining host. They knew they were very close to their destination and were making good time. After the meal, they would drive straight to Baghdad through a small town named Miqdadiyah.

TWENTY-NINE

It took Suleiman the entire next day to collect what he thought they would require, including servicing his old black Range Rover, and another half day to plan and spread the rumour that he was taking his new client out on a tourist visit to the Nineveh ruins. On hearing about it, Eric was impressed. 'Fulfilling dreams and wishes…you truly are a man of your word, huh!' And they both had a good laugh.

Suleiman arranged the required permits to strengthen their story. It was reasonable enough in any case. There were always some history buffs among the regular tourists to Samarra who went to Nineveh, either for the history on the surface or in search of the history still hidden. People of Samarra and Mosul were happy as long as their foreign visitors left some of their money behind.

They had a quick brunch and stepped out.

'Into the truck, my friend, and I will take you for a ride,' Suleiman said with a mischievous smile.

'I was afraid you were going to say that!' Eric chuckled.

They drove in the north-western direction along the arrow-straight two-lane Baghdad–Mosul highway via Tirkit. Suleiman was at the wheel. Large plastic jerry cans that Suleiman had bought the day before and filled with drinking water were stored in the back of the truck. And along with other supplies, a few fifty-litre emergency fuel cans were bolted with iron ties to the floor of the cargo compartment in the rear. Both men sat in the bench-like front seat that seemed to take 'hardass' rather literally.

Suleiman had already explained the drill he'd planned for the trip. For an hour and a half, they would drive on the Mosul highway until they reached Mukeshefah, from where he would guide the truck down a dirt track leading into a depression that went through the desert. If there was a problem in Nineveh, Suleiman thought it was strategic for them to be cautious and move tactically. 'No reason to take the highway and announce our arrival in Nineveh with a loudspeaker, eh?' he said.

Right on schedule, they reached a point where the safety bars on both sides of the highway had been taken off to make way for vehicles to exit. Suleiman guided the truck down a barely visible track and it thumped off the road onto the hard-packed sand in one abrupt movement. They swung into top gear in a bid to get as far from the highway as possible until it was lost behind them in the rolling dunes. After a few minutes, Suleiman slowed down the vehicle, then reached beside the shift lever and dragged down a black-knobbed stick.

'What are you doing?' Eric wondered aloud.

'When going off-road, engage four-wheel drive,' Suleiman smiled. 'My father taught me a long time ago.'

'What happened to him, if I may ask?'

'You may not,' Suleiman said coldly.

'You are good at your job, Mr Suleiman.' Eric smiled, impressed with the short man.

'Just enough to drive this old fellow on the sand,' he laughed.

There was nothing around them but sand in every direction. After half an hour of driving, they saw a water body shimmering in the distance to the south. Eric thought it was a mirage until Suleiman said, 'Lake Buhayratath-Tharthar, but your Google map might just call it Lake Tharthar. It is a huge artificial lake and located roughly a hundred kilometres north-west of Baghdad between the Tigris and Euphrates rivers. Look to your left; that's the depression we call the Wadiath-Tharthar. Now all we need to do is carefully navigate the truck to stay parallel to the depression, keeping it on our left, and it will take us straight to Al Fatsi.'

'So it's not a mirage after all!'

'Every single thing in this world is a mirage, my friend. Every human being is a mirage for someone, every dream is a mirage, every desire is a mirage,' Suleiman smiled dryly.

Eric frowned. 'Not a very good thing to say, for someone who calls himself an artist!'

The desert gradually merged into rocky terrain, interspersed with small pockets of vegetation every now and then.

The grey-haired man hauled around the big wheel which looked bigger in front of his short stature. The oversized mud tyres gripped well with the 'four-wheel drive' and were doing fine on the hard-packed sand.

'You seem to know your way around the desert, Suleiman—even without GPS!' Eric said, stretching his arms.

'I told you, my father was an archaeologist and worked extensively in this area. He developed several maps of almost the entire southern and northern Iraq. And those were my only inheritance. I have put them to good use over the years.'

'In fulfilling dreams and wishes, you mean?'

Suleiman glanced over at him and smiled meekly.

'Is it going to remain this rocky all the way?' Eric seemed concerned.

'It's both rocks and sand till Al Fatsi.'

'How much longer till we're there?'

'Al Fatsi is four hours from here, more or less. Once we reach there, we'll take a right turn to cross the Tigris by an old bridge and drive further down to the Nineveh ruins. There are small hamlets around the ruins, and I know some people. It shouldn't be a problem for us to stay close by for a couple of days and investigate.'

At this point, Eric decided to tell his companion the other part of the story that he'd kept to himself so far. He wanted to tell Suleiman about Marina's distress call because he thought if this man was going to help him find her and if he had to depend on him to figure out what happened in Nineveh, he no longer had any right to hide such important details as might help their mission.

Suleiman rolled the truck carefully along the base of the ranging lines of sand dunes on their right. On their left, they could still catch a glimpse of the shimmering water of Lake Tharthar.

◆

They travelled for another hour before pulling over under the shade of a rock jutting out of the rugged landscape.

'Why are we stopping?' Eric asked with surprise.

'Toilet break,' the short man muttered, 'along with a watch. Stretch yourself, young man; I'll just take a minute or three.'

As Eric climbed out of the truck, Suleiman dragged a small knapsack out from beneath his seat and yelled from the other side, 'You still don't believe me, right?'

'Why do you say that?'

'You still have suspicion in your voice.'

'You are right,' Eric nodded.

Suleiman shrugged and started walking towards the rocks.

Running after him, Eric said, 'But that doesn't affect our deal, of course!'

'Don't worry, my friend, Suleiman is a friend to a friend and a real foe to a foe.'

'You know, Suleiman, there's a little more to the story I told you.'

'Tell me.' The grey-haired man kept walking up a steep pathway that went up to the top of the rock.

'Actually, I know what happened at the site.'

Suleiman reached the top of the stone ledge, gave a quick look around and came down.

'Did you see anything from up there?'

'A great deal of blankness,' said Suleiman, panting from the exertion. 'Now tell me what you know.'

'Well, I've learnt that the site was massacred and almost all the people were killed some four or five days ago. Quite possibly there is only one survivor—the one who called me. She's a girl named Marina, who is currently hiding out in Mosul.'

Suleiman scratched his chin for a while and looked out at the distant lake. 'So what's the mission going to be like now? Is it a "rescue and run" or a "rescue and revenge"?'

'Rescuing the woman is primary, but I don't think I am going back without my friend Dr Huntley either.'

'Take my suggestion—find the girl and just get the hell out of this mess. You have no clue who all might be involved in such a brutal act of violence.'

'I have to find Dr Huntley, Suleiman, I really have to. He is like family.'

'I understand, but you must know one thing. For this kind of thing, the stakes must be very high, and the racket behind this must be very complex. So the people at Nineveh might not talk to us, and if they do, they might mislead us.' Suleiman paused and nodded thoughtfully. 'My friend, I have learnt—money has always been the key to buying silence, but then again, it is also the key instrument to free tongues. You can never know how much of the silence around you is bought and how many of those who talk to you are speaking the truth!'

'Suleiman, I don't want to, but I know I should believe you,' Eric spoke, 'because you're all I've got at the moment. Let's just reach Nineveh and decide on our next step. How about that?'

Suleiman grimaced and walked towards the truck. Squatting on the ground, he took out a couple of magnetic tin-plate signs from his knapsack and put them up on both doors in the front of the truck.

'What exactly are those?'

'This is the logo of the Road Construction Authority of Iraq.' He stood back and examined his work. 'Luckily for us, they use the same kind of truck for their patrolling teams as mine.'

'That's luck by chance or by strategy?' Eric pointed out.

'Well, you can say both, but this can make our journey a little disturbance-free and save us from unnecessary questions and checks.' He shrugged. 'It won't stand close inspection, but it will certainly pass a cursory surveillance.'

'Are you expecting to encounter something like that on our way?'

'Well, it's not uncommon in this region, given that the border security forces patrol this area frequently because of its proximity to unrestful borders and because of previous attacks at the ruins and on this highway. In fact, it has happened to me once.'

'How far are we from Nineveh?'

'About six and a half hours from here—eight if we drive in the dark. And we're going to wait until it's dark.' Suleiman looked at his wrist watch, 'And one more thing—are we still going to Nineveh, or do we go straight to Mosul and find the girl?'

'That's a good question. I think I need to take a look at the site first. I have to find out what exactly happened there and look for clues.'

'For the last time, I suggest you get the girl and run, because it is my responsibility as your guide to make you aware of possible threats and dangers.'

'Thanks for the advice, Suleiman,' Eric replied, 'but I really need to check out the site for myself.' What he didn't say was that he could not give up on his mentor just like that.

◆

They waited for nightfall while Suleiman dozed under the stone ledge and Eric paced on the sand, looking idly at the line of water glistening in the distance. In due course, a herd of sheep led by three men approached them from the direction of the highway and trotted past them towards the water.

Not for the first time in his life, Eric found himself thinking about borders between countries and why men fought over such artificial boundaries. The Genghis Khans, Alexanders and Hitlers of the world were not the only ones to fight and kill for territory, and there were more to come for sure.

The thought of Sid Patel, the metallic seal from the desert of Bikaner and the newly discovered mystery around it flashed through his mind for a moment, but Eric pushed the thought away. This was a different game, a different mission. His friend and mentor's life was at stake and the problem was—he didn't have any clue what the stakes were.

◆

Evening came early in the desert. The sun receded behind the rolling sand dunes, leaving a frail magenta curtain over the dark skies. Suleiman woke up from his hibernation, and in no time they were back in the truck.

The air had turned chilly, and Eric shivered as Suleiman started the engine and went around the base of the rock.

'We will be driving close to the border area. Please remember, if there is any trouble, I am the one who handles it—you keep calm,' the half-Iraqi said bluntly. They drove on quietly as the ground got rougher and stonier than the hard-packed sand they'd left behind. The headlights were insufficient, and the darkness near-opaque, and Suleiman navigated the truck along the wadi more by instinct than sight. They didn't know what lay ahead of them or what they had left behind in the endless desert, in the infinite darkness.

THIRTY

Suleiman drove the old truck carefully, picking the way slowly. 'At this rate we'll never get there,' Eric complained.

'Speed is not the key,' replied Suleiman, 'caution is. This is the most treacherous part of the journey. A little bit off the track and you could easily land up in the lake or sink in the desert sands. And then, my friend, you really won't get there.'

The sandstorm hit them relatively lightly at first. Eric sat back in his seat. 'This isn't so bad.'

'If it doesn't get any worse,' Suleiman said as he hauled the truck through the sand that bombarded its metal body, making a distinct sound. 'Sandstorms tend to fall into two broad categories: one is effectively a dust storm, hundreds of feet high, that blocks out the sun and is disorienting without being particularly brutal. The other—like the one we're in—is a true sandstorm, a fierce wind picking up grains of sand from the dunes and firing them in every direction like shotgun pellets.'

It wasn't long before Eric was regretting his earlier comment. The wind was coming at them so hard that the truck creaked back and forth on its suspension, and the bodywork and windows seemed certain to crumble any second under the constant bombardment of sand particles at crazy velocities. The headlight's visibility had deteriorated exponentially, and Suleiman could hardly see the track any more. He kept on sinking into soft sand that slaked beneath their wheels or tumbled over stray sharp rocks that threatened to rip open their tyres. He had to go down to first gear and slow the truck almost to a crawl.

'Shouldn't we stop?' Eric suggested.

Suleiman shook his head. 'Stop for even a minute in this storm, and the wind will blow away the sand beneath your tyres, causing the truck to sink like dead weight into the sand pits. Then the wind will pile on a drift against the sides of the truck until it is completely buried in the sand, with its doors pinned. And the chances of being rescued from a situation like that are as slim out here as those of making it out on your own.'

The winds were growing fierce, and the truck rocked precariously. The left wheels were suddenly lifted up in the air as a vicious gust of wind blew against them. For a moment, the two men felt as if the truck was about to be turned on its side.

Eric clutched the door handle as the truck slammed back into its spot on its four wheels. 'Have you been through one like this before?' he asked Suleiman.

'Twice.'

'How long did it last each time?'

'Five days, and three days.'

'You are kidding, right?'

Suleiman allowed himself a little smile. 'You're right,' he nodded. 'The first one was more like five and a half days, and the second perhaps closer to four.'

They drove through the sandstorm at a snail's pace for what seemed like several hours. The whines and roars of the furious monster got to them both, and they did not talk for most of the journey. The wind continued scraping at the truck's metalwork, trying to get inside and wreck it beyond repair. The engine was increasingly strained, while unsettling glugs and belches came from the radiator and worried Eric. After an eternity, the storm finally began to subside, and then, within a moment, the wind died away altogether. They were through the ordeal with nothing but open desert all around them.

'You know where we are?' Eric spoke up. 'What about the moon?'

'No, I think we drove off the track sometime during the storm,' Suleiman replied nonchalantly, 'and there will be no moon, at least not for the next few hours.'

'I'm assuming you know what is to be done now.' Eric remained calm.

'Don't worry, there are rocky trails which I'll find,' the little man smiled, climbing out of the truck.

'I am not worried. Not any more.'

◆

The only way Suleiman could think of navigating was to drive the truck close to the base of an uneven trail of rock somewhere on their left. He found that they had some sense of the terrain around them that actually came from looming chunks of blackness in between frequent patches of a starry sky. Another such mound ran parallel to them some fifty yards on their right. The ground beneath their tyres was rough and the suspension of the truck rattled, jarring the lumbers of both the passengers. The moon was beginning to rise on their right.

After a while, Suleiman took out a small device from his pocket, switched it on and placed it on the dashboard.

'You had a GPS device with you all along, and you didn't use it?' Eric was beside himself with shock. 'Why? And why do you need it now?'

'I just don't want to miss the turn at Al Fatsi, that's all. We are fifteen minutes away from it. If there is any trouble, I will handle it,' Suleiman said quietly. They drove on, the desert getting rougher with way more stones and much less sand. When they reached the juncture from where they were supposed to take a right, there was a brief pinging sound from the GPS unit.

'This is it,' Suleiman chimed, 'we take a right to reach the Tigris and then on to Nineveh.'

◆

They drove on in silence, the two rocky walls on both sides closing in on them as if the landscape was going to change. Eric could hardly see anything when Suleiman said, 'We are about to step on the bridge over the Tigris.'

In a minute or two, he heard the tyres rattling over a wooden structure and the silent growl of water far below.

'When do we reach Nineveh?'

'Very soon. It's almost dawn.'

Eric peered out to find the sky had suddenly turned a rosy pink. They were there. Exiting the narrow passage between two huge slabs of wind-carved rock, they saw Nineveh spread out in the distance below them, looking like a child's clay model of a toy town. Most of the houses were weathered by the ravages of time and looked ancient. Some of them were crumbling, some still had signs of life in them and some looked like nothing more than ancient foundation stones.

'Our destination lies on the other side of the town,' Suleiman told Eric as he guided the truck to the left, onto a narrower lane.

They drove past some old ruins, keeping steadily to the left. They hadn't seen a car or even a person on the road since the break of dawn. Just then an army truck appeared from behind a large rock on the left of the road ahead of them. The upper body of a soldier in Iraqi army fatigues was visible through the opened hatch of the truck, with both his hands gripping the firing handles of a big .50-calibre machine gun.

'Problem?' Eric asked.

'Don't think so,' Suleiman replied, not once taking his eyes off the army truck. 'These guys are sluggish. If they stop us, they'll have to file a report. And as you know, all soldiers hate paperwork. That's just how it is, no matter where you go.'

'Is there a military base around here?'

'Just a small squad for basic law enforcement duties,' Suleiman said. 'They must be out on their morning round. It shouldn't be a problem, I am telling you.'

Suleiman was right. The army vehicle slowed down to let their truck catch up, and when Suleiman drove up his truck parallel to them, the driver saw the sign on their door and waved at Suleiman. He waved back, smiling, and slowed down. The army vehicle steered away, and within a few seconds, it took a left turn from a crossing and disappeared. Eric exhaled.

'You see,' Suleiman shrugged, 'not a problem at all!'

'May I ask you something?' Eric blurted out.

Suleiman looked at him and nodded with a smile.

'Why does my sixth sense tell me there's something wrong?'

'Because there is,' Suleiman said curtly.

Eric straightened up, turned to face Suleiman, and said, 'You knew who I was right from the beginning, didn't you?'

'Of course, just as I know that you have one of my weapons in the left pocket of your cargo pants—the same one you took from my jacket pocket when I dozed off under the stone. Be a good man and remove it with your thumb and forefinger. Then put it on the dashboard.' Suleiman slowed down the truck and exclaimed, 'The welcome party has arrived!'

'So that's your art,' Eric nodded.

'You got me!' Suleiman smiled. 'Didn't you ever hear the famous Arabic saying, *The wise man doesn't insult he who has a gun*, or should I say *big guns* in this case?'

Eric took the palm-sized machine pistol out of his pocket and kept it on the dashboard.

Then he looked directly at Suleiman and asked, 'Where are the guns?'

'There they are.' Suleiman jerked his head towards the right and then stopped the truck abruptly on a narrow turn of the road.

Two hundred feet away, a dozen armed men stood blocking the road. Behind them, in the courtyard of a crumbling structure, stood their camels.

The men were dressed in black thawbs, and the bottom halves of their faces were covered in long black kaffiyehs. Some of the men carried Chinese Norinco guns, automatic rifles that were cheaper Chinese versions of the Russian AK-47. And some of them had rocket-propelled grenade launchers of the same make strapped tightly across their shoulders. All of the camels in the back had the same unpleasant expression on their faces as if they didn't like the taste of their breakfast cereal.

'Meet my fellow fighters from the brotherhood of the Tomb of God.'

THIRTY-ONE

Suleiman held his gun on Eric's temple and pushed him towards the door. As they both climbed out of the truck from the same side, two men from the armed lot walked forward and got into the vehicle. The sun had risen over the crumbling buildings by now and cast long shadows on the ground. The Range Rover's engine purred and one of the men drove it in the direction it was being driven in minutes ago. Another man walked up to Suleiman, and they spoke briefly. Then the man in the menacing black thawb handed him a small knapsack.

Twenty minutes later, Suleiman and Eric were dressed exactly like the armed men and were atop two camels moving east through the older part of the city, followed by the men on their camels. Eric had been relieved of his soft luggage, his wallet and cell phone, which were now being carried by one of the men behind him.

They rode continuously for half a day and only stopped for bathroom breaks and a quick lunch. Eric had no idea where he was being taken, but he could tell they were heading eastward. Suleiman did not make eye contact with him throughout the day, even though they ate in a group, and he rode as far from Eric as possible.

Sometime in the afternoon, they reached a ravine and followed it due north. After an hour, their caravan reached a place where a long extrusion of sandstone blocked their way. The wall was at least 500 feet high, but it was climbable for the camels, since there were several dried-up streams filled with sand running up the wall, and a number of goat tracks ran alongside them. They climbed up the escarpments following the winding trails of sand. By the time they reached the top, it was dark, and they decided to camp. Eric tried creating a mental map of the region. *This is probably an extension of the Zagros Mountains,* he thought, *though there's no point in asking. None of these guys looks interested in chit-chat.*

The first half of the next day was spent moving across the top of the plateau. They edged down a goat path slowly. The unprotected drop was around seven inches away from their camels' slapping hooves, and every lurching, swaying step threatened to be their last. Eric had never had a problem with heights, but after a few minutes on that path, he decided to shut his eyes to ward away the sickening vertigo building up inside him.

They reached the bottom and travelled further east, but the escarpment never went out of sight. Every now and then, they would pass abandoned ruins of mud-and-brick villages, some of which looked ancient and some comparatively new. By noon they reached another, much narrower dry channel, and instead of crossing it, they took an abrupt right towards the high sandy wall they had left behind and eventually reached a greener clearing at the bottom of the wall. The surroundings included shrubs, thorn bushes, the occasional desert beetle and a great deal of hard, crusted white sand. Gradually they began to see herds of goat led by men in long dresses with a part of their turbans covering their faces, leaving out the eyes. A little further, they saw what appeared to be a permanent camp in the distance.

The closer they got, the larger the encampment seemed to be. The goat-and-camel-skin tents were much bigger than the ones Eric and the group of men had slept in the previous night. Taking a quick count as they passed the tents, Eric estimated that there were at least a hundred men living there. Interestingly, the location of the camp was such that, except at high noon, it would continuously lie in the shadow of the escarpment or its long extension, making it almost invisible from up in the air. *An effective strategy for an ancient-style cluster against modern enemies with airplanes and satellites,* he thought.

At the far side of the camp, the group stopped in front of a medium-sized tent, and Suleiman gestured to Eric to get off. Before he could react, one of the armed men barked a command and Eric's animal instantly dropped down on its front knees. Eric climbed down. The man who had commanded the camel also climbed down and gestured Eric towards the tent opening. With a quick look to his left and right, Eric walked into the frying interior of the tent.

The tent was spacious inside. The floors were covered in woven rugs that had more than ten colours and patterns, none of which gelled with the others. Heavy pillows were propped up against the walls. Eric saw an extension at the far end of the tent with a curtain guarding the entrance, and he figured it was to be his temporary toilet, which would surely be no more than a hole in the sand. The guard turned and spoke to him in broken English, 'Stay here…we guard outside…do not run.' He punctuated his sentence with a wild gesture using his gun. Then the man in the black robe turned on his heel and walked away from the tent.

Eric looked at the stack of pillows and sighed. 'After such a long journey on camelback, I at least deserve these pillows. Not for my head, but for my bum!' He smiled at his own joke.

'Hello, hello, hello there…'

Startled, Eric turned around. At the entrance of the tent, a man stood with both his hands raised in a welcoming gesture. He was in his mid-fifties, a little over six feet tall, lean, tanned but good-looking, with long salt-and-pepper hair. His face was clean-shaven and he wore a pair of thin round glasses on his sharp nose. He wore a light-yellow t-shirt over khaki cargo pants and Timberland boots.

'Welcome to my little camp, Mr Eric Roy,' the man said. 'You have arrived at an excellent time, my friend.' His accent sounded Canadian.

'You seem to know me,' Eric noted with an expressionless face. There was something he didn't like about the man, though he didn't know what it was.

'Of course,' the man smiled, 'I know a lot about you. For instance, I know you teach history at a reputed Indian university. You lost your parents many years ago. I know you lost your girlfriend as well. More recently, I know you annoyed some highly connected people on a treasure hunt. Above all, I know you are one of the finest archaeologists the world has ever produced. And that last part is the reason you've been brought here.'

He couldn't have got all of this from just a quick chat with Suleiman, Eric thought. 'Who are you?'

'Oh, yes, where are my manners! Well, the media knows me, or rather mentions me, as the nameless and faceless leader of the brotherhood of the Tomb of God. My real name is Dr Zaid Nassar. I am an archaeologist just like you, among other interesting things.' The man smiled pleasantly. 'I am also the man responsible for kidnapping you and bringing you to this secret camp, which lies absolutely hidden and isolated from the world you come from.'

THIRTY-TWO

'Why did you bring me all the way here?' Eric demanded. 'How am I connected to your bullshit brotherhood's agenda?'

'Aha! What exactly do you know about my brotherhood's agenda, my friend?'

'You are a terrorist, and I know terrorists' agendas pretty well. What more is there to know?' Eric's face was flushed with indignation.

'Yes, of course! You are absolutely right in that terrorists' agendas are really bullshit, because if you look deeper, there is hardly any issue worthy of terror. But my brotherhood is no bullshit. A terrorist is as a terrorist does. And I am not one.' Nassar paused and smiled at Eric's face for a moment. Then he continued, 'I was born in Vancouver, Canada, to Lebanese parents. They were both paramedics working in Kabul, Afghanistan, when the Russians bombed it to rubble. I was fifteen years old at the time. I was raised in a Catholic orphanage in Kabul and have a blurry memory of my parents. I studied well, went back to Canada to complete my higher studies, and then decided to take my revenge.'

'Revenge?'

'My parents were stolen from me by the so-called civilised superpowers, and I am going to take my revenge.'

'No political motivation at all?' Eric was suspicious.

'Only the politics of thievery…of people snatching things from people. My people here have lost everything—their lands, their cultural history, their women, their children—all stolen in the name of big projects, wars, corporate mergers…' Nassar's eyes were bloodshot as he uttered his next words. 'Did you know that none of the Iraqi archaeological sites were excavated by any Iraqi archaeologist till the early twentieth century? British, French, American—by all the colonial powers, yes! But never by the people who owned the land. I am no terrorist, Mr Eric. I am just a man avenging himself and his people's rights.'

'What about the brotherhood then?' Eric asked bluntly.

'Initially, when I was recruiting people, I thought I would make money from our historical ruins—by stealing and smuggling small artefacts, which was how it started. But then things became bigger, and we started operating throughout Iraq and got connected with the global artefact market through Baghdad, Cairo, Udine, Tehran, Herat, etc. Herat is actually where I met Suleiman, you see. He was kind of an expatriate, and so was I. He was an army washout, and I was planning to raise an army, so we joined hands, and he got me connected to larger markets in Alexandria, Tripoli, India, Pakistan and a lot of places. The business was getting bigger by the hour, and then people at the other end of the smugglers' chain started asking questions. Now these were bad people, and I mean really bad people.

'So we invented the brotherhood of the Tomb of God to add

political colour to it. The stories of this legendary brotherhood have sustained through the folklore of the region for millennia, so no one questioned us. It sounded deep, and it made us look dangerous to the bigger fishes in the chain. It also earned us friends in the world of politics, and weapons. My people especially loved it, because calling themselves the brotherhood reminded them of their warrior past and accorded them a higher status among the local tribes. Problems still exist, and for now we are hiding out here. But far too many people now know about the things we do and the things we know. Eventually the trouble will come to hit us head-on, I know that. But I also know I will act before that happens.'

'The recent massacre at the Nineveh site was your work, right?'

'Hold it there,' said Nassar. 'That's the second-most interesting bit. Truly speaking, we were not involved in that mishap. We didn't even know there was an excavation already planned in that area until the team landed at Baghdad Airport. Later, when I came to know about the mishap from you—I mean, from Suleiman after you told him—I figured a bigger game was afoot in my land than I was aware of. So I wanted you here in my camp to find out more. And I was sure you would help.'

'How did you find out I was coming?'

'Silly question, Mr Roy,' Nassar furrowed his eyebrows. 'I have my men everywhere, from Baghdad Airport to Samarra and from Mosul to any place you name in Iraq. Every single entry into Iraq is reported to me if the person doesn't fit his/her travel story. Period.' Nassar moved his right hand menacingly in the air like a butcher's knife.

'Why don't you tell me about the first most interesting thing, Mr Nassar?' Eric smiled now. 'I am curious.'

'You got me!' Nassar smiled from ear to ear and continued, 'I have found something really big, but I'm not sure what it is. With the kind of archaeological reputation that precedes your name, I believe I would need your expertise in this matter as well.'

'What is it?' Eric asked with a hint of excitement in his voice.

Looking deep into Eric's eyes, Nassar took a rather long pause to create anticipation for his answer.

'What have you found, Mr Nassar?'

'We have found a tomb,' said Nassar. 'It could be the legendary Tomb of God, but I am not sure yet.' And then he turned and walked out of the tent as abruptly as he had entered.

THIRTY-THREE

The bikers were finally on the last leg of their long journey to Baghdad. They headed west for an hour, eventually finding their way through single-lane narrow roads to the two-lane Route 48–AH2 highway. There was nothing to see around, but dry arid landscape scorched by the blinding sun on both sides of the road. They stopped for tea at a place called Kermanshah. Alex climbed down from his bike and walked up to Aurin and Father Smit, studying his map. 'It says there is a mosque a few kilometres ahead, from where you can take a right and go straight to Mosul, which makes most sense for you.'

'Ummm, let me see,' replied Aurin. 'I think I'll go to Baghdad with you guys and complete the formalities of the event.'

'Okay, as you wish!' Alex walked back to his bike.

'I am beginning to wonder if this whole thing was a good idea,' Aurin muttered to Father Smit.

'What do you mean?'

'We are taking a big risk. Even if we *do* find Dr Huntley, what do we do then?'

'The target is to find Dr Huntley as well as that girl. If we get to them, we'll take time to think about what is at stake, and we'll find a way!' Father Smit reassured him. 'Don't worry, Auri boy, we have people like your brother, Mr Naidu, Sid Patel, all of them backing us.

Let's make a move.' Aurin smiled weakly, and the two men hopped back on their bike.

♦

Mahmod Jamal was a taxi driver from Mosul. Just like any other taxi driver operating within three hundred kilometres of Baghdad, he would consider it his lucky day if he was hired for a trip to Baghdad, because it meant half the work and double the money. He would charge a two-way fare for a ride to Baghdad and on the way back use his taxi as a poolcab.

Mahmod lived with his family. He was usually particular about forgetting all about his work once he'd closed his front door for the night. But three days ago, something had happened to him while he was driving back to Mosul from Baghdad. Since then, he had lost his sleep. On any given day, no matter how tiring, his wife and daughter were like a tonic to his spirits—but not any more.

His anxiety did not subside even as he bent down to let Heena throw her little arms around his neck and lift her off the ground. Every time he had come back home since the incident, he would try his best not to let her sense the change.

After carrying the unspoken burden alone for days, he decided to share it with his wife, Shad. He carried Heena through the bead curtains into their kitchen before dinner that night. Shad looked up from her cooking, her eyes tired and her skin shining with sweat.

'Something smells good,' he said. He proceeded to help himself to a morsel from the pot, but she smacked his hand away. They exchanged smiles. Thirteen years of marriage and he was still often surprised by the freshness of their affection. Heena sat cross-legged on the floor, a pad of paper on her lap, drawing pictures of animals, birds and trees. He watched over her shoulder, praising the smell of the curry, asking her about her day. But then he fell into a contemplation, thinking about the demons and evils that plague the world. And only after a few minutes, when Shad touched his shoulder, he realised that she'd been talking to him. He shook his head with raised hands to clear the web of evil thoughts in his mind and flashed as warm a smile as he could at her. 'Yes?' he asked her.

'Something is not right,' she said. 'What is it?'

'Nothing in particular.'

'Heena, love,' said Shad gently, 'could you please go into the other room and draw?'

Heena looked up at her parents, puzzled. She'd been brought up to be obedient, so she gathered her things regardless and left quietly.

'Well?' Shad prompted.

Mahmod sighed. Sometimes he wished his wife didn't know him so well. 'Some days ago, I found a man on my way back from Baghdad, half-dead. It looked like he had been walking around in the wilderness for days without water or food. He lay on the road, his clothes bedraggled and hair in disarray. I gave him water, and he opened his eyes. They were insane, Shad, and then he convulsed. I was so afraid. He convulsed, and he mumbled and mumbled and mumbled!'

'What did he say?'

As if her words had brought back the memory, Mahmod's eyes widened and his body shivered. 'The man was getting more hysterical with every passing second. All he kept saying was "The Devil's army has come…they will kill us all" over and over. Mahmod paused for a moment and continued more softly, 'Then he fainted. I carried him to my car and took him to the hospital. But I can't erase the incident and that man from my mind, Shad. Over the past few days, my thoughts have again and again veered towards him, as if some sign is trying to tell me we are all going to perish soon.'

♦

'Sometimes I wonder why borders even exist,' Aurin mumbled as Father Smit pulled up alongside an old SUV going the same way. The steel grey giant looked like it belonged to the World War II era. Father Smit wanted to overtake it, but then thought better of it. All the other bikers of their group had already overtaken the SUV and gone out of sight. They rode on in silence, each of them lost in their own thoughts.

They were approaching a bridge that went over a dry canal. Father Smit tried a lower gear for extra thrust. A hundred and fifty metres ahead of them, the SUV suddenly lurched and then swerved to the side, hitting the low railing of the bridge.

'Shit!' Aurin exclaimed even as the vintage truck climbed over the rails and toppled off the bridge to a twenty-foot drop. Father Smit quickly checked the rear-view mirror over his left handlebar and hit the brakes. 'Could be a flat tyre!'

'Maybe,' Aurin muttered. He looked around. The only outstanding feature of the unfriendly landscape they were riding through was a low, stony ridge on both the sides of the road along the canal. On their far right there were some hillocks.

'What do we do?'

'Let us first find out if anyone survived,' Father Smit said as he pulled the bike over and parked it on its side stand. 'Aurin, bring some rope from the box please.' And he ran across the empty highway to the railing of the bridge. He looked down into the dry canal. The Land Rover lay on its back, smoke and steam blowing up from the front hood. In this part of the world, chances that the vehicle was equipped with seat belts were extremely slim, which meant the driver and passengers, if any, would have been thrown around like dice on a roulette wheel. It was unlikely that anyone would have survived the fall.

Aurin approached with a bundle of rope as Father Smit stood deep in thought.

'How much do we have here?'

'Thirty feet, that's what is written on the tag over here.'

'Should be enough.'

Father Smit looped a double-figure-eight knot around one of the metal poles of the bridge railing. He pulled the rope with both hands to check its strength and then crossed the railing and climbed down over the edge. The side of the bridge was a blend of rock, hard-packed mud and crumbling sand. Without the rope, climbing down to the upturned truck would have been virtually impossible. He reached the ground and stepped back from the rope to look up.

Aurin was already on the rope, their small first-aid kit dangling from a strap on his shoulder. Father Smit decided not to wait for him and approached the overturned truck. The driver's side door hung open, twisted and loose on its hinges. The truck was groaning as if it was in great pain. Father Smit had to squat next to the open door to reach inside the truck. The windshield had been crushed, covering the driver's body in tiny shards of glass. The man was bleeding from his mouth and one side of his temple. His eyes were closed. There was a bright red stain all over the chest pocket of his light-coloured shirt.

The man was alive but barely breathing. Father Smit eased him out of the driver's seat and onto the mud. It was at this point that Father Smit noticed the hole in the back of the driver's seat and the matching wound in the man's back.

'We've got trouble!' he exclaimed as Aurin joined him. 'He's been shot, whoever he is. Shot with a large-calibre rifle…the injury is not close to his heart—he can be saved if we take him to a medical facility right now.'

'Bandits?'

'Bandits couldn't possibly be this accurate. This guy is a trained sniper. There's a pro killer lurking somewhere behind those rocky hillocks.'

'What if he shoots us?' Aurin whispered.

'Chances are slim.' Father Smit sounded grim.

The resonating thump of several Enfield engines rented the air the very next moment. The rest of the group had come back for them.

'We have an emergency, boys. Need to take this man to a hospital,' Father Smit yelled out. 'Rob, please check if your phone has enough data speed to google the nearest hospital. And Alex, if you can, please take the closest exit to come down here on your bike...'

'Why this guy? He's just a cab driver,' mumbled Aurin.

'You need to check his wallet to find out who he really is,' Father Smit said.

THIRTY-FOUR

Things began to settle for Eric when he was offered warm water for a sponge bath. His dirty clothes were taken away, and he was presented with a fresh thawb to wear. Feeling clean and resuscitated after ages, he eased his exhausted body onto a rug and propped it up with several pillows, hoping to get some rest.

'I thought of sharing a cup of tea with you, Professor,' Nassar entered the tent as Eric's eyes were about to close. A man followed him with a tray full of fine bone china crockery.

'That's a good gesture for a terrorist, Mr Nassar.'

Nassar laughed. 'Well, I am sorry, Professor, it's just your bad luck that you walked straight into my world, that too at the moment when I needed someone like you.'

'What do you want from me?' Eric asked between sips of tea from the cup he was handed by the other man.

Nassar stood across from Eric on the rug. 'I'd like your opinion on something. From an archaeologist's point of view, I mean. Do that for me tomorrow and I'll be happy to let you go!'

'It's the tomb, right?'

Nassar gave a little nod. 'We'll head for the tomb tomorrow morning. I'll send your dinner in sometime. Eat and then get some rest, or feel free to wander about the camp if you like. Try to escape and you are dead. But I'm sure you understand that part.'

'Very well,' Eric muttered.

'Good,' Nassar smiled and turned on his heel. He threw back the flap of the tent and disappeared outside.

'Fascinating,' Eric said to himself, leaning back against the pillows and staring thoughtfully at the opening of the tent where Nassar had just been standing.

◆

Eric was awakened at dawn the next day with the rest of the camp. Throughout the night he could hear someone singing to himself outside his tent. Eric knew he was being guarded. The guard hummed local songs about journeys through the wilderness, and Eric dreamt about the two days he had spent journeying through the Iraqi desert. He woke up in a sweat several times during the night, and his thoughts inevitably turned to Dr Huntley every time. His thought would also find Marina sometimes, but his primary concern was Dr Huntley.

Breakfast consisted of extremely strong coffee and thick bread made from millet flour and goat's milk with no sugar. A guard, with his face covered, brought him the bag he had carried from Samarra, and Eric changed into fresh clothes. Afterwards, he was escorted out of his tent, and for the first time Eric had the chance to see the camp properly. The guard led him in the direction of the rapidly rising sun. It gave Eric enough time to observe the layout of the camp: a three-hundred-by-three-hundred-metre square arena in a dry sand ditch where the tents were laid out in rows. He figured the big tent in the middle to be Nassar's. They climbed out of the ditch at the eastern corner, where a couple of guards stood drinking tea or coffee from earthen mugs with rifles slung across their backs. They both eyed Eric for a moment and then went back to their teas. *C7 assault rifles*, Eric thought, *most probably knockoffs made in Canada—Nassar's Canada connection at play*. The guard walked with him for two hundred metres beyond the other guards and then stopped.

Eric could see a sheep-and-goat enclosure in the north-west corner of the camp. He turned around and looked out across the open stretch in the north. He could see a dark rocky extension a mile away from the camp where some costumed guards were patrolling, and then his eyes captured something odd: a darker strip of hard sand about half a mile long, but strangely, it didn't go anywhere.

What kind of a road doesn't go anywhere? Eric asked himself with a frown.

And then it struck him. 'A runway!' He looked around him. 'These bastards have a plane!'

THIRTY-FIVE

Eric was in the passenger seat of a new black Toyota Land Cruiser. Nassar was at the wheel, steering the truck through the undulating sand dunes, dodging the boulders and rocky outcropping every now and then. A sign on the driver's side of the vehicle read:

> Society of Iraqi Studies
> Department of Antiquities
> Royal College, London

Underneath the sign was what read like the Arabic translation of the sign in English.

Crouching in the cargo section behind Eric and Nassar, there were three more people with covered faces and weapons hidden within the folds of their thawbs.

'If we get stopped, you say nothing. Speak, and my man Rafiq behind you will slit your throat. But then, don't worry, because no one is going to stop us anyway,' Nassar smirked. 'Groups from Iraqi soil testing and mineral agencies have been working in this semi-rocky desert area for over a decade; field workers come and go all the time. No one recognises anyone any more, which is of great benefit to us.'

For fifteen minutes after they left the camp, Nassar drove

eastwards. Then he put the cruiser into four-wheel drive and turned northwards, driving through the part-sand, part-stone landscape for over half an hour. Eric knew they were going in the direction opposite to where he had come to the camp from.

'Professor, I want to ask you something,' Nassar said without taking his eyes off of the uneven road in front. Eric turned towards him and furrowed his eyebrows.

'I believe you are well aware of the Sumerian King List,' he continued.

'Which one are you talking about?'

'The one more popular for its "Ram and Bharat" debate than for its actual historical value.'

'Oh, you mean the Rim-Sin and Warad-Sin version?'

'That's the one,' Nassar smiled and then, without warning, he swung the truck to the right and they clambered onto a paved road. 'Do you remember, Professor, who was mentioned as the father of Rim-Sin and Warad-Sin in the King List?'

'My Sumerian is kind of rusty, Mr Nassar, but as far as I remember it is Kudur Mabug who ruled the ancient Elam and who probably had some connections with the Indus Valley people as per some historians.'

'Right you are, Professor,' Nassar beamed. 'I have also read some of the reports by these historians on Rim-Sin. Many of them claim that studies of Sumerian history provide a vivid picture of Ram from the Ramayana. Names such as Bharat-Sin and Ram-Sin appear in the Sumerian King List. I know "Sin" is a reference to the Moon God—Chandra—and the cuneiform symbol for "Rim" is also read as Ram, which gives us the names Ram Chandra and Bharat Chandra.'

'Yes, several historians, including some famous European ones, connect Rim-Sin, the king of Larsa, with Ram Chandra of the Ramayana. The Sumerian texts suggest Rim-Sin was from Elam and had links to Indus Valley people. But if you ask me, Rim-Sin was the longest reigning monarch of Mesopotamia and ruled for sixty years, after his brother Warad-Sin, who ruled for twelve years—from 1834 BC to 1822 BC. And that's it.'

'But that's the point!' Nassar exclaimed. 'That is exactly what the *Dasrath Jataka* mentions. It says Ram reigned for sixty years, and prior to that, Bharat reigned for twelve years when Ram lived in the forest. It tallies with the timeline of Warad Sin's reign from 1834 BC to 822 BC, obtained from the Sumerian King List by the Assyriologists.'

'But that doesn't make Kudur Mabug Ram Chandra's father!' Eric said.

'Why not?' Nassar argued. 'I understand Kudur Mabug does not clearly equate with present versions of Ramayana's Dasrath, but that's because of the Aryan layers that were added to the Elamite epic in India, probably at a much later stage.'

'The argument is strong, no doubt.'

'Yes, it is, my friend,' Nassar smiled. 'I have studied this an awful lot.'

'What I don't understand is why you are interested in this person at all!'

'As I was saying,' Nassar went on, ignoring Eric's comment, 'Dasrath is more of a military title or epithet, and so is Kudur Mabug. It means the lord of the land.'

'And Dasrath means the one with ten chariots,' Eric said nonchalantly.

'Good!' Nassar laughed out loud. 'It looks like we both read books. As a professor, you read history to teach your pupils, and as an antiquities dealer, I read history to optimise the prices of my finds.' He continued laughing like a mad man.

'Yeah, something like that!' Eric mumbled, his level of interest in the history lesson waning with every bump in the ride. Nassar looked at Eric out of the corner of his eye and didn't say anything else, a smile playing on his lips.

A little while later, they saw an old tin sign mounted on an iron pole. It had nothing to say any more, the colours and texts all faded with time.

'This was a pre-World War II British excavation site. They found nothing here, because they miscalculated the location of the site. But I managed to find what they were looking for,' Nassar said with a hint of pride in his voice. 'The Kudur Mabug that I am talking about,' Nassar continued, 'came from a place called Der, which resonates with your Mohenjodaro.'

'What is this endless *your this, your that*? I am not the President of India,' Eric scowled. 'Come on, you're getting on my nerves now.'

'Sorry for that,' Nassar said. 'Anyhow, as I was saying about Der…'

'Yes,' Eric chimed in, 'some scholars do think Der was Mohenjodaro, which was probably derived from Maha-Anga-Dvara.' He paused, then said, 'But my question is, did the "Elam" of the Sumerians include the lands as far out to the east as that? The standard Sumerian texts make no mention of it.'

'Mr Roy,' Nassar grinned, 'even the important points that *are* mentioned in the Sumerian texts were not noted by the western historians, let alone the ones that are not mentioned. For instance, Rim-Sin or Ram-Sin was one of the most significant figures of ancient Sumer; yet reputed historians have missed the point time and again that Ram was anyway a popular name in the ancient Sumerian Civilisation. An early ancestor of Darius-I was Arya Ramanna, whose name bears a clear resemblance to Ram. The name of the first Sassanian king, Ram Behist, also has the resonance of Ram.' Nassar paused his monologue as he slowed the truck to dodge a broken part of the paved road. 'I have even read that Ayodhya could be Agade, the capital of Sargon that has not yet been identified.' He changed the gear, took his eyes off the road and turned towards Eric.

'It is possible that Agade was near Der or Herat as we have a Harayu or Sarayu river in Herat,' said Eric. 'Some scholars wrote that Rim-Sin's father could be from the Herat area of Afghanistan, you know?'

Nassar's eyes lit up as he replied. 'It is widely believed that the Cambridge Ancient History department contains priceless information that was never brought to light because of several conspiracies.'

'I have another question. Why in the first place are we even talking about all of this?'

'Because this is all a precursor to the thing I am going to show you now, Mr Professor.' Nassar smiled, with a twinkle in his eyes.

♦

They continued eastward along the paved road for a good forty minutes, huge dunes of shifting sand visible on both sides of the valley. The sun was much harsher now, casting smaller and smaller shadows behind the truck as they continued on their way.

'We are going to enter the ruins through the back door,' Nassar declared. Eric remained mute, staring through the window at the ruins that had begun to appear in the distance, the roofless mud-brick remains of a small town.

'This isn't where we are going?'

'No, what we have found is much older than this. It would date around 2000 BC,' Nassar replied as they drove past the ruins, veering steadily to the right. The paved road ended and Nassar once again drove the vehicle through undulating sand dunes.

Twenty minutes later, they reached a strange field that was full of half-pyramidal structures. Nassar eased on the accelerator, weaving his way through the maze of brick structures. The field appeared to Eric as the eerie ruins of a ghost town. Each structure was made of rough brick a shade or two darker than the dry dirt around it and had the appearance of a ten–twelve-foot high pyramid, only without the top—as if the topmost sections of the pyramids had been chopped off with a sharp weapon. Some of them had square windows on one or two sides, and some were solid. Each of the pyramidal structures was separated from its closest neighbour on each side by around twenty feet of empty space.

'Most of the pyramids you see here are false—there's no tomb beneath. They were erected to deceive tomb robbers and thieves. The real tomb is the farthest one to the north. And that's where lies our interest,' said Nassar, pulling the vehicle to a stop in front of one of the ancient structures.

Eric noticed that the structure had been worn out by the wind, losing its shape and turning into an almost-natural mound. *The false ones must have been erected at different times,* Eric thought, *some at the same time as the original tomb and some much later.*

'Come along, gentlemen,' Nassar instructed, grabbing a powerful flashlight from beneath his seat. He opened his door and said, 'We have arrived. The Tomb of God awaits.'

THIRTY-SIX

'How do we get inside?' Eric wondered, looking at the smooth surface of the mound of ancient mud-brick. There was no hint of a door or an entrance of any kind. Eric was amazed at how anything made out of mud could have lasted for that long. If his hunch was correct, the tomb had to be at least four thousand years old.

'Follow me,' said Nassar and headed towards the far side of the tomb. Eric followed suit, with Rafiq and the other guard behind him. Once there, Rafiq advanced to the front of the line and took out a corkscrew-shaped device from the folds of his robe. For the first time, Eric registered how huge a man Rafiq was. As he squatted down and peered at the wall, his shoulder muscles moved like a python under his robe. He finally found an invisible hole in the slanted wall. He pushed the 'worm' of the spiral device into the fine hole, gave it a twist, and then pulled. 'And…there we go…!' Nassar exclaimed theatrically as a crack appeared in the mud-brick that quickly became a two-foot-by-two-foot square. He dragged the corkscrew through the slim opening, and the entire brick-square came loose. With the guard helping Rafiq, they both lifted the trapdoor and set it down on the side.

On closer examination, Eric marvelled at how ingenious the trapdoor was. The mud-brick on the exterior was a cleverly made fake layer—no more than a couple of inches thick. From outside, the fake four-square-foot section fit in perfectly with the rest of the wall, concealing the secret entrance completely.

Nassar spoke in brief, incomprehensible sentences to Rafiq, and both men nodded in response.

'We'll have to duck,' Nassar turned to Eric. 'Follow me, Professor.' He got onto his hands and knees, then crawled through the small opening and disappeared inside the tomb. Eric looked at the two men and then ducked after Nassar into the secret gateway. Rafiq and the other man stayed where they were.

The inside of the tomb was roasting hot and poorly lit by the hint of sunlight filtering in through the secret entrance. All Eric could see of Nassar was a blurry spot of darkness in the centre of the small chamber. Nassar didn't waste any time. He called out to Rafiq and had the men re-insert the trapdoor in its place while he switched on his powerful flashlight. Eric looked around in the sudden blaze of light; the chamber was depressingly grim.

It was a very small chamber, ten feet on each side. The interior walls were plain and undecorated, made of brick and left unplastered. The floor was a few rough slabs of basalt, slightly larger than the trapdoor.

There was a slab missing from the exact centre of the floor. In its place was a dark opening with a wooden ladder descending vertically into the shaft below. On the far side of the room, there were remains of a wooden box about six feet long. The top had been shattered to pieces. Even from where he stood, Eric could make out several faded symbols on the side of the box, including bows and arrows and a large ornamental moon at the centre. Eric tiptoed towards the broken box. It appeared to be a coffin, but there was nothing inside. On a closer look, Eric saw fragments of tobacco-coloured bandage strewn about inside.

'His name was Kudur Mabug,' Nassar ventured from behind him.

Eric froze. 'You mean the father of Rim-Sin of the Sumerian King List you were discussing with me a few minutes back?'

'Yes, Professor, it was him in that coffin. At least that was what was written on a tablet on the sarcophagus.'

Eric turned around with eyes gleaming and exclaimed, 'Where is it? I need to see it.'

'I pieced together fragments of the clay tablet and deciphered the inscription when I first came here. Everything was already destroyed, and we couldn't save the remains,' Nassar grimaced. 'Someone had already broken in and stolen everything of value. When they were done, they re-sealed the tomb and placed the trapdoor exactly where you saw it today. The sarcophagus had been in an upright position in the centre of the chamber, protecting the ground stone that hid the shaft. The grave robbers tipped it over to get at the jewellery the mummy had been decorated with.'

'Do you even know what you are saying?' Eric whispered. 'I mean, do you have any clue how big it could be if this was really Kudur Mabug's grave?'

'Yes, I know.' Nassar said. 'I know the probable worth of such a tomb. This is exactly my line of business.'

'But do you understand...' Eric whispered, 'if this is it, then a closed door will be opened on a lost world. It will validate the idea seeded by great scholars like Sir Aurel Stein and Sir Charles Eliot about the Indian and Mesopotamian traditions being inextricably linked.' Eric looked directly at Nassar. 'I repeat my question, are you sure about this?'

'I am,' Nassar replied confidently. 'The inner lid of the coffin also had a metal plate, and the cuneiform inscription on it repeated his name.'

'In Akkadian?'

'Yes, sir—in Akkadian.'

'And where is the inner lid, if I may ask?'

'That has long been removed...for safekeeping.' Nassar's face reddened.

'Let me guess...the inner layer of the coffin was made of gold or some other metal studded with precious gems?' Eric scoffed.

'Yes,' Nassar said through pursed lips. The muscles around his jaw had stiffened.

'So what do you need my help with?'

'I need you to tell me what he was doing here.'

'I don't understand.'

'Of course you understand. You are an archaeologist,' Nassar snorted. 'I know Kudur Mabug was the king of Larsa in Ur, and this place is far too north of Larsa. I want you to tell me, what was Kudur Mabug doing here?'

'Aha!' Eric's interest was piqued.

'Yes, Professor, I told you I have researched a lot about them, because I want to get the highest possible price for this.'

'That's rather honest of you.' Eric looked at Nassar.

'But I need your help to figure this out.'

'Indeed,' Eric rolled his eyes. 'What was Kudur Mabug doing here? That would be the most obvious question to ask if you wanted to tell the world about this discovery.'

'Do you think Kudur Mabug was Dasrath?' Nassar's question startled Eric for a moment.

'Though Rim-Sin and Warad-Sin's periods of rule exactly match with that of Ram Chandra and Bharat Chandra respectively, as mentioned in the Ramayana, Kudur Mabug doesn't as clearly equate with Dasrath of the Ramayana. But as you have mentioned earlier, that is mostly due to the Aryan layers that were added to the original Elamite epic when it reached India. And as we have already discussed, Dasrath and Kudur Mabug are both military titles. So it is not impossible that they were the same person.' Eric paused for breath. 'That is why, over the last several decades, historians and archaeologists have been looking for Mabug's and his sons' tombs.'

'As a matter of fact, that is the second point I would like to discuss with you today.' Nassar's face brightened.

'I am listening.'

'It was all fate!' Nassar said. 'Inshallah—as God wills it. If the robbers hadn't knocked over the sarcophagus, I wouldn't have seen what they missed—the cracks around the central paving stone, revealing the shaft beneath.'

'When do you think it happened?'

'No way to tell, really! But probably not long after the original burial.'

'I see your point. But what is there in the lower chamber?'

'Patience, Professor, patience! You will see it with your own eyes.' Nassar smiled. 'There are hundreds of such tombs. Whoever broke into this one knew there was someone important buried here. It's like the grave robbers of Victorian England. They would read death notices of wealthy people and attend the funerals to see if they were being buried with their jewellery.'

'Aah! Gross!' remarked Eric, and yet, he couldn't resist smiling at Nassar's story.

'Wouldn't you call it practical—or ingenious even—if that was the business they were in?' Nassar smiled playfully.

'I'll wait until you are done with your theatrics,' Eric evaded the question. *A seasoned crook*, he thought, *swallowing his anger only to get my help...once his purpose is solved, he'll have me killed the first chance he gets.*

'You have to walk a little more, Professor.' Nassar smiled.

'Are we going down the hole?' Eric asked.

'Claustrophobia or vertigo?' Nassar's smile broadened.

'None. I just want to get on with it, if you don't mind.'

'Of course, Professor,' Nassar stiffened, 'your wish is my command.'

'If that were true, you wouldn't have kept me in captivity.'

'Patience, Professor, you don't know how lucky you are and what you are going to experience today.'

'Then, like I said, let's get on with it.'

'You first,' Nassar said, handing Eric the flashlight. 'I am not sure if I'm ready to turn my back on you yet.'

'Believe me, the feeling's mutual.'

Eric put the nylon strap of the light over his head to keep his hands free and climbed down the ladder into the hole. He dropped down into a small, low-ceilinged chamber lined with mud-brick. It was at least ten degrees colder in here than the upper chamber. A few moments later, Nassar joined him. Without a word, he took the spotlight dangling over Eric's chest and focused it to their left. Eric saw a set of stairs curving directly into the stone bedrock beneath their feet.

'Good looks before age, please!' Nassar gestured with his right hand towards the staircase.

Eric went down the stairs quietly, the stone on either side brushing against his shoulders. At the bottom of the shallow flight of steps, there was an extremely narrow corridor.

It was even colder here than the previous chamber. Eric could smell death in the corridor, which seemed to him like a forgotten part of space lost in the passage of time. The tunnel-like corridor must have been dug through the bedrock, considering the depth they had climbed down to. The walls still bore chisel marks of the quarrymen who had dug it thousands of years before.

The flashlight beam threw long, dancing shadows ahead of Eric as he walked. At the end of the passage, about a hundred and fifty feet from the stairs, was an antechamber, also empty, with walls decorated in cuneiforms and colourful relief work. As Nassar appeared beside him with another torch in his hand, Eric observed the same set of symbols repeating over and over again. As Nassar moved his torch to the right, Eric saw a small doorway and another corridor that connected the chamber with a second antechamber.

This next room had a pile of unmatched furniture and small artefacts, thrown together like junk. There were piles of decorated boxes, jars, statuettes of gods and animals and several small models of houses and ships. It looked like the precious items in the chamber had been looted and then the not-so-valuable stuff had been pushed to the side to make space for a walkway.

'But why?' Before Eric had finished uttering the question, Nassar's torch illuminated a third doorway on the wall across from them.

'I am afraid my men are not the most careful workers,' Nassar said.

'You are the boss, aren't you?' Eric smirked.

'Come, Professor, let me take you to your surprise!' Nassar said, paying no attention to Eric's denunciation.

They walked past the clutter of discarded artefacts and stepped into the third chamber.

'Welcome to the burial chamber of Warad-Sin, or Bharat,' Nassar announced with unmasked glee. As you know, Warad-Sin ruled Larsa...'

But Eric could not hear the rest of the sentence as he froze in his tracks. Nassar's torch beam danced around the large room. In the centre of the chamber stood a giant stone sarcophagus. The lid of a coffin leaned against its side.

The visible sides of the vault were covered in images of Sumerian gods: Enlil, the god of wind and storm; Enki, the god of water and human culture; Ninhursag, the goddess of fertility and the earth; Utu, the god of the sun and justice; Inanna, the goddess of sex, beauty and warfare and Nanna, the god of the moon.

Led by Nanna, the entire pantheon was present in the chamber, either carved in stone or drawn in vivid colours on the walls, as bright as if they had just been painted.

'How do we know this is Warad-Sin?'

'There was a metal tablet with a cuneiform inscription of his name on the inner cover of the sarcophagus, of course.'

'I understand that has also been removed for safekeeping?' Eric said without the slightest hint of sarcasm.

'Of course! Now would you please have a look at this?'

Nassar shone his light around. It revealed an enormous panorama, seemingly captured from a high vantage point. The entire wall at the head of the sarcophagus had been given over to a single large relief of a ship with fifty oars of gold. Two figures, much larger than the others, stood at the bow of the ship. The smaller of the two held a sapling in his hands, and the other pointed his royal stick ahead like a commander giving a command.

The ship was painted against the point of confluence between two rivers. The banks were thick with tall grasses, the shoreline populated with people wearing kaunakes—fur skirts made from sheep's or goat's hair. The upper bodies of women were covered with an additional piece of animal skin and men's upper bodies were bare, their hair long and mostly in buns. All men and women seemed bent in reverence to the two men at the bow of the ship. Above the scene, a stylised crescent moon shone a single beam of light upon the voyagers that went all the way down to the sapling.

'Any guesses?' Nassar asked expectantly.

'Hmm, interesting indeed.'

'Can you make anything out of this?'

'If this is indeed the tomb of Kudur Mabug and his son Warad-Sin, then I think I have a theory.' Eric scratched his chin, his eyes glassy.

'What is it?' Nassar asked impatiently.

'I think this relief depicts the mystical voyage of Kudur Mabug and his son Warad-Sin from Larsa to somewhere in this region—possibly where we stand now. The two rivers are most likely the Tigris and the Euphrates. The topography and vegetation along with the depiction of the worshippers in the mural all collectively suggest that it was somewhere close to Larsa, from where they must have started their voyage. As people represent settlement, their position in the mural suggests that the ship was sailing towards the north, which can lead to this place. I understand, standing here some three thousand seven hundred years back, we could have been close to the Tigris on its ancient course. Depicting the place of the joining of the two rivers was important, I think, because that's how in a single artwork it could easily be shown that the journey started in the south and continued northwards.

'Not bad!' Nassar beamed. 'That was pretty good, actually.'

'The only thing I don't understand is the emphasis on the sapling in the painting. Why is it blessed by the sacred-looking moonlight?' Eric stared at the relief and muttered. 'Most ancient civilisations had their versions of the Tree of Life, and the Mesopotamians or Sumerians were no exception. There are plenty of early Sumerian reliefs with the Tree of Life as the centrepiece. But then again, this one looks different. As a matter of fact, this one seems far more real than the other ornamental depictions.'

'I think you need to take a look at this as well...'

Nassar swung the light beam towards the foot of the sarcophagus, and Eric saw yet another panoramic relief covering the entire wall behind the sarcophagus.

The mural portrayed a series of death scenes. The two men from the previous artwork were each shown on their deathbeds in two consecutive scenes, with several people weeping around them. In the older man's death scene, he was shown handing the sapling to the younger one, and in the next, the younger man was handing it over to another tall man in a king's attire. The third scene showed the ship from the earlier mural in the background and a crescent moon casting a single beam on the sapling, illuminating the face of the third man who now held it.'

'Rim-Sin,' Eric's mind prompted, 'the king who was worshipped as the Moon God by his subjects, as mentioned in several Larsa tablets.'

'What do you think about this one?' Nassar asked.

'This mural doesn't indicate that they both died at the same time, but it does probably imply that this is the resting place of both Kudur Mabug and Warad-Sin.'

'But why here?'

'There can be many reasons.' Eric seemed immersed in deep thought. 'One probable answer is that they were trying to hide something precious from Hammurabi and came to this region to hide it.'

'But Hammurabi, the sixth king of the first Babylonian dynasty, was from a different time!' prompted Nassar.

'According to some scholars, Hammurabi was a contemporary of Rim-Sin. And Warad-Sin's reign was when he was planning a campaign against Larsa. Coming back to the artwork,' Eric scratched his chin, 'during the voyage, one of them—most probably Kudur Mabug—might have died and handed the secret, in the form of knowledge or some treasure, over to Warad-Sin. Later, when Warad-Sin died, his body might have been brought here to be buried with his father. This could support the idea depicted in the last scene—that the secret was passed on further to Rim-Sin.'

'What could that secret or treasure be?'

'The sapling can be a metaphor—and it could be anything, from something of immense material value to some kind of secret knowledge.'

'But where is it?'

'Well, I didn't find any map here. Maybe it was removed for safekeeping?' Eric did not ease up on the sarcasm.

'Well then, I think we are done for now!' Nassar declared stiffly. 'We should be on our way now.'

'Whatever you say,' Eric shrugged, 'you are my captor.' He turned towards the stairs, although it was clear from the look on his face that he would have rather stayed in the ancient chamber for several more hours. They climbed out the same way they'd come, back through the antechambers to the narrow corridor, their footsteps ringing on the rough-quarried stone floors. They climbed the few steps leading to the bottom of the shaft, went up the groaning ladder, and got to the upper chamber.

Eric scurried out of the tomb under Nassar's watchful eye and got up to face the light of the sun, much closer now to the dunes in the west.

◆

Nassar drove the jeep cautiously on the concrete road they had used in the morning. Darkness hadn't set in yet, and a chilly breeze blew in from the front of their open jeep, turning their fingers to stone. Nassar kept his headlights on; the possibility of finding people out here was far less than the risk of hitting one of the rocks that lay hidden in the sand like mines ready to explode.

Eric felt strangely calm. He still couldn't believe what he'd just discovered. Its implications could potentially be far more significant and earth-shattering than his discovery of Job Charnock's treasure the previous year. The third man on the relief was Rim-Sin for sure, but what was that secret his father had handed down to him, and why? Whatever it was, it was related to the last wish of Kudur Mabug and had to be something highly precious, otherwise it wouldn't appear on the main walls of his burial chamber. Questions swirled in his mind, but he knew this was not the time to think about the past. His present and future were still full of uncertainty. Eric knew the situation was out of his control. What he didn't know yet was that, like always, luck was on his side.

◆

They drove back to the camp in silence and without incident. Nassar let Eric out of the truck in front of his tent. 'I'd thought we could have dinner together, but I changed my mind.' He nodded curtly at Eric while putting the truck in gear and drove off. Eric nodded to the guard, who stood outside the tent with an AK-47 propped up on his shoulder, then turned and ducked inside.

THIRTY-SEVEN

Marina Martinez woke up to the sharp sting of vomit bubbling inside her stomach.

She shut her eyes, trying to piece together anything that might help her understand where she was. She faintly remembered being in her motel room in Mosul and the room service bringing her food. As she'd stood up to thank the waiter, he had taken a handkerchief from his pocket and covered her face with it. Then everything went dark.

The vomit must be her body's way of getting rid of the potent chemicals that had been used to keep her unconscious hours—or days. She had no clue how long she had been unconscious. She looked around her. Faint light was entering from somewhere—it must be evening. It looked like she was in a tent. Her left hand was cuffed to one end of a long iron chain, and the other end of the chain ran through an eyebolt securely anchored onto a pillar in the centre of the tent. The floor around her was dry, with warm sand and hardened dirt everywhere.

She closed her eyes again, trying hard to focus. She had fleeting visions of a cramped bazaar and glimpses of faces she had encountered as she was being carried away. But no one had intervened. No one seemed to care, as if this sort of thing was commonplace in Iraq. Still reeling under the influence of drugs and the nausea they caused, it took Marina several moments to notice that her feet were bare. She also realised that the shackles that tied her would allow her to stand up, though her movement would be restricted to a three-foot circle around the pillar.

Marina felt sweat beads slithering down her face as she pawed ferociously at the iron clamp encircling her wrist. As the severity of her situation began to set in, panic and the sweltering heat inside the tent kept her from catching her breath. Her face and clothes were soaked in perspiration as she desperately tried to slip her hand out of its restraints. The moisture allowed the metal to slide an inch or two, but it couldn't help Marina escape. Each time she tried to pull her arm free, she succeeded only in chafing her skin a bit more. When her efforts began to draw blood, she knew it was time to give up.

She would have to find another way.

Marina took a deep breath and steadied herself. She knew she could only get through this if she kept her calm and worked methodically.

Until a year ago, this kind of self-confidence would have been unthinkable for Marina. Back then, real-world dangers would have left her paralysed with fear. Despite having worked for universities on archaeological documentation projects, her real talent lay in fieldwork, in archaeological excavations. But her seniors thought she lacked the confidence and attitude for real fieldwork.

It was Dr Hussein with whose help she'd started working on building courage and confidence for fieldwork. Under his tutelage, she had worked really hard to bridge the gap.

Right before this field trip, Dr Hussein had advised her to get enrolled for a survival training course. During that course, she had learnt a few survival tricks. Starting off with the basics such as how to blend into a crowd and hide in plain sight, she had worked her way up to complicated tricks such as avoiding surveillance cameras and circumventing standard security measures such as window alarms and motion detectors. She had also learnt how to pick locks.

Now, with a clear head and some composure, when Marina studied the clamp that bound her hand, she could sense her fortunes shifting. She had yet to master the art of picking tumbler locks, like the ones found in homes and cars, but handcuffs were right up her alley. Handcuffs were usually designed in such a way that a single key could open a variety of models and sizes. All she needed was something sturdy and small to trip the internal mechanism.

Marina scoured the floor for something she could use as a makeshift lock pick. Finding only sand and dirt, she checked the pockets of her jeans. On the verge of desperation, she ran her fingers through her hair, hoping to find a stray bobby pin, even though she seldom wore any. Not surprisingly, she got none.

Then it came to her.

In an instant, she had unfastened her belt and pulled it out from the loops of her jeans. She rolled the buckle in her hands, considering how to best use it. It was a fake Gucci she had bought off the streets of Vancouver. The prong of the clasp was skinny, with a slight curve at the end. As far as improvised tools went, she couldn't have asked for more.

Now Marina was confident she could make it work.

Slipping the curved end of the prong into one of the cuffs, she slowly rotated it inside the keyhole, searching for resistance. All she had to do was find the right pressure point.

The moment she felt the prong catch on to something, she adjusted the angle and pressed hard. The resultant brief click was the sweetest sound she had ever heard in her life. The metal cuff popped loose from her wrist, its well-oiled hinge releasing her from its grasp.

Marina beamed as she tossed the cuffs to the floor. She had freed herself, and she had done it all on her own, without anyone's help.

Her heart swelled with pride, but she kept her emotions in check. Just because her hands were free, it didn't mean that she was too.

Marina crept up on her feet. Her steps were unstable still, but she managed to walk to the corner of the tent opposite to the entry. She looked down at her bare feet, wondering how far and how fast they could carry her. She took a deep breath, summoning all her reserves of energy and courage and clearing away the last few cobwebs from her mind. She took a mental vow not to stop sprinting until she had reached someplace safe. To survive, she only needed to outrun her captors.

Marina nodded to herself.

It was do or die.

She aligned her ear with the tarpaulin of the tent and listened for any signs of her captors. Hearing nothing, she pulled up the heavy tarpaulin wall of the tent and slipped her head out.

The evening light had cast a translucent veil over the landscape. There were several tents surrounding hers. Just when she pulled her whole body out of the tent, she noticed, with panic, the vigorous shaking of the tent in front of hers. The very next moment, a head popped out from the bottom of the tent a few feet away from her.

It was a man.

He instantly put his finger to his lips, gesturing to her to keep quiet.

Then they both heard the distant rumble of helicopters.

THIRTY-EIGHT

Even without seeing the helicopters, Eric knew they were Italian Augusta Westlands.

He leaped forward, dragging the woman by her hand back into her tent. He saw the handcuffs and chain on the floor and looked up at her eyes. She was beautiful, her doe eyes set in a chiselled face with well-defined jaw lines. Holding his breath, Eric whispered, 'Please don't worry; I am not one of them. I am also a captive here. Now tell me, who are you?'

The woman looked at Eric with a blank face, her mind seemingly unable to register anything.

'Do you speak English?' Eric continued softly. 'The camp is under attack, and we don't have time.'

'I am Marina.' The woman burst into tears. 'Marina Martinez.'

'What?' Eric couldn't believe his ears. 'You look different from your driving license photo,' he added, and without wasting any time, he took Marina's hand and led her towards the entrance of the tent.

Before they could get out, a man appeared at the entrance in an olive green combat outfit, a dark green balaclava covering his face and a Spectre M4 machine gun in his hand. He also had an automatic pistol tucked into a nylon holster on his left thigh, a commando knife visible from under its Velcro sheath on the right thigh and a lightweight body armour covering his chest. Eric didn't waste a second. In a reflex motion, he dropped to the ground and kicked the man between the legs.

The man screamed and staggered back as the machine gun in his hand shot a line of bullet holes across the ceiling of the tent. Eric didn't have to change his position to knee-butt the commando at the same spot, just a little harder, and the man toppled backwards. Barely pausing for breath, Eric sprung up from the ground on one leg and dropped down with the other bent, smashing the fallen man's ribs with his knee. He reached out, pulled out the commando's knife from its sheath and raised it in the air to plunge it into the man's chest. But a soft yet firm hand held his forearm from the back.

'He will not be a concern for us,' Marina said, moving forward and pulling Eric's armed hand down, 'at least for the next several hours.' She added without moving her eyes from Eric's face, 'Who are you?'

Eric did not reply. Instead, he dropped the knife, grabbed the man's Spectre and hung it on his right shoulder. Then he took the automatic pistol, a Beretta M9, from the commando's thigh holster. He tossed it to Marina. For a moment, the young woman looked as if she had a snake in her hand. Then she looked up at Eric with curious eyes.

'Point, and pull the trigger,' Eric instructed. 'The safety catch is on the left…shoot anyone who looks at you funny. All right?'

'Okay!' Marina chimed. 'But I think I have the right to know who I am taking my orders from…' 'Of course, you should know that, and you will know it sooner than you thought.' Eric hesitated for a moment, then added, 'My name is Eric Roy.'

'The one I spoke with a few days back?'

'The same one.'

'You actually came all the way for me?' she cried and threw her arms around him.

Struggling to keep his balance, Eric said, 'Well, that's technically half-correct, since I have come for both you and Dr Huntley.'

There was a ripping sound behind them. Eric and Marina both turned to find a blade appearing across the wall of the tent, ripping it all the way down. Marina raised her M9, and Eric saw her thumb flipping down the safety catch. A face appeared across the slit in the tarpaulin. Eric expected a balaclava-wearing commando. Instead, he came face to face with a familiar pair of eyes.

It was Suleiman. The double-crossing dwarf of a smuggler.

THIRTY-NINE

'This way!' Suleiman beckoned urgently from outside as the knife ripped down to the base of the tent. 'Come now; the camp is under attack!'

'Why should we come with you?' Eric asked, brandishing his machine gun in the man's face.

'There are a bunch of helicopters out there, and at least sixty heavily armed men. Unless you come with me, you two will die.'

'I am not sure if we'll live to see the next morning with you either!' Eric smirked.

'I know a way out of this fucking place,' Suleiman said.

'Why should I trust you again after what you did?'

'Because I am your only chance!'

Eric knew Suleiman was right. With nowhere to go, a hundred enemies were a little too many to fight. They'd be slaughtered in no time. For a fraction of a second, he began considering who the attackers might be and then put the thought out of his mind. There would be plenty of time for that kind of an analysis, he told himself, if only they managed to get out of the present mess.

'Lead the way,' he said to Suleiman, lowering his gun.

Suleiman's face withdrew from the slit in the canvas wall. Eric and Marina stepped out and followed the man into the flimsy twilight.

Suleiman was dressed in an all-black military outfit with a beret on his head. He carried one holstered pistol and no other arms. With Eric and Marina in tow, he tiptoed through rows of tents, working his way towards the north-western side of the camp. Eric remembered he had seen the sheep-and-goat enclosure on that side earlier.

Behind them, there were frequent bursts of gunfire followed by the muffled screams of dying men. Camels and goats squealed, panicking and tearing at their picket lines, unable to do anything more than stagger into each other. Fires leapt up as grenades burst into tents and bullets found their targets.

Climbing up a dune, in the last of the evening light, Eric caught a flicker of movement and instantly turned to his right. A figure rose out of the darkness; a robed member of the camp—Rafiq. He was carrying a sword, three-and-a-half-foot long with a simple wooden crosspiece and grip, and the blade shone as it swept down in a deadly arc.

Eric had a momentary flash of a turbaned Pakistani attacker wielding an immense curved pulwar at his camp in the ruins of a village in northern Sindh, on one of Eric's earlier excavations. He did exactly what he had done then: he ducked. Rolling to one side, keeping low to avoid Rafiq's backstroke, he then came up on his knees, tearing the commando knife out of its sheath and thrusting it into the man's fluttering thawb. Cutting through the fabric, the blade sliced into the tendons in the back of his right leg, crippling him instantly. As Rafiq fell, he managed to pull a lethal-looking dagger from his right sleeve, bringing it down to Eric's lower abdomen. Eric backed away, but he knew it was too late. The dagger was going to draw blood.

A single shot rang out right then, and Rafiq was thrown backwards. His wounded body rolled down the sand dune, leaving behind his turban caked in a mess of blood. Eric looked up. Marina stood over him, one hand extended, the other holding a smoking pistol.

'Point and shoot, right?' the girl said, cocking her head to a side.

'That's right.' Eric took her hand and pulled himself up.

'Come on!' Suleiman whispered from a distance.

They reached the sand rampart and struggled upward behind Suleiman. Once at the top, Eric looked back. Much of the camp was on fire now, and he could see the silhouettes of robed soldiers against the flames. He could also see the attacking commando force and realised they were herding the native force against the far eastern wall.

As Eric looked on, a fresh line of fire emerged from the top of the far rampart. It sounded like it came from some heavy weapons. It was an ambush. A squad had been lying in wait to catch the native forces in a deadly crossfire.

Eric turned back. He was in the exact spot he'd been that morning, except now the area between the rampart and the near-invisible runway was blocked by four huge helicopters. They were red-and-white Augusta Westlands, as Eric had thought. They had the longest range of any medium-sized transport chopper in the market.

Following Suleiman, Eric crouched, pulling Marina down with him. Standing up, they'd be perfect targets, silhouetted as they were against the rising flames behind them.

'What now?' Eric whispered to Suleiman.

'There,' said the little man, pointing at the parapet. 'Keep low.'

Without any signal, Suleiman began to run along the sand-pile wall, heading towards the north-western corner of the structure. Eric followed, pulling Marina behind him, keeping low as he'd been instructed and checking every few seconds if anyone had seen them from the helicopters. Marina was following Eric, but then all of a sudden she stopped running. Eric looked back to find the body of a native guard blocking the narrow running track, his throat slit by one of the commandos. Eric stepped over the body and helped Marina, and then they again followed after Suleiman.

When all of them had reached the corner of the wall, Suleiman pointed down to the ditch below. Waiting on the other side of the dry trench was a truck. It looked a lot like the army patrol vehicle he had seen a couple of days ago near Nineveh, but much older for sure. It was an open vehicle with a big machine gun perched on a hinge mount in the rear.

'Can you work that?' Suleiman asked in a hoarse whisper, pointing at the big machine gun.

'Probably,' Eric peered down at the monster truck. The gun looked much bigger than an American MP-40—probably a Russian version. But then again, a machine gun was a machine gun, and the Russians had a penchant for making weapons strong, simple and user-friendly. That was the reason the AK-47 was considered the cheeseburger of all automatic rifles.

'You'd better be able to work it,' Suleiman cautioned, 'because those copters are in our way, and I am sure they have left behind someone to guard them. Watch your back!' Suleiman suddenly yelled.

Eric twisted his upper body, bringing up the machine pistol he'd stripped off the dead soldier in the tent. A commando was charging up the hill, another two men right behind him. As Eric fired his Spectre, the charging man looked up.

'Merda!' the commando called, lifting his own weapon.

Eric squeezed the trigger on the Spectre and sent the man tumbling down the hill in a heap. Watching the body roll, the other two men stopped in their tracks and took a moment to bring up their machine pistols. Eric took advantage of the moment and swung his weapon from right to left, firing until the clip was empty and both men had been sliced in half. Behind the dead men, at the base of the wall, two more commandos looked up.

'Run!' Eric yelled, turning and throwing himself over the edge of the sloping sand as firing erupted from below. He lost his footing and tumbled down towards the ditch at the base of the rampart.

Eric fell to the bottom with a thump that knocked out his left shoulder. As he struggled to his feet and scrambled up the far side of the ditch, he felt a burning sting as a bullet shot through the sleeve of his shirt. More shots were fired through the sand around him as the commandos, now high above him, tried to throw him off. He reached the truck and flung himself into the back, grabbing the grip underneath the machine gun and swinging the weapon around on its hinge.

As soon as he saw Marina pull up beside him and Suleiman start the truck, Eric dropped the firing lever, locking the belt feed in place. He flipped off the safety catch and angled the gun upward, checking, out of the corner of his eye, to see if the belt feed ran smoothly into the large ammunition box. Then he took a deep breath and pulled hard on the trigger.

The heavy-barrelled weapon came alive in his arms, jumping like a beast while shooting a pulse train of .50-calibre shells that chewed up the crest of the sand rampart like grass razed by a lawn mower. Anyone still on the summit would be dead meat by now.

Once this line of threat was removed, Eric spun the gun around to face the helicopters as their truck roared towards the runway. The copters were standing in a rather staggered formation, in a curved line of defence that blocked their way. The fat-bellied flying machines had sliding doors like a minivan and a ramp at the rear end. Eric scanned the scene to find out if there were any commandos inside and noticed a mini-gun behind one of the three giant windows of the second helicopter.

'If you see a gun strategically positioned, always remember there might be a man behind it,' his trainer Professor Naidu's voice reverberated in his head. As if on impulse, Eric shot a train of shells into the line of choppers, firing in short bursts at the centre of each passenger compartment. Even from over a hundred and fifty metres away, Eric could see the windshields exploding, metal sheets being torn apart and chunky engine parts flying in all directions. A bright flare illuminated the third copter from the left, and a split second later, a huge fireball erupted from its windows with a deafening sound. Jet fuel.

Suleiman swung the truck away from the exploding copter even as Marina held on to the back of his seat to save her head from crashing against the insides of the truck. In the light cast by the exploding chopper, Eric saw figures running about in the foreground.

Suleiman yelled, 'RPG at eleven o' clock!'

One of the running figures had a familiar-looking launcher on his shoulder. 'An RPG-7,' Eric mumbled. 'This little thing can stop much bigger things than this tin truck!'

Eric heaved the gun in that direction, pot-shooting at the line of men who promptly dropped like puppets with their strings mercilessly cut, including the man with the RPG.

The men were through, as was the line of choppers behind them; one lit up like a torch and two others were badly damaged. Even if they were heavily armed, stranded without transport, the commando group could do nothing.

Suleiman pulled up their vehicle beside the runway. The plane Eric had been thinking about in the morning was visible now. Tied down under an awning beside a line of fuel drums, the eight-seater was right next to the runway. Both the cockpit doors were wide open.

'I can't see the pilot!' Eric exclaimed, climbing down from the truck. The cockpit was indeed empty. He shuddered as an explosion sounded behind him. He turned to discover that the fire had spread; a second helicopter was ablaze now. The commandos had planned for a quick rendezvous with minimum casualties, and now their plans had gone up in flames.

'Well, I am the pilot,' claimed Suleiman, approaching from behind.

'Are you kidding?'

'I have a Canadian license, and I *have* earned it!' Suleiman rolled his eyes matter-of-factly. 'I was flying even before I could drive a car.' He walked around to the pilot's side and got in behind the half-moon wheel. Marina and Eric climbed in after him, Eric taking the co-pilot's seat and Marina the one behind it.

Suleiman shut the door with a bang and started flipping random switches as if it was what he did all day every day.

'I have also completed my mandatory military service stint here in Iraq,' Suleiman continued. 'I spent a year flying one of these.'

He switched the fuel mixture to 'rich', set the RPMs at 'high', and held the ignition switch down. The engine coughed, then died. Suleiman waited for a couple of seconds and repeated the drill. This time the engine purred. There was a shrill cracking sound from the rear section of the aircraft, followed by a louder second one.

'They are shooting at us,' said Marina.

Eric looked out of the window on his right. Except for the flames rising from the choppers, the night was dark.

The engine roared as Suleiman pressed down on the throttles. More bullets hit the plane from behind.

'Let's fly,' Suleiman hissed, releasing the brakes. The aircraft rolled out from beneath the cover and took a hard turn. With his feet set on the pedals, Suleiman pushed further down on the throttles than he had ever had cause for. The old two-engine aircraft made a huge noise and hurtled down the runway, slowly rising into the dark of the night.

FORTY

'Where are we heading?' Eric asked, raising his voice over the steady roar of the engines as Suleiman levelled the aircraft.

'North-west, towards Italy, if you are not about to give me another option.' The only light in the aircraft came from the control panel. The radar screen in the centre of the dashboard cast an alien glow over their faces.

'My option would depend on where the choppers came from,' Eric said.

'I saw a logo that said HAC on the side of one of the choppers,' added Marina from the back.

'That's the logo of the Helicopter Association of Canada,' Suleiman muttered.

'They are one of the biggest chopper-hire companies in the world!' Eric recalled. 'They serve most oil rigs and several governments, providing rescue helicopters during disasters.'

'But they have their offices everywhere in the world, and anyone from any country can hire them,' Suleiman said.

'Yes, of course, the logo doesn't necessarily mean anything—you should know it better!' Eric said. 'Hey, one second!' He paused for a moment, trying to remember something, then said, 'The man on the outer wall said "merda" just before I shot him...'

'That's Italian for shit,' Marina chimed in.

'So these people are from Italy! Though I understand they can come from anywhere much closer. But why are they doing this? Is it some kind of revenge?'

'Why not!' Suleiman said. 'It isn't like all the people Nassar deals with are good. Recently he was in touch with the Vatican for some business I know nothing about.' He smiled.

'Or maybe these guys were looking for something else?' Eric scrunched his face.

'Like what?'

'Like the tomb of Warad-Sin that Nassar has found!' Eric quietly said.

'That's possible. Mercenaries working for someone very powerful...' Suleiman muttered half to himself. 'Someone very powerful must have got a hint of this tomb,' he said with his eyes welded on the dashboard.

'I know Italy well, and that's the only place where I can organise papers for us—if you guys recall, we are people without identities right now!' Marina said.

'That's immensely sweet of you,' Suleiman smiled at her.

'But before that, it's time we did an analysis of our situation,' Eric said, raising his voice a little more than what they were chit-chatting at. 'How far can this aircraft take us?'

'A little over three thousand kilometres, with the additional fuel cans Nassar stores at the back section.

'Can we make it anywhere close to Rome?' Excitement pulsed in Eric's voice.

'Yes, that would be around 2,900 kilometres. Nassar keeps the fuel tank full at all times, in preparation for unanticipated events.'

'I guess he didn't anticipate this particular event,' Eric sniggered.

'He was a fool. He should have seen this coming!' Suleiman grunted, his eyes looking straight ahead. 'Keeping that big an archaeological discovery a secret is a foolish thing to do...it's a bad-luck-catcher anyway! By the way, he lied to you,' Suleiman turned to Eric and added with disgust in his eyes. 'He is no archaeologist. He is a filthy smuggler, and he was the one behind the massacre at Dr Huntley's site.'

He adjusted the controls. Eric watched as the compass needle swerved on the illuminated dial. They were now going due west and slightly to the north. He wanted to say something, but then thought better of it and nodded.

'The sand is absolutely hard there. We can smoothly land,' Marina mumbled to herself in the back.

'Where?' Eric had caught her words.

'I know a secluded hard-sand beach near Porto de Enya where you can land this thing.'

'Yes, of course, I've seen the place,' said Suleiman, 'less than three thousand kilometres from here. Five and a half hours tops. We'll be good for a late dinner, Italian time, at the Marine Village restaurant close to this isolated marina where we plan to land.'

'And from there, if you wish to visit the Vatican, we can take Via Litoranea and then Cristoforo Colomboto.' Marina completed the itinerary. 'A little over an hour, and we're knocking at the gate of the Vatican!' she beamed.

'Yes, indeed. If you are still as excited when we reach, we will make time to say hello to the Pope as well!' Eric sneered.

FORTY-ONE

Directed by the long stretch of sodium lights paving Via Litoranea, running parallel to the isolated beach, and keeping the phosphorous-lit waves on his other side, Suleiman readied himself for an unorthodox landing. When the turboprop was right above the hard sand, he gave it rudder and straightened it out against the wind. A moment later, they kissed the sand as lightly as a feather's touch. Rolling across the sea breeze, Suleiman slowed the plane and brought it to a grinding halt. He shut down the engine and proclaimed, 'I am hungry; now we shall get some food!'

With their part-time pilot leading the way, Eric and Marina walked westwards along the sand towards a line of trees perched on higher ground. The night sky was starry enough for them to watch their step. The air smelled of fish and had the typical salty taste of coastal towns. The cool sea breeze kept hitting them in the back. They reached the high ground with the line of trees and climbed up.

Even in the dim light from the stars they couldn't miss it. A few metres away from them stood a strikingly tall, well-built man, backed by a squad of armed men. The man wore loose-fitting clothing, and his heavy arms were folded on his chest.

'Mr Eric Roy, Ms Marina Martinez, I presume?' He turned to his squad and nodded. One member of the group lifted his weapon—some kind of handgun Eric couldn't recognise at first glance. He never got a chance, for the man took aim and fired at point-blank range.

FORTY-TWO

Mahi Dasht medical facility,
Fifty kilometres from the accident spot

Accompanied by a hospital attendant, Jojo climbed a ramp carrying the wounded cab driver on a handheld stretcher, followed by Alex, Aurin and Father Smit, to reach the porch that led to the main hospital building. It had the look of a typical middle-eastern medical facility: the stairs along the ramp, the wrought iron railings, the stone walls and the wide porch that led to a large balcony with a series of cabins on both sides. The layout was identical on the second floor.

They stepped through the balcony where an Iraqi family stood squabbling in strained voices. An obese woman was stretched out on a bench. Signs were posted everywhere in Arabic and English. Aurin found one that said 'Reception' in English. He followed the arrow and pushed through double doors into a small room crammed with a large desk and rows of aluminium benches. As they entered, a flash of cool air hit them in the face. They had never expected to find air-conditioning machines in a medical facility like this, and that too in perfect working condition. It was quite a feeling for the bikers after several days of riding bikes under the scorching sun through the obscure wilderness. A receptionist in a white burqa looked at them from over the rim of her round glasses.

'How may I help you?' she asked in unaccented English.

She was a small woman with large eyes. Aurin moved closer to the desk, pressing against it and leaning over, as if to keep from being overheard. 'We found this guy on the highway. His car fell off the road and into a gorge. He is badly injured. Please do the needful to save him.'

The receptionist sat up straight. 'Do you know him?'

'No, we only know his name from his driving license—Mahmod Jamal.'

'Did you see the accident occur?'

'No,' Aurin lied.

'Here's a form you need to fill up.' She pressed a single digit on an old-fashioned phone kept on her desk. As Jojo started filling in empty squares on the form, two men came in through a side door and carried the stretcher inside.

'Put him on bed number twenty-seven and inform Dr Abbas!' the receptionist called and waved after them with her manicured, henna-patterned left hand.

FORTY-THREE

Eric came to his senses feeling as if someone was driving a road-roller through his head. For a long time, he lay there with his eyes closed, letting things come back to him very slowly. The last thing he remembered was the tall man and his group of armed men standing before them on the beach at Porto de Enya.

It had looked like the men had been waiting for them. Who were they? How could they have known about their arrival? Where were Suleiman and Marina now? Were they alive? A barrage of questions and fears closing in on his mind, Eric's heart sank at one thought. Could it have been Suleiman?

Eric remembered the men firing at him from a few yards away. He should have been hit hard. But all he had felt was a painful sensation to the left of his ribs. After that, everything was a blur. He decided to take it easy. He took deep breaths, inhaling as much oxygen as he could. He was not injured—at least not visibly—that was clear. But he had been drugged for sure, and the rattling of the road-roller inside his head was the after-effect.

As he lay there, trying to quieten his mind, the blur of activity that had led to his present circumstance began to resolve itself. In the back of his mind, he heard the purr of an engine. The distinct thumping of an army truck. His exhausted mind played tricks on him, bringing up memories from other times, other memory folders. Eric was reminded of the soft yet forceful thump of a Jiefang military truck, the likes of which were used by the Chinese People's Liberation Army. It was a copy of the Russian ZIL-157 army truck. The truck must have been waiting for them behind the screen of trees on the high ground where they had run into the armed men.

Then there was the sound of a big diesel engine and the reek of dead fish.

Then a boat, possibly a trawler. But how long had he been out, and where was he now?

Eric sniffed. His clothes smelled like a Chinese wet market, the air moist and musty. He was very close to the ocean, certainly close enough to smell the moist air. Probably a place that hadn't been inhabited for a very long time.

The cobwebs were beginning to fade away, so Eric tried to open his eyes. His eyelids were sticky. He'd been out for over twelve hours at the very least. He squinted against the bright light in his face. It was not natural light, just a low-watt bulb enclosed within a wire cage hanging from the ceiling. There was nothing else.

He pulled himself up into a sitting position and took stock of his surroundings. He was in an old-fashioned cot that could very well have been an army issue at some point in time.

There was a wooden box next to the cot on which lay two objects—a couple of protein bars and two half-litre bottles of packaged water. Eric suddenly realised how hungry and thirsty he was. But his army training kicked in, and he ate only one of the two bars and drank half of one bottle. Who knew when he was going to get food or drink again?

Four bare walls of pressboard, left without any paint, surrounded him. The ceiling was made of the same material and stained by leaks. The floor was concrete. The door was plain wood and had been fitted with a new lock.

It was all starting to make sense. It could be Suleiman playing one of his tricks again. They had flown to Italy because Suleiman had seeded the idea of Italy in their minds, and if his story about Nassar doing business with the Italian mafia was correct, then Nassar actually had the required connections in Italy to take care of things.

No one would care about a fishing boat leaving a secluded marina with the day's catch. Wherever they were now, they would probably be kept there until they had been thoroughly questioned.

But the most urgent question at the moment was—was he alone, or were the others somewhere near? Eric racked his brains to come up with a plan. Looking around, he wondered if the walls were actually as flimsy as they looked. He decided to take a chance. 'Let me count to ten, then hit the wall with my shoulder and see what happens.'

He had only reached as far as seven in his count when the door opened of its own accord and a huge man in army camouflage stepped inside the room. This time there was no tranquiliser gun. What he held in his hand was a Remington 870 combat shotgun. He also had a Sig Sauer P226 in an open holster on his hip.

'Outside,' he gestured, 'and no tricks.'

Eric nodded and did exactly as he was told.

◆

As Eric stepped out of the little room, the man with the Remington backed up with the gun aimed at Eric's belly. They stood inside an old-fashioned tin-roofed factory shed of sizeable proportions. There were big sliding doors both on his left and right. The one on the right was open, flooding the entire space with natural light. Beyond the open door waited an old white SUV. Just then, Marina and Suleiman appeared at the entrance along with another guard holding a Remington. Marina looked a bit dazed, but Suleiman looked alert.

The second guard pushed Marina inside the SUV, and Suleiman followed her.

'Walk,' barked the first guard and gestured towards the door. 'Into the van.'

Eric moved forward without any resistance. Inside the truck, Eric looked at Marina with concern. 'Are you okay?'

'I am fine.'

The three of them were huddled in the middle seat of the SUV with the first guard in the front seat, next to the driver. The second guard climbed into the rear of the truck, keeping his gun perched over the heads of the trio. The driver waited in silence and, when the rear door was closed, started the engine.

'What about you, Mr Double Cross, or should I call you Mr Triple Cross?' Eric smirked. 'How are you doing?'

Suleiman looked at him and sniffled, 'Believe me, Eric...!' But he was cut short.

'Shut up!' Eric growled. 'I am not interested in listening to any of your stories! What I want you to tell me is who have you sold us to this time?'

'Both of you shut up!' the guard bellowed from the rear. They both went silent while the driver hummed an unfamiliar tune and drove on.

'Does anyone know where we are? And where are they taking us?' Eric whispered.

'I think I know,' Marina piped. 'Suleiman and I weren't tranquilised like you. From the bits and pieces I heard them saying in Italian, I have a strong hunch that they transported us from Porto de Enya to Pescara by a truck, then ferried us to Grado, which is a six- or seven-hour journey over the sea.'

'Aha! We are in Grado, Udine!' Eric smiled. 'That's remarkable, Marina. Fantastic work.'

'Shut the fuck up!' the guard in the front seat yelled this time.

If this was indeed Udine, it was Eric's first time there. He looked out of the window.

The historical capital of the Friuli region, Udine was an Italian town known for its rich history, excellent wine and great food.

The town had some great attractions, including an old castle at its centre, numerous festivals and fairs and great shopping opportunities. Located just above the northern tip of the Adriatic Sea, Udine was also a quick drive away from some of Italy's best beaches. Eric wished he was a tourist with a picnic basket complete with cake, fruits, coffee, a good book, a bottle of wine and plenty of time.

The SUV drove up along the marina. On their left, the Adriatic Sea and the Laguna di Maranog gleamed in the morning light. It was the fantastic coral-blue waters of this lagoon that had made the Udine coastline popular among tourists. The sky over the marina was overcast, with migratory birds crossing over from Central Europe. The masts of the fishing boats in the harbour clanked like flamencos in the light breeze, which brought with it a faint acidic smell. Eric leaned his head back, using his hand to shield his eyes from the sun as it glared on and off from between hotel towers, apartment blocks and offices pockmarked with satellite dishes. His head still throbbed; he needed coffee.

The place was gradually coming to life with a big yawn. Udine was a late riser compared with most of the other northern Italian cities. Cafeterias were taking time lowering their striped canopies, some shops were still raising their steel shutters and groups of men sat around sipping coffee at myriad roadside joints, watching calmly as ragged boys and girls sold packs of paper napkins, flowers and cigarettes to passing cars. The alleys leading away from the main street were narrow, dark and menacing. A bus already crammed with passengers paused at a stop to take on more. A policeman in a dashing black uniform and a flat cap held up his hand to divert their truck towards the right. A vintage van crawled with taunting slowness across a junction. Elderly men played chess on plastic tables outside pastry cafes scattered all over the city streets.

Eric looked intently at the buzz of activity all around. Udine was one of the few places in Europe that he had always wanted to visit. But he had planned to do so as a tourist, not as a prisoner—

especially not with zero clue about what he had gotten himself into.

FORTY-FOUR

The SUV rolled into a walled property through a manned wrought iron gate, driving over a pebbled pathway and coming to a halt under a portico. Eric was helped out of the car by an armed man from outside. Marina and Suleiman remained inside the vehicle as the driver turned the key into the ignition and backed the car away through the exit.

On his right was a landscaped garden, and on his left were marble steps leading up to an extravagant door. Two guards escorted him up the stairs to an ornate wooden door fitted with shiny brass bolts. One of the guards rang the bell. Eric could hear the strains of chamber music coming from inside. Gustav Mahler's Piano Quartet in A-minor. *Good taste*, he thought. The door was opened by a butler, and the music accosted them like a breath of fragrant air. Eric could tell that it was a recording of a live performance. Piano, violin and cello played in perfect harmony. As a child he'd hear recordings of his father performing. His father was a brilliant musician who played several instruments, including the acoustic guitar, but was too humble to shine in any field. He never made a name for himself in music and died early.

'Yes, Signor?' the butler asked the guard nearer to the door.

'The Count wants to see this man.'

'*Sicuro!*' the butler nodded. 'The Count is in his study. Please follow me.'

They stepped into a marble-floored hallway. Masked by the sound of Mahler's music, Eric heard the faint chatter of mixed conversations that suggested a gathering or party raging down the hall to his left. The butler took a right, went around a flight of centrally positioned stairs and paused in front of a closed door. He knocked, then opened the door and stood aside. The guard stepped into the study, followed by Eric. The room was large and masculine. A huge oriental carpet covered the floor. The ceiling was panelled in dark oak with two large chandeliers lighting up the entire place, and waist-high built-in bookcases ran along the walls, interrupted by a pair of French windows at one end and an ornate wood-burning fireplace at the other. There was a Rococo-style desk on the right side of one of the windows, and next to it was a matching sideboard serving as a bar; the rest of the furniture was dark green leather and the gilt-framed paintings above the bookcases were oil on canvas, all of them. Eric recognised several Renaissance paintings, including Madonna by Filippo Lippi and an angel by Giovanni Angelico, both of them early Renaissance painters from Italy. He suspected that, like all the other paintings in the study, these two were originals, even though he knew for sure they were both supposed to be safely tucked away in different museums—the first one in Florence, Italy, and the second one in Michigan, US. Eric smiled to himself. *In this century, an excess of money and good taste can't exist without a mandatory third partner—a criminal mind.*

A man in a dark suit, with a broad forehead, long face and thinning salt-and-pepper hair swept back, stood by a bookcase. He was in his late fifties and had a tall, frail structure. His lips were dark from smoking. The man had a strange air about him, something Eric couldn't put his finger on, so he made a mental note of the guy, thinking that he might come into the picture again later on. Little did he know that their paths would cross again and again, with more interesting and twisted outcomes every time.

'Do I know you?' Eric asked.

'No, you don't,' the man said in an Italian accent. 'Please sit down.'

'Why am I here?' Eric found himself a club chair and sat down tentatively. 'Certainly doesn't look like I was invited for dinner!'

The man in the dark suit smiled gently. 'Not dinner, but you shall be treated to high tea as a guest of Count Delfino—that would be me.'

'Nice to meet you, Count,' Eric said, scanning the place. 'Nice art collection, I must say!'

One of the guards from before pulled the man a leather-upholstered vintage chair. He sat down next to the bookcase, pulled a silver cigar case out of his suit pocket and lit up what Eric assumed was a very expensive cigar. The lighter he used looked like a vintage Zippo.

Eric eased up a little and sunk back into his chair. His head still throbbed and his shoulders and back muscles were numb from pain and dehydration. He looked at the Zippo and said, 'People envy that kind of stuff, you know; you'll be in trouble in a bar or a place like that.'

'I don't go to bars. And I rarely meet people,' the tall man declared calmly. 'But I can tell you a thing or two about the cigar I'm smoking since you seem to be a connoisseur yourself.'

'Go ahead,' Eric smirked. 'The day I chose archaeology, I knew my career would lie in ruins. I just didn't know the different forms and shapes,' he added with a shrug.

'As a non-smoker, Mr Roy,' Delfino completely ignored his sarcasm and said, 'you might only have heard that premium Cuban cigars are much desired for their impeccable quality and rich flavour and are considered a symbol of luxury. What you might not know is the reason they are so premium.'

Eric nodded, thinking to himself, *I feel I am going to enjoy this high tea.*

'It is because of this very reason that the process of their creation is shrouded in legends. One such legend claims that the cigars are rolled on the thighs of virgin women.' Delfino closed his eyes and cherished a long puff of his cigar.

'Well, thanks for the trivia.' Eric drummed his fingers on the armrest and blurted out, 'What about Suleiman? Is he working for you?'

'Yes and no,' Delfino said, his eyes still closed. The Count didn't say anything for several moments and then continued, 'We discovered Suleiman quite some time ago. He was on his own, and at times he worked with someone called Nassar in Iraq. It was during one of these stints that we found him. Like any man, he had his price.' Delfino smiled. 'He's been rendering a sort of consultancy service to us of late—acquisitions, assets, contacts development, etc. So, you see, I can't really say he is working entirely for me.' Delfino crossed his legs, lifting the razor crease on his trousers.

'Honestly speaking, I am not interested in knowing how Suleiman is associated with you, Mr Delfino. I already know he is working for you. What I really want to know is why I am here.'

'Okay. Fair enough. I'll tell you our story, because to work with us you'll need to know it.' He took a long drag of the cigar and blew the smoke towards the chandelier. It swirled and faded as it ascended.

'For a few years, we have been looking for priceless ancient relics. Then we found out that your friend Dr Huntley was about to start an excavation for something similar. We decided to let him do it and keep an eye on the progress. But then everything went haywire when some desert tribes massacred the whole site and killed almost all the people.' Delfino grimaced. 'So we tried connecting with people who knew the region and could offer some help. That's how we found Suleiman, and then we found you.'

'Why did you have to kill all those people?' Eric cried out.

'You are not listening, Mr Roy,' Delfino said, 'we didn't. We only wanted Dr Huntley to carry out his excavation to the end, so that when he'd get something, we could swoop in and simply snatch it. It was probably Nassar's group that killed those people.'

'What about the attack on Nassar's camp?'

'Yes, that was us.' Delfino nodded. 'As I just said, Nassar did things he shouldn't have done…we wanted him to know there are bigger players in the game. We wanted him to come to us seeking support.'

'What do you want from me?' Eric asked coldly.

'Not much! We just want you to pick up from where Dr Huntley left off. But you would be working for us.'

'And why exactly do you think I'd do that?'

'Oh, believe me, you will!' Delfino narrowed his eyes on Eric.

'We have something that will inspire you to.'

'What's that?'

'It would be more appropriate to ask "Who's that?" Mr Roy.'

'What do you mean?'

'I mean you'll never see Dr Huntley again if you don't do this small favour to us.' Delfino smiled. 'We have him.'

'Before I believe your words, I need to talk to him.'

'Sorry, that can't happen.' Delfino said with a smile.

'But…' Eric couldn't hide the look of relief on his face, 'I hardly know anything about what he was upto!'

'He was looking for a certain tomb and a relic,' replied Delfino. 'We know you pretty well by now, Mr Roy. We know you are one of the finest archaeologists the world has seen, we know your track record, and we know you can figure things out very fast.'

Eric laughed, his voice ringing in the large space. 'What is it with you people and relics? Do you really think a Holy Grail or an Ark of the Covenant is going to give you supreme powers?'

Delfino shot Eric an amused look. He said nothing.

'You don't really believe that these relics have some kind of power that you can use like some sort of interstellar battery, do you? Because you would be no less mad than Hitler himself. And that guy was nuts.'

'Go on, I am listening.' Delfino's expression remained impassive.

'Indiana Jones books and movies are good as stories, but they aren't real. Where we live, on the other hand, is the real world. You know that, right?'

'Are you finished?'

'For now,' Eric shrugged.

'I don't have time for this, Mr Roy, but I'll give you some food for thought. Better still, let's take your namesake, for example. What do you think of the work of Erich von Daniken?'

'His work's fake, and he's a loser.'

'Well, a loser who made billions of dollars from selling millions of copies of books in several different languages and fuelled a new billion-dollar genre of sci-fi movies. All of this generated solely from a strange strain of racism. Don't you call that power?'

'I am listening.'

'The Masons, the Weeping Mary statues, Dan Brown's books, and closer home, your Ganesha statues drinking milk,' Delfino continued, 'what do you think about these...?'

'Faith is the word you are looking for, I think.'

'Yes, faith. It can move mountains, start wars, kill millions of people. And, most importantly, it is invisible and intangible. It's not the relic, Mr Roy. It's the idea of the relic that wields power.' Delfino raised the hand holding his cigar, and one of the guards instantly appeared with a crystal ashtray. He tapped his cigar on the edge of it with a slick movement of his fingers and continued with a smile. 'If there's anything I love in this world and am seriously attached to, it is *power*. There's one Dr Hussein who's the actual initiator of this project. I am getting him on this mission, along with you and Marina.'

'I am highly obliged.' Eric smirked. 'Has he volunteered?'

'Not exactly. The emotional card of Dr Huntley worked in his case as well.'

'I see!' Eric sneered.

Delfino ignored Eric's remarks and went on, 'What we don't have is time. I am giving you a month and two people who know some of the *hows* and *whys*; now I want you to figure out the *what* and the *where*. Bring me the result I want, and take Dr Huntley back. Period. Well, one more thing,' Delfino said, taking out a translucent plastic folder from one of the drawers of the bookcase and handing it over to Eric. 'This might help you in your quest.'

Eric peered inside and found a sheet of printed paper taken out of an old book. Both sides had notes pencilled in English at the bottom.

'What's this?'

'This is the key to the relic. Pencil notes made by seeker and academician Luigi Tessitori on a page of the *Ramcharitmanas*.'

'I know who Tessitori was,' Eric said.

'Well, I believe Tessitori stumbled upon something during his excavations in the Indus region. He figured out the existence of this relic and wanted to find it. These were his notes for his own use. I tried deciphering them and met partial success—my team was able to decipher one page. But I have learnt that the scribbling on the second page is the actual key to an ancient relic which is the source of unthinkable power.'

'What is it?'

'I don't know yet, but I hope you'll help me find out. Here, look at the first one.'

'Sets of alphabets,' Eric noted, 'all gibberish. DA.JF, EG.BA.'

'Gibberish at first glance, yes, but they are not meant for reading; they stand for numbers. A is for 0, B for 1, C for 2, and so on.'

'You mean the alphabets stand for numbers, and the numbers then represent something else?'

'Right, you are getting there. And what would the numbers represent?' Delfino asked, nodding slowly.

'I would pick latitudes and longitudes.'

'You are absolutely right,' Delfino smiled. 'They are coordinates, and Tessitori noted five such sets of coordinates here. Five places where he thought the relic could be found. I tried a few of them with advanced machinery and further zeroed it down to four places. The first is Tell el-Muqayyar in Iraq, which stands on the ancient site of Ur; the second one is Nineveh, where Dr Huntley planned to dig; the third is in the Syrian desert and the fourth site is some hundred miles from a small area called Musa Laka in the north-eastern range of the Zagros Mountains in Iraq.'

'Where do you want me to go?'

'To Musa Laka. My instinct says it is to be found in Musa Laka. But before that, you need to visit the British Museum to find out the exact location of the relic.'

FORTY-FIVE

Aurin and Father Smit walked out of the reception with smiling faces. After some initial hassles, Dr Abbas had finally attended to Mahmod and confirmed that he had survived the accident with only a flesh injury below his collar bone. He remained uncertain about the cause of the wound. It could be from a broken metal rod, from something that came out of his seat, or even a bullet wound. Whatever it was, he said the man should be fine in a week. He got one of them to sign the register book and asked them to leave a phone number in case of a police enquiry, before rushing back to his chamber.

Aurin and Father Smit discussed plans for the next part of their journey as they walked past a series of curtained cabins where patients rested. They crossed a door that had no curtains, and a chill ran down Aurin's spine that had nothing to do with the air-conditioning.

His eyes hadn't seen anything in particular, but his subconscious mind had sensed something. Aurin pulled on Father Smit's arm and returned to the open door for a second look. The ward looked like an extension of a large storeroom: unopened boxes of hospital equipment, a series of privacy screens, several cold storage units for vaccines and stacks of boxes of medicine supply lay around. Amidst these odds and ends, there were three empty beds in the cabin. As they stepped into the entrance, a fourth bed came into view, placed against the back wall of the room. It was not vacant. A bearded elderly man lay under a thin blanket, an oxygen mask fitted over his face and a saline IV drip hanging from a stand beside his bed. Aurin's heart skipped a beat.

He rushed forward and yanked the oxygen mask away. He put it back and then fell to his knees, weeping silently.

FORTY-SIX

Eric and Marina stepped into a small cafe and inhaled deeply, savouring the rich aroma of freshly brewed coffee and the freshly baked breakfast cakes that had caught their attention outside on the sidewalk. The warm and welcoming interiors were in contrast with the early November morning chill in the air. The place was tiny, but there was an open table by the bay window that overlooked the Thames. The cafe was within a few hundred metres of the Cutty Sark Maritime Museum and half a kilometre away from the historic Old Royal Naval College.

The table, much like the whole area, was perfect for their need. They were about to meet Dr Hussein. The previous night, a little after midnight, they'd been dropped in the middle of the Salisbury meadows by a small aircraft and then picked up by a black Porsche that brought them to Greenwich by morning. Both of them were famished and dying to have a proper breakfast.

Delfino had taken charge of things. Eric and Marina had new clothes and had got their credit cards back, all neatly arranged by Delfino's men in Udine. The only thing they didn't have were clean cell phones. Their mobile phones were bugged. Every second of their lives was being tracked; every moment was a silent threat to Dr Huntley's life.

Although Eric enjoyed panoramic landscapes, shimmering water bodies and all kinds of scenic beauty, none of those were the reason he had picked this place. He had chosen Greenwich because it was so far off the commercial grid that it barely had any CCTV cameras in the streets, a rarity in the UK. As a regular intelligence practice, Eric always did his best to avoid cameras, but privacy was of particular importance on this mission. The situation had forced him to work for the bad guys. He didn't want to be caught on camera doing that, and he knew Delfino's men would also try to track their movements through CCTV cameras wherever they went.

They ordered a full English breakfast and looked out at the easy-flowing Thames through their own reflections in the glass. A swanky cruise ship swayed by the City Cruises' private pier.

It was not a busy cafe, and their waitress didn't take long to serve them. As she arrived with the food and a large pot of tea, Eric saw the man they'd been waiting for.

Dr Muzahem Hussein was walking down the cobbled street in their direction, the limp of an injured soccer player distinguishing him from the morning crowd. Eric knew him from the photographs he'd been shown while he was briefed about Dr Hussein's work in Udine. A thin man in his fifties, Dr Hussein had a clean-shaven face that had seen a lot of sun. He wore a light brown fedora hat that made him look a little bit like Gene Hackman in *The French Connection*. Dressed in a brown tweed jacket with light brown patches on the elbows, he carried a black backpack. The only splash of colour on his outfit came from the autumnal scarf around his neck.

Eric stood up as the man entered the cafe. 'Good morning, Dr Hussein.'

Hussein smiled warmly. 'Same to you, Eric.' They shook hands like old friends before settling at the table. Somehow, the common cause of saving Dr Huntley's life—which had brought them together—had also brought their hearts and minds closer. Marina hugged her senior and tried hard to control her tears. 'Oh sir, I wish I hadn't been a part of the Nineveh team!' she sniffled.

'Would you like something to eat or drink?' Eric asked, hoping to make things lighter.

Hussein nodded as they all took their seats. 'Some tea would be good. I was working through the night.'

'What's the plan? Where do we start from?' Eric asked as he poured tea in a cup.

'We want Dr Huntley back, and for that we need to give Delfino what he wants. At least something that looks like it!' Hussein said, grabbing his cup. 'I have some ideas.'

Eric leaned forward. 'You have all my attention, Professor.'

'There is an ancient Sumerian tablet in the British Museum that has scripts similar to the coded message I have been trying to decipher for some time. I have a hunch that this message is one of the keys to the relic as well as the tomb I have been searching for all these years.'

'What does the Internet say about it?' asked Marina.

'It's not available on the Internet.'

'Why do you think this tablet can help?'

'Because what we are dealing with here is a kind of coded message written in cuneiform. The code we need to decipher is nearly four thousand years old, and the only script that comes any close to it is on this tablet in the British Museum, which is probably from the same group of keepers. I hope it will give us a lead.'

'Okay. Let's go to the British Museum then!' Marina piped. 'We'll take some pictures and then check into a hotel to freshen up before we sit down to explore how to decipher it.'

'Well,' Dr Hussein cleared his throat, 'I am afraid this tablet I am talking about is not on public display.'

'Okay, then how do we get to see it?' Eric asked softly. 'I am sure you have something in mind?'

'I have contacted an old colleague of mine, who is a member of the curators' committee of the museum and has access to the research repository where this tablet is kept. She has agreed to help us and will meet us at the museum at three.'

'May I ask who this person is?'

'Of course, Mr Roy, she is Dr Tracy Layard, a direct descendent of Austin Henry Layard, the British archaeologist who excavated almost the entire collection of exhibits displayed in the Sumerian section of the British Museum, including some twenty-two thousand clay tablets recovered from the ancient city of Nineveh in 1849. To be honest, Layard's work was what inspired me to get into archaeology.'

'Yes, of course, I am aware of Henry Layard's contribution to European expeditions and archaeology. I have read about these clay tablets as well.' Eric cut a piece of bacon and put it in his mouth. 'But at present, I am a little more interested in knowing how all of this is going to help us find the relic.'

'I am coming to that, Mr Roy,' Dr Hussein calmed him.

'*Eric* will be better, actually.' Eric smiled at the professor.

'All right,' Dr Hussein returned the smile, 'coming back to Layard—as a result of his expedition, many of Nineveh's archaeological remains were transported to the major museums of the nineteenth century, including the British Museum and the Louvre.' Dr Hussein stopped to take a sip from his cup. 'Layard brought many things, including more than half a dozen pairs of colossal figures that stood guard outside palace entrances and were called lamassu. They were statues with a male human head, the body of a lion or a bull and a pair of wings. In 1847, Layard brought two of the colossi, a lion and a bull, weighing nine tonnes each, to London along with a series of Stela. After eighteen months and several near-disasters, he succeeded in bringing them to the British Museum. This involved loading them onto wheeled carts towed by three hundred men, then loading them onto a barge that required six hundred goatskins to keep afloat, and finally, building a ramp in London to haul them up the steps and into the museum on rollers.'

'The tablets...?' Eric tried to bring Dr Hussein back to the topic.

'Right, the tablets we were talking about...they contained cuneiform inscriptions made by the Sumerians some six thousand years ago, and Henry Layard figured out how to read them. I was with Tracy in college, and we worked on a few projects together. She is a brilliant linguist. Like her great-grandfather, she also specialises in ancient Sumerian and Harappan scripts, and I believe if there is someone who can decipher this message, it is her. Oh, and Tracy also specialises in spoken languages and phonetics.'

'Quite an illustrious CV she has,' Eric nodded.

'I only hope it works in our favour,' Marina mumbled.

'It should,' Dr Hussein said. 'This tablet we are going to look at in the museum can be the key to decipher the messages I have photographed, and then the messages should lead us to the relic Delfino is after.'

'Amen,' Marina smiled.

'Inshallah.'

◆

Father Smit touched Aurin's shoulder. 'Look up, Auri boy, Dr Huntley is fine.'

Aurin, still crying on the floor near the bed, pulled himself up and hugged Father Smit.

'Seek, and you shall find—the Bible is never wrong,' Father Smit said. 'Mathew 7:7 says, "Ask, and it shall be given you; seek, and ye shall find; knock, and it shall be opened unto you".'

'Yes, we sought him, and now we've found Dr Huntley. I just hope he is fine.'

'He *is* fine. Let us talk to the authorities now.'

Aurin breathed a soft Amen, and the universe smiled.

FORTY-SEVEN

The black taxi drove past London's Russell Square park on its left. Reaching the T-point, it took a right and pulled into a driveway several metres from the main gate of the British Museum.

'Can't you get any closer?' Dr Tracy Layard asked the driver. Although she had landed at the airport with three hours to spare before her meeting with Dr Hussein and his friends at the museum, customs and mid-day traffic had eaten up most of that time. Now she had less than thirty minutes to get to the museum director's office with her friends and show them a specific artefact before the director's assistant left for the day. She could have called and said she was running late if she had had the time to charge her cell phone.

'This is as far as I can go,' the driver said in broken English laced with a Turkish accent. 'They might have started the old people's shuttle by now, if you want to try,' he added with a grin.

'Here's some advice,' Tracy retorted, 'don't make fun of the client till after you've got your tip.'

'Here's *my* advice,' he replied. 'Don't assume the tip is not already built into the fare—they mostly are when the driver owns the car.'

◆

In a region where beautiful women are the norm, at thirty-eight, Dr Tracy Layard still made heads turn. Tall, with hazel hair and blue-green eyes, she was blessed with a slender figure that required neither constant dieting nor endless exercise to maintain. Her lips were full and her teeth straight, but her striking eyes and glowing skin were what left a lasting impression.

Tracy was very popular with men and women alike, not for her looks but for her infectious personality. She had a cheerful nature and was always optimistic. Tracy Layard was content in herself; she knew how to get the most out of every day and spread light and positivity while at it. It was no wonder people flocked to her like bees to a flower in bloom. For her meeting at the museum, Tracy wore an ivory linen shirt and a pair of khaki chinos, with a hand-painted floral scarf draped around her neck.

The British Museum in the Bloomsbury area of London was the world's oldest public museum and a rival in popularity to the Louvre of Paris and the Metropolitan Museum of Art of New York. Established in 1753 to house the collection of physician Sir Hans Sloane, it had gradually grown to possess more than seven million objects, illustrating and documenting the story of human culture from its genesis to the present.

Tracy entered the Great Court at the museum's principal level. It was flooded with natural light streaming in from above and was surrounded by galleries on all sides. Within the quadrangular space there were also several bookshops and cafeterias.

Tracy hasted towards the cafe on her left, and there they were.

After a quick hug, Dr Hussein introduced Eric and Marina to Tracy. She shook hands with both and beamed warmly at the little party. Then she turned and said, 'Let's go.'

With one hand gripping Dr Hussein's elbow, Tracy led the visitors through the Great Court, past the entrance to the Egyptian Gallery, which was followed by a series of banners publicising various museum events. On a different day, Eric wouldn't have missed the pair of fifteen-foot-tall silk banners on his left announcing a lecture by Dr Jennifer Roberts at one of the exhibition galleries, where she would be recounting her recent adventures, including a treasure hunt in India and solving a three-hundred-year-old riddle.

Unfortunately, Tracy's team members were neither in a position to pay attention to the banners nor in the right mood. They walked right past the infamous crystal skull that had inspired an Indiana Jones movie and climbed down the stairs to their destination—a small office next to the Sainsbury galleries beneath the courtyard.

Despite their best attempts at a timely arrival, they were late. The Director's office was closed. It appeared that the assistant had also left for the day, leaving behind a locked office door.

Tracy looked dejected for a moment and then suddenly dived into her purse. 'We are lucky that some of the research material and the artefact we came looking for are kept in the assistant's office and I have a key to that lock.'

She opened the door and switched on the nearest light. The room was full of desks and cabinets spilling with files. Three of the four walls had large Renaissance and modern paintings, and the fourth wall had two large glass-fitted cases with several small artefacts on display.

Tracy walked straight towards the glass cases, but then she stopped midway. Following her wide-eyed gaze, Dr Hussein found the body of a middle-aged woman on the floor behind a desk in front of one of the cases.

Eric was at Dr Hussein's heel and could see a part of the body. He took a step forward to get a closer look. The woman lay in a pool of blood, her throat slit across the middle. Eric observed the blood and whispered, 'Roughly ten minutes ago.' He looked up to find Tracy pale and breathing heavily. Under her arms, dark circles of sweat were spreading into her ivory shirt.

'She's Martha, the director's assistant. What's going on?' she trembled.

'Where is the artefact?' Eric asked in a low voice. Tracy looked at the glass display and her eyes widened.

'It's gone,' she gasped.

FORTY-EIGHT

'What do we do now?' Marina said with panic in her voice.

'Shhh! Let's not talk here. We need to get out of this place quickly,' Eric whispered. He held Tracy's trembling hand and led her out of the room. He locked the door without making any noise, then took out Tracy's key from the lock and rubbed the metal knob with his handkerchief.

'This is far too well-timed to be a coincidence. It could be a trap set especially for us,' Eric said.

'What we know is, we don't have much time,' Dr Hussein said.

'We should expect a welcome party any moment now,' Eric said, checking the walls around them for cameras.

'Thank god there are no cameras,' Marina said, following his gaze.

'Yes, I heard they were replacing the old ones with upgraded models,' Tracy offered.

'That's good news,' Marina said. 'But we still don't know if this was a trap.'

'I hope our hunch is just a hunch.' Dr Hussein grimaced.

'But what will we do if it's not?' Marina remained pensive.

'We make some noise and create a little mess,' Eric muttered. 'Tracy might be able to tell us how best to do it.'

◆

Following the directions Tracy had given him a minute ago, Dr Hussein walked ahead of the group, climbed down the main staircase of the museum building and found the first payphone booth on his left. He used the payphone to call the phone number Tracy had written down on one of her business cards for him.

After pressing zero to get the operator, he carefully enunciated the phonetic pronunciation of a single word. Then he hung up the phone, held his jacket in front of him and plastered a smile on his face. On Eric's cue, he walked back to the group waiting at the exit gate, and they walked out amidst blaring alarms and a fleet of guards darting towards the main building.

◆

Inside the sealed lecture hall of the museum, hearing the wail of the alarm, Dr Jennifer Roberts shook her head in amazement at the whole scene. She leaned close to her sister Sarah, who had also been a part of her *Riddle* adventure, and whispered, 'Every time I come here, something bad happens.'

'Stop complaining, Jenny,' Sarah frowned. 'You know as well as I do, if something bad happens, you drag me into it with you!'

There are times the universe plays this trick of bringing people close and at times keeping them close yet apart...and all of it depends on its whims and fancies.

◆

'At the moment, they're combing the museum grounds for a stranger with a bomb who just called in the threat. If you had taken seven more seconds to end the call, you'd be flat on a table or pinned up against the wall right now, with guards searching your pants...' Tracy muttered grimly. She was still struggling to come to terms with the murder scene she had just witnessed.

'Please, I can do without the details,' Dr Hussein grimaced, visibly relieved to be out of the museum compound. 'Can they put you in prison for calling in a false bomb threat?'

'I didn't call it in, you did,' Tracy said, attempting humour in a bid to recover from the shock. She had led the team well out of sight of the guards and into the bustling street.

'By the way, here's the card you wrote that phone number on,' Dr Hussein said. 'I never got the chance to throw it away!' He chuckled, handing Tracy a small card.

'Never saw it before,' she threw up her hands. 'It's not the one I gave you.'

Dr Hussein looked down at the card and said something in Iraqi that could be loosely translated as *Oh shit!*

'What now?' Eric demanded.

'You need to have a look at this.'

Eric took the card from Dr Hussein.

The next moment, his eyes widened in surprise and he cried out, 'Shit!'

Tracy peeked over Eric's shoulder and read what was written on the plain piece of card in pencil.

Cafe Museum Tavern, 6.30 p.m., table no. 3.

FORTY-NINE

Cafe Museum Tavern

Dating back to the fourteenth century, Museum Street was just opposite the museum's main entrance and was lined with an attractive collection of small memorabilia shops, bookstores and quaint cafes well worth exploring. There was a traditional seventeenth century pub by the name of Museum Tavern at one corner of the street. The cafe served food and drinks but remained untainted by the scourge of gaming machines, TV screens and any other modern intrusions.

A couple of gloomy drinkers sat at a table, staring at their bottles of The Smoked Brown from Anspach & Hobday. Old men ignored each other at the bar, drinking four-pound pints of lager. A group of young white and black men stared aggressively at Dr Hussein and then at two beautiful women who stood behind him, like male stags during rutting season.

Dr Hussein waved his hand at them with a firm stare. *Come on then*, he thought, *I am descended from one of the deadliest tribes of Iraq. My great-grandfather killed five armed men in a single sword fight and my grandfather singlehandedly killed two grey wolves with his dagger. You think you are stronger than me?*

There was one thing about Dr Hussein: he never hesitated in working up his temper. He had an almost blind confidence in his physical capabilities, which came in handy in addition to his deceptive frail structure. He recalled the day he'd beaten up a group of boys in a Baghdad alley, giving them a thrashing for trying to molest his sister's friend when the police refused to do anything.

Don't let anyone push you around, son, unless they have a gun. But then depending on the situation, you can always go and get a gun. That's what his father had always said to him when he was young. His mother was different; she made him strong from within, teaching him how to leash his punch and how not to raise a gun and yet display power.

Eric was busy finding table no. 3 when Marina whispered in his ear, 'I am thirsty; can we order some beer first?'

'Of course, we all need beer after putting up such a show!' Eric smiled. 'The Smoked Brown?'

'The Smoked Brown it is!' Tracy nodded wearily.

FIFTY

Carlos Clemente pulled his weary body out of bed at his normal hour and climbed up to the terrace of his Florida-style beach house to look at the sun rising over the horizon. As usual, the weather in Ostia Lido beach was fantastic—cloudless skies, the Tyrrhenian Sea stretching out to infinity, a gentle sea breeze and a temperature that was nearing twenty degrees Celsius already.

Clemente returned to his bedroom, slipped into a pair of bathing shorts and gave himself a quick once-over in the full-length mirror on the bathroom door. At seventy-eight, he still had most of what he'd had at twenty, except some of it had been chemically or mechanically enhanced over the decades. A pacemaker kept his clock ticking inside his chest. A good transplant job kept his hair full and his looks intact. Well, almost intact. Expensive contact lenses maintained his twenty-twenty vision, and two sets of customised dental arrangements embellished his smile. For some reason, unlike most of his friends, he still had the liver and kidneys of a thirty-year-old. He was tanned, fit, always in good spirits, always in command of his senses and absurdly rich. What else could a man want?

He descended down another curving staircase to the hand-finished, all-white kitchen and poured himself a cup of coffee. Standing by the sink and looking out at the infinity pool in front, he shook his head, savouring the rich bitterness of the brew just the way he liked it.

It was such a strange thing: there was a time when he could count his lifespan in seconds. The thought of living out the last part of his life in a place with beach houses, swimming pools and machines that kept coffee ready for him before he woke up was almost too much to comprehend. He had made it through wars, hurricanes, so many other untold disasters, and had more than just survived—he had prospered. And the only reason for such tremendous change in his life had been the Church.

At the age of twenty-seven, Carlos Clemente had barely been a human being. He was more of a pest haunting the dark alleys of Rome. One day, as he was being roughed up by a bunch of guys on the street, a priest from the Catholic Church saved him and took him under his wing. He stayed there thereafter and got a chance to study. He did well and became a clerk in the Vatican library. Then he studied further, became a researcher and worked his way up to becoming in-charge of the Vatican Archives.

He was doing fine in the Archives until, one day, a young man from Udine named Delfino visited his office. He brought with him some secret documents to ask for Carlos's opinion. And after that day, his life changed. Until then, Carlos had been an academician, passionate about research—someone who wasn't afraid to take chances and fight for something he believed in. But the secret knowledge that the documents helped him gain began to change his persona. He slowly grew wicked—malicious—immoral. And all of it was fuelled by a single idea that sparked in his mind when he understood what those documents could lead him to.

With the help of his mentor from the Vatican, Carlos planned for an intelligence wing outside the Vatican to protect the image and sanctity of Christianity by a constant study and pursuit of other religious forces and knowledge from around the world.

And thus, the Salvation Knights were born under the secret leadership of Carlos Clemente. Initially operating from outside the Vatican, they eventually entered inside the holy walls. Whatever the mission of this secret army, in his mind Carlos knew it was going to be a source of power and unimaginable wealth. Because far beneath the proposed façade, another plan was already brewing in his mind.

◆

Clemente finished his coffee, rinsed out his mug and put it on the rack to dry. He crossed the tile-floored living room, through the screen door onto the covered porch, and then down the steps to the pool. People had made fun of him for building an indoor pool when his house was a mere seventy feet from the Tyrrhenian Sea, but he enjoyed the convenience. Less than twenty kilometres away from Rome, Clemente's house was on the peaceful side of the Ostia Lido beach, away from the crowds and close to nature.

The pool was filled with saltwater pumped in from the Tyrrhenian and then filtered and warmed to thirty degrees, night and day. There was no surf to get in the way of his exercise, and no currents or riptides to fight against.

He walked down the concrete floor around the pool, took off his slippers at the foot of the diving board and picked up his goggles from the plastic bucket he kept nearby. He proceeded to walk the length of the board, bounced twice, very lightly, and then jumped, slicing into the breeze-rippled water with the ease of a professional.

Clemente began his usual laps, his mind clearing as he went through the routine of alternating crawl and breast stroke, and thought through his plan. The one he knew would bring the Church down at his feet.

FIFTY-ONE

Mahmod awoke abruptly, frightened out of his senses, though not sure why. The room was pitch dark except for the occasional glare of passing headlights that painted yellow rectangles on the walls. Opening his eyes to look around him made him more anxious, for he didn't recognise his surroundings. He tried to lift his head, but he felt no strength in his neck. He tried to push himself up, but his arms felt numb and useless. He worked his eyes instead, left, right, up, down. A catheter was taped to his forearm. His gaze followed the translucent tube to an IV drip on a stand next to his bed. He found three beds of the same kind around the room, albeit empty. Hospital!

At least it explained why he felt like shit. He had no recollection of what might have brought him here.

Another car passed by, its headlights casting the silhouette of a man standing by Mahmod's bed and looking down at him. He yanked the pillow from beneath Mahmod's head, holding it squarely in his hands, and beckoned to place it over his face. Mahmod's eyes widened and his throat choked up.

Heels started clacking on the tiled floor outside, drawing closer by the second. The man vanished into the shadows. Mahmod tried to call out for help, but no sound emerged. The heels passed on by, pushing through swing doors somewhere and fading away, leaving behind their echo, and then nothing.

The man re-emerged by Mahmod's side, pillow still in his hands. He placed it over Mahmod's face and pressed down.

Until that moment, the entire experience had felt like a waking nightmare. But as the pillow pressed down on his throat and he couldn't breathe, Mahmod's heart kicked into overdrive, pumping adrenalin and giving him extra strength. He lunged at the man's hands, kicked with his feet and knees and tried to twist his mouth sideways to get some air. But he had no leverage; his muscles were already tiring, his systems closing down from lack of oxygen. He flung up an arm in a last-ditch effort to claw at his assailant's face, in the process tugging at the IV tube so hard that the stand wobbled and clattered to the floor. The pillow was instantly whipped from his face and flung onto the floor, allowing Mahmod to heave and take in great gasps of air. As the oxygen flooded his bloodstream, Mahmod knew he could easily have been dead at that moment.

The door swung open. A nurse came in, switched on the light, saw the fallen IV stand and Mahmod gasping. She stepped back into the corridor and shouted for assistance, her voice panicky. Mahmod lay there, terrified by the thought that his assailant could have finished him off in a few more seconds. A doctor finally appeared at the door. A three-day-old stubble covering his face, eyes bleary with tiredness, he picked up the IV stand, checked the tube, then reaffixed the catheter. 'Why do you guys do these things in the middle of the night? I haven't slept for seventy-two hours!' He said under his breath, 'I'd be grateful even for a couple of hours of sleep right now.'

Mahmod tried to speak, but his mouth couldn't form words. The nurse stepped forward, checked his pulse and raised an eyebrow. 'Panic, yes?' she said. 'Is normal. You have a bad crash, or so I hear. But you are okay now. You are in hospital and nothing bad happen here. You need rest.'

'That is all any of us need!' the doctor muttered, shaking his head as he exited the cabin.

The nurse picked the pillow off the floor, fluffed it and put it back beneath Mahmod's head. Then she nodded in satisfaction and went back to the door, turning off the lights and leaving Mahmod at the mercy of a stranger waiting to kill him.

FIFTY-TWO

Inspired by a time when London brewers used to dry their malts in flame-heated kilns, The Smoked Brown by Anspach & Hobday had a subtle smoky flavour and aroma. A fruity bitterness underpinned by an oaky dryness in an unusual beer full of intrigue, The Smoked Brown was a favourite with people who liked to taste adventure even in their beer.

Table no. 3 was in the farthest corner of the pub. As they carried their beer mugs carefully to the table and settled down, someone whispered behind them: 'No one looks at me under any circumstances. We will continue to talk this way until I walk out of this place.'

'We'll fill you in later,' Eric breathed in Tracy's ear. 'Just go with the flow for now.' Then he raised his glass and muttered, 'Let's bring Dr Huntley home.'

Everyone raised their glasses silently.

Out of the corner of an eye, Eric glanced at the person talking to them from the adjacent table. A tall, thin young man with hair touching his shoulders, he sat with a cup of coffee and a laptop. He wore a long-canopy baseball cap and had his back turned towards their table.

'No one can track or eavesdrop on our discussion,' he said in a low yet clear whisper. 'I have set a high-frequency deflector that would be effective over a fifteen-metre radius.'

Eric heard the same whisper as all the others in the group, but then again he heard something more. Even in that whisper, he could sense a familiar voice.

'Sid! Sid Patel!' he whispered as softly as he could.

'That's right, Chief,' said the man without moving any muscle except his mouth. The happiness in his voice was unmistakable.

'What the F are you doing here, Sid?'

'I am here to help you get out of this, Chief.'

'That's nice to hear. I really appreciate your showing up! But tell me, how did you find us?'

'I have been tracking you since you met Delfino. With some luck, I was able to follow almost every conversation between that meeting and now...but that's a long story. We don't have much time, so here are a couple of important things. First of all, Dr Huntley is safe and reaching his facility at Trongsa, Bhutan, in two days.'

'What?' They all blurted in unison.

'Yes. For now, all you need to know is that Aurin and Father Smit found him a couple of days back in Mosul, and on receiving Aurin's SOS call, I requested Dr Naidu for the necessary papers for all of them to get out of Iraq. In a few more hours, they'll be flying out of Baghdad.'

Marina sobbed quietly, both palms cupping her face. The mention of Dr Huntley brought back ugly memories, but she was relieved to hear he was safe.

'That means we are free from the Delfino deal,' Dr Hussein breathed.

'At least for now,' Eric cut in. 'But we are not dealing with petty criminals who will simply let us walk away without delivering on our agreement. Delfino is a big fish in the international game. His corporation has enough clout to swing deals with governments, steal top-secret documents and find anyone in any corner of the world with the click of a few buttons. There is no way in hell that Delfino would let us turn our backs on him without finding the secret he's looking for.' Eric looked at Dr Hussein and Marina and continued, 'Now we are loose ends that they are going to discover soon, and then they'll come for us.'

'Let's push on then,' Dr Hussein said.

'Yes, you are right! But we'd have to do it in a carefully planned way.' Eric smiled. 'Delfino is going to come after us anyway, but we can slow him down for sure.'

'Yes, I suggest you get rid of the mobile phones you were handed, along with the SIM cards,' Sid whispered, 'and use the ones I've got here. I'll also check for bugs in your body and deactivate them.' Sid pushed a small knapsack from under his table to theirs using his foot. 'I have three clean handsets and SIM cards in there for you guys to use. Dr Tracy wouldn't need one, as she is out of Delfino's grid for now.'

'Then what?' Marina asked, composed by now.

'Then we vanish.'

'From where?' Dr Hussein sounded taken aback.

'From Delfino's grid!' Eric said curtly. 'We'll try our best to stay out of sight of his trackers and pursue the quest in our own way.'

'But we need at least a couple of days to figure things out,' piped in Dr Hussein, 'gather our clues, decipher the ancient message... We can't just rush like that!'

'Of course, we need some time to take stock of the situation and get a direction,' Marina added.

'And we need a safe place to hide during this time.'

Tracy had been waiting patiently all this while for someone to fill her in. She jumped in now. 'I have a small cottage in Windsor. If that helps.'

'Can you accommodate us for a couple of days there, Dr Layard?' Eric asked.

'Tracy or Trace—any of the two would be nicer. I quite detest that formal prefix when I am out of my office!' she chimed. 'And yes, I will welcome all of you into my house, but on one condition!'

'Please go ahead,' Eric prodded her with some uncertainty.

'I want to be a part of it,' she half-smiled. 'I am curious to know what this whole thing is all about—and I sense it is a hell of a mystery.'

'You are already a part of it!' Eric chuckled. 'We can't take our next step without your help.'

'Please write the address on a piece of paper and pass it to me,' Sid whispered. 'I'll walk out of this place first and make my way to your place in a few hours if that is fine with you, Dr Tracy.'

'Great.' She scribbled a few words on a chit of paper and pushed it towards Sid.

Sid laid a crumpled note on the table for the attendant, wiped his mouth with a paper napkin, shut his computer and packed it away in his backpack. He paused by a giant mirror by the front door to admire his thick mane that fell in light curls over his shoulders and framed his oval face. Then, wrapping his woollen muffler tighter around his neck, he walked out into the darkness around the corner of Museum Street.

FIFTY-THREE

Tracy tried firing up her dead mobile phone but her phone charger didn't fit into the slot of their rented car. After a few unsuccessful tries she thought better of it. She looked up and caught Eric's eye in the rear-view mirror. 'Do we have a problem?' she muttered.

Eric smiled. He'd been watching the silver-grey sedan following their rented hatchback for over twenty minutes. Since they had left the petrol station after Brentford, it had stayed about a car's length behind them. The M4 motorway running between London and South Wales had several connecting roads, but the sedan remained steadfastly stuck to them.

In an attempt to be absolutely sure, Eric switched on the hazard lights of their car and slowed down to a crawl. The sedan slowed to a matching speed. There was no doubt about it. They were being followed.

'I think we need to get them off our tail,' Eric surmised.

'But this is a motorway; there is no space to play hide-and-seek!' Dr Hussein said.

'You can take the first exit, and then you'll find plenty of roads criss-crossing each other,' Tracy said, bringing the GPS map alive with a gentle touch of her finger on the small digital screen of the car.

'Sounds nice,' Eric shrugged.

'Nice and easy!' Tracy smiled through clenched teeth.

Six minutes later, Eric spun the car towards their left and kept on driving.

The turn surprised and impressed their tracker. He knew Eric was performing a Surveillance Detection Route (SDR), and that Eric was going to make a series of seemingly random turns, attempting to figure out how far the follower would go. Eric's SDR could mean a detour of a few minutes, or it could take hours. In any case, the tracker couldn't turn left and continue following the car, for he would be caught. He had no choice but to continue driving on the London–South Wales motorway.

◆

Eric and his team had no idea there was a black London taxi driven by a greyhound disguised as an old man still following them. Neither did they know that more than one enemy would soon be aligned against them. In that moment, they remained in blissful ignorance.

FIFTY-FOUR

Tracy's house was a classic English countryside cottage in the old style, even though it was clearly very new. Covered and screened porches were wrapped around the ground floor, the second floor accommodated a master bedroom and a guest room and a spiral staircase led from the master bedroom to a ten by twelve terrace with flowers and fancy plants in pots of different shapes and sizes.

The ground floor had living and dining rooms—both had pretty views of the small garden at the front of the house. The dining room led off into a kitchen, and behind that was another small bedroom. Across the hall from the bedroom was a large study. These two had doors leading out to a small kitchen garden with a single wrought-iron bench.

Even those who had no idea of Tracy's family background could pick up on a couple of things as soon as they set foot on the property—or maybe even before. The car in the garage was a top-of-the-line Mercedes SUV and the furniture inside the house was mostly Edwardian, visibly antique and expensive. The family had money and good taste.

Tracy lived all by herself. Apart from a brief live-in relationship in her early thirties, she had never spent much time on men, always preferring to dedicate her time to her work. She was happily committed to her work and didn't care much for other things in life.

The group assembled in the study with two crates of beer from Tracy's fridge. She quickly put together some ham and cheese sandwiches and served them with roast beef and mustard chips from a large brown-and-violet Brannigans packet. For herself, she poured some gin in a Copa De Balon glass and added tonic water before settling on the wooden floor. Dr Hussein began, 'I am really happy to know Dr Huntley is safe.'

'Yes, of course! I am glad too,' Eric sighed.

'Let's raise to that!' a chipper Marina said.

They all raised their glasses and laughed as they clinked.

Unfortunately, it was to be the last time they all would ever sit together and share a laugh.

◆

Hours had passed. Dr Hussein and Eric had taken Tracy through the entire series of events up until that point and given her an outline of everything she needed to know.

'Okay, let's put together what we have,' Eric spoke, looking in Dr Hussein's direction and wiping his mouth with the back of his palm. 'The first thing we have is a photograph of the partially deciphered coded cuneiform script from the wall of the first tomb that I had discovered in Nimrud in 1991. The translation says, *Ninki, a girl inside this after-world chamber, has the key to the Tomb of God. The tomb is in between a river and a mountain range far in the north.* Secondly, we have a couple of round tablets—one recovered from the corpse of a slave girl inside the same tomb, which is most probably the key mentioned in the message on the outer wall. The other one is from a general's tomb inside an antechamber that I had discovered later in a different site in Nimrud.'

'Round tablets! That's interesting,' Eric stroked his chin. 'Clay tablets?'

'No, they're made of some kind of alloy, I haven't been able to figure out what,' Dr Hussein answered.

'A metallic round-shaped tablet with a hole in the centre?'

'Yes!' Dr Hussein furrowed his brows at the rising excitement in Eric's voice.

'Thin concentric grooves on both sides and ancient Indus scripts on one?' Eric went on with more delight in his voice.

'Yes. But how do you...'

'Because he found a similar one in the Thar Desert a few days ago,' Sid Patel spoke up from the doorway to the study.

'Wait... Before we get into that, how did you enter my house, for God's sake?' Tracy screamed. 'Everything here is secured with a high-end password-protected system!'

'Well, I hacked into your smartphone and cloned the system on my phone.'

'What? This guy must be kidding...!' She mouthed in mock anger, grudgingly impressed by Sid's wiles.

'Tracy, please, let him be,' said Dr Hussein. 'I am more interested in hearing about the other thing he just said.'

Eric sat up straight on the sofa, making space for Sid. 'Do you have the tablets with you?'

'Yes, I have them in here,' Dr Hussein said, unzipping his backpack.

'That's great,' Eric said. 'We'll check them out in a bit, but for now, let's have all of our leads listed first. What else do we have?'

'I have some clues,' Sid said, settling down on the sofa.

'You do?'

'Yes, Chief.' Sid nodded. 'It all started with the cell phone you had found at the site in Thar Desert, which belonged to Haban Sangma, an oil explorer. Amidst the retrieved data, there was a series of photographs sent with an email to the Nobel Oil Company. It looked like he had stumbled upon some ancient treasure inside a mound or a cave somewhere in the desert. The pictures showed a cavern full of pre-Harappan artefacts...unfortunately, the mail didn't reach Haban's boss at the Nobel. Instead, it went to some bad guys—it is highly probable that it was intercepted by Delfino, who, in turn, organised the missile attack and erased everything for reasons yet unknown, of course.'

Eric nodded but said nothing.

'After you left for Baghdad,' Sid continued, 'I used the Internet and randomly checked the coordinates of the Thar Desert massacre and of Dr Huntley's camp. To my surprise, I found one match. An Italian academician named Luigi Tessitori had conducted surveys in both the locations.'

'Yes, I know about Tessitori and his immense contribution towards uncovering the lost pre-Harappan era,' Tracy spoke up. 'In fact, he exchanged a couple of letters with my great-great-grandfather. And another thing, he was a fan of one of your great Indian epics.'

'Which one?' Dr Hussein asked.

'The Ramayana.'

'Yes, for sure,' Sid smiled at Tracy and nodded. 'Now here's what I got from further research.'

'One sec…one sec, please!' Eric raised both his hands in the air to stop Sid. He had suddenly recalled an important link—the tomb in the Iraqi desert that he'd visited with Nassar—Warad-Sin's tomb, or at least that was what Nassar had claimed. 'Why do I hear Ram Chandra's name so often? And why do I have this strange feeling that Ram had something to do with this quest?' he asked in a low voice.

'Because he did.' Sid smiled.

◆

'What do you mean?' Eric demanded.

'I'll explain everything. If you would just let me share my findings with you all…'

Tracy pulled up a chair and sat across from him, bent forward with intrigue.

'One, I found a hand-drawn version of a round-shaped tablet just like the one Chief had found in Thar. Two, I got a page where Tessitori compares the Sumerian cuneiform script with the pre-Harappan. There's a footnote that says, *I came this far in search of knowledge.*' Sid held up his mobile phone and showed everyone two images. He looked at all the curious faces and added, 'He probably meant that it was the final result of his comparative study of both ancient scripts.'

INDIAN SIGN	SUMERIAN SIGN	APPROXIMATE DATE OF USE	PHONETIC VALUE	PICTURE VALUE
		2800 -2700	KHA	Fish
		2400	SAR	360
		3,000	GAL	great
		3000	SAG	heart, in
		2800 2400	BAD	dead
		3000	KU ŠU	to
		2800	ŠU	hand
		2800	UŠ	member, male
		3000	E	house, plot of land

INDIAN SIGN	SUMERIAN SIGN	APPROXIMATE DATE OF USE	PHONETIC VALUE	PICTURE VALUE
		2750	BAR	a kind of shrine
		3000	GI	reed
		3000	GAN	a land measure
		3500	MAL GA	a dwelling
		3000	—	—
		2400	GIL	(a doubled form of GI above)
		3000	GIR AD	a scorpion

'This is fantastic!' exclaimed Tracy. 'I clearly remember one of Tessitori's letters had this kind of a very preliminary comparative study of the pre-Harappan and Sumerian scripts, on which he wanted my great-great-grandfather's opinion. Now that I've seen this, I can guess he had not only deciphered the Sumerian script but also figured out the phonetic values attached to the scripts, that too some hundred years ago.'

'Now for the best part of my story...' Sid looked at Eric and smiled in undisguised excitement.

'Wait, wait...wait!' Dr Hussein yelled. 'Please show me the images once again.'

'Sure, here.' Aurin handed over the phone to Dr Hussein after a quick look.

'Alhamdulillah!' he muttered. 'I spent twenty-seven long years searching for a pattern in the writing on the wall but failed. And today, as I look at this image, it hits me like an electric wave!'

'What did you find?' Tracy asked, impatient.

'This guy, whoever he was, had a fantastic brain. You'll be amazed at what he actually did.' Dr Hussein smiled.

'This person could well be a she as well,' Marina said, half to herself.

'Oh, yes, of course. It could in fact be the same girl as the one found inside the after-life chamber with the tablet.'

'Please, Dr Hussein, do tell us if you have really deciphered it!' Tracy begged.

'Of course I have. Look at this...she had me fooled with this trick even two thousand seven hundred years after her death. All along, I thought I was deciphering a Sumerian script, while all she had done was mix both the Sumerian and pre-Harappan scripts, making it almost impossible for anyone to decode the writing!'

'Clearly, she had to,' Eric thought out loud. 'We must not forget, she was writing on an open surface—she had to make it tough to decipher.'

'Guys, look at this. She simply replaced the most commonly used cuneiform signs in the Sumerian script with their closest counterparts in the Harappan script. Sheer genius!' Dr Hussein declared.

'This is great! We're surely getting closer,' Eric addressed the gathering. 'So far, one part of the mystery is solved. But what does the message say?'

FIFTY-FIVE

Dr Hussein took some time deciphering Ninki's message in his notebook. Once done, he recited:

There is a secret tomb of God
There is a divine blessing for all
The key to the secret place is
hidden with Ninki here in this tomb of Queen Yaba

I ... Ninki, and my brother Ina
We two are the last of the keepers
The brother has gone to the land of seven rivers
To leave a clue about the secret
I am going to die
Our family was the keeper of this secret since ages
The clue is hidden in a round tablet ...
Today I give my life to keep the secret safe
With me one of the last two dies
But I shall hold the clue in my hand till the end of time

'That's what it says,' Dr Hussein took a deep breath and sighed.

'Hmm, so you were at least half correct,' Eric remarked.

'How?'

'You had identified and collected the round tablet, and you also guessed quite rightly that the clue was hidden in the tablet itself.'

'Yeah, I guess, now that you put it that way,' Dr Hussein nodded.

'All of this is fine, but will I ever get a chance to share my findings?' Sid pleaded once again.

'Sure, Sid, we're sorry—please go ahead.' Eric pursed his lips and raised a hand towards the rest of the group.

'Well, when I found out Delfino was running one side of the show, I hacked his super secured personal system and found two documents. One had Tessitori's coordinates, which he had already shown Eric, and the second was a small note on the margins of the same copy of *Ramcharitmanas*. Most likely Tessitori's translation of an ancient riddle.'

'How did you find it?' Tracy blurted out.

'If I can break into a sophisticated and well-protected house like yours,' Sid smiled enigmatically, 'don't you think I can also hack a personal server and download some files?' Sid brandished his cell phone in the air.

'I know what you mean,' Tracy grinned sheepishly.

'Thanks, Ma'am,' Sid said. 'My phone has found a digital printer nearby. May I shoot a print, please?'

'Go ahead. It isn't as if you won't if I said no!' Tracy shrugged.

She got up and walked out of the room. A minute later, she returned with an A4-sized paper printed over on both its sides.

Sid took it from her and read it aloud.

The knowledge is green, the knowledge is pure
The knowledge is alive, the knowledge is cure
The knowledge is hidden in ancient layers
Layers of words by many soothsayers.

The knowledge is a garden, a life to proclaim
The knowledge is restored under a king's emblem
The knowledge is life, the knowledge is breath
The knowledge can heal a strike of death.

The source of the two lost rivers marks the place,
River—the God named Pison with grace,
The other one is Gihon and a garden was the source,
The secret is hidden in a godly discourse.
The knowledge is hidden on a lofty cliff,
The path is rough and also steep.

A large stone covers the secret and the key—
The key to life, and the life-tree.

The knowledge of life and life for all—
Climb up the steps, or you may crawl.
The God will protect and keep it till the end—
The words are said and no one can amend.
The God is…

'This is wonderful, Sid!' Eric remarked. 'Now we know what intrigued Delfino.'

'But it's incomplete,' Tracy frowned.

'Yes, ma'am, I know…but this is all I could find in Delfino's repository. I checked it thoroughly; there's nothing more.'

'That's okay. You got us off to a good start, Sid. I have a hunch that the knowledge Tessitori wrote about and the divine blessing for mankind that our girl from the tomb mentioned are probably the same thing,' Eric said.

'Highly possible!' Dr Hussein piped in. 'Tessitori excavated extensively in the pre-Harappan sites, and the girl also used pre-Harappan scripts and mentioned her brother's journey to the land of the seven rivers, which could be the Indus, its tributaries and the lost river Saraswati.'

'This might be helpful at some point in the future, but not right now. We now know about a cliff, but we need to know where the cliff is, to start with,' Dr Hussein said, shaking his head slowly. 'And, to add to the list, I need to mention the small replica of a ship that I found in the antechamber along with the second tablet.'

'Do you have that with you too?' Sid's eyes lit up.

'Yes, I have all of them—the replica of the ship and both the tablets that I found in Nimrud. I carried them along for Eric.' He took a cardboard box from his backpack and passed it to Sid.

'And here's the one you had found in the Harappan mound.' Sid held up in his right hand a six inch by eight inch white envelope that looked puffed up and heavy.

'Thanks, both of you!' Eric half-smiled at Dr Hussein and Sid. 'Now, as we have all the three tablets, let's give them numbers to keep track. The one I found in the desert—let that be number one, and tablet two and three could be the ones Dr Hussein discovered in the first and second excavations at Nimrud, respectively. Is that fine with everyone?' Eric looked around. Dr Hussein, Marina and Sid nodded in unison, and Tracy thoughtfully moved her head up and down, still trying to get a grip on things.

'Tessitori must have had some additional clue,' she mumbled. 'Pison, Gihon—these rivers were only mentioned in the Bible.'

'We might never know it!' exclaimed Dr Hussein.

FIFTY-SIX

Cast in pure gold, the long neck of the ship had the Moon God Nanna's head at the end. The beautiful piece of art shimmered in Dr Tracy's dimly lit living room. It was a ten-inch replica, but it seemed to have been modelled after a bigger one. Originally built from overlapping wooden planks, the 'twenty-rower' lower deck was neatly carved out of solid gold along with the rowers in position on their benches. The mast was a thick rod of gold perched in the middle of the upper deck. The helmsman's platform at the end of the rowing benches had an odd-looking tiller that extended and broadened to turn into a rudder that stuck out like a handle from the side of the ship. The rudder went further down towards the imaginary water. 'Sumerian ships sailed on the Euphrates and Tigris as early as in the fifth millennium BC, when the geography looked very different and those rivers fell via separate mouths into the Persian Gulf,' Dr Hussein offered with a smile. 'This one would be more recent, probably from the second millennium BC—still some hundreds of years prior to Queen Yaba, the lady whose tomb I found the first tablet in.'

'Looks like all the three round-shaped tablets we found,' Eric said after some thought, 'are made of the same alloy and bear the same Indus scripts on one side.'

'And each of them is very different, in every possible manner, from the catalogued seals of those eras…except the popular Indus scripts,' Marina added to Eric's stream of thought.

'And they were all found in different places!' Sid finished.

Marina still toyed with the ancient replica of the ship, lost in confusion. Dr Hussein smiled at the look on her face. 'But I don't understand the connection,' she said, 'as we know that you found two tablets from two different tombs and the second site was nearly a thousand years older than the first one.'

To help her connect the dots, Dr Hussein said, 'Tell me, Marina, have you ever been to the Roman ruins in Bath?'

Frustrated with the irrelevant inquiry, Marina snorted. 'No. Why do you ask?'

'Well,' he said, remembering the quaint little town of Somerset on the River Avon, 'when in Bath, you are in the middle of the English countryside, and yet you are surrounded by relics from ancient Rome. It seems surreal. But do you know what the most amazing thing is? Built by the Romans in the first century, AD 60, and restored by the English in the seventh, the baths still work. The warm springs still bubble up from the ground, and the architecture still stands proud. Ancient pillars rise to the heavens from the magical water below. It is fantastic actually, if you think about it…'

Marina stared at him with an uncomprehending look. 'Sorry, I still don't understand what you want to imply.'

'Think about it, my dear. I found the second tablet at a site near Queen Yaba's tomb. However, that doesn't mean it was also made in Queen Yaba's era! The world's ancient civilisations were always ahead of their time. We all know that, right? Those bath houses I talk about were not built by the Brits—they were built several centuries before, but they still work to this day. In the same way, the Sumerians could likely have developed ways to pass on secret messages down the generations.'

'That means,' Eric chewed on each of his words before speaking, 'the girl was trying to tell someone to follow the trail of a secret that was already a thousand years old at the time of her death, at the very least.'

'That's right!' Tracy perked up. 'You know what? I have a feeling her family, who were the keepers of this secret, had actually developed some unique tool in the form of this round tablet and carried the secret through generations.'

'May I take some photographs of the ship and the tablets?' Sid interrupted, but before Dr Hussein could respond, he started taking photographs of the ship. After finishing with the ship, he gestured to Eric to raise the tablets one by one so that he could shoot them as well.

Tracy took one of the tablets from Eric, kept it on her palm and caressed with her finger the scripts on one side. 'They are so commonly used on so many Indus seals…but what are they trying to tell us?'

The question buzzed in their minds for a while, until they heard another kind of a buzz—a distinctive one that could only be produced by chopper rotors.

FIFTY-SEVEN

Less than one-fourth of a square mile in area, it is the smallest independent state of the world. A city inside a city, encircled by the Italian capital, Rome. And yet, Vatican City is also one of the most powerful states in the world, crossing lines of nationality and race and politics to exert influence over a billion people across the globe: the followers of the Roman Catholic Church.

Vatican City and Rome were places Eric had always wanted to visit—but as a tourist with a lot of money and time to spare, not as a captive with the threat of death hanging over his head. A threat that could be dismissed—or just as easily carried out—on the word of one man. The man he was just about to meet.

Once the armed group that raided Dr Tracy's house had collected most of Eric's belongings, including the three tablets, they took him along on a long and chilly chopper ride to Vatican City. All Eric could make out in the intervening moments was that someone in the Vatican was going to give him an audience and decide what his next day was going to look like. This was almost how the threat had come in from the leader of the attack group.

♦

It was sometime before dawn when, exhausted and jet-lagged, Eric was brought into the Vatican in a black Mercedes SUV with blacked-out windows. Two armed men aimed small firearms at his stomach. The vehicle passed through a side entrance as Eric caught the barest glimpse of the majestic St Peter's Basilica before being driven into an ordinary building somewhere near the small city-state's only railway station.

The guns were put away, but Eric felt the threat still looming over his head as he was ushered inside. A tall man with a bull's shoulders in a black suit led the way, and as they entered a large courtyard, several men in black suits came into view, guarding the plain but huge three-storey building with their cold, hard faces.

Not all the Swiss guards wear colours. Eric knew that the original blue, red, orange and yellow uniform with the distinct Renaissance appearance was not for all of them. Major importance has been given to the non-ceremonial roles of the guards since the assassination attempt on Pope John Paul II in 1981. They have different ranks, arms and dress codes now. The Swiss guards are responsible for the safety of the Pope, including the security of the Apostolic Palace, and serve as the de facto military of Vatican City.

The huge building's interiors were equally elegant and serious. This was a place of serious business, not worship. It was quiet, their footsteps reverberated like drumbeats through the polished lobby, still Eric felt that a lot went on behind each of the closed doors they passed. There was a feeling of tremendous power, discreet yet indisputable.

The tall man took him up a flight of steps to a door at the end of a long corridor. He opened it and said almost inaudibly, 'Go in.' Eric hesitated for a moment, then composed himself and went through. The man followed him.

The room was a cross between an office and a small library, with two of its walls lined with stacked bookshelves and filing cabinets. The cabinets made space for three baroque landscapes, all of them lonely. There were high windows covering the third wall, against which stood a heavy wooden desk and a chair overlooking the dome of St Peter's. The fourth wall was almost covered by a stone-curved fireplace, with flames gently snapping in the grate. Beside it rested two club chairs upholstered in red leather.

An elderly man—tall, lean and dressed in dark grey—sat in one of the leather chairs, staring thoughtfully at the fire. His skin was overtly tanned, and a gentle smile played on his lips. The guard accompanying Eric walked up to the elderly man and whispered with his head lowered, 'Cardinal!' The man looked up and said something. Eric didn't know the language well enough to understand what they were talking about but figured from their tone that they knew each other well and that the guard probably reported directly to the elderly man.

The only thing he understood during their conversation was his name.

The elderly man stood up to face Eric, revealing the dark grey robe he was wearing, which was in stark contrast with a Catholic priest's robe. The only colour and decoration on the robe was a crucifix made from two gold-coloured swords on the chest. 'Mr Roy,' he said, gesturing towards the empty chair, 'please sit down.'

Eric sat on the chair, looked straight into the man's eyes and said, 'May I know what is going on?'

The man settled back in his chair. 'Well, I think you could do with a coffee first.'

'That's right,' Eric found himself saying, 'thanks for asking.'

The stately man shot a glance in the guard's direction and nodded.

'I am sure you have several questions, Mr Roy, but I suggest you hold on to them for a little while.'

The coffee was brought in by a male attendant on an elaborately designed silver tray. The attendant left, and the old man embarked upon the coffee-pouring ritual, offering Eric sugar, which he gratefully accepted, and cream, which he did not.

'I am Carlos Clemente, and as you can see, I run an office here in the Vatican,' the man spoke. 'I understand you have too many questions, but the most important question at the moment is, do I need you?' He fixed Eric with a searing gaze typical of a mercenary.

Eric looked at him for a while, then took a slow, deliberate sip from his coffee and smiled. 'The answer is, you do, and that's why you've flown me all the way to the Vatican. But before we come to that, let me tell you a story,' Eric went on, unfazed by Clemente's quizzical looks. 'My grandfather was a freedom fighter, and there was a time when people of our ancestral locality in India had deep respect for him. But with time, people changed. He would say "hi" to them, and they'd rarely respond. People changed further. He'd say "hi" to them, and they would say, "Do I need you, old man? No. So don't bother me—oil your own machine!" At times, my grandfather would be irritated and would take out his machine, a Sig Sauer, and show them, "See, it is perfectly oiled; that's why I have enough time to say hi to imbeciles like you!", Eric finished his story and said, 'Well, that was an old story, but tell me, anyway, what you think. Do you need me…or don't you?'

'You live up to your reputation, Mr Roy,' Carlos Clemente smiled. 'But as you said, times have changed, and individuals don't run the show now—institutions and corporations do. You need to convince me that I need your help in finding that relic we are looking for. And then I'll decide if you should live, along with your brother and two of your friends…what are their names… Father Smit and Dr Huntley! How about that?'

Eric's jaw stiffened. 'They are with you?'

'I think,' the man said, his Italian accent unflinching. 'And hereon, I'll be the one asking questions. But to answer this last one—yes, we had them picked up from Baghdad Airport a few hours ago.'

The tall guard in the dark grey suit moved to stand behind him— in a position, Eric realised, that would give him the easiest shot should he choose to draw his gun. 'So,' Eric said calmly, trying not to let the gunman intimidate him, 'are these the headquarters of a secret brotherhood or something like that?'

'Those things only exist in fiction like *The Da Vinci Code*,' said Clemente.

'That's your official comment, I believe?' said Eric without moving his eyes from Clemente's face.

'Yes.' Clemente smiled.

'And what would your unofficial comment on that be?'

'Yes, there are many,' Clemente continued, 'but they are all shadows. Nothing but groups of phantoms…'

'Which one do you work for?'

Clemente paused. 'Some call it the Salvation Knights, but then again, it doesn't exist.' He smiled. 'As I said, it is a shadow—its work is only known to a chosen few.'

Eric looked through the windows at the great floodlit dome of St Peter's. 'Even the man on the highest podium here—you know who I am talking about—doesn't know about us.' Clemente added, 'Isn't it astonishing?'

The tall man made a low guttural sound to show his displeasure at the conversation. Clemente, however, leaned back in his chair. 'That's the rule we follow—he should *never* know. His Holiness should be kept out of these kinds of political things. So whatever we do, we do it in secret. I am a cardinal too—a cardinale della salvezza, or a salvation cardinal. I run this secret agency of the Catholic Church.'

'Aha! The secret chief of the secret agency,' Eric sneered. 'What is it that is bothering the Church? Is it the non-Abrahamic linkages of the "Tomb of God" that contradict Christianity? Or the secret of your connection with the brotherhood of the Tomb of God? Or is it the secret of the Sumerian relic that, all of a sudden, several people are interested in?' Eric noticed the slight upward twitch of the cardinal's eyebrows at his remarks.

Carlos Clemente finally smiled, a hint of surprise visible in his eyes. 'I understand, Mr Roy, that you indeed know a lot about things. I would have clapped for you, but despite everything you have learned, there is one thing you have not—why is the secret of the Tomb a threat to the Church?'

'What?' Eric demanded, suddenly realising that the cardinal had been trying to manipulate him to understand the limits of his knowledge. 'What secret?'

Clemente smiled again, infuriating Eric. 'None of what you know matters to the Church. If that were all it was, the Salvation Knights would not even need to exist.'

Eric looked at his face for a while. 'So what's the secret?'

'You tell me!' the cardinal said, his eyes fixed on Eric's.

'Well, it's surely something that is such a threat to Christianity that all knowledge of it has to be erased and all evidence destroyed.' Eric paused. 'Did I make sense?'

'Carry on, please,' the cardinale della salvezza nodded.

Suddenly, like a flash of lightning, it struck Eric that if he did pretend to know the truth, he would be signing over his own death permit. But something drove him on. He *had* to know…he'd been on the scent of this trail for several days now. He had a right to know the cause for all of this.

'But it cannot be just that this civilisation existed long before Abraham!' Eric said. 'There must be something about it that contradicts some key beliefs of Christianity. That's the threat, right? And you know what it is.'

'Of course, I know, but the question is—do you?'

'Why?' Eric asked, stealing a glance at the man behind him. 'Are you going to kill me if I do?'

The cardinal sniggered. 'Not in here for sure; the carpet is very expensive.' He fixed Eric with yet another stare. 'And perhaps not at all. But that depends on you. You need to act responsibly, Mr Roy, for three more lives depend on your decision.'

'So, if I give you the right answer, you might not kill me?'

'The answer doesn't matter, but the beliefs that lead up to it.'

'What do you want from me? Tell me, for God's sake!'

'You tell me.'

'Hmmm…something that contradicted the faith so much that the Salvation Knights would kill to stop it from becoming known?' Eric wondered aloud. 'Science has contradicted the Bible enough in the past. In everything, from geology to zoology and astrophysics. But you never killed Einstein or Stephen Hawking. So, it must be something bigger… I just hope it's not the alien theory this time!'

A long silence descended upon the room, broken only by the crackling of the fire.

'How long have the Salvation Knights been around?' Eric asked, keeping his voice mellow.

'You might be surprised to know that the Salvation Knights, in their current form, have existed only since the 1970s. But a similar secret agency existed for around two hundred years after the Mesopotamian excavations began in the mid-nineteenth century, which was formed by scholars with biblical and classical backgrounds. That was the time the Church developed an interest in learning about ancient civilisations and the non-Abrahamic religions.'

'To either borrow and include, or destroy and erase,' Eric added with a grin.

'Subtlety is not one of your strongest suits, is it, Mr Roy?'

'Looks like it's not one of the Salvation Knights' methods either. You are no different from terrorist organisations like the Islamic State of Iraq and the Levant,' Eric sneered. 'ISIL announced their intentions to destroy several ancient civilisation sites of Iraq for their "un-Islamic" nature. You are doing the same thing, albeit in a more polished way. If they are using bulldozers and explosives to destroy ancient ruins, you are using scholars and intellectuals to tweak history to either link it with the Bible or erase it entirely. And if both fail, you simply drop a missile and wipe it off the face of the earth.'

Cardinal Clemente tented his hands under his chin and looked at Eric with an amused expression.

'You claim to be men of God?' Eric continued. 'After all the people you've killed over the years in the name of protecting the faith, how can you still have the nerve to say you're doing it in the name of God? Eric breathed. 'Aren't you ashamed?'

'We are,' the cardinal admitted, his face revealing signs of a long-harboured guilt, 'and when the time comes, we shall all be judged. Perhaps we'll even be damned. But, for now, protecting the faith seems like the right thing to do.'

'Protecting the faith or your own personal agendas?' Eric fixed Cardinal Clemente with a look as intense as the one he had earlier given Eric. 'I believe it is all about personal gains. You are afraid that if we discovered what we are in search of, your individual goals would be shattered. Please admit, Mr Salvation Cardinal, that it is all about power, as it has always been. You need the relic for yourself, either to make money or to gain more power, and to keep its price high, you are destroying all the other centres that are connected to the secret.'

'You overestimate yourself, Mr Roy,' the cardinal said. 'The Church has survived Copernicus, Galileo and science…it will survive the forthcoming obstacles too. I and my goals have survived situations and people you can't imagine even exist, so chances are high that we will survive yet again. I know what your Mesopotamian quest stands to bring out. I also know your discovery will likely turn allegories into historical facts.'

'My discovery?' Eric blurted out, feeling an odd spark of energy. 'What do you know about the Tomb of God, and how are you so sure about the find?'

'From our previous findings, and from findings at other sites and from relevant written documents, we have learnt that the Mesopotamian Tomb of God is also the source of the two lost rivers mentioned in the Bible.'

'You mean Pison and Gihon?'

'Yes. And therein lies my interest because that find alone will change the status of the Church in the present global religious context and will greatly strengthen the faith.'

'But the Bible says, "a river went out of Eden to water the garden; and from thence it was parted, and became into four heads…"'

'Yes, what is written in the Holy Bible is right. We had engaged groups of geologists and historians to figure out the possibilities, and the results have been positive. The quest of the tomb might lead you to that one river and the place where it became four.' Clemente paused and scrunched up his face. 'Geography changes, Mr Roy. Fertile lands turn into deserts, water bodies dry up, rivers die. So the situation demands that we get someone other than us to discover the two lost rivers of the Holy Bible.' Here the cardinal's intense gaze returned. 'Perhaps you…you are certainly qualified for the job, and more than that, I am told the media likes you.'

'Me?' Eric barked. 'Are you guys insane? Minutes ago, you were ready to kill me, and now you offer me a project?'

'Ummm, I would rather call it *a special arrangement*, Mr Roy. There is still a big chance you and your people will get killed, if things don't go well.'

Eric looked into his eyes, and he knew what the cardinal was offering wasn't his best hope, because he couldn't escape the feeling that the current chain of events were an effort to mask something far more sinister than what was visible on the surface.

'Find the Tomb of God and don't get killed, right? Eric smirked.

'There's more, actually,' the cardinal smiled. 'Find the rivers, and the four of you live!'

'And what if I turn this overwhelming offer down?'

'You cannot. You care too much for your friends.'

'I'll need all three of them with me if I decide to help you on this.'

The cardinal stared at the fire for a while and finally said, 'That shouldn't be a problem, since Niccolo and his men will also be with you.' He turned towards Eric and said, 'The point is, now that we know the rivers existed, we will eventually find them. If you help us, it will be good for you and your friends, but even if you don't…' he bored his eyes hard into Eric, 'we have several empty cells under this building where you'll spend every moment of the rest of your life praying for death to come.'

Eric felt the heat of the threat but tried to conceal his uneasiness. Above everything else, he visualised that piece of paper with Tessitori's poem and the names of the two rivers on it—Pison and Gihon.

FIFTY-EIGHT

The tall man standing behind Eric said, 'This is the best opportunity you will ever get in your life!' He nudged his weapon into Eric's back.

'Niccolo!' the cardinal waved him down. 'I think he understands the threat all too well. He understands that it is not only about him but about each of his associates who know about this secret. We can only hope he understands the gravity of the chance he's being given.' He stood up from his chair. 'Come on, agree to help us, and you will be the one to discover Pison and Gihon. Imagine—it would be one of the greatest discoveries in history...far bigger than your Job Charnock treasure,' he smirked. 'And yes, there is an additional secret waiting to be discovered at the end of the journey.'

'What's that?'

'I don't know. But I know something very important does exist at the end of the road.'

'You know it all right. Why don't you just tell me right now?'

The cardinal smiled. 'Because then you would have no incentive to find out for yourself. I know your kind, Mr Roy; you are driven by the "need to know" force; to discover what is hidden. I think I understand you, because I am much the same.'

'No, we are not the same!' Eric sneered. 'I seek knowledge to share it with all, and you suppress facts from becoming public knowledge to protect your so-called faith.'

'My faith is strong; it doesn't need any protection.'

'Then why are you trying to destroy ancient civilisations?'

'Because unlike mine, faith is fragile for the majority of the people.'

'That's relative,' Eric said coldly. 'I'd rather put it this way—the Church survived Galileo, that's true,' Eric returned the glare he'd received some minutes before, 'but his *ideas* have survived your ideologies. The Church survived Copernicus, but the fact is, his theories will survive your very existence.'

FIFTY-NINE

The cardinal's words had confirmed at least one thing: whatever the secret of the long-gone civilisation might be, it must have conflicted strongly with Christianity.

Eric knew the value of the discovery of Pison and Gihon, but he didn't know what the other secret could be. Well, he would figure it out for sure, he told himself.

For now, Eric's and his associates' only chance of survival was to accept Clemente's offer and hope that he could thread out the small fragmented pieces of information he had to unearth. And, of course, there was something else. What if…what if he *did* discover Pison and Gihon, along with that *something big* at the end of the puzzle? The cardinal was right. It would surely be one of the greatest discoveries of the modern world. And if he were the one to make it…

'All right,' he spoke, standing up from his chair. 'Cardinal, I accept your offer.' Eric held out his right hand. 'I will find the Tomb of God and the lost rivers. But I want all three of my friends with me in Iraq, and I want all our belongings back.'

'You'll get your belongings back. But your communications will be restricted and monitored. Welcome to the big leagues, Mr Roy.'

SIXTY

Villa Sospisio, Rome

Sandwiched between Vatican City on one side of the river Tiber and Sant' Agostino on the other, Villa Sospisio was an extraordinarily beautiful place that Carlos Clemente had arranged for Eric to stay at for a week. Aurin, Father Smit and Dr Huntley had joined Eric, and together they were tasked with solving the unsolved parts of the puzzle and planning the journey that lay ahead of them.

Skirted by a landscaped garden and built around an outdoor pool, Villa Sospisio had a brilliant sun terrace and was perhaps a place best suited for the small team to relax and think clearly. Most of the brainstorming was to be done by Eric and Father Smit, for Dr Huntley was still recovering from the trauma, and Aurin was nursing him.

◆

It was a lesson Dr Naidu had taught him and the other six trainees in their first training: sometimes you could get so involved with the day-to-day, hour-to-hour, minute-to-minute tactics of a focused situation that you would lose sight of the overall strategy, the bigger picture that was going to win you the battle, or even the war.

Ever since he had landed in Iraq on this mission, the bigger picture had faded into the background of his mind as he'd dodged kidnappers, bullets, grenade launchers and double- and triple-crosses. So when he actually gave himself time to think about things, the masks from many faces began dropping one by one.

Surrounded by sheaves of loose paper and piles of open books, Eric sat at a long table in the study, completely focused on his work. Aurin came and stood in the doorway for a moment, hoping to be noticed and to tell his brother about their Hindukush adventure and the success of their mission to find Dr Huntley. When that didn't happen, he pulled out a wooden chair and sat across from Eric, who finally looked up and nodded with a smile.

'Fancy some pizza for lunch?'

◆

The group settled down in the living area of the villa after a light lunch of pizza and coffee at the poolside. It had been a lazy day. They had a long session over a hearty brunch up on the sun terrace through the late morning, where Eric briefed everyone about everything he knew. He also passed around the three round-shaped tablets he and Dr Hussein had found in Bikaner and Nimrud.

In a way, it was good that the troopers had collected most of the articles from Tracy's Windsor house when they came for Eric. What they had missed, however, was the replica ship that Dr Hussein had found in the third Nimrud tomb. The last thing Eric remembered before his being taken from Dr Tracy's house was that Dr Hussein had been showing the vessel around, and Sid had been taking photographs. But then everything had been jeopardised, and this morning, when Eric had tried calling them, their cell phones had been unreachable. Not one of them—Sid or Dr Hussein or Marina or Tracy—could be reached on their phones. And without Sid or Dr Hussein, Eric had no way of figuring out where that artefact was.

'We are fucking fucked', Aurin punched his palm. 'Dr Huntley is unwell, and our clues are inadequate. We hardly know anything about Sid's findings, and he is perhaps the only guy who has got some grip on the mystery! We don't know where Dr Hussein, Sid or Marina are, we are not allowed to connect with anyone, and, above all, we've promised some deadly fanatics that we'll solve the entire mystery and find the relic for them. I think even if God almighty wanted to save us, he wouldn't be able to do it now!'

'Doesn't sound very religious to me,' Eric remarked. 'Settle down, boy...let me think.'

'He is not totally wrong, Eric...' Father Smit began. Eric turned towards him and sat up, smiling. Father Smit looked leaner and far more energetic than any sixty-seven-year-old he knew. He flaunted his usual pop singer spectacles from the nineties that fitted tightly on his sharp nose and wore a white shirt over a pair of faded jeans. 'I don't know how many groups and brotherhoods are involved in this, but I know one thing—this is much messier than our previous adventure,' he added.

'I gather the Salvation Knights have been destroying archaeological sites for a long time,' Dr Huntley said, 'but now they want us to dig out secrets for them—so that they can renew the world's faith in the Catholic Church? Wonderful!' he smirked. 'And then there is Count Delfino, who has always been after treasures and relics for the price they fetch. And as I understand, Nassar is simply a smuggler with a militia branding, singlehandedly responsible for the massacre of my entire camp. What a bunch to deal with at once!' He quivered for a moment.

'You are recovering very well, Dr Huntley!' Eric said cheerily, realising that Dr Huntley was again visualising the massacre in his mind.

'Of course,' Father Smit added, 'your brain is analysing things perfectly! Congrats, Dr Huntley, you are almost back in action!'

'My point was,' Aurin cleared his throat, 'Nassar, Delfino and the Salvation guys—they are all brutal killers. They all have been killing people for their own sets of agendas. They have even gone as far as killing people just because they knew something!' Aurin paused for effect and then added, 'To sum up—one wrong move, and we all die!'

'So, what do we do now? If three ruthless and really powerful groups want us dead, then we've got a big problem at our hands.' Dr Huntley grimaced.

Father Smit sat on a couch with one of the three tablets in his hand, while the other two rested next to him. Beside the couch was a square end table with an antique turntable and a collection of classical music in long-play records. A decorated lampshade flooded the corner of the room with soft light.

'Does anyone mind if I play some Bach?' Father Smit asked, looking at a particularly colourful record cover.

Aurin smiled and said, 'Fantastic idea, let me help.' He got up from the fluffy club chair he'd been parked in and walked up to the record player. He ran an admiring hand over the well-kept hard board cover and its design. Taking the shining black record out, he caressed the disk with a magician's finesse and placed it on the spindle. He switched on the player, but nothing happened. Then he positioned the stylus on the record, but nothing moved still.

Eric watched Aurin's theatrics and rolled his eyes with a sigh. 'That thing's not plugged!' he said, stretching his arms out in Aurin's direction, and then...

...at that very moment, with his arms stretched in front of him, Eric had a vision. In that momentary flash, he discovered the missing pattern. He whirled around to look at the turntable and yelled, 'Jesus Christ!'

'What happened, Ric da?' Aurin was startled.

'Aurin,' he breathed urgently, 'give me one of the tablets.'

'Sure!' Aurin mumbled. 'Are you okay?'

Eric gestured with a raised index finger—*give it to me*—his eyeballs fixed on the turntable, as though his mind was racing through gigantic columns of data, like a supercomputer looking for a match.

Eric stared with growing excitement at the inscriptions on one side of the tablet when Aurin handed it to him. 'I know what this is!'

'What?' Aurin cried.

'Father Smit!' Eric said, looking squarely into his eyes. 'We were in ninth standard, studying sound, and you gave us a demonstration. That day I'd asked you a question, and your answer enlightened the entire class. Today I ask you the same question again: Why did Edison call the sound-recording machine he developed the *phonograph*?'

Father Smit rolled his eyes and said, 'Because phonograph literally means *sound-writer*. As per Edison's notes, it had a wooden cylinder with a thin sheet of foil wrapped round it and a sturdy needle with a horn attached to it, pressed against the foil. Edison spoke into the horn, and the sound energy from his voice, funnelled and concentrated by the horn, made the needle vibrate up and down. As Edison cranked a handle, the cylinder rotated, and the needle cut a groove into the foil. Since the needle was moving up and down, the depth of the groove varied according to how loud or soft his voice was. In other words, the groove was a recording of the sound of Edison's voice translated into a mechanical form. That's about it.'

'And...?' Eric prodded.

'And to play back the recorded sound, Edison noted, he simply had to run the process in reverse. He put the needle back at the start of the groove and cranked the handle. The needle ran along the groove, jolting up and down to follow the pattern it had cut previously. As it moved about, it vibrated, and the noise of its vibrations was amplified by the horn, recreating the sound of Edison's voice, albeit in a very scratchy fashion.'

'Can I pester you to draw that same diagram for all of us?'

'Before that, we need to understand how sound is produced,' Father Smit said, getting into teacher mode. 'Sound is produced by vibration. When a body vibrates, it forces the neighbouring particles of the medium to vibrate. This creates a disturbance in the medium, which travels in the form of waves. This disturbance, when it reaches the ear, produces sound. Like this,' he picked up a bunch of paper napkins from the top of the empty pizza box and started drawing a diagram with a pencil he found on the corner table.

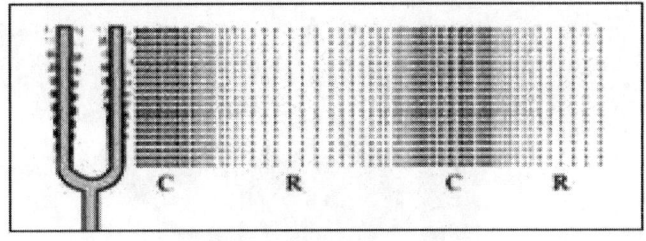

'When a vibrating body moves forward, it creates a region of high pressure in its vicinity. This region of high pressure is known as a compression. When it moves backward, it creates a region of low pressure, known as a rarefaction. As the body continues to move forward and backward, it produces a series of compressions and rarefactions, represented here by the Cs and Rs. This phenomenon can be represented with this simple diagram,' he drew a box with a pattern of lines on a napkin.

'Thanks for bringing back my middle-school physics memories,' Aurin said mockingly.

'Now let's get back to Edison!' Eric pleaded.

Father Smit drew another, rather complex diagram on a fresh napkin. 'Let me show you how the phonograph worked.'

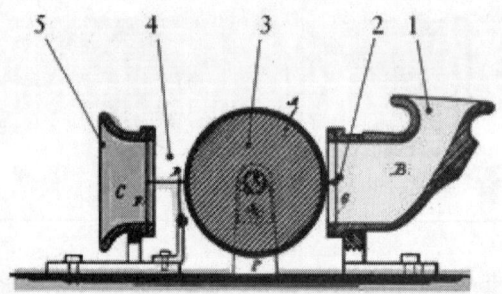

'If you want to record sound, you speak into the tube numbered one. The sound energy from your voice makes a diaphragm, which is like a mini drumskin, vibrate, pushing a needle, numbered two, back and forth and cutting a groove into some metal foil wrapped around the cylinder, numbered three, which is slowly turned by a clockwork (wind-up) motor. Playback runs this process in reverse. Another needle, numbered four, presses into the groove, bouncing up and down in the pattern previously cut there. Another diaphragm and horn number five amplify the sounds and turn them back into sounds you can hear.

'Now let me try to explain the next part of the mystery, which I believe I have solved in my mind.' Eric picked up where Father Smit had left off, pointing at the Indus scripts etched on one side. 'These scripts are so common in the Indus seals that we have been seeing them almost everywhere for ages. They were in our history books, they were in museums, they were in articles and magazines…but we only always looked at them as scripts.'

'I think because that's what they are,' Dr Huntley interjected.

'This is a special moment for all of us, Dr Huntley, because this is the moment when we find out they are *not*.'

'Then what are they, Eric?' Dr Huntley asked, curious.

Eric looked at all of his friends, one after the other, savouring the moment before he eventually said, 'They are pictograms, and believe me, they have always been.'

'What are you saying, Eric?' Father Smit straightened up.

'I am saying, in all of those famous Indus "bull" seals, through all of the last century, these pictograms were trying to communicate only one thing.'

'What?' Aurin asked, his eyes wide with anticipation.

'They were trying to pass on an instruction. Probably the most iconic instruction from a lost time, from a lost civilisation,' Eric offered.

'And you are saying you've decoded it?' Aurin and Father Smit asked in unison.

'Yes! But I need a couple of things first. Roberto!' Eric called out to the caretaker of the villa. 'Excuse me, can you tell me how to get to the nearest hardware store?'

SIXTY-ONE

Eric worked on a small table in the study of their villa. From his trip to the store he had brought back several sheets of chart paper, rolls of packing tape, pieces of wooden dowel, thread, a lamp stand, an electric screwdriver and a set of large needles of the kind used to repair tarpaulin and other heavy fabric.

'What are you up to, Eric?' Father Smit placed an inquiring hand on his shoulder.

'Let me find out first…it could just be a hunch!' Eric smiled. He used a piece of packing tape to fix the electric screwdriver to the side of the small table with its empty chuck up. He then put a short piece of wooden dowel to one of the screwdriver's bits. He had already drilled a fine hole on the other end of the dowel. He inserted the bit into the empty slot of the chuck. Setting the screwdriver to its lowest speed, he pulled the trigger. The wooden dowel spun as he wanted.

'All right, that part works! I wish the turntable was in a working condition. It would save us a lot of time. Now let's see about the rest...'

He made a cone from the chart paper he bought and secured it to the lamp stand by its narrow end with some tape. Once it was in place, he took one of the needles and carefully inserted its eye-side into the point of the cone. He used some more tape to make sure it was fixed there. Then he slid the lamp stand across the desk in such a way that the needle hung just above the piece of the wooden dowel.

'Perfect!' Aurin smiled, 'this is almost half the Gramophone Company logo.'

'Truly fantastic work, Eric!' Father Smit exclaimed.

Dr Huntley stared at the construction with disbelief. 'You have indeed built a gramophone, Eric!'

◆

'May I have a paper napkin and your pencil, please?' Eric asked Father Smit.

'Here you go!'

What Eric drew next were the Indus scripts from the famous bull seal that almost every school-going child in India sees in their Class V or VI history books.

'Guys, look at this... I think we are on the verge of deciphering a coded message that was created for this day about four thousand years ago,' Eric yelled. 'I know what this is!'

'You do?' the others asked in unison.

'Yes...look at this.' Eric started labelling each script with his pencil.

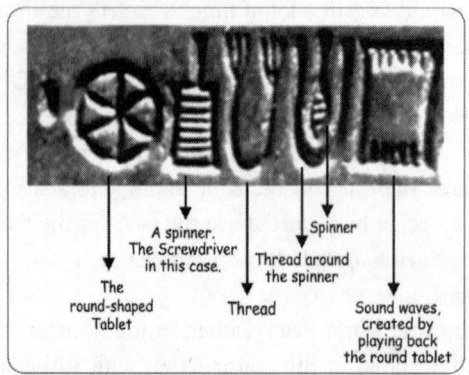

A spinner. The Screwdriver in this case.
Spinner
The round-shaped Tablet
Thread around the spinner
Thread
Sound waves, created by playing back the round tablet

Everyone looked on with bated breath.

'These pictograms were simply trying to tell us how to play the disc!' Eric held his temples. 'This is huge! They had to use the thread, since they didn't have electricity to propel the disc. They must have threaded the spinner with a handle to rotate it manually instead.'

'Let's check if it really works!' Father Smit said.

'I don't know what I would do if I heard a voice that was recorded some three thousand seven hundred years ago,' Aurin whispered, his voice echoing with excitement. 'This is a frickin' CD!'

'Yes, a four-millennia-old CD.' Father Smit nodded.

Picking up the metal tablet from the desk, Eric replied, 'That's what this is—it's an audio recording! Look at the grooves; they are absolutely similar to the ones on the LP record.'

'Yes, I see your point,' Father Smit said. 'There have been examples of pottery accidentally recording ambient sounds while they were being inscribed with a stylus on the potter's wheel.'

'I think the people who made this developed the technique into something with practical applications,' Eric surmised, indicating the card-paper cone. 'I think they must have used copper along with some other metal for the cone as well as for the tablet, though the principle remains the same—the cone is used to pick up the vibrations of sounds and transmit them through the needle on to the heated, soft copper alloy of the tablet when the recording is being made. Then they are amplified as if by a loudspeaker when the cooled and hardened tablet is played back.'

Dr Huntley gazed at the second and third tablets. 'So, what did they record on them?'

'Voices, presumably. Religious sermons. Speeches by their kings...' Father Smit offered.

'Maybe even poetry!' Dr Huntley chuckled. 'You never know; we might hear a recital of *Gilgamesh*.'

Eric lowered one of the round tablets on to the makeshift turntable, sliding the dowel into the hole at its base. 'Let's find out.'

Aurin looked unsettled. 'So, you are saying that if this works, we might hear a voice from a lost time, from an era long gone?'

'A four-millennia-old message at the very least, if my calculations are correct.' Eric moved the lamp stand until the needle's tip lightly touched the start of the groove near the tablet's top. 'Here we go...'

Holding his breath, he switched it on.

The tablet rotated and the screwdriver's motor moaned because of the weight of the tablet. But, even over all the noise, the makeshift loudspeaker generated some specific sound that they all could clearly hear.

It was a voice for sure. But they had never heard anything like that before.

'What's that?' Eric exclaimed.

It was an unnatural sound, a low, almost shrill moan. The fear of something eerie started overpowering the excitement they all shared a few moments back.

'Most probably it is not the right speed,' Father Smit came forward. He stopped the motor, adjusted the makeshift device and then he moved the needle back to the starting point. 'Let's try once again.'

This time, the voice came much closer to the human voice, though it was still indistinct. It uttered five discrete sounds—'words', as Eric pointed out—before adding.

'Its not right yet!' Eric exclaimed.

Dr Huntley, fascinated with the results of the impromptu experiment, said, 'It needs to go faster.'

Father Smit increased the screwdriver's speed and restarted the motor once again. The sound came on again, now clearly a male voice with a strange baritone to it. Eric strained to listen to the voice through all other mechanical noises. The speech lasted for over four and a half minutes. And then Eric quickly unplugged the screwdriver.

◆

'Please play it once again, and let me record it, Ric da,' Aurin broke the stunned silence. Eric nodded at him and replayed the disc, while Aurin recorded the entire speech on his mobile phone. 'We've successfully digitised a voice that is four millennia old, and we have no clue what is being said by it. But we might seek the help of people like Dr Tracy, who is an expert on the subject.'

'Auri boy is right!' Father Smit chimed. 'We need special help to decipher what is being said.'

'I agree. And I am really excited...' Dr Huntley's eyes twinkled. 'For the first time in human history, an ancient audio recording is going to be archived in one of the world repositories. And that would be my knowledge hub in Trongsa, Bhutan!'

'I know how you feel, guys,' Eric said, 'but before all that, let's digitise the contents of all the three discs.'

The second disc had a longer speech of nearly six minutes, replayed in a similar mechanical voice. But they were unsuccessful in playing the third disc. Throughout the evening, they replayed the contents of the two discs on Aurin's mobile phone but failed to make out anything from the speeches. The voices on both the discs were so emotionless and mechanical that none of them could figure out whether they were sermons or religious chants, recitations or political announcements, or indeed directions to a place.

They all agreed to reach out to Dr Tracy for help if they were permitted to call her. Finally, when they got the permission and connected with her on phone, they briefed her and sent over the two MP4 files via encrypted email.

She informed them she was fine and was worried sick for all of them. She didn't know anything about the whereabouts of Dr Hussein, Marina or Sid. She thought they had all been taken by the same group of people who took Eric. She just said one of the troopers had knocked her out, and when she came to, it was morning and no one was around.

SIXTY-TWO

Ancient Egypt had one primary spoken language, but it was written using a number of different alphabets. The first was hieroglyphics, the stylised pictograms familiarised by temples, tombs and Hollywood movies. These had first appeared around 3100 BC. Pioneering Egyptologists had assumed the language to be pictorial, each symbol representing a single concept. But after the Rosetta stone was found with identical text inscribed in hieroglyphics, Demotic and Ancient Greek, Thomas Young and later Jean-Francois Champollion deducted that these pictograms had phonetic as well as symbolic value. That they were, in short, letters that could be combined in multiple ways to form words and thus form a broad vocabulary, and that this language had its own syntax and grammar too.

Hieroglyphics, while they looked fantastic on the walls of temples and palaces and formal documents, were far too elaborate to be practical for everyday use. Therefore, from the very start, a simpler and quicker alphabet had developed alongside. This was known as the Hieratic, and it had become the language of literature, business and administration in ancient Egypt, which is why it was usually found inscribed on cheaper materials like wood, papyrus and ostraca. Then, around 600 BC, a third written language called the Demotic had evolved, reducing Hieratic to a series of strokes, dashes and dots, somewhat like Egyptian shorthand. To make matters worse, it had neither vowels nor breaks between words, its vocabulary was large and vernacular, its alphabet varied significantly from region to region, and it evolved massively over the centuries, so that it really became a family of related languages, not just one language. Mastery took years of dedication and a set of dictionaries the size of a Volkswagen Beetle. Likewise, given the challenge of deciphering a long-lost spoken language from several ancient Sumerian and Mesopotamian languages, Tracy didn't know where to start, because she didn't know how mainstream this recorded language was. She didn't even know what resources to tap into to decipher this language.

The only thing she knew was that the decipherment of something like this could take anywhere from weeks to months.

SIXTY-THREE

It had been six days since Eric's conversation with Cardinal Clemente. Dr Huntley had taken four of those days to recover fully from his trauma, and then the three of them had taken the better part of the fifth day to plan for their impending trip.

On the evening of the fifth day, Eric had received a video call from Tracy. She greeted him with her usual charming smile and cheery eyes filled with enthusiasm, clad in a floral scarf over a white shirt, a damp lock of hair falling onto her freshly rinsed cheek. Tracy swept her hair back with both hands, holding it there in a quick, makeshift ponytail, and she trembled as she shared her findings. 'I have to tell you about my wonderful experience deciphering this almost four-millennia-old dialect!' she beamed on Eric's mobile screen.

'We are equally eager to know, Tracy!' Eric smiled. He understood that even for a linguist of Tracy's stature, this must have been the challenge of a lifetime. It must have taken all her research, education, and knowledge to work on this. 'I am sure you have done it exceptionally well for us!' Eric added with a broader smile. 'If you don't mind, I want my friends, Dr Huntley, Father Smit and Aurin Roy, to also be a part of this discussion.'

'Of course!' replied Tracy, as the rest of the group came up behind Eric's chair. 'Hello, all of you! The initial problem was,' Tracy started, 'that apparently, leaving aside a few research pieces, no articulate information was available on how the Sumerian or Harappan language would sound, because...' she laughed, 'no one could have ever imagined that a four-thousand-year-old disc with recorded human voices would just pop up out of the blue one day, or that the human race in the twenty-first century would actually be listening to the Sumerian spoken language, complete with the underlying tones and nuances.'

'I understand exactly what you are saying,' Father Smit nodded.

'As we know, humans had been speaking for a couple of hundred thousand years before they got the inspiration to mark their ideas down for generations to come.'

'Yes, of course,' said Dr Huntley. 'By 3000 BC in Sumeria, and then soon after in Egypt, and by 1500 BC in China, people were scribbling, sketching and telling the world about their culture in a permanent way.'

'But 5,000 years ago,' Tracy smiled, 'when the Sumerians finally did scratch out a few book-keeping symbols on clay tablets, they unknowingly started a whole new era in what we call, well, *history*.

'Today, because of a lack of native speakers and transmission through the filter of Akkadian phonology, it is difficult to read out the cuneiform scripts out loud. Scholars say that when we try to find out the morphophonological structure of the Sumerian language, we must remember that we are not dealing with a language directly but rather reconstructing it from an imperfect mnemonic writing system which was not aimed at the rendering of morphophonemics. By the way, to bring everyone on the same page, morphophonology, or morphophonemics—morphonology for short—is the branch of linguistics that studies the interaction between morphological and phonetic processes. It chiefly focuses on the sound changes that take place in morphemes, which are the minimal meaningful units that combine to form words. Now, at the very beginning of this challenging work, I decided to study the available research work on finding the phonetic values of both the Sumerian and Indus languages. That's how I came to know that in 2004, historian Steve Farmer, computational linguist Richard Sproat, who is now a research scientist at Google, and Sanskrit researcher Michael Witzel at Harvard University caused a stir with their paper comparing the Indus and Sumerian scripts with a system of phonetic symbols similar to those of medieval European heraldry or the Neolithic Vinča culture from central and south-eastern Europe.'

'That's interesting!' Eric interrupted. 'I didn't know people had done that kind of research!'

'Taking a cue from that research,' Tracy continued, 'I started digging out similar kind of work and, as luck would have it, two specific works caught my attention. One was a study on Akkadian and Sumerian language done by an American institute, which concluded that being a Semitic language, Akkadian was very similar in grammar and structure to Arabic and Hebrew. Sumerian, on the other hand, was quite different. In terms of structure, Sumerian was much closer to the American-Indian languages than it was to Akkadian. Modern languages that structurally resemble Sumerian are Turkish and ancient Tamil.

'The second was a very interesting project by Martin Worthington at the University of Cambridge, who got a few Assyriologists and recorded them reading verses from the Babylonian *Gilgamesh*, the world's oldest epic poem. As per my great-great-grandfather's personal diary, ancient Tamil had certain connections and similarities with the spoken language of the Indus Civilisation as well as the spoken language of the Sumerian Civilisation, and ancient Tamils must have been well aware, through their trade links, of how the Sumerian spoken language functioned.'

Tracy paused for breath, then continued with renewed vigour. 'The universal features of most of the spoken languages are a *sequential ordering* of the phonetical values and an *agreed direction* of voice. Based on this theory, I decided to complete the gaps in phonetic values of the Sumerian language with phonetic symbols from ancient Turkish and ancient Tamil, which are still spoken today. Though both the languages have gone through lots of changes, their frameworks are still intact. But I didn't know how to go about it, till someone told me to try a digital approach. This colleague of mine shared an Internet link where I found out that working with geo-information, scientist Andreas Fuls at the Technical University of Berlin has created the first electronic corpus of Indus, Sumerian and ancient Tamil phonetic values.

'A related article on the said work led me to another path-breaking work by a group led by computer scientist Rajesh Rao at the University of Washington, who took a digital approach to find the phonetic values of ancient language scripts. The team was able to calculate the conditional entropies, that is, the amount of randomness in the choice of a token, given a preceding token, in natural-language scripts, such as the Sumerian cuneiform and the English alphabet, and in non-linguistic systems, such as the computer programming language Fortran and human DNA. The team found that the conditional entropies of ancient Tamil were much similar to those of Harappan and Sumerian cuneiforms.

'The most amazing part was,' Tracy's eyes shone as she related her complicated research process, 'the team followed the trails of some Eastern Aramaic languages from the Mesopotamian region and found that even today, a minority of Jews and Mandaeans speak some varieties of it.

'At this point, someone informed me that the work I wanted

to do, filling phonetic gaps of a digitally scanned language file with phonetics from some other languages, could be done using a software. She, in fact, joked about the idea, referring to Steven Spielberg's film *Jurassic Park*, comparing my idea with what they had depicted in the film. The film showed the DNA gaps of dinosaurs being filled with DNA from today's reptiles. I was told that the software was available with BBC's futuristic tech-lab, The Blue Room, in London. I immediately talked to the director and asked to borrow their technical team as well as the technology to work on this, and...'

'And what?' Dr Huntley cried impatiently, seated on the edge of his couch.

'The phonetic values of about 31 per cent of our Sumerian voice recording matched with the phonetic values of a known version of ancient Tamil, and about 76 per cent of it matched with the still-spoken Eastern Aramaic.' Dr Tracy paused to clear her throat.

'What happened then?' Eric prodded her.

'Then I contacted Michael Witzel at Harvard University—he's the Sanskrit researcher I mentioned earlier. I found out that the group had worked on Eastern Aramaic...' her voice lingered.

'And?' Everyone asked in unison this time.

'...and deciphered over 71 per cent of the first recording and over 75 per cent of the second recording.'

'Is that really true?' Dr Huntley asked with marked disbelief.

'Yes, sir, it's true.' Tracy smiled. 'Do you think I would otherwise chat for this long over the phone with people I barely know?' she laughed.

It was as if the tension in the air had been cut with a knife. Suddenly they were all laughing. 'You have done it, Dr Layard!' Dr Huntley threw his hands up in joy.

'I am sending a few scanned pages where I have written down the content of the two audio recordings. I have also added my notes in italics on the margins. I think you will figure everything out from these pages...'

'I don't know how to thank you, Tracy!' Eric's voice betrayed deep emotion.

'You will find chances, I am sure!' Tracy smiled. 'Guys, come back safely to tell me the whole story...over and out,' she signed off.

TABLET 1 (the one Eric found in the Thar Desert)

In the land of Sumer	
There lies a blessing for mankind	
The secret belonged to the land of seven rivers near _____	*(This must be the Indus valley.)*
and was taken to Sumer to save a king	
This message was sent back as a gesture of the people of Larsa	
To the people of the land of seven rivers	
The key to this ancient secret was	
hidden in the tomb of Queen Yaba at Kalhu	*(Kalhu was the ancient name for Nimrud.)*
Ninki giving her life to keep it there	
I and my sister...we pledged to bring one key here	
Ina and Ninki we two were the last of the keepers	
_____	*(couldn't figure out this sentence)*
Our family is the keeper of this secret since ages	
Generation after generation we kept it	
We have discovered ways to hide it from the wrong hands	
Here is one	

If a blessed soul _____ this message
He must find the tomb of Queen Yaba at Kalhu - Sumer
The message we carried to this land of seven rivers
to leave behind a key to the trail for the people of this place

_____

_____ *(couldn't figure out this part either)*

TABLET II (the one with the ship replica)

The father and the two sons
I have buried them all

(This guy, probably the commander of the voyage, is talking about Kudur Mabug, Rim-Sin and Warad-Sin…)

(Most probably, the keepers carried his version through ages and then archived it in the tablet at a later point in time, in one of their voices.)

The fateful voyage took two lives
Two souls left—the father and the son

(Kudur Mabug and Warad-Sin)

To let them sleep in peace and to save from the enemies
We buried them both in a small pyramid unsung
In a northern desert far away from Larsa

That was when the secret was handed over to me
And I took care of it
It was the blessing of life
that came from the land of seven rivers

(as he was the commander of the voyage)

(the Harappan Civilisation)

The one that saved a king's life
Many years passed.
The Son of the Moon God ruled the earth

(This is Rim-Sin—his people called him the son of the Moon God.)

and finally when he left the body
we took his body to the cliff of the moon
and buried with the secret
The cliff is the one that enlightens us on moonlit nights
The secret place where the son of the Moon God slept

(also interprets as— spreads the light)

———————————————————————

(couldn't figure out this part)

Zabu ēlū they called the flow

(This is Akkadian for The Great Zab river of Iraq.)

which was close to the mountain slope

(This should be Zagros Mountains of Northern Iraq.)

In between the mountain range and the flow
there is a secret cave that we know
the burial place for ancient men

(This might be the Shanidar Cave of Zagros where several Neanderthal remains were found. It's amazing to know that four thousand years ago also they knew about this place.)

There is a strange cliff near the cave
Moonlit nights make the cliff glow
That is the one with a hidden flow
this cliff has a circular path around
and a passage hidden behind a large rock
Many steps inside the cave
there are stairs to the heaven
The stair gives way to a hidden world
no one has ever seen… and no one ever told
The one door that one need to unlock
has the key hidden in _____

_____

_____

(couldn't figure out this part)

The path is hidden inside the
waterfall that drops in a lake
The lake gives birth to four rivers
This is the place where the son of the moon
god sleeps in the garden of heaven

(I am not sure if they are talking about the garden of Eden.)

Here is the true source of the four rivers that is hidden
one will find what they hide from the enemies
one will find what they called the key of life

_____

(couldn't figure out this last sentence)

SIXTY-FOUR

'So, do you actually know where we're going?' Niccolo asked Eric from the back row as their pilot guided the Eclipse 550 twin-engine jet towards a landing on the dusty private runway at the outskirts of the Erbil Governorate of Iraq. He and three of his heavily armed men accompanied Eric, Aurin, Father Smit and Dr Huntley.

'More or less,' Eric replied. 'Do you know anything about Shanidar Cave in northern Iraq?'

'Yes,' Niccolo nodded. 'It's an archaeological site in the Zagros Mountains. The remains of Neanderthals, several tens of thousands of years old, have been found here.'

'Ten in number,' Aurin interjected.

'I beg your pardon?'

'I said there were remains of ten Neanderthals.'

'All right!' Niccolo said with a surly expression. 'I read that the cave also shelters two cemeteries, one of which dates back about ten thousand years and has the remains of several prehistoric individuals.'

'You are a learned mercenary!' Eric smirked, sweeping the landscape with a careful eye.

'So, that's where we are heading?' Niccolo asked, ignoring Eric's sarcasm.

'More or less!' Eric peered at the desert below. 'This Zergeta plain, with its surrounding desert and lunar terrain, looks as desolate as the Sahara,' he said. 'Okay, maybe less rather than more.'

'What are the coordinates?' Niccolo asked.

'Latitude 36° 48' N, longitude 44° 14' E would be the approximate coordinates of the cave, but we'll have to go further.'

'Any landmark?'

'Yes, a particular cliff,' Eric said, 'which is supposed to *enlighten the seeker*!'

◆

The plane touched down, its hot wheels hitting the ground with a squawk. They were all thrown forward in their seats. 'Sorry,' said the pilot, braking. 'I'm not exactly thrilled to be here.'

'You have a problem with the Iraqis?' Aurin asked from his seat in the second row.

'Yes, Iraqis and Iranians, both. They just won't stop killing innocent people and vandalising history!'

'You are right,' Father Smit shook his head in dismay. 'Where are you from?'

'There are only three things you can be sure of finding in this region,' the pilot continued, avoiding Father Smit's question, 'sand, rocks and death.' He brought the plane to a sudden stop.

'That should be all, Lorenzo,' Niccolo said in an authoritative voice. 'You can fly back now.'

Lorenzo switched off the engines, the silence unsettling after the continuous mechanical drone throughout the flight. 'I think here comes your Uber,' he grinned, looking ahead through the windshield at two battered SUVs rolling towards the aircraft. One of the vehicles had a small satellite dish perched on its roof. 'We haven't hired the drivers, so you guys drive,' said Lorenzo. 'Hey, Niccolo, one more thing,' the pilot called out with a snigger, 'try not to get killed here, you won't get a proper burial. It's an Islamic country, after all!' He ended his advisory with booming laughter.

◆

'Where are we?' Dr Huntley asked, looking around.

'Northern Iraq—the Zergeta plains,' Eric replied, 'not very far from the Great Zab river. This was the only deserted field we could land a craft on without alerting the authorities.'

Carrying all the four backpacks on his shoulder, Eric climbed out of the aircraft followed by Father Smit, and then Aurin helped Dr Huntley out. They all looked at each other in eager silence and headed for the rundown trucks.

Niccolo carried his own duffle bag and followed the group at a distance along with his men. 'How long will it take for us to reach the site?' He had to raise his voice to be heard over the noisy hum of the warm breeze blowing in from the Zagros Mountains to their east.

'Can't say for sure,' Eric yelled back. 'Rugged desert, river, mountain, an almost uncharted territory…it should take six to seven hours at the very least, if our rides cooperate.' He took a deep breath, blissfully unaware of the dangers and obstacles waiting for them.

SIXTY-FIVE

Seventy kilometres to the north of where the group had landed, a convoy of four high-mobility multipurpose wheeled vehicles, popularly known as humvees, pulled over by the side of an old concrete road. Painted grey rather than in camouflage colours, the 4×4 vehicles appeared civilian. But their ex-military camouflage colours remained intact beneath two layers of paint.

Despite their humongous size, the powerful armoured XM1114-model trucks only had four seats, save for the leading truck. Accompanied by Rafiq and three of his goons, Nassar was driving this one. This humvee had been modified with an additional seat attached to the left side of the hood, occupied by Rafiq. The second truck carried two armed men and some captives, and the third and fourth carried four armed men each.

Nassar's squad was in full strength, all fifteen men emerging from their humvees to form an armed crescent as they waited. Soon, a group of horsemen emerged from behind a rocky escarpment half a kilometre away from them.

When they came within thirty metres of the armed group, they halted. 'These are the Mountain Rifles—the deadliest military tribe of this region,' Nassar announced to his men. 'Unfortunately, we have to collaborate and work together with them over the next few days, because this is their territory, and for this mission their support is crucial. Our fight is to save our heritage and history from the foreign looters, and that's the need of the hour, my brothers!' He looked into the eyes of each of his men, and then he turned and strode across the sand to meet the lead horseman.

The riders wore thick headscarves and layered clothing to protect them from the sun and wind. The topmost layer was military fatigue in green and brown camouflage. They carried AK-47s, the universally popular rifle of the Third World. One of the men carried a rocket-propelled grenade launcher: new military weaponry in the hands of supposedly civilian militia. Despite the heat of the desolate landscape, the men's eyes were stone cold. The narrow, unblinking gaze of warriors who were used to being feared by everyone.

Nassar talked to the lead rider for a while and then walked back to his truck. 'As per the arrangement between us, they have been tracking the entire region for suspicious movements but have found none. They know the probable location of an ancient tomb around here, and they are going to lead us there now.'

The horsemen led the convoy of vehicles through the empty deserts of northern Iraq in a south-eastern direction. The sun was a fat, flaming half-circle on the horizon to their right by the time they stopped.

♦

Aurin gazed into the distance in the scorching desert. From the middle seat of the SUV, he remarked, 'Looks like we are at the end of the road, literally!'

'If you call this a *road*,' Eric said dryly, looking back at the rutted track they had followed north-east from a place named Bujal, towards the Great Zab river.

'It's better, actually!' Niccolo chuckled. 'Lesser chances of being spotted.'

'Going off-road is not going to be any worse for the truck, I'm sure!' Eric smiled and banged a hand on the solid dashboard of the rusting, sand-scoured 1980s Toyota Land Cruiser that Lorenzo's contact had arranged for them.

Eric drove the car into never-ending nothingness reeling under the late afternoon sun on their far left. He looked at the SUV's GPS display that indicated they were still at least ninety kilometres from the location of the cave. And then, the next moment, he spotted a rock poking out from the sand and swerved the truck's wheel to dramatically change course. He jammed his foot on the brakes, and the truck came to a dead halt just shy of the mysterious protrusion.

It wasn't only the bluff; Eric spotted something else too—a column of black smoke rising into the sky some four or five kilometres ahead. 'Aurin, check the map—are there any villages on the route we are following?'

Aurin and Niccolo had seen the smoke too, only Dr Huntley didn't, for he had been dozing, his head resting on one of the Salvation guys' shoulders. Father Smit was in the second SUV behind Eric's, riding along with the three armed Salvation men.

'No! Not for a long way,' Aurin spoke after consulting his map. 'Are we off the course, Ric da?'

'Niccolo,' Eric ordered, 'connect with your HO—if they have sent any "team B". Also confirm if we should be expecting any visitor they have the slightest hint of.'

◆

Eric's mind and body had been trained over the years of adventuring to push their limits, enduring what other people couldn't even think of.

He eased into the driver's seat and took a deep breath, then looked around him—the sun was almost on the horizon and was changing colour fast. As was his method, Eric was allowing his mind to loosen up. He killed the engine. In a moment, it was calm; the only sound was that of the wind blowing from the Zagros Mountains. The wind carried the hints of a chill, a gentle warning about the unbearable cold it would unleash after sundown.

It was Eric's way of introspection, first cleaning his mind of all information and thoughts, then looking at everything from a third person's perspective. He hadn't found this kind of a peaceful moment until then on this mission. He had just never been in control of the situations and events—the massacre at Dr Huntley's site had brought bad news, and since then he'd been flowing with the unfathomable tides of the tsunami. Finally, after his talk with the cardinal in the Vatican, he'd tried regaining his foothold. And he knew it was high time he learned more about the invisible stakeholders in the game—the players who controlled everything from somewhere beyond the clouds.

His formula for success in any mission had always been simple: gather maximum information, focus on the objective, blur out the rest, accomplish the goal, and take the first chance to get the hell out. Everything else was meaningless.

But this time, things seemed much more complicated. His sixth sense warned him of a problem. A big problem. But he was unable to put his finger on it. When all of this had started, he'd thought the massacre was a muscle-flexing act by local fanatics. But then with Sid's help, he figured out that the Thar Desert bombing was also a part of it. Along the way, he started feeling that it was a bigger mess, where far more dangerous mafia groups and far deadlier religious fanatics were involved. Every time he'd think he had figured out the key motive, he was proven wrong soon enough. After his meeting with the cardinal, he had come to know of yet another side to the mystery, which gave him a sense of confidence. Now at least he knew how far humans driven by religious fanaticism could go. But, actually, he still didn't.

The problem was that he would know nothing about what they were dealing with until he jumped headlong into it. So he did. He had made a deal with one of the biggest stakeholders. And now, the time had come when he would get to know the others better.

◆

'There's no village, we are not expecting visitors, and we've not lost our way. We'd better take a look.' Niccolo announced after speaking to his HO on the satellite phone he carried.

'Are you sure that's a good idea?' Aurin asked, his tone making it clear he thought it was not.

'If no one's supposed to be out there, then someone might be in trouble, or maybe we have company. Either way, we need to check. We need to know who and where they are before they know who and where we are.' Eric put the truck back in gear and pushed down on the accelerator, aiming towards the smoke.

A little less than an hour later, Eric slowed down the truck and then came to a grinding halt. They were close to the base of a rocky rise—an extension of the lower range of the Zagros Mountains. The smoke was coming from the other side, still glowing eerily against the blinding desert darkness. Eric wound down the window, listened for a moment, then took Niccolo's Enfield rifle from his lap. 'Come on,' he said to Niccolo.

'What is it?' Aurin asked as Eric climbed out.

'I hear faint voices from the other side of the rock. You guys stay low,' Eric said. 'Niccolo and I will have a quick look and be back soon. Aurin, you take the driver's seat and use the comm to inform the other truck. Ask everyone to check the guns Lorenzo's contact had arranged for us. And most importantly, at the first hint of trouble, or at a signal from me, start the truck and lead the other one back to the rock we last halted at, okay?'

'Okay, Chief,' Aurin nodded.

Eric crawled up the shadowed face of the rock. Pulling out a shotgun from behind his seat, Niccolo followed suit.

SIXTY-SIX

'Shit!' Eric cried, scanning the fire-lit encampment through the rifle scope.

'What is it?' Niccolo asked from the side. It was pitch dark, and they lay just beneath the crest of a low rocky rise, observing the activity from a safe distance.

'Oh my God!' Eric whispered. 'He was the last person I had expected to see here!'

'What? Who?' Niccolo asked anxiously.

'This is Nassar and his gang—the so-called brotherhood of the Tomb of God,' Eric whispered. 'But it's not just them. There are several horsemen who I can see belong to a different group or tribe. Probably working together on something.' He scanned the camp for clues. 'But, then again, there have to be some other people, a third party, involved… I don't think Nassar and these thugs could arrange for four humvees in the middle of this rocky desert all by themselves.' He kept scouring the entire camp with a careful gaze. 'There are around sixty people in the camp, mostly young. The four humvees are pulled together in a circle, like a wagon train.' Eric went on with his narration of the details, as if Niccolo was taking notes. 'Looks like the local tribesmen got their own trucks—battered old military pickups, stripped to their bones to weld machine guns onto the rear beds.'

The tallest man of the lot stood next to the main fire. He looked different. From his white headscarf, Eric assumed he was the leader of the tribe. The man had an AK-47 slung over his shoulder, a Syrian shamshir across his back and a face of cold, hard stone.

Nassar emerged from one of the humvees, strode up to the tall man, and began talking. During their discussion, he pointed towards a white tent that stood next to the circle of humvees.

Eric adjusted the focus of the rifle eyepiece and scanned the tent. 'What the hell…' He breathed in disbelief. He had just picked out a very familiar head of red hair and an equally familiar jacket through the half-open flap of the tent.

'What?' Niccolo inquired.

'They've got Dr Hussein and Marina!' Eric hissed.

'You see them?' Niccolo's eyes widened. 'They actually brought Dr Hussein and Marina with them all this way?'

'Yes, of course, they must need them to work out the location of the tomb.' Eric shifted the sights, pinpointing their exact position.

'Oh!' Niccolo wondered aloud. 'He must have made a deal with them. His life in exchange for the location... I should have picked them up as well, along with you!' He punched his palm.

Eric glanced at him out of the corner of his eye. 'I don't think he would do that.'

'Are you sure? Because for all he knows, you and Dr Huntley are dead. And he had no other hope.'

'I don't think so!' Eric snapped, looking back through the sight with newfound purpose. A couple of Nassar's men were patrolling inside the circle of humvees, while more tribesmen did the same on the outside. Both the sides seemed to regard each other with mutual suspicion. Eric surveyed the camp's perimeter. Away from the fires, everything was cast under flickering shadows.

Eric sat back up and handed the Enfield to Niccolo.

'I have a gun,' Niccolo muttered.

'You'll need this one to cover me; it has a scope. I am going out there; give me your shotgun!' He removed the chocolate-coloured leather jacket he had pulled on after the temperature fell post-sunset and gave it to Niccolo. For what he was planning to pull, he couldn't allow the scraping sound of leather and zippers to give him away.

'Why?'

'I am going to rescue my friends.'

'From there?' Niccolo exclaimed. 'There must be at least sixty heavily armed men all around!'

'The numbers will decrease very soon.' He drew a long knife

from his high paratrooper boots. 'I am going to get a smaller gun from the truck if I can find one, then I am going in. You cover me from here, okay?'

'Okay!' Niccolo shook his head. 'Do you seriously think you can just stroll in there, get Dr Hussein and Marina, and walk back without anyone stopping you?'

'No, I don't,' Eric flicked the blade of his knife against his left palm. 'I'll probably have to silence some of them first…' He smirked. 'Let's rock and roll.'

SIXTY-SEVEN

Eric crept across the low rising rock, the shotgun slung over his back. He hunched over to avoid being spotted. He took a Beretta 3032 Tomcat from the truck and slipped it into his cargo pocket before heading for the camp. He had observed the camp for long enough to get an idea of the routes of the patrollers, and he could make a confident guess about their attitudes through the cold night. There was a big fire at the centre. The furthest side was marked for the tribesmen, and the side close to the escarpment where Eric stood belonged to Nassar's men. Within ten paces from the fifth tent on Nassar's side, some pickup trucks were parked.

Two men were on duty, lazily walking along the perimeter of the camp. Both the men were clearly bored and irritated from missing out on the campfire activities. They didn't expect anyone to be out there in the wilderness at that hour.

Eric dropped to his chest, sprawling flat on the uneven surface, as he heard the footsteps nearby. Raising his head, he saw one of the guards heading in the opposite direction, his head turned towards the fire instead of checking the black nothingness of the desert for threats. Nobody was covering the man from the back—the coast was clear.

Eric crawled along the ground until he reached a barbed bush and lay down next to it. The nearest tent was around forty paces away, with three horses tied beside it.

One of the tribesmen came from behind the tent and started walking towards where Eric lay.

Careful not to make the slightest sound, Eric lifted his gun to his shoulder. Even in the low light, the man was bound to be able to spot sudden movements.

He was still advancing, one hand almost touching his gun. Had he seen him? Eric couldn't figure out how, but he was pacing right towards the bush. Eric brought his shotgun up, ready to fire at a second's notice.

The man stopped a few feet away from him, only the leafless thorny branches of the bush separating them. He spat on the ground…

Then he pushed the folds of his thawb aside and opened his fly.

◆

How much had the bugger drunk? Eric wondered. The torrent of urine would just not stop. The thick undergrowth saved Eric from being sprayed directly, for which he heaved an inaudible sigh of relief. Finally, the flow eased off, the man straightened himself up, and quickly turned to leave. By now, the man on watch had also come around. The two men talked in a low voice before the second man went back to join the campfire activities, and the guard on duty trudged on.

Eric gazed beyond the bush. He waited for both men to move far enough, then swiftly crossed the open space to the nearest tent. As he negotiated the open space, he was uneasily aware of the fact that Niccolo was certainly tracking him through his gun's scope. If, for any reason, he thought that Eric had outlasted his worth, he could be dead long before he'd even hear the faint crack of the gun.

Eric reached his destination with his life and cover intact. Looking around the tent, he found the circle of humvees wasn't far away as it seemed earlier. He could see the reflections of flames in their bulletproof windows as they were close to one of the tribesmen's campfires.

Eric ducked on his way through the spot where the horses were tied, not wanting to give them a chance to get startled and make a noise. He rushed to another tent, then into the cover between three parked mounted trucks. One of them was a Toyota Hilux pickup and was in a relatively better condition than the others. He glanced inside, finding the key still in the ignition and a Rubik's Cube key ring dangling from it. Eric moved to the front of the truck.

The nearest humvee was actually very close to him. Most of the men around the fire had their backs to him. Nobody in sight was looking in his direction. He stood up, looking for signs of movement inside the circle of Nassar's vehicles.

A man emerged from a nearby tent and his eyes fell on Eric.

For a moment, neither man moved. Eric's gun hand was hidden from view behind the pickup. He began raising it slowly in preparation.

The man sneered at him after a few seconds, then he turned and walked towards one of the groups of merry-making brutes. Then Eric realised what had happened. The militiaman had assumed he was one of Nassar's troopers. In the shifting half-light, his dusty clothes could easily have been mistaken for their fatigues.

Eric held back until the man was out of sight, then he paced to the humvee. He made sure nobody was looking in his direction, then dropped to the ground and rolled underneath the vehicle.

He could see one of Nassar's men approaching. He waited for him to pass, then he rolled out from under the humvee and headed for Dr Hussein and Marina's tent, having marked the location from his observation post earlier.

He stopped as he saw another of Nassar's troopers sitting on a wooden case outside Hussein's illuminated tent. A Chinese Norinco rifle lay across his lap.

'Shit,' Eric whispered to himself. There was enough open space between the tents for the guard to spot him and prop up his gun much before Eric could get close enough for a knife attack. The problem was that if he fired a single shot, the entire camp would be alerted.

He needed another idea.

He stopped and then followed a circular route that would take him around to the back of Dr Hussein and Marina's tent, constantly alert for any sign of the men on patrol. One passed within close range. Eric dashed towards his aim, the knife in his hand. It wouldn't be long before the other man came around, and if he didn't make it inside the tent in time, his cover would be gone. He punched his knife into the base of the tent's frame and drew it across to cut a slit through the fabric. He ducked inside when it was wide enough to fit through. He tried looking up and hit his head against the heavy base of a battery-operated lantern hanging from a hook.

'Eric!' Marina cried, unable to believe what she saw.

'Shhhh!' Eric hissed, placing a frantic finger on his lips. He glanced back through the hole—the man on patrol had just walked past.

Marina took the lamp and set it down beside the slit as Hussein ran across the tent to where Eric stood, and they both enveloped him in a hug.

'Oh my God!' Marina whispered. 'You found us! I can't believe it; you found us!'

'I can't believe it either. Honestly, I didn't expect Nassar to already be out here, ahead of us.'

'Us?' Hussein raised his eyebrows.

'I met Dr Huntley, my brother Aurin and my friend Father Smit on the way...long story!'

'I am afraid we too have a long story about getting nabbed by Nassar's men minutes after you were taken away.'

Eric frowned, noticing a hand-drawn map and some notes on a wooden case next to Dr Hussein's laptop sleeve. 'And you told them?'

'No! Not exactly.' Marina answered. 'Dr Hussein was stringing them along.'

'Yes,' muttered Dr Hussein. 'I don't even know where the damned place is exactly!'

'Well, we all had some idea the last time we discussed things. And you got them so damn close!' Eric grimaced. 'This is a big desert. Not that I am complaining, but why'd you bring them so close?'

'Can we discuss these things later? I mean, once we are, y'know, out of this shit?'

'Yeah, we need to hurry the fuck up!' Eric remarked as he darted to the tent's flap door. He pulled down the zip slightly and had a look outside. He could see the back of the sitting guard's head. He hadn't heard anything yet.

Eric came back to Dr Hussein and Marina as they gathered their things, including the papers, and stuffed them into two backpacks. 'Over sixty armed men all around us!'

'Shit!' said Marina.

Dr Hussein smirked. 'Did you bring *any* good news?'

'Yeah,' he smiled. 'I'm on your side!'

'Okay, once the patrol guard goes past the tent again, run out and hide under one of the humvees.' Then he realised neither of the two was looking at him, but staring at the door instead. 'What?' He turned his head to see.

'Shadows!' Dr Hussein whispered, just as Eric also realised what was happening. The lantern on the floor was casting their huge shadows across the fabric. Three large silhouettes dancing against the light.

And then he heard the screech of a wooden box.

The man outside walked towards the tent and began to unzip the tent's door.

Eric flung his knife just as the trooper glanced inside. The blade got lodged into his neck almost silently. The man gasped, then gurgled and toppled in through the door, shaking the entire tent.

'Let's go,' Eric told them, pulling the trooper inside, and picked up his assault rifle and his Browning.

Dr Hussein and Marina dropped on the ground. Marina lifted the cut fabric from where Eric had entered and peered outside.

What she saw was a pair of boots.

Almost simultaneously, the slit was opened from outside and Marina looked right into the face of the man who pointed his gun between her eyes...

Eric fired the Norinco, sending a series of bullets through the tent's fabric just above Marina's head. The trooper didn't get a chance to scream. He fell instantly backwards.

Eric yelled, 'Guys, get under the humvee, quick!' and sprinted towards the gate to find the other patrolling guard. Dr Hussein and Marina scrambled through the slit, leaping over the body of the fallen soldier and plunging beneath the nearest 4×4. Barks arose from all around, the tribesmen and Nassar's thugs retorting to the gunfire.

Eric spotted another guard ducking behind a nearby tent. He shot yet another round from the stolen rifle, the bullets slashing through the nylon sheet, and the soldier fell right into view, with a single bloody wound on his forehead.

There were more movements beyond the circle of the humvees. Groups of tribesmen came running from different directions to investigate with raised guns.

Eric raised his gun and fired again. Blood spurted from the back of one of the running men's heads, and he fell in an instant. The others scattered, taking cover behind the parked vehicles. One militiaman looked round the side of a humvee and recognised Eric.

Unlike the last time, he wasn't about to ignore him again. He ducked back and shouted at the top of his lungs. More men were coming. Eric fired a series of shots, felling a few more tribesmen, then ran back into the tent and exited through the slit.

◆

Niccolo heard gunfire from his vantage point atop the rocky

escarpment. He had been tracking Eric through the scope until he reached the cluster of tents. Now he was sweeping his sight back and forth, and looked for targets.

He found one. 'Well, well…,' he said as he focused the cross hairs on the man Eric had referred to as Nassar.

Nassar stood with the tribe leader and a few troopers, the latter engaged in an argument with him. The militiamen had jumped up to protect their fellowmen against the sudden attack. 'One of your men shot at us,' the militia leader yelled in his native dialect.

'I don't know what's going on,' Nassar replied, 'but it wasn't us.'

One of the militiamen—the one who had seen Eric—ran towards them. 'I saw him! It was not one of us!' He pointed his finger at Nassar, shoving him in the chest, pushing him back a couple of steps.

The next moment, the militiaman's head blew apart in an explosion of blood and tissue that splashed across the faces of the men all around.

For a while, nobody moved, frozen in shock. Then the guns on both sides came up.

Nassar's goons, better trained, fired first and took down five men in an instant.

But there were more. Rifles blazed as the militiamen fired wildly. Several men went down on both sides. Nassar made a run, the few remaining troopers covering him. The militia leader dived the other way, using his men as shields. 'Get to the humvees!' yelled Nassar.

Niccolo was puzzled at the aftermath of his shot. He tried to track Nassar, but the scene had turned too chaotic. 'Shit!' he mumbled, searching frantically for Eric.

Eric joined Dr Hussein and Marina underneath the humvee. 'This is not what I had planned, but it'll do,' he said in the middle of the AK-47 shots against the clatter of the more modern weapons wielded by Nassar's troopers.

'They're fighting each other!' Dr Hussein remarked.

'But we are right in the middle of all of this—that's the problem!'

Marina shrieked. 'How are we ever going to get out?'

Eric looked over the parked pickups. 'We can borrow one of those.'

There was more gunfire and shouting behind them. Nassar's men were forming a circle. They used the humvees for cover. 'If we could just get to the pickups!' Eric muttered thoughtfully. Then he saw another militiaman running from a tent, carrying a rocket launcher. 'This is the time to try!' They crawled out and ran for the pickups.

Shots whizzed past their heads as a tribesman spotted them. Eric grabbed Marina and dived behind a tent as more bullets tore through the fabric. 'Dr Hussein, stay low!' he yelled as he switched his gun into auto mode. He twisted his upper body to return fire. The spray of bullets almost sliced the gunman.

Then there was a sound close by, the click of a rifle's charging handle. Eric turned to see another militiaman run out from behind one of the pickups, confusion painted all over his face.

Eric flashed his gun, pulled the trigger, and—

An empty click reverberated.

'Shit!'

A vicious smile appeared on the militiaman's face. The next moment, a ragged hole blew open in the middle of his chest as the impact of a 303-rifle bullet slammed him to the ground.

A second later the distant crack of the Lee-Enfield reached Eric's ears. 'Thanks, Niccolo!' he breathed, raising his empty gun in the direction of the hillock in the distance. 'Okay guys, we...' he saw a militiaman hoisting a rocket launcher onto his shoulder, lining it up with the humvees, '...need to get the hell down! *Now!*'

He threw himself onto Marina as the rocket-propelled grenade tore away from the tubular launcher. Dr Hussein was already on the ground. The grenade slammed into one of the humvees, the explosion tearing off its wheels and flipping the vehicle up and over a couple of tents that belonged to Nassar's men. One of the troopers was torn apart by shrapnel, another crushed under the massive 4×4. It came to rest with its smouldering underbelly pointing into the air at an angle, its nose half-buried in a devastated tent. But Eric didn't have time to stop and stare at the devastation. He helped Dr Hussein up and took Marina's hand, then he made his way towards the pickups. Gunfire sounds continued all around, bullets clanging off the humvees and pickups, screams piercing the ambience of the fire-lit night.

Eric crouched lower, coming round a collapsed tent to reach the pickups. He pointed at the one with the Rubik's Cube key chain. 'That's our ride! The Hilux.'

'It's pointing the wrong way!' Marina exclaimed, realising that the pickup stood facing the camp. 'Towards the humvees!'

'Believe me, they solved that problem by inventing steering wheels!' Eric yelled.

Dr Hussein noticed that the tribesmen's attention was focused on Nassar's group. 'No one's watching the fringes of the camp!' he remarked as they reached the first pickup, a rust-stained old Ford. Eric walked round the truck's rear, keeping his eyes on one of the campfires, now abandoned. Waving his companions on, he headed for the remodelled pickup fitted with a machine gun.

A militiaman jumped down from the back of another pickup near the fire, carrying a case of RPG rounds. He saw Eric and shouted out in warning. Dropping the box of ammunition to the ground, he proceeded to take out his AK-47.

Eric fired his Browning, catching the man in his arm. He went spinning in the air and hit one of the petrol cans strapped to the pickup's side. He reeled, mouth open in a silent shriek, and fell right onto the fire in an explosion of flying sparks. The man finally found his voice as he leapt up, clothes and hair ablaze, eyes wide with terror. Four militiamen came around the first pickup with raised guns.

Eric fired again—not at the burning man but at the petrol can. A jet of fuel sluiced from the hole and splashed all over him. The can immediately exploded, liquid fire spilling in all directions. The man flared up from head to toe even as a second can blew up nearby and threw the pickup truck in the air towards the approaching militiamen.

Shielding his face from the heat, Eric reached the Hilux and looked around to see if there were any more militiaman posing a threat.

There was a man near the humvees holding a pin in one hand and a grenade in the other. He raised his hand and was about to throw the grenade at the Hilux, when—

A stray bullet came charging, and his wrist was blown apart. Niccolo's bullet had found its mark. The grenade flung out of his hand and exploded on another humvee, adding more fire to the blazing night.

Eric looked at the pistol in his hand and then at the weapon in the pickup's rear bed. It was an old Kalashnikov PK, a light anti-aircraft gun, loaded with a belt of ammunition.

'Definitely more firepower than a Browning!' he muttered. 'You drive,' he told Dr Hussein and climbed into the back of the Hilux. 'I'll shoot.'

'Drive where?' Dr Hussein asked while helping Marina up into the Hilux. He followed suit and put the engine into ignition.

'I'll let you know once I've shot a hole big enough to fit through,' Eric replied from the back. He swung the gun towards the humvees and pulled the trigger.

High-velocity shots rang out of the Russian gun, streaking across the camp like lasers, but Eric could barely see them through the constant blazes erupting from the muzzle. Tyres of the vehicles bursting and dropping them onto their steel inserts, shattering all the armoured windows, the machine gun created havoc before the ammo belt reached its end, bringing the thundering to an abrupt close. Eric jumped into the driving section through the glassless divider and slid between Marina and Dr Hussein. 'Drive,' he said.

'Which way?'

'Left.'

Dr Hussein released the clutch and the Hilux lurched into

motion, kicking out sand from under its tyres. He turned left, only to find a group of militiamen running towards them. He spun the wheel to the right.

'Don't!' Eric cried. 'The man who destroyed the humvee has reloaded his rocket launcher and is aiming at us—go straight!'

'Bad news!' Dr Hussein said, jamming the accelerator down to the floor. Eric shouted over the noise of the screeching tyres, 'Keep it going, and drive straight—let me take care of that rocket launcher.'

He pulled out his Browning from its holder. Bending his upper body at an angle, he took aim through the broken divider in the back and fired. Dr Hussein couldn't resist finding out what was happening. Out of the corner of his eye he saw Eric's bullet hit the man with the rocket launcher, and the man about to fall into a pool of fire, the launcher dangling from his lifeless shoulder.

Dr Hussein turned back to see a humvee directly ahead. He yelled out and swerved frantically, narrowly missing Nassar. Flaming debris flew all around—tents burning, embers raining from the night sky—and for a moment, Hussein saw a vision of his grandfather fighting against two grey wolves with his dagger. He pressed down on the accelerator and aimed to drive the truck out of the encampment.

'Now?' he asked Eric.

'North-east,' came the reply as Eric pointed towards the escarpment where Niccolo and the SUV waited.

'Who are you?' Marina clutched Eric's shoulder, her eyes wide with wonder.

'A history professor,' Eric replied with a brief nod.

'I had that impression too, until I found out you handle guns like Jack Reacher!'

'Times are bad; single jobs are not enough!' Eric shrugged. 'You need other part-time jobs to survive.'

◆

'Where are we going?' Dr Hussein inquired.

'We'll pick up a friend from that escarpment...'

'And then, the next stop...' Marina punctuated the thought with a pause and added, 'the Tomb of God.'

SIXTY-EIGHT

They drove through the night, crammed into their newly acquired Hilux and one of their two original vehicles while the second one carried Niccolo and the three Salvation troopers behind them. None of the passengers of the two lead vehicles complained about claustrophobia since they all found the body heat of their co-passengers a necessary shield against the freezing cold of the desert night. The road twisted and turned through rocky and barren plains, past ruins of villages that were bulldozed by Saddam.

Father Smit and Eric guided the Hilux and the SUV, while Niccolo drove the third truck across the wilderness. There was no sign of any pursuit by either the tribesmen or Nassar's men. Even so, the going was slow, over treacherous terrain and with a single working headlight to guide them. More than once they had to dig the lead truck out of soft sand that bogged it down.

'I couldn't get any sleep over the last three days, guys, so I would love to grab a nap while you drive. Please don't mind,' Dr Hussein said to no one in particular and closed his eyes.

Hours passed, with Dr Huntley, Dr Hussein and Marina managing to doze off in short spells despite the bumpy ride. They crossed the Great Zab river over a wobbly bridge on the Bujal–Bekhama road and drove steadily north-east through the wasteland to avoid being spotted by any patrolling troops. Hitting the Shanidar–Erbil road, they turned towards the north, once again avoiding the road and driving through rocky terrain.

Despite the steady groan of the engine and the rocky drive,

a strange silence had settled over everything, and Eric found his thoughts wandering into strange places they hadn't been to in years.

Another wilderness from many years ago; his small team was moving through a mountainous region in Turkey. They were on a recce, and Harvinder 'Harry' Bhatia, one of his team members, was walking ahead of him when a particularly thin strip of stone cracked beneath Harry's feet, pulling him inside a deep, narrow gorge with a whoosh. The faint thud took several moments to reach Eric's ears. But Harry's right forearm, wrist and hand lay in front of Eric's eyes, clinging onto a crack in the stone, still trembling from the shock. On his dismembered wrist was the Seiko his dad had gifted him when he had graduated from high school. Harry always had it set to New Delhi time, so it read five-fifty in the evening even as the harsh afternoon sun blazed overhead. Eric couldn't push away the thought—that Harry was dead, but his watch was still telling the time. Harry's dad would, at the very moment, be sitting down with his evening tea on the balcony of their Paschim Vihar apartment in Delhi, and he was dead in the Turkish wilderness, and the Seiko still worked... It was all there, but none of it fit together.

Then he remembered sitting next to his girlfriend Kuhu's bed in a Kolkata hospital on another sun-soaked morning, holding her hand in his...and then feeling the life go out of her in an instant, like a sad beginning to a rejected love letter tossed into a waste paper basket. Huddled up in the navigator's seat of a battered pickup truck, travelling in search of an unknown place, Eric felt his tears beginning to fall for her, and for Harvinder 'Harry' Bhatia...and he realised he hadn't cried for a very long time.

♦

By the time Father Smit stopped to refuel the Hilux from one of the battered jerry-cans of fuel they carried up on the SUV's roof, the moon was directly above their heads. The third truck pulled up on the side of their pickup.

'Okay,' Eric began, throwing the empty can back onto the carrier and tapping Aurin on his shoulder, 'now that we can see things, let's work out where we are.' He looked at the GPS and surveyed the surrounding desert for landmarks, then looked up to find the misty outline of the Zagros Mountains over the north-eastern horizon. 'Give me the rifle.'

Niccolo dragged a Barrett M82 semi-automatic rifle from the back of the truck. It was fitted with a Leupold Mark 4 scope. Eric noticed the rifle looked new and in much better condition than the Lee-Enfield they had used the previous evening. He wrung his hands in disgust. 'You always had this? Why did you take the Enfield then?' Niccolo shrugged, handing the gun over, and slid himself into the front seat. Eric peered through the scope, scanning the horizon. Distant shapes resolved themselves into distinct mountain tops under the pale yellow moonlight.

'Okay, I see one…no, two weird mountain peaks,' Eric noted. 'One of them has a bizarre cliff-like shape… We are not too far from our destination!' he announced, handing the rifle to Aurin.

Aurin followed Eric's direction. The nocturnal landscape that materialised in front of his eye through the scope blew his mind. The two mountain tops Eric had mentioned were some forty–fifty kilometres away, and for some unknown reason, the odd-looking cliff gleamed like a well-photoshopped picture.

'The first one's where Shanidar Cave is located, and the taller one behind that is our destination,' Eric said as Aurin silently handed the rifle to Father Smit. Still amazed by the mind-blowing nocturnal scene, he knew why his big brother hadn't said anything while handing the scope over. Because that was the moment where the magic lay, and he wanted Aurin to experience it first-hand. He didn't utter a word to describe the miracle he saw, because he knew any kind of hint would destroy the whole effect. He knew now why Eric always said, 'It's the grandeur of the adventure that makes everything look larger-than-life; people are just a small part of it.'

Father Smit smiled with the scope attached to one of his eyes. 'This is why we are born. This is why we live!' He placed the rifle on the roof of the truck and closed his eyes. 'Our souls do not speak the human language,' he whispered, 'and they don't need to, for they communicate with us through signs, visions, poetry, music, intuition and magic like this.'

'Life is beautiful with a blessed B!' Aurin muttered into the chilly night air.

SIXTY-NINE

The eastern sky was starting to brighten up. A flock of birds flew across the horizon. Eric stood on a rock on the bank of the Zab river and stared up at the enormous cliff. The sky above was dark. Wisps of translucent clouds drifted past faint hints of stars. A soft morning breeze stroked his face, whipping strands of hair back over his ears, and he felt, almost to his surprise, that after a very long time he was…happy.

The top of the cliff was at least three kilometres above ground, invisible from where their small team stood. Vegetation clung to the mountainside for only the first five hundred metres or so, beyond which it was an unclimbable wall of stiff rock. Eric, Aurin, Father Smit, Marina, Dr Hussein and Niccolo, along with the Salvation troopers, stood there looking up, spellbound for several moments.

'Let's gear up, guys! Pack all your stuff: guns, ropes, knives, compasses, flashlights and, of course, coffee—which we're going to need a lot of. It's going to be tough.' Eric looked around at everyone. 'Anything else anyone can think of that we might need?'

'Just some luck!' Father Smit said, casting an intimidated look at the glowing cliff.

◆

They had reached the foothills of the Shanidar Cave two hours before. Since it was the last motorable point on their arduous journey, they decided to set up camp there and leave Dr Huntley behind to take some rest. They also had to leave the vehicles, along with a Salvation trooper, to guard the camp. From there, they continued on foot with necessary equipment, weapons and some supplies in their knapsacks. Like always, Dr Hussein refused to leave his heavy backpack behind and carried it along, strapped to his shoulders.

'Why didn't we ever read anything about this magnificent cliff, Ric da?' Aurin asked.

'You mean about the fact that it glows, right?'

'Yes.'

'This is not a very uncommon phenomenon, actually,' Eric said. 'Zinc and sulphur are found in many rock formations. In its natural form, it occurs as a white or yellow patch on the rock, but when the substance is exposed to light, it stores energy and re-emits it at a slower pace and a lower frequency, giving rise to the glow you see when you turn out the lights.'

'Adding silver as an activator also produces blue illumination,' said Father Smit. 'And, because of the moonlit glow, it's actually common for several ancient cultures around the world to think that these kinds of places belong to the Moon God,' he finished with a theatrical hand gesture.

'Now let us find a way up to the top,' Eric said, scanning the surroundings.

Soon he found a narrow path curving upwards around the cliff. Apart from mountain goats and the occasional wolf, it looked unlikely that any human had used the path in a long time. Yet, the setting of stones on the path forced them to believe it had probably been made by ancient men. Shortly, the team began ascending the narrow trail.

'What an unrestful place!' Father Smit huffed as he climbed. 'Many of the places we passed along the road so far were autonomous regions of the Iraqi Kurdistan and are quite populated. But in the last few decades, this place has developed into one of the most violent hubs of the Middle East. In the eighties, Saddam Hussein targeted the centre of an ethnic Kurdish belt that extended from eastern Turkey to western Iran in an effort to stamp out a series of rebellions. He razed nearly 4,000 Kurdish villages to the ground, slaughtering over 50,000 civilians. And then, in 1991, Saddam's forces drove hundreds of thousands of Kurds across the mountains into Turkey.' He shuddered.

'Yes, I think President Bush was the one to demand the withdrawal of Iraq's troops,' Eric said, 'which later helped the Kurds form an autonomous government. It was only after the US invasion of Iraq in 2003 that the Kurds began to develop their own economy.'

'We are the human race; destruction and killing comes easy to us,' Aurin smiled.

◆

The cliff they climbed was not only enormous in height but also in its circumference. As they trudged along on the path, they calculated that the base of the cliff was easily ten kilometres around. Eric suddenly turned towards Father Smit, who was right behind him, and chimed, 'Prehistoric upthrust! Looks like this place is over three-and-a-half billion years old.' But Eric had to let the words hang mid-air, incomplete, as he detected a strange buzzing sound in his ear.

SEVENTY

Something was buzzing inside Eric's head. It was such a bizarre experience that he startled into an abrupt halt. Moments later, the sound got clearer and he heard someone talking inside his head.

'Eric, can you hear me? Please say something if you can!' a familiar voice said.

'Yes, I can...who is this...and what the hell is this?'

'Suleiman here! It's a life-and-death situation, Eric, and I badly need your help. In return, I can help you find the tomb you are looking for!'

'What is it now, Mr Triple Agent!' Eric said exasperatedly.

'For God's sake, you need to believe me, Eric; my children and wife have been held captive by Delfino and Nassar all through the last few months, forcing me to offer my services in return for their lives. They are still captives of these two ruthless thugs. Now please, listen up. As you guys went up the cliff, Nassar's group stormed in, killed your guard, seized your camp and was on the verge of killing Dr Huntley when I reached the scene. I could somehow save him, but he is unconscious. In the combat, I was shot and am bleeding badly. Dr Huntley and I are hiding in the Shanidar Cave.' Suleiman breathed heavily.

'Is this true?'

'Yes, Eric, all of it is true,' Suleiman panted. 'I'll help you find the tomb and the relic you are looking for. But I need you to save my life.'

'Tell me, how did you reach here?'

'I've been tracking you on Delfino's instructions with the help of the same device through which I am talking to you right now.'

'What do you want from me?' Eric pursed his lips.

'In eight to nine hours, I will die of bleeding,' Suleiman pleaded. 'I want to live, Eric...only to see my wife and children once again. Please help me!'

'What do you know about this place? And what do you know about the Tomb of God?' Eric asked. 'And how?'

'All you need to know for now is that I am a scholar and have worked with The Society of Biblical History, a secret wing of Mossad.'

'I *thought* you were a military washout,' Eric said, 'judging by your ways.'

'I did have the finest military training, thanks to the Mossad,' Suleiman whispered. 'Boy, you're a smart-ass, and the best I've ever known. But Eric, you are too emotional... And believe me, I am banking on that one trait of yours at this moment.'

'Wow! I never thought I'd ever meet a foe I'd be able to quote in my biography!' Eric scoffed.

Suleiman ignored the jibe, for he had little time. 'There are two more things you should know,' he said. 'One, I had secretly planted this chip behind your right ear when Delfino got you in Udine, because Allah knows I wanted to tell you everything at some point in time. It also helped me eavesdrop on everything you discussed with your people. Two, I stole the second clue from Delfino as my insurance. That was Luigi Tessitori's complete write-up on the *Ramcharitmanas* page he'd stolen from the museum long back...' Suleiman cleared his throat.

'But Sid has retrieved it from Delfino's online repository.'

'What Sid Patel has retrieved is not even half of it. That's why you missed a significant part of the final clue. And...' Suleiman paused, 'I was also the one who got the tablet stolen from the British Museum and deciphered the key of all keys to this mystery.'

'Key of all keys? What do you mean?'

'The most important pieces of this enormous puzzle, that I hold now, are from that single tablet Dr Layard had discovered some hundred and seventy years ago.'

'What is it, Suleiman?'

'There was a metal tablet hidden inside the clay casing. The metal tablet had a message etched in cuneiform with directions to the tomb and the relic. The killing of the secretary in the museum wasn't part of the plan, though.'

'That means you know what the relic is?' Eric exclaimed.

'Yes, but before I tell you that, you need to promise me that you'll help me!'

'Let me tell you one thing, Suleiman. I will help you anyway. Even if this turns out to be a trap, I'll still go ahead and try my best to help...you know why?'

'No, I don't.'

'Because you've reached out to me for help. We'll talk about the relic or whatever it is later.' He breathed for a while, mentally checking off all his options. 'At this moment, you tell me how I should go about it. I want Dr Huntley to be safe, and I also want to help you. Can we just climb down and come to you?'

'No, Eric, you can't! You have come too far on your journey... you need to finish it and gather your blessings from the Moon God Nanna and his son. Where are you right now?'

'I am trying to locate the hidden entrance to get into the cavern mentioned in one of the tablets we found.'

'Call out to me whenever you need help with something. Until then, you carry on, Eric, I need to check how Dr Huntley's doing. Over and out.'

It took the group over two hours of trekking up the narrow pathway around the mountain before Eric and Father Smit identified a large boulder almost blocking their way that looked out of place. Eric had already briefed the team about his chat with Suleiman. It had been an embarrassing scene, as everyone had seen him talking, yet no one knew whom he was talking to and how.

Covered in thick vegetation, the place around the boulder was damp. It was nearly three hundred feet above the ground. The boulder was enveloped in creepers and mosses that seemed to have gathered over the course of several millennia.

'Matches the description Dr Tracy gave of the entrance to the cavern, doesn't it?' Father Smit said.

'Absolutely!' Eric exclaimed. 'This looks like our door number one to the Tomb of God.'

'Let's check it out,' Aurin went ahead and started clearing out the creepers behind the boulder. But it was Niccolo who, with the butt of his rifle, cleared the final mass of dirt and plants before they found a narrow gap to pass through. The gap led them into a dark passage. It was so dark that the group felt like walking with paper bags over their heads.

Niccolo switched his flashlight on to find the passage broadening ahead. After another few metres' walk, the darkness softened, and they saw a hint of daylight. Till that moment, no one could have imagined where they were about to enter.

'*Santa Maria!*' Niccolo shouted.

'Out of this freaking world,' Marina whispered, looking up towards the roof of the cave. Even the entrance had suddenly surpassed cathedral-like proportions to reveal a towering arch four or five hundred feet high and half a football field across. A tinge of yellow mixed with the dust particles suspended in the air as little rays of sunlight tried penetrating the darkness through cracks in the gigantic cave wall. But mostly it was dark and dreary inside, like an omen carried in by an evil wind. They discovered that the cave itself was twenty times the width of the entrance, and the roof, barely visible, at least two thousand feet above their heads.

Eric instantly thought that the enormous cave was large enough to land several helicopters. A gurgling sound of a waterfall reverberated through the thick air. The group saw, towards the far end of the unbelievably large space, a waterfall dropping down out of the darkness. The water's half-a-kilometre-high fall turned into a silken mist as it hit the cavern floor, feeding a chain of small lakes joined together like pearls on a string by a wide bubbling stream.

There was something menacing about this place, so real that Eric found himself wishing he had a powerful automatic gun with him, more powerful than the Tomcat or the Norinco rifle. On his numerous archaeological trips to Egypt, Afghanistan and Turkey, he'd seen some really dangerous places, but this was different. Somehow he knew that stepping into that cavern was like stepping off the edge of the known world and that once inside, he might never find his way out again. Eric suddenly remembered something his grandfather often said to him, *Don't play with the devil, he always cheats.* He didn't remember who had originally said the words, but the thought was so strong, it had stayed in the back of his mind. Even till this day.

'The Garden of Eden!' Dr Hussein muttered.

'No! I think there is more to it than this; this can't be the Garden of Eden. Eden can't be a stuffy, smelly place like this.'

'I agree with you, Ric da,' Aurin said, taking a few steps forward, 'it looks like the source of this fall is elsewhere.'

Eric walked towards the fall and knocked on his temple thrice with his index finger as he said, 'We are here in the cavern, Suleiman— it's literally gigantic, and there's a waterfall pouring in a chain of lakes at the far end of this place. My trail ends here, and I am not very happy about it, because this place is a stinking dump of a cave!'

'Eric, believe me, there is more to it. You can't imagine what lies ahead.'

'Why don't you tell me then, Suleiman?'

'How large is the cave?'

'Eight or nine full-size football fields wide.'

'Think about the perimeter of the cliff you just trekked, Eric. Your cave should have been much larger than this; have you considered that?'

'Yes, you are right, Suleiman. What we have here has to be less than half of it. But we were expecting steps to take us up, and we see none here. I need to figure out what to do now!'

'Check if there is any vegetation around.'

'There isn't.'

'Around the lakes?'

'No, only moss.'

'Go closer to the fall and look up around it; see if you can find a way up.'

Eric led the group along the inner perimeter of the cave for a thousand feet or so, bypassing huge, sharp-edged boulders and long tongues of scree that had fallen from the roof perhaps millions of years ago.

Marina touched Eric's shoulder. 'There,' she said, pointing to a pile of rocks and boulders. 'Up there!'

They looked up to find a dark spiralling shadow that seemed to run up the entire height of the cave. As she stepped closer, Marina's eyes widened. 'That can't be the way up! No way!'

'It *is* the way, I am afraid,' Eric answered, scanning the area. The 'way up' was a chimney-like narrow cleft in the rock. It had been pegged with narrow slabs of rock pushed into deep cracks in the walls, and where there were no pegs, there were rickety lengths of stone-crafted stairs. 'Thanks, Suleiman, you've shown us the way! I'll be in touch. Stay strong till we reach you.'

'Roger that,' Suleiman chuckled.

'Over and out,' Eric talked back to his head.

◆

'The Serpent's Throat!' Father Smit exclaimed in awe.

The whole thing looked like a single curling strand of DNA rising up into nothingness. At the base of the stairs, there was a bubbling pool of bright yellow mud. It smelled foul, like hundreds of rotten eggs had been left there to fester.

'Sulphur dioxide,' noted Father Smit. 'We smelled a diluted version of this thing when we entered the cave.'

'Do we have to climb that now?' Marina asked, her voice shaking.

'It's already noon, and we could have taken rest here,' said Eric, 'but we all know Dr Huntley and Suleiman are injured and need our help—we need to do it now.'

'Is there any way to avoid the smell as we climb?' Marina crinkled her nose.

'Climb as fast as you can,' Aurin giggled.

SEVENTY-ONE

Count Delfino, robed in his favourite silk dressing gown, sat at the breakfast table in one of his many luxury apartments in Udine, overlooking the Piazza di Spagna, the Spanish Steps, while Major Bill

Robins sat opposite, enjoying a cup of strong Italian coffee. Scrambled eggs, bacon and freshly baked croissants lay heaped on ornate trays between the two men as Delfino had decided to finish this meeting over breakfast.

Delfino folded his copy of *Messaggero Veneto* and set the newspaper down beside his cup of coffee. Bill poured more coffee for them both, then tore a flaky croissant in half and slathered each piece with butter and the tart fig balsamic jam he loved.

'How bad is it?' Delfino began.

'Worse than we could have imagined.'

'Tell me about it!'

'Everything about this project has gone out of control.' Bill chewed on a piece of cornetto, then wiped his mouth with a paper napkin and said, 'We've lost all contact with Eric Roy, Dr Hussein and everyone we wanted to track. The last time they were seen was in Windsor. Then we lost track of them.'

'What about the miniature GPS tracker we had planted on Eric's body?'

'No signal from that as per last night's report.' Bill grimaced.

'Is it Suleiman? Is he playing us?'

'Don't know. I never could gauge that guy,' Bill shrugged. 'Anything from your other sources?' He took a long sip of his coffee.

'Yes, of course, I have a backup plan as always.' Delfino smiled wickedly. 'I have someone keeping a track of everything. When the time comes, we will strike.'

Someone knocked at their door.

'Who's it?'

'It's Angelo, Signor.'

'Come in,' Delfino called out. 'Do you have something important?'

'Yes, Signor, I need to show you something.' With these words, a square-faced man in his mid-fifties entered the room.

Nodding in approval, Delfino lit a cigar with his Zippo and took a sip from a silver flask that contained tea-flavoured vodka.

Angelo switched on a giant screen built into the wall with a remote handset.

'What are we dealing with here?' Delfino asked.

'Your favourite, agent X, has finally patched us up with a satellite, Signor. It looks like some people have found something.'

'That's wonderful!' Delphino smiled, 'Yes, X is the best!'

'There's been some concentrated effort in the Zagros Mountains of Iraq, Signor.'

'Show me,' instructed Delfino, 'I'd like to know who is crashing my party.' He smiled in excitement.

The huge screen instantly switched from idle mode to a satellite image of the Zagros Mountain Range. The man zoomed in on a large area of dull green and grey with a fist-sized patch of red in the centre. Patterns of dark blue ran through the entire frame.

'What am I looking at?'

'An infra red image of an area about fifteen miles across, with Shanidar Cave at the centre.'

'The red is Roy's group?'

'Yes, Count.'

'How many?'

'Seven or eight, maybe more,' he replied. 'They are inside a cave or something, making it tough for the satellite to track them.'

'Excellent!'

'What is your order, Signor?'

'Contact Nassar and ask him about his hired guns. You know what the aim is.'

'Right, Signor.' Angelo left the room.

Delfino smiled. 'It's getting interesting now. Get ready, Bill, you need to move your ass!'

'What about Nassar then?'

'I don't trust him. Thugs like him aren't loyal to anyone—they only work for their own benefit.'

'Who is Agent X?'

Delfino looked at Bill squarely and said, 'Well, now I can safely say you've ruined my morning.' He rolled his eyes. 'Bill, need I remind you this is the twenty-first century? And in this century, anonymity is a rare commodity. Something to be protected. Something to be valued. Now move your butt, will you?'

♦

The entire group gathered by the Serpentine Throat, as Father Smit called it. Light inside the cave had reduced drastically. 'The sun has risen over the top of the mountain, beyond the cracks in the wall,' Eric remarked. 'We should use our flashlights.'

'Let's do this,' Marina announced, taking one out of her knapsack for herself. 'The longer we wait, the more nervous I'll get.' She shone the light upwards, but the beam failed to hit anything. It faded away in its search for the roof.

'Shhh! Wait a minute,' Father Smit said. 'I have a bad feeling.' He crouched and brought his ear close to the ground. 'I hear a rumble... guys, please step back a few feet from the messy pool.'

'Why?' Marina asked, not willing to let anything lessen her resolve. 'Let's climb up!'

'Wait, I say!' Father Smit rebuked her. 'Something bad is about to happen...I have a feeling.'

As if on cue, there was a low rumbling from the ground beneath their feet. The noise reverberated through the cave, ebbing and flowing like a tide. It continued for about a minute, then the sulphur pool at the foot of the rock funnel began to boil.

'What the hell...!'

A gout of ulcerous mud rose fifty feet into the air, steam hissing as it shot up. There was another deeper-rooted explosion under their feet, and the sulphur mud became white-hot steam that rose higher and higher within the chamber, until it subsided a few seconds later. The raging came to an abrupt end, leaving behind no sign that anything had happened.

'We would certainly have been killed,' Dr Hussein said.

'You're right. Now we should wait for the steps to cool down and dry before we begin our climb,' Eric said.

'Can it happen again while we climb?' Niccolo inquired.

'There is no way to tell,' Father Smit replied.

'Either we stay here, or we take our chances,' Eric declared. 'No one has to follow, but I sure am going up to the top.'

'I am coming with you, Ric da,' Aurin followed.

'Me too,' Father Smit raised his hand.

'Glad to have company.' Eric smiled.

'Well, you're certainly not leaving us behind,' Marina said, clutching Dr Hussein's elbow and pulling him forward.

'I can think of no better way to die than seeking entrance to the heavens, and if not that, I would very much like to see where God chose to sleep,' Father Smit grinned. And they all proceeded to climb up the wall.

Initially, the climb was fairly tough, with everyone feeling as if they were hard-boiled eggs left for too long in a pot of hot water. But it became progressively tougher with the increase in altitude, especially on the rickety stairs where there were no pegs. On one such unsteady stair, an unexpected buzz in his ear caught Eric off-guard, and he almost lost his grip. He wasn't really expecting a buzz from Suleiman, but even more surprisingly, the thing in his head had a different voice this time. Barely had Eric managed to steady himself when it rang in his ear.

'This is Sid Patel, Chief, can you hear me?'

◆

'What the...' Eric was afraid of losing his grip again, so he steadied himself before continuing, '...hell is this, Sid?'

'I have been scanning through frequencies for all kinds of communications in this region. Thanks to my stars, you spoke to Suleiman, and I got you.'

'Sid, it's a life-and-death situation out here!'

'I am sure it is, Chief! But I have good news to deliver.'

'I and seven other people are dangling midway between heaven and hell, and you offer me *news*, that too in my freaking head! I could have slipped and died!'

'I had to inform you about one thing, Chief. There are movements close to you. At least fifty people have gathered around with high-end ammo. Please operate with extra care. And let me know when you need the next key. Because I think I have it.'

♦

The ascent took more than an hour, and their lungs were aching by the time they reached the topmost peg. The roof of the cave was still not in view, but there was a long five-foot-wide ledge on the wall where all of them could park and stretch their tired bodies.

On the ledge, they came face to face with a door. Carved out of the rock in the wall, nine feet in height and six feet across, the giant door had beautiful plants and floral motifs carved on it, in addition to a few human and celestial figures. The carvings on the door were so intricate and fine, it seemed as if the artist had just finished the job some minutes back and would be back any moment with his chisel and hammer to marvel at his work. But there was something beyond the beauty of the carvings that bothered Eric.

'I have seen this floral motif and this plant somewhere!'

'The concept of a "tree of life" has been used in several ancient civilisations and contexts,' Father Smit said.

'Please enlighten me on this, Father Smit,' said Aurin. 'We aren't going anywhere until we find the switch of the calling bell.'

'In philosophy, in mythology, in biology and in religion— particularly Indo-European, Siberian and Native American religions,' Father Smit said, resting his back against the wall, 'a tree of life is a common motif. The term "tree of life" is also linked with the concept of "knowledge". These two kinds of cosmic trees are portrayed in various religions and philosophies as the same. The Tree of

Knowledge, connecting heaven and the underworld, and the Tree of Life, connecting all forms of creation.'

'That's right,' Dr Hussein said, probing the edges of the door with his fingers and then pushing against the stone with his shoulder. 'But how do we open this...?' He breathed heavily, but it did not budge, and he walked back, shrugging. 'As you know, the Tree of the Knowledge of Good and Evil is one of the two trees in the story of the Garden of Eden in Genesis 2-3, the other being the Tree of Life. A cylinder seal, known as the temptation seal, from post-Akkadian Mesopotamia...'

'Which is?' Aurin interrupted.

'The post-Akkadian period in Mesopotamia was between the twenty-third and twenty-second centuries BC, and the temptation seal I just mentioned has been linked to the Adam and Eve story,' Dr Hussein clarified.

'I remember from my second-year papers,' Marina added, rubbing the back of her neck, 'Assyriologist George Smith had described the seal as having two figures, male and female, seated on each side of a tree facing each other, holding out their hands towards the fruit, while between them is a serpent.'

'Right,' Dr Hussein nodded in agreement, 'the temptation seal is evidence that the account of the fall of man was known in early times in Babylonia.'

'Specific world tree names are pretty interesting actually,' Eric said. 'Világfa in Hungarian mythology, Ağaç Ana in Turkic mythology, Modun in Mongolian, Yggdrasil in Germanic and Scandinavian, the Oak in Slavic and Finnish mythology, and in Hindu mythology there are Mruthasanjeevani and Kalpa-Vriksh. Mruthasanjeevani is believed to have brought people back from near-death to life.' Niccolo pulled Eric by his arm as he was finishing his trivia session and got him to shoulder-butt the huge stone. Again, nothing happened.

'And as per the Ramayana,' Aurin continued, 'this is the plant that saved Ram's brother Lakshman when he was hit with an arrow by Ravan's son Meghnad and had fallen into a state of near-death.

Hanuman approached the Lankan royal physician Sushena for advice. Sushena asked Hanuman to rush to Dronagiri Hills and fetch four plants: Mruthasanjeevani, the restorer of life; Vishalyakarani, the remover of poison; Sandhanakarani, the restorer of skin and Savarnyakarani, the restorer of skin colour.' He looked around at everyone and added, 'Hanuman, not able to pick the four from the multitude, brought back the entire hill. And Lakshman was revived from near-death and brought back to life.'

'But this is not a tree!' Marina exclaimed. 'This is a mere sapling!'

'Did you just say *sapling*, Marina?' Eric arched an eyebrow.

'Yes, Eric, I just did,' Marina grinned. 'It's not a swear word, I presume?'

'Oh my! How could I be this stupid! *A sapling!*' Eric punched into his palm. 'Thanks, Aurin.' He nodded at his brother. 'Yes, that's a sapling, and now I remember where I have seen it!'

'Where?' Marina asked, stepping forward to take a good look at the ancient door.

'In a pyramid somewhere in the north-eastern deserts of Iraq,' Eric replied, 'not very far from this region.' He scratched his stubble, his mind somewhere else. 'These artworks are very similar to the ones I had seen in the tomb of Kudur Mabug and Warad-Sin in the Iraqi desert. Similar not just in style but also in form. I think *sapling* was the word I had in mind when I found those murals...the word and the visual were tagged in my memory together.'

On closer inspection, they found twenty panels of carvings on the door, and almost all of them had the sapling. Some showed a God-like figure handing over the plant to an authoritative-looking man, while others depicted a naval voyage like the one Eric had seen in the desert tomb.

SEVENTY-TWO

More than once, Eric had been in places where he had felt the past and present occupy the same space and time: at the Cellular Jail in the Andamans, where you could almost hear the echoing footsteps of the British guards in their heeled boots and the shrieks of the inmates; or in the remote forest called Belleau Wood in Picardy, in the north of France, where the soil had been fertilised with the blood of ten thousand US Marines and an undetermined number of their German adversaries.

Back in the cave, he wondered what waited for them on the other side of the door. And then his head began buzzing again.

'Where are you, Chief?' Sid Patel's voice came on.

'We have reached a door we can't figure out how to open.'

'None of your clues match?'

'We never had any clue pointing to a closed door made of solid stone.'

'I think I can help.'

'What? How can you help us, Sid? You are not even in the same country, let alone region!'

'Chief, please do me a favour and check if Dr Hussein is still carrying his backpack.'

'Yes, I can see him carrying it right now. He refuses to part with that backpack for some goddamn reason.'

'Good that he does, because the key to this door is in his backpack.'

'Okay...'

'You need to play one of the tablets.'

'Sid? We could play two of them but not the third one. We tried all the ways we possibly could to play it.'

'Yes, Chief, Dr Tracy told me that yesterday when I finally could connect with her. Let me tell you, you couldn't play it because this one needed a special player.'

'Balancing on a stone ledge hundreds of feet above the ground, how do you suggest we build that special player to play this tablet?'

'You don't need to build anything, Chief,' Sid said calmly, 'as I had slipped it into Dr Hussein's backpack before I snuck out of Dr Tracy's house during the raid.'

'What do you mean?'

'I mean the replica ship is the special player that can play this tablet. You remember, they came together?'

Eric's eyes widened. 'Yes...yes, I remember...Dr Hussein found both of them in a vessel. But how do we play it?'

'The mast is fitted on a one-inch-tall base. I think the mast will come out, leaving behind a spinner at the base. Now if you'll look at the odd-looking tiller and its handle-like radar end, you will realise that the handle is designed to actually run the spinner...'

'Where's the pin?' Eric interrupted, unable to digest what he was hearing.

'I think the bottom tip of the upper section of the mast might act as a pin. You will figure it out when you unscrew and free the upper part of the mast from its base...and make sure you play the pictogram side of the tablet.'

'Stay on the line...let me check if this works.'

◆

They all crouched around the model ship on the ledge in front of the ancient door. The small ship rested on a mid-sized boulder that came in handy as a table. To their collective surprise, with a couple of twists and turns and a few spins by Eric's trained hands, the mast loosened on its base, leaving only a little portion attached to the deck. Hanging by a handful of thin gold wires that held it up from both sides of the upper deck, the lower end of the mast now looked like the nib of a pen. 'The pin that will replay the recording...!' Marina whispered in awe.

Holding the round-shaped tablet like a CD, Dr Hussein placed it on the base section of the mast. The hole at the centre of the tablet perfectly fit the base of the mast, and the tablet finely settled in its place. Eric then held the dangling pin-end of the mast and positioned the needle gently against the tablet's circular groove—the one at the edge.

'We need to spin it with the handle now,' Dr Hussein said.

'Right,' Eric nodded, taking hold of the jutting section of the radar with two fingers of his right hand.

'Let's rotate it!' Father Smit reached out to touch Eric's shoulder.

'Where is the speaker cone?' Aurin looked around him frantically.

'Look at the top section of the mast,' Father Smit said. 'It's much broader than its base and hollow as well.'

'Let's find out what message has awaited us in this tablet for over four millennia,' Eric smiled in anticipation.

Closing his eyes, Eric concentrated all his mental energy on those two fingers and slowly rotated the handle of the radar.

The handle only moved fractionally, still jammed from disuse, but the tablet on the base of the mast creaked in unison. They were linked for sure.

Eric turned the wheel again. 'I hope we get the right speed...'

'The electric screwdriver did well, actually,' Aurin remarked.

Eric turned the handle, spinning it at what he thought was roughly the right speed. An unpleasant scraping noise came from somewhere inside the model ship.

'That was how the blackboard of my sixth-grade classroom sounded ever so often,' Aurin grinned.

'Hold on.' Eric adjusted the needle and spun the handle again. This time, it worked. A slurred, uneven voice came from the mouth of the figurehead of Nanna, the Moon God.

'We probably need to go faster!' Father Smit cried, remembering their earlier experience with the tablets.

'Okay,' Eric spun the wheel faster, waiting for the next words to emerge.

But no words were uttered.

What came from the mouth of Nanna was more likely a hymn. Eric kept turning the handle. The hymn was a long series of ascending and descending notes sung by a group of people, now distorted by the variations in speed due to manual rotation.

Time stood still inside the strange mountain cavern as everyone listened to the chorus belonging to a different era. The volume of the sound increased gradually, the ancient voices touched the next octave, then suddenly dropped before rising again. The chorus reverberated against the visible and invisible walls around them. Then it stopped. It was a beautiful piece, yet somehow left the group a little unsettled.

The very next moment, there was a sharp metallic click. They looked around but couldn't find the source of the sound.

'What was that?' Marina whispered.

'I am not sure about the click, but I heard something similar to the hymn in a Spielberg film, *Close Encounters of the Third Kind*—the five-note theme, to be precise!' Aurin chuckled.

Before anyone could comment, there was a loud creak behind them. Everyone turned in unison to see the heavy stone door moving. Very slowly, the door slid into the wall on their right.

◆

'How the hell did you figure this out, Sid?' Eric asked, his mind reeling from the sudden turn of events.

'I told you I'm a smart-ass nerd. Do you remember, I had photographed all of our findings at Dr Tracy's residence in Windsor?'

'Yes, and then you vanished.'

Sid sounded amused. 'Their primary target was you, Chief...and my advantage was that I had already checked out all the exit points before entering the house.'

'That was smart!'

'I knew that wherever they took you, if I were out, I would be able to track you down and connect.'

'Great work, Sid. Now tell us, how did you figure out the key? We anyway need to wait until the dust settles in the doorway.'

'The next day I flew back to India. Back in my office, I scrutinised the photographs of the model ship using a 3D software. The first thing that struck me as odd was the dismantling mechanism of the mast at its base. I calculated the diameter of the base and of the centre hole of the round tablet; they were just made for each other.' Sid began to speak faster. 'My next discovery was the uncanny similarity between the radar end of the model ship and the handles of early manual record players. I tried checking the hole the radar jutted out from and could see hints of a watch-like mechanism inside. The rest was just guesswork.'

'Intelligent guesswork, Sid. I appreciate your enthusiasm. You are one hell of a smart nerd!'

'Thanks, Chief,' Sid said softly. 'I believe all the three tablets can be played on this small ship. And they all could open this door, because from their pictures I could see they all have these fine grooves on one side—five in count, and finer than the main playing-side grooves of the tablets…that's probably why you missed them!' He paused and added, 'There's one more thing…'

'Yes, Sid?'

'I had also left a zip-pouch in Dr Hussein's bag containing three sets of high-end satellite comm earplugs. As you're entering the unknown, I request three of you to wear the plugs so that I can track and communicate with you.'

'That's a good idea, Sid. I think Father Smit, Aurin and I can wear the earpieces—just make sure whenever you talk, you do so gently as there's already another comm system lodged in my head.' He said, gesturing to Dr Hussein to check his bag for something that didn't belong to him.

SEVENTY-THREE

Through the shifting dust that had gathered over four thousand years, they saw glimpses of what lay on the other side of the door. Everyone stood staring, mesmerised, bodily numb.

Eric took a couple of minutes before he remembered to share Sid's warning about the armed men following them with the others. He finally did and added, 'We do not have much time; let's quickly find out what awaits us on the other side of this door!'

'If we don't find another way out of here, we'll be trapped inside when the army gathering below arrive,' Dr Hussein pointed out.

'We don't want to wait here for them; let's go!' Father Smit said, taking a decisive step towards the doorway. A dusty darkness lurked inside. 'Please get me a flashlight,' he said. Aurin tossed his torch to Father Smit, who caught it and switched it on, leaning forward into the opening. All he could make out beyond the door was that the cave went deeper into the rock for some distance.

Not a cave. The shape was too regular. *A tunnel...*

'It's man-made!' he announced, excited. He bent to duck through the doorway over the rubble. 'Come on, there's a way through!'

'Wait,' Eric called, but Father Smit had already scrambled inside.

Followed by Aurin and Dr Hussein, Eric made a dash for the doorway, while Father Smit was a little ahead, picking his way down the tunnel through heaped stones and debris.

'Check it out,' he said, shining his light around. The tunnel was taller than it was wide, some ten feet at its broadest.

'Holy cow!' Aurin whispered.

As the beam of the flashlight moved around, it revealed enormous panoramas on both their sides. The walls were adorned with brilliant relief work capturing what looked like a mountain range, a cliff, a giant cascading waterfall and vegetation, all down to the minutest detail. Every climber, every plant, every leaf, every flower, every rock came alive on the walls, not only due to fine stone craftsmanship but also a fantastic use of colours like greens and ochres, blues and whites and vibrant yellows. The magnificent arc of the rainbow over the waterfall dropping into a foaming canyon—it was as perfect as a photograph.

'These artworks are nothing short of masterpieces...' Aurin mumbled, '...perfect lifescapes at the entrance to the Garden of Eden...' He let the last part of his sentence hang in the air.

'Also perfect dream scapes for the sleeping God. Beautiful enough to make him stay on earth till eternity!' Eric leaned in to survey some of the artwork.

The tunnel ahead curved towards the right. 'It must lead to the hidden part of the cliff...the other two-thirds of it,' Eric thought to himself.

Father Smit bounded across the entrance, with Eric at his heels and Aurin jogging after both of them. 'Slow down, Father! You don't know what's down there!'

'And I won't until I see for myself, will I?' he called after him. 'Eric, pardon my enthusiasm, it's just...it's the Garden of Eden we are about to witness! If it's real, if it's down this tunnel, then it changes *everything*! And we're going to be the first ones to find it.'

◆

The tunnel twisted and turned as they progressed through it. Suddenly, after a sharp turn, their torch beam was no longer the only light in the passage.

Father Smit stopped in his tracks and switched off the flashlight. The other source of illumination was just ahead of them. 'It's daylight,' he whispered, 'and listen—can you hear something?'

Eric strained to pick up any unusual sound over the residual ringing in his ears from the resounding waterfall they had crossed on their way up.

Aurin cocked his head. 'It sounds like running water.'

'Could be the source of the fall we saw,' Dr Hussein suggested, catching up with the group along with the two troopers trailing him. He could hear it too.

Father Smit switched the torch back on. 'It's not far away.' And he set off again, speeding up to a jog in his eagerness to see what lay ahead. The rest of the group had little choice but to keep up with his pace. They rounded another curve and emerged out of the end of the tunnel into a large opening, stopping short in amazement at the sight that greeted them. A vast meadow covered in foliage spread from left to right in front of their eyes. No lesser than fifteen football fields, this huge space was walled from all sides and the ceiling was at least two hundred feet high.

'Oh God...' Eric whispered.

'We found it!' Father Smit breathed.

SEVENTY-FOUR

'Wow!' Aurin cried. 'This can't be real, can it?'

'Oh, it's real,' Eric replied, 'it's absolutely real.'

The walled space was enormous, spread out more to their right than to their left. The walls rose up in an inward sloping manner to form a dome of rock overhead. There were holes in the top of the cliff ceiling through which sunlight poured in long slanting beams to illuminate the giant space below.

The landing on this end of the tunnel was at a slight height in the south-western corner on their left, and they walked over to the spot to come face to face with a panoramic view of the colossal chamber and the lush green jungle sprawling in front of their mesmerised eyes. The air smelled crisp and fresh; exotic trees and the greenest grass swayed in the gentle breeze below. They could hear the faint hubbub of birds chirping in the dense foliage.

'Jardine Del Eden,' Marina whispered.

'Yes, this is the Garden of Eden,' Aurin exclaimed, filling his lungs with the scented air. Steam rose from the trees where the sunlight touched the leaves, only to condense on the rocky ceiling and drip back onto the vegetation underneath. The water was easy to spot—a large lake occupied most of the cavern's south-eastern corner on their far right. A cloudy mist rose from it. The sound of running water came from a small waterfall originating somewhere above the lake and dropping directly into it.

'Look at that!' Father Smit said, slowly raising his right hand. Everyone followed the direction of his pointed finger. 'One, two… three and four,' he said, 'four rivers, all fed by the same source!'

Four streams emerged from the far side of the lake. The first three disappeared one after another behind a series of hillocks beyond the lake. The fourth one fell into a giant canyon that split a large section of the jungle in two, starting right below their vantage point and continuing to the right. The canyon seemed bottomless. Only the distant rumble of the churning water told them there had to be an end to the fall.

I bet at some point in time they all flowed out of this mountain.' A broad smile appeared on Father Smit's face.

'Four rivers,' echoed Aurin, 'Pishon, Gihon, Tigris and Euphrates.'

'The four biblical rivers flowed from the Garden of Eden. But they don't any more,' Dr Hussein said, 'because for some unknown reason, two of them were lost centuries ago!'

'And yet, we have just discovered them,' Niccolo exclaimed, finally joining in the conversation, 'and the lake—the original source of the four rivers of the Genesis.' In a trance, he grabbed the sleeves of both his troopers. 'But what about the Tigris and the Euphrates as we know them—what are they actually?'

'They are probably just two rivers originating in the Armenian Highlands of eastern Turkey,' answered Father Smit, 'that people started calling Tigris and Euphrates after the original rivers went underground.'

'We have to go down, cross the canyon, and walk through the jungle to reach the fall,' Eric interrupted.

'Yes, as per the last part of the message, the path is hidden inside the waterfall that drops into a lake—the lake that gives birth to four rivers,' Father Smit said.

Marina glanced across the canyon and then looked at the lake and the fall and then at her wristwatch. 'We need to get going, and fast... Suleiman and Dr Huntley need us.'

Eric looked at her. 'Right, Marina, we need to move fast...we are losing precious time!'

Aurin moved ahead of the group and climbed down the man-made ledge they were standing on.

'We can't jump across this chasm, guys; it would be quite a bit of a jump!' Niccolo shouted before following after Aurin.

'Maybe it is narrow enough somewhere below this ledge,' Father Smit said. 'We can see it broadens further up on the right.' One by one, the group made their way down the ledge. There were stone pegs driven into the rock surface here and there which made their climb a bit easier. 'Must have been a pretty big earthquake to cause a rift that deep,' Father Smit noted. Ahead of them, a smattering of large boulders lay about, moss clinging to their sunward sides. Eric looked up. Directly overhead was a longish hole in the ceiling. 'It probably made that too,' he said, pointing upwards.

'Well, I have a theory,' Dr Hussein declared. 'Some geologists think water arrived in comets as they struck the planet. For a moment if we believe there was a shower of comets millions of years ago, the multiple fractures in the ceiling and the earthquake-like massive crack in the chamber floor would suddenly make a lot of sense. Also, as per this theory, the water actually came along with the comets and created this lake and the four rivers.'

'It's a good theory!' Father Smit looked up and announced. 'There's our bridge to cross the chasm!' A little ahead, they noticed a tree had fallen with its trunk spanning the gap in the ground.

'It looks slippery!' Marina said, alarmed.

Eric jogged to the fallen tree and examined the broken end of the log, then the ground beneath it, before testing the strength of the makeshift bridge with his foot.

'Feels solid enough.'

'After you,' Aurin smiled.

Eric gave him a caustic look, then climbed onto the log. He began to walk across, arms outstretched for balance, then looked down and thought better of it. He dropped down on all fours, and slowly but safely crawled to the other side of the chasm.

'You were right,' he called from the other side and winked, 'it is a bit slippery...now come on!'

9'The ceiling has survived well over a hundred thousand years,' Dr Hussein remarked. 'Why would it collapse now?'

'I am talking about a meteorite, Dr Hussein,' Aurin smiled, 'and don't forget—wherever we go, destruction has a way of following us!'

They followed Eric as he led the way to the waterfall. Once there, they found a large outcropping of rock hung over the lake right next to the fall. As Eric went near it, he discovered there was an entrance to a cave under the outcropping. Stepping through the opening, he realised the cavern was hewn out of stone by human hands.

At the far end of the man-made tunnel-like structure, there was a wide spiral staircase descending into the ground. As they began to go down the steps in single file, Eric noticed the stairway was naturally lit by the light coming in through finely carved slots in the rock wall, casting eerie patterns on the stairs.

About twenty or twenty-five feet down, the stairway curved towards the right and began ascending.

♦

Marina felt it here more than she'd ever felt it before: this adventure was pulling them into a world of madness, deep into the heart of darkness, beating like a monstrous drum. She shivered, even though it was warm inside the cave. She tried to shake off the feeling, but it lurked in her thoughts as she took each step. Every nerve in her body screamed—*run*.

She clutched her flashlight like a weapon and climbed on instead.

◆

The long stairway spiralled its way up for a good ten feet, until they found themselves in a narrow corridor. It was flanked on both sides by a long line of archways, each leading to a different chamber. Aurin ran ahead and peeked inside the nearest archway. His eyes flew wide open. 'Holy cow!' Before the others could respond, Aurin disappeared into the room. His voice echoed from across the wall, 'You guys need to see this!'

They followed his voice and found Aurin holding a crown made of gleaming yellow metal: gold. Everywhere around them lay massive piles of artefacts: vessels, figurines, jewellery, thrones, utensils. All yellow in colour, gleaming in the faint rays of light filtering in from the skylights in the corridor.

Smiling at Aurin, Father Smit and Eric walked inside the chamber to take a closer look. Eric reached down and grabbed a crown. 'Definitely Larsa,' Father Smit commented.

'Yes,' Eric replied, 'between 1700 and 1800 BC.'

Marina and Hussein followed them into the chamber. Everywhere they looked, piles of gold glinted in their torch beams. Centuries of accumulated dust and moisture could do nothing to reduce their glitter. 'Do you think all the chambers will be like this?' Marina asked.

Eric smiled and motioned towards the exit. 'Come on, let's make sure we find what we've come for.'

'What you've come for is the Tomb of God!' a voice buzzed in Eric's head.

'Suleiman! We've just found the treasure chambers!' Eric replied excitedly.

'One thing, Eric,' Suleiman said, 'the tomb should be in an open ground, not in a chamber. That's what Layard's tablet said—*There's no wall around the burial chamber; it is surrounded by heavenly flowers; the sky is its roof, and the birds sing for the God.'*

Eric looked towards the far end of the corridor. It was brightly lit.

'Daylight,' he whispered, dragging Father Smit by his arm in the direction of the light, with Dr Hussein and Marina at their heels. As they drew closer, they discovered a circular open field double the size of a football ground. Covered in fresh green grass and strange-looking shrubs and with exquisite flowers swaying in the heavenly breeze, the place was a visual treat. Far to their left, a small waterfall plunged from a grotto in the south-western wall.

'One of the four rivers, coming down from the lake at the upper level!' Dr Hussein said.

Sunlight came in at a slant through the hole, casting a dramatic spotlight on the object at the centre of the field covered with foliage and flowers.

It was a stone sarcophagus, eight-and-a-half feet long, four feet across and three feet high, cut from huge slabs of dark basalt. The sarcophagus rested on the backs of four crouching lions made of the same black stone. On the sides were carved extraordinary scenes: a kingly figure holding up a blooming plant towards the moon and a beam of light from the moon piercing it; soldiers approaching with their standards held high. On top of the sarcophagus was a stone effigy of a king gripping a sword in his left hand. On his free arm was a shield made of solid gold and etched in cuneiform script.

'I wish I could stay here forever,' Aurin pined, stepping forward from behind the group with his tiny digital camera out and recording everything. 'Perhaps then I would know what peace feels like!'

'Not if the Devil finds you first, and I'm afraid he's coming. For all of us,' Eric smirked. 'That large hole up there—it looks pretty much like the devil's hole mentioned in that *Angels & Demons* book.'

'Big enough for a Volkswagen Beetle to drop through,' Marina breathed, her eyes fixed at the hole some hundred feet above them. Looking around, her heart felt like a steam engine pounding against her rib cage. She took a deep breath, trying to cope with the rush of adrenaline.

They all paused, soaking everything in—the towering roof of the beautiful valley, the sparkling waterfall, the majestic tomb, the invigorating breeze, the flowers and the fragrance—each in their own way.

SEVENTY-FIVE

'Dr Hussein, you must take a look at this!' Eric announced, suddenly breathless. 'Let us once and for all find out who he is.'

Dr Hussein walked up to the sarcophagus, wiped the layer of dirt on it with his hands, and let his fingers trace the stone carvings—a world within a world, plots within plots, stretching out through the centuries until that moment. He smiled to himself.

'It's Akkadian,' he remarked, 'because in Rim-Sin's time Akkadian became the official language of literacy.' He took a deep breath and started reading aloud. 'Here rests the son of the Moon God. The king of all kings. Rim-Sin of Larsa.'

He looked up from the stone and smiled. Most of his companions had gathered in a circle around the sarcophagus, their eyes shining with enthusiasm.

'Shouldn't we open it?' Marina asked.

'Yes! Let's open it!' Eric said, circling the sarcophagus to find the opening. The lid appeared to be hinged at the back. 'Give me your bag, Father Smit.' He came round the coffin and, taking the backpack from Father Smit, pulled out a claw hammer. 'Okay, I'll try to lift the lid. If Dr Hussein, Aurin and Father Smit can hold it up for a couple of seconds, I'll prise it open. Meanwhile, Marina, would you mind filming this epic historical moment?' He ran his fingers along the edge of the lid. Finding a slight imperfection, he pushed the claw end of the hammer into it.

'Ready?' The three men moved into position and nodded as Marina pressed the record button on the camera and started walking around the sarcophagus. 'Okay, here goes...' Eric exclaimed.

Straining, he pulled the hammer's shaft down with all his strength. The lid rose by half an inch as the hammer's head crunched against the heavy stone. The three men pushed up hard. The gap widened to about three inches, revealing a slit of blackness underneath. Eric quickly jammed the hammer in deeper and pushed down again. 'Push it up!' he shouted, breathing heavily.

The men lifted the lid a little higher with all their strength combined. The hammer slipped, spitting tiny stone chips on Eric's face, but the men managed to hold it long enough for Eric to grip its edge and shove it upwards. The lid swung, then fell backwards to the ground with a deep thud.

Aurin quickly picked up a flashlight from the ground and shone it. Inside was a figure tightly wrapped in an astoundingly well-preserved cloth shroud.

'The stone coffin must have been practically airtight,' Dr Hussein marvelled.

'The last time this mummy saw any light was sometime around 1763 BC!' Father Smit said.

'And the intactness of the mummy proves,' added Dr Hussein, 'that the Sumerians were not just as good at this job as the Egyptians, they were better. All Sumerian mummies found in previous excavations are newer than this one. This is one of the world's most valuable finds—enough to challenge the whole contemporary idea of Sumerian Civilisation, let alone settling the Rim-Sin and Ram Chandra debate.'

'Do you find the theories of Zecharia Sitchin or Erich Von Daniken interesting?' Eric asked, looking at Dr Hussein.

'I know what you mean,' he smiled. 'Until recently, the primary advocates for testing Sumerian DNA have been followers of Zecharia Sitchin...'

'Daniken I know, I've read his *Chariots of the Gods*, but who is this Zecharia guy? Do I know him?' Aurin interrupted, scratching his chin.

'Zecharia Sitchin is the preacher of this belief that the ancient Sumerians socialised with extraterrestrials and may have carried alien genes,' Dr Hussein explained. 'But there are several other conventional reasons to study Sumerian DNA: it can tell us where the first city builders came from and who their contemporary descendants are. The migration of the Sumerians is one of the great unsolved mysteries of human civilisation. If we want to solve it, DNA is the best tool we have.' He smiled at Aurin. 'And for that, what could be better than the 3,700-year-old mummy of King Rim-Sin, who called himself the son of the Moon God. In fact, his Elamite name, Eri-Aku, also means the son of the Moon God.'

'The "Chandra" in Ram Chandra takes on a whole new meaning now,' Aurin remarked.

'Yes, and the debates regarding Ayodhya from the Ramayana—that it can actually be the city of Agade in the north of Sumeria—will also become much more interesting now,' Eric shrugged. 'The explanation that Rim-Sin's legends travelled over the trade routes and inspired the Ramayana tale will become more believable.'

'But how do we get this mummy to the civilised world?' Aurin asked, walking around the tomb. Then he stopped.

'The flowers around the tomb…the flowers!' he yelled.

'What's wrong with the flowers?' Eric asked, visibly vexed by the interruption.

'Look at the plant growing around the tomb. And look at its flowers!' Aurin panted. 'Don't you see it?'

'O God!' Marina exclaimed. 'This was carved on the stone door that we entered from. This plant was on the walls of the tunnel as well!'

'That is exactly what everyone has been looking for,' a voice buzzed in Eric's head. It was Suleiman.

'That's what has brought all of you here. Directly or indirectly.'

'Why is this plant so significant, Suleiman?'

'Because that plant, my friend, is God's gift to mankind. That plant holds the secret of life that mankind has been trying to unlock since Genesis...'

'What is it?'

'God made mankind mortal,' Suleiman said, dodging Eric's question. 'God also created ambrosia for immortality. But he was smart enough to hide the knowledge from humans!'

'You mean to say this plant is ambrosia?' Eric exclaimed so loudly, everyone looked at him in alarm.

'In ancient Mesopotamia, the medicine man—the asu—treated wounds using three basic techniques: washing, bandaging and making plasters after applying medicines,' Suleiman said. 'You will be surprised—all three of these techniques of the asu appear in the world's oldest known medical document, written in 2100 BC.' He paused. 'A 1700 BC tablet mentioned ambrosia as a life-saving medicine in the post-Rim-Sin era. The tablet stated it was brought to Larsa from the land of seven rivers.'

'Suleiman, please tell me, are you saying this plant is ambrosia?' Eric was on tenterhooks.

'Yes, Eric, this is supposed to be the sanjeevani from Ramayana,' Suleiman said, 'the life-saving plant that Larsa kings wanted to hide from Hammurabi, since they knew Hammurabi was planning an attack on Larsa during Kudur Mabug's reign.' There was a pregnant pause. 'Now please collect enough samples and come back fast; I don't have much more time. I couldn't stop the bleeding, but this thing just might!'

'So this was the divine blessing!' Eric blurted.

'The key of all keys, which saved Lakshman's life! It might save my life as well... I really have to take this chance for the sake of my wife and children. Come fast. Over and out.'

'This might be the sanjeevani, the ambrosia, from the Ramayana!' Eric announced to everyone. 'Aurin, get samples of the plants with the roots intact,' he instructed. 'Make sure to collect as many as you can and store them in the zip-pouches you're carrying in your knapsack.

Also collect soil with each sample—it needs to be tested as well.'

Father Smit went near the flowerbeds around the tomb. He kneeled and touched the leaves and flowers of one. 'One of my favourite topics—medicinal plants and the sanjeevani herb. I had even developed a few theories around it.' He recited in a whispering voice, '*It could refer to a particular plant with rejuvenating properties; alternately, it could be a metaphor for any good medicinal plant.* I always wondered what we should look for before dismissing the sanjeevani as the imagination of the narrator of the Ramayana.'

'And they are?' Dr Hussein asked, kneeling down beside Father Smit to examine the plants for himself.

'First of all, I strongly believed we need to look at different versions of the Ramayana across the regions and tongues of India. Do all of them have references to a plant with a name similar to sanjeevani? Then we need to find out if all of those versions mention this plant having medicinal, or resurrection, potential.'

'Right,' Eric nodded. 'I had read about these researchers—Ganeshaiah, Vasudeva, Uma Shaanker—who actually searched through the Indian bio-resources database methodically for the term sanjeevani or its synonyms and phononyms. They found three such plants, based on the widespread use of the terms across languages.' He scratched his forehead, then added, 'I think those were *Cressacretica*, *Selaginellabryopteris* and *Desmotrichum fimbriatum*.'

'In fact,' Father Smit added, 'I recently read about some biological experiments being done by some researchers in India using biochemical and cell biology methods. And the experiments showed that *S. bryopteris* contained molecules that protect and help recover rat and insect cells from oxidative and ultraviolet stress, both of which can affect nerve cells.'

'But this one doesn't look like *Selaginellabryopteris*,' Eric demurred.

Father Smit smiled. 'This will be a new entry to the sanjeevani debate and will show us what wonders it can do.'

'I still can't believe that we are this close to finding out which plant the real sanjeevani from the Ramayana was. And, more importantly, maybe we'll finally discover something that can cure incurable diseases and save human lives,' Eric said.

♦

'Have you guys noticed one thing?' Aurin asked, still kneeling on the ground collecting samples religiously.

'Yes, I noticed Niccolo and his men entering the artefact room,' Marina said, 'but they never came out.'

'No, no!' Aurin laughed. 'I wanted to point out that we've eaten nothing since those early-morning cookies and coffee, and yet we are not hungry—at least I am not!'

'Auri boy!' Father Smit smiled. 'The Garden of Eden is the Garden of God. You can't experience mortal feelings here. *The Book of Genesis* in the Bible refers to it as the Garden of God, with no mention of Eden, and the magical plants of the garden are mentioned in Ezekiel. *The Book of Zechariah* and the Psalms also refer to the garden and plants without explicitly mentioning Eden.'

Dr Hussein nodded, 'Traditionally, scholars have favoured the theory of the name "Eden" being derived from the Akkadian edinnu, in turn derived from a Sumerian word "edin" meaning "plain" or "steppe". It actually draws subtle connections between the Sumerian Civilisation, the Akkadian language and the Garden of Eden.'

A little away from all of this, Eric paced on the grass, deep in thought. 'This mummy is our proof,' he suddenly spoke, turning towards Father Smit and pointing at the body. 'DNA and carbon-dating tests will provide unquestionable evidence as to whether he had a genetic connection with the Maha-Anga-Dwaror Der people. This will prove whether Rim-Sin's father Kudur Mabug was actually from Der and whether the bloodline of this Sumerian dynasty had a connection with the Indus Valley people.

'It seems,' a thick voice sounded from behind them, 'as if you are breaking your deal with the Salvation Knights, Eric Roy.'

They all whirled around to find Niccolo and the two Salvation troopers with their guns raised towards the group. 'If this evidence can unearth a new anthropological connection between Mohenjodaro and the Sumerian Civilisation, the Salvation Knights cannot allow it to come to light.'

'You mean, if this mummy proves to be historical proof for one of the oldest myths of the world, that too from the Indian subcontinent, the Salvation Knights won't allow it to surface?' Eric groaned.

'The important question is, what do *you* plan to do about it?' Father Smit asked. 'You have the guns and the goons—take your pick.'

'Father Smit is right, you are the one representing them now. It seems to be entirely your decision,' Eric joined in.

'So it does,' Niccolo said. He stared at the mummy and said, 'In the past, things were simple. The Salvation Knights had a specific purpose: to locate and destroy evidence of civilisations or historical knowledge that were non-Abrahamic, or could not be aligned with the Bible even by fabrication. Basically, anything that could undermine Genesis and the Creation story in the Bible and the other holy books. We would simply have obliterated this entire place.'

'So what's stopping you now?' Aurin butted in. 'You have the guns and the goons, as Father Smit just said!'

'I think Eric knows.' Niccolo gestured at the scenery all around them. 'Up here, this is the holiest place in the history of the earth. The Garden of Eden! Paradise on earth, where God himself talked to the first man and woman! Destroying it would be…blasphemy. The greatest earthly sin.'

'Worse than all your other ones, you mean—' Eric blurted out.

'The discovery of the Garden of Eden doesn't undermine Genesis,' he continued, ignoring Eric's sharp comment, 'it confirms it. If Eden is revealed to the world by *you* along with Dr Huntley and Dr Hussein, as per the discussion between you and our cardinal, the world media will have no reason to doubt the credibility of the story. The news will spread, rekindling faith in billions of people. The faithful would be reassured that what they believed in has been right all along.'

'You might be right,' Eric said, still not sure where the argument was heading, 'but the world will miss a major discovery if we do not bring this tomb to light.'

'Listen up, Eric,' Niccolo said, assuming an authoritative tone, 'you have found the Garden of Eden. And some significant medicinal plant. I will not have these destroyed. They must be revealed to the world—the Garden of Eden to rekindle faith and the plant for scientific experiments. I do understand the tomb of Rim-Sin is also a very important discovery, but I cannot let it be revealed to the world. Perhaps we should hold on to it for the moment and figure out a way later.'

'I'm starting to see what you have in mind,' Eric nodded.

'Yes, I reckon we can gradually introduce this idea of there being connections between Abrahamic religions and non-Abrahamic religions and civilisations, just like we did with the Big Bang and Evolution theories...strategic introduction over a period of time works best.' Niccolo shrugged. 'What do you think? Are you okay with the idea...?'

'Not really. But I hate the other idea of destroying everything.'

'Good! Once again, we agree on something,' Niccolo smiled. 'Let's get the mummy packed then,' he gestured towards his troopers, 'so it can start its journey to the Archive of Ancient Finds in the Vatican.'

'You mean, Area 51 of the Vatican, right?' Eric sneered.

As if on cue, a loud noise caught everyone unawares. They all craned their necks to find out what was going on.

'I have a bad feeling...' Dr Hussein whispered.

Unfortunately, those turned out to be the last words they would ever hear him say.

SEVENTY-SIX

It was a coordinated attack. The Hercules choppers stationed steady over the roof of the cliff and dropped a forty-man army of paratroopers, descending down ropes, one after the other, through the hole in the roof into the Garden of Eden. Meanwhile, two MI-26 helicopters landed a contingent of highly trained commandos at the base of the cliff. The troopers from the Hercules dropped with pinpointed accuracy at the mouth of the treasure chamber corridor the group had come through, and five of the commandos took up their positions at the same spot, sealing the exit.

'They are not military,' muttered Father Smit. 'The colour scheme's all wrong for the Iraqi Ground Force or the Iraqi Special Operations Force.' Eric could also not figure out who the guys might be. *Were they Delfino's men? Was Suleiman behind this? Could it be Nassar?* In his mind, he scanned through all the possibilities.

'I am guessing they are private contractors who play by their own rules,' Eric said, pushing everyone towards the sarcophagus.

'We must leave immediately,' a frightened-looking Marina cried. The paratroopers dropped in by the dozen and began firing at the group. Niccolo and his troopers dived behind the sarcophagus, Eric tried covering Dr Hussein and pushed him to the ground and Father Smit hurled his body towards Aurin and Marina, dragging them behind the sarcophagus. They all crawled behind the large stone structure.

Eric asked, 'Everyone fine?'

Each one of them replied in the affirmative, save for Dr Hussein. Marina remembered being in front of him when the firing began, so she looked behind her. She let out an audible gasp as her eyes caught Dr Hussein falling to the ground, blood gushing out in spurts from his abdomen. Before anyone could react, a rapid firing of bullets hit the sarcophagus, sending stone chips flying everywhere. One of the two Salvation troopers was hit, his AK-47 landing at Eric's feet as the man fell. He grabbed it even as Suleiman's voice buzzed in his head.

'I hear the gunshots. Now listen up, Eric,' he said, 'do you see a waterfall somewhere around you?'

'Yes!' Eric said, his eyes still on Dr Hussein as he lay writhing in pain on the ground. Tears were beginning to well up in his eyes.

'You can't get out the same way you entered the cave,' Suleiman continued. 'Two choppers and at least twenty commandos are covering the entrance and the foothills on that side. The waterfall is your only chance.' Suleiman took a brief pause. 'As per Layard's tablet, the flow of the water should take you below the layers of rocks and bring you straight to the Great Zab river in front of the Shanidar Cave. The keepers of the tomb had designed their way back in such a manner because, for some reason, many of them met their deaths while returning through the main entrance.'

'Copy that,' Eric said. 'Let me see what I can do…over and out.'

Another bullet spray rained on their hideout, from more guns this time, chipping off more stone from the tomb. One of the bullets hit the second Salvation trooper. One moment he was aiming at a paratrooper, and the next moment he was lying dead on the grass.

'You are going to die, Eric Roy! This place is sacred, and all of this belongs to us—to the people of this land. I won't allow you to plunder our lands!' a thick voice reverberated through the cavern.

'I am impressed, Nassar!' Eric's eyes lit up. 'I see you've left your village mob behind and gathered a bunch of trained pests instead!' he sniggered.

'Don't try to play any tricks, Mr Roy, or all of you will die here today.' He laughed. 'Isn't it considered a good thing—dying in Eden?' The sound of his laughter seemed to rise, and then he appeared above their heads, being pulled up by a steel cord towards a helicopter that hovered over the cliff.

He was flying away from the war zone.

Eric bent to check Dr Hussein's pulse but found none. He looked up and growled, 'You are nothing but a liar and the scum of the earth, Nassar! And you know that!' He gestured to Marina and Aurin to get ready to run. 'I know you were behind the massacre at Dr Huntley's camp...your hands are smeared with the blood of twenty-five innocent archaeologists, and now with Dr Hussein's!' He closed Dr Hussein's eyes with a gentle touch of his fingers and hissed at Nassar. 'If you think I'll let you go, you are a fool. I'll find you wherever you hide and I'll kill you.'

◆

They had taken his dear friend's life. Now he would take theirs. When it came to his loved ones, no logic or better sense could prevail on Eric. He became a different thing altogether. A monster.

'You and I will do the killing together, Eric,' Niccolo muttered from behind. Eric looked at his crew—a sixty-something preacher, a couple of college kids, a professional gunner and an operative. But then again, he didn't know what wonders Father Smit had up his sleeve. All things considered, Eric liked their chances.

He dragged one of the Salvation troopers' dead bodies by the hand and checked his AK-47. Some rounds were still left in the magazine. He collected three spare magazines from the dead trooper's pocket and then secured his small Tomcat in the knee pocket of his cargo. 'It's time for action...' he whispered.

'More of them are coming in, Eric!' Father Smit warned.

'Father, we'll have to take a different route to get out of this place,' Eric said. 'Aurin and Marina, listen up—you two run to the waterfall, check the flow of the water and dive into it. Take Dr Hussein's bag, split the plant samples between the two of you, and carry them carefully. I'll cover you.' He took a deep breath and whispered, 'The waterfall will take you straight to the Great Zab river. Now go, go, go, go!' He pointed with his left hand at the fall, curling his shooting finger around the trigger of the AK-47.

Niccolo silently handed a Benelli shotgun to Father Smit. His face was flushed, but he looked ready to face hell.

Aurin and Marina rose from behind the stone structure and ran, keeping their heads low, while Eric mowed down Nassar's troopers like targets in a shooting range. His special training of close combat came in handy as he avoided bullets like a spry grasshopper.

Blood and brains spattered all over the lush foliage as Eric continued firing. Round after round he tore through the attackers, shredding their bodies.

The troopers never stood a chance in front of an enraged Eric Roy.

When the magazine was consumed, he ducked behind the sarcophagus and checked if Aurin and Marina had reached the waterfall safely.

Father Smit hurdled over the corpses of the Salvation trooper and Dr Hussein and touched Eric's shoulder. 'Are you okay?'

'Yeah,' he lied as he tossed the empty magazine and replaced it with a new one. 'What about the other two?'

'They both went in nice and safe, I saw,' Father Smit assured him.

'Their lead guy has taken shelter behind those rocks across the fall...after killing both my men,' Niccolo said, tight-lipped. 'So what's the plan?'

'We can't take the mummy. We need to get out of here safely with the plant samples,' Eric said. 'I am sure Aurin has documented everything well; let's just make a move.'

'It's a fifty-foot open run. Do you think we have a chance of making it without cover?' Niccolo said, shaking his head.

'There will be cover.'

They both turned to find Father Smit ready with Niccolo's shotgun.

'That's impossible!' Eric said angrily. 'Who will cover you?'

'Don't worry, Eric, you know I'll finish the rest of them by the time you reach the fall!' He grinned. 'Go, go, rush now!'

'Let me stay, Father Smit, you go with Niccolo,' Eric argued, the alarm clear in his voice. 'There must be more of them coming; I can't just leave you here like that!'

'Don't waste time, Eric, I'll clean up this ground and join you soon…you go, Eric! Run!'

Unfortunately for Father Smit, Nassar's lead trooper Rafiq was having the same thoughts right then.

SEVENTY-SEVEN

Eric held Father Smit's arm for a moment, then reached out to touch Dr Hussein's forehead.

In an odd way, this little act felt like proof to Eric that all of this was real. Until that moment, he hadn't fully comprehended the magnitude of what had happened. Now he knew. He would never see Dr Hussein again. He would never be able to hold a debate with him again. His friend was dead. He wrapped his fingers slowly around the grip of his AK.

Turning towards Father Smit, he nodded and smiled, then rose from his crouching position and sprinted across the meadow towards the waterfall. At the same time, Niccolo handed three Adaptive Tactical Magazines to Father Smit and started shooting with his AK in the direction they had last seen Nassar's troopers. Then he fell in step behind Eric.

'Sid, we are on the go,' Eric said, 'keep talking to us so that you know what's happening on the ground. Aurin has a headstart, I am following him, and Father Smit is backing us up.'

'You need to see this, Ric da,' Aurin's excited voice came from the comm, 'it's amazing!'

'What is?' Sid asked.

'There's yet another strange tunnel in here. The water from the fall comes down as a roaring stream, but there is something far more astonishing here, and you need to see it!'

'Wait up, I'll join you soon. Make sure you cover Marina,' Eric yelled as a series of gunshots reverberated through the prehistoric walls. Father Smit was raising hell with the Benelli.

'...*And I will strike down upon thee with great vengeance and furious anger...those who would attempt to poison and destroy my brothers. And you will know my name is the Lord when I lay my vengeance upon thee...*' Father Smit kept reciting Ezekiel as his gun spat bullets like a hailstorm, putting the killers to sleep.

SEVENTY-EIGHT

Reaching the waterfall, Eric was startled at the discovery. Carved into the stone were steps leading down into a grotto adjacent to the small lake at the base of the fall. The sound of gushing water came from the depths of the tunnel-like cavern. Eric and Niccolo climbed down the steps to a spot where the grotto broadened all of a sudden. A stream of water flowed in from the lake through another opening on their right and went leftward. Next to the steps, a few feet away from the opening stood Aurin and Marina. Gaping.

There was a giant object about twenty feet further into the grotto to their right, on an open expanse of stony ground across the stream. The object rested on its cofferdam, cradled by several huge tree trunks on each side.

It was a twenty-foot version of a huge ancient Mesopotamian ship.

'Unbelievable,' Eric mumbled.

'Yes, this is the one they made the gold replica after,' Aurin said, still awestruck at the sight.

'You are right,' Eric said. 'The figurehead on the bow of the ship is the Moon God Nanna, just as he was depicted on the replica.' He advanced towards the ship, wading through the waist-high water of the gurgling stream. He climbed up the support tree trunks and peeped over the deck. 'Ten rower benches sans the rowers and the same odd-shaped tiller of the replica. There's no doubt our replica was modelled after this ship.'

'But why did they build it here?'

◆

'I just hope it still floats,' Niccolo said.

'What do you mean?' Eric asked.

'What? Don't you see? It was built here specifically to sail out of the cave through this tunnel,' Niccolo explained. 'Look at the low mast, the short oars! Notice the robust capsule-like body? The unorthodox rounded bottom? My father was a seaman. Believe me, I know what I am saying!' He shouted, 'The troopers will be here soon, and then we will all die in this freaking tunnel! *Meglio morire combattendo che pregare.*'

'Translation please!' Aurin yelled back.

'Better fighting than praying.'

'Father Smit,' Eric spoke into the comm, suddenly sensing the oppressive silence that had dawned over the valley, 'how are you doing?' He waited for a response. None came. 'Sid, I don't hear gunshots any more...can you please check on Father Smit?' His voice betrayed his panic.

Before Sid could answer, they sensed the presence of a fifth person in the cavern. With a sudden splash, Rafiq had entered the tunnel.

Rafiq flung himself at Aurin in a full-body attack, pushing him away from Marina's side and tumbling into the water. His arm wrapped around Marina's throat and his machine pistol pointed at her temple. Marina had barely been able to raise a hand to her face before Rafiq's iron grip was around her neck. Luckily, the grip wasn't as effective due to Marina's hand being trapped in between. Rafiq hesitated for a split second at the unexpected resistance. Then the man strained harder, tilting his head back. Standing on the cofferdam a few feet away, Eric knew Rafiq was a few precious moments away from getting a solid grip on Marina and announcing his threat. He dived into the water. Moving with a panther's stealth, he reached Aurin and secured him with his left arm. At the same time, while squatting in the shallow water, he slid his right hand in his cargo pocket and gripped his Tomcat. He didn't try to take the weapon out. He simply fired from inside the pocket. The .22-calibre bullet struck the man right under his chin, slicing through the tongue and palate and drilling through the skull, until it pierced into the brain and got lodged somewhere in the chewed-up remains of his corpus callosum.

The scum was a corpse even before he realised he'd taken his last breath. There was almost no blood. Marina, on the other hand, was struggling for breath. Rafiq's lifeless body fell to the floor with a huge splash. Aurin staggered out of the water with Eric's help. Marina lumbered up to the stone steps and sat down, still breathing heavily. She leaned back on the cool stone, her neck throbbing. She sat there for what seemed like a long time and prayed that the light-headed feeling would go away fast. Along with that she wanted to erase the events of the last few seconds from her memory.

SEVENTY-NINE

'Father Smit,' Sid called out, 'can you hear me? What's your status?'

Eric waited anxiously for a response. It wasn't in his nature or in his training to panic, but considering all that had gone wrong on this mission, the prolonged silence was deafening for him. 'Sid, I need an update. Where is Father Smit?'

'He's at the same place as before, Chief. I last heard him when you had reached the fall. After that, he might have been attacked by the troopers. I heard a barrage of shots from more than one gun.'

Eric had also heard the shots. Not only in his earpiece but also through the echoing walls of the cavern. But he couldn't pay heed then, for he was busy ensuring the safety of the rest of his entire team. Now that Sid had confirmed the gunshots, he needed Father Smit to check in. Because if he didn't, Eric would have no choice but to track him down himself.

'Father Smit, it's Sid, are you okay?' He waited for a few seconds. 'If you can hear me but can't talk, just tap on your earpiece to signal. Chief will come to you.'

'I am fine,' the familiar voice reverberated.

Eric, Aurin and Sid breathed a collective sigh of relief. 'Where were you? You had us worried!' Sid said.

'Don't be worried. It is them who need to worry right now.'

Eric didn't like the ominous tone of his voice. *This wasn't the time to lose control*, he thought. Not with danger lurking all around them in a lost world deep inside a prehistoric mountain.

'Where exactly are you, Father Smit? Are you still behind the sarcophagus?' Eric asked. 'Stay there; I am coming to get you.'

'None of you will. Eric, you need to concentrate on your team's safety and carry on in this journey. I'll stay here.'

'What are you saying, Father?' the brothers exclaimed together.

'I have a bunch of AKs and ten-odd magazines; I'll hold this post and kill all of them—one by one.'

'No, Father Smit, please…don't do this!' Aurin whimpered.

'Carry on, Auri boy! You've been a hell of a young man to know. Have a great life.'

'You can't do this, Father, we are going to get out of this place together and introduce this brilliant find to the world as a team,' Eric pleaded. 'You can't ruin all of this for mere vengeance…you are the truest man of God I know, Father!'

'One must stay here to make sure no one follows you. Go ahead, Eric.'

'No, Father, you can't do this…' Eric's voice broke, 'you know I lost my parents early…you've been more of a father to me than a mentor. Please don't do this to me! Please, Father Smit…let me come and get you...'

'Eric, don't do anything that you might regret later...you have lives to protect. There is a female member in the team as well. Focus on their safe return after the successful completion of the mission. Understand?'

'I understand, Father,' Eric sighed. Then a thought struck him. 'Are you hit?'

'You remember the verse from the Bible I used to recite?' Father Smit asked elusively. The sound of fresh gunshots echoed in the background.

'Yes, I remember, Ezekiel 25:17,' Eric cried. 'I can hear them shooting at you, Father...please don't do this to me, let me come.'

'*Blessed is he, who in the name of charity and good will, shepherds the weak through the valley of darkness, for he is truly his brother's keeper and the finder of lost children...*' his voice reverberated in Eric's head. He knew it was coming from the comm unit, but it seemed as if the entire cave was billowing with Father Smit's deep voice, and his ominous recitation. His breathing was increasingly strained, but he continued, '*...and I will strike down upon thee with great vengeance and furious anger those who would attempt to poison and destroy my brothers. And you will know my name is the Lord when I lay my vengeance upon thee...*' He paused. 'They used this part in a Hollywood film, you know! That's how it became popular.'

Eric took a deep breath and nodded. 'Yes, I know, Father.'

'I have sent too many people to God, Eric...it's my time now. And rest assured I die in peace, for I think it was my job to arrange a meeting between God and all those bad men.' His voice was beginning to take a menacing tone.

It was a tough moment for Eric, but he had been there before.

He felt Father Smit's agony and his anger. He also knew he was too far away to extend any kind of help to him without jeopardising lives. But Eric knew this wasn't about Father Smit losing control, but reclaiming it. He must have taken a bullet or two and been unable to move. The thought that he was unable to save Dr Hussein must have been weighing down heavily on him. He couldn't do anything to bring Dr Hussein back to life, but he knew he could even the score by killing the people he held responsible for Dr Hussein's death and for the situation his friends were in. The fact that he could help the mission along from the back end by killing their pursuers was just another reason to stay behind.

Eric knew he couldn't—and shouldn't—stop him. He had to let Father Smit have this. He wanted to die with dignity, doing something he thought he needed to do. Eric had to respect that.

'Stand down, Chief, I repeat, stand down,' Sid said into the comm. 'Focus on the safety of your team, and finish the mission. Father Smit has disconnected the comm.'

'Yes, Sid. I got it. I'm standing down,' Eric whispered as he stood there with misty eyes.

EIGHTY

Time is a fuzzy concept during battle. Most of the D-day survivors from the combined American, British and Canadian forces said, 'It took us eternity to establish a beachhead,' when, actually, it had taken a little less than three hours, from 6.29 a.m. to 9.17 a.m., almost the same amount of time we generally take to get up from bed and reach our workplaces every day.

In the same three hours on D-day, twenty thousand casualties were reported by the Allied and German armies combined, just about two every second. Time is truly relative during battle—it takes eternity to ensure survival and only a fraction of a second to die.

◆

Had there been a Hollywood cinematographer waiting at the mouth of the secret tunnel that opened up over the Great Zab river, he could have caught on film a once-in-a-lifetime stunt performed by an ancient Mesopotamian ship as it burst forth from the side of a cliff, riding on a waterfall, and plunged nose-first into a churning river whirlpool twenty-five feet below. It could win the cinematographer several awards, get him unbelievable film offers. But none of that actually happened. No one aboard the ship knew what was happening or where they would end up on their crazy two-kilometre free-roll on the secret waterway through the tunnel. Certainly none of them would ever know how mesmerising a sight it was to watch their ship dive into the Great Zab river seemingly out of nowhere.

◆

When the cofferdam was opened, the ancient vessel pushed out on the stream with Aurin and Niccolo at the oars on each side and Eric at the tiller, controlling the ship's direction. Marina, embracing the mast, hung on for dear life.

For the small group, the two-kilometre journey through the tunnel was like a roller-coaster ride inside a rickety capsule. The oars somehow helped maintain a safe distance from both the walls of the tunnel, while the tiller only came in handy to prevent the ship from crashing at turns. By the time they saw the first hint of daylight, they were thoroughly exhausted and soaked to the skin. The vessel hurtled past the mouth of the cave and whooshed down into the churning river below.

Like Daenerys Targaryen's dragons coming up from the depths of the water in a nine-hundred-million-dollar TV show, the ancient vessel rose again. Moon God Nanna's figurehead streamed water from its spout. The golden border around the ship glistened in the surf. A sudden wind helped the sail as the oarsmen dug their oars into the murky water and thrust the vessel forward. 'What a ride!' Eric exclaimed. Every one of their faces looked bedraggled, but they reflected an exhilaration they'd all assumed was long gone.

◆

The ship steered nimbly out of the whirlpools clustered at the foot of the falls. It became clear almost immediately that Shanidar Cave was much closer than they had imagined.

'It will be dark soon,' Niccolo spoke. 'We need to reach the cave as soon as possible and rescue Suleiman and Dr Huntley, so that we can drive out of this menacing place at the earliest.'

'You are right, we need to reach the pickup point by sunrise tomorrow.' Eric sounded grave. His mind was still in thoughts of Father Smit and Dr Hussein. The people they had left behind.

Suddenly, heavy breathing filled the comm. 'Promise me something, Eric...' The breathing was erratic, interspersed with coughing.

'Father Smit!' Aurin cried.

'Are you okay, Father Smit?' Eric whispered. In his mind, he knew what his raspy voice meant. A cry rose from deep within him, and tears welled up in his dry eyes.

'Listen, Eric, I don't have time... Don't...don't let the samples get into the wrong hands. Something tells me they are immensely powerful.' He coughed and spluttered.

Eric could almost see the clot of blood Father Smit had coughed up.

'Promise me...Eric.'

'I promise... I will always hold on to you tight, Father Smit...' he mouthed into the comm.

'I know, my boy...you were always my favourite...you always will be!' There was a pause as Father Smit gathered his breath. 'Now, there's one more thing...'

'Yes, Father?'

'I have a box hidden inside my bed at the Chinsurah Church quarter. You need to remember two things to access its contents... first, a line from the Lord's prayer: *Lead us not into temptation*. And then, *Blessed are your eyes because they see, and your ears because they hear*. Promise me you will find it and take care of whatever's hidden inside...'

'I promise.'

'Thanks, Eric! You know, duty and honour always seemed an essential part of my life...but it just didn't seem like I would ever regain honour. So I stayed and fought. I wish...I wish you would be happy for me...for I die in peace...in the Garden of God...to the sound of running water from the source of Gihon, Pison, and who knows, maybe the original Tigris and Euphrates... Well, time to go. These scum have set explosives before flying out...they are going to blow the top of this place up very soon...but I'd suggest you come back looking for the mummy even if this place is blown apart. Goodbye, friends...over and out!'

Before anyone could move a muscle, a series of explosions lit up the evening sky. From a distance, Eric and his team gazed at the cliff they had evacuated only a few minutes before. The first explosion shook the gigantic structure. The second caused the top of the mountain to spew fire and then the top of the cliff crumbled and caved in.

The Garden of Eden was gone. Father Smit was gone, Dr Hussein was gone. And along with everything of beauty and value inside the enigmatic mountain, gone was the big secret—the Tomb of God.

EIGHTY-ONE

When they heard the whirring sound, Eric and his team were anchoring the ancient vessel along the bank of the sluggish river. In the last light of the evening, against a flaming auburn sky, they saw the silhouettes of two helicopters descending in front of Shanidar Cave. They made a pinpoint landing some five hundred metres away from the entrance to the cave. The bigger helicopter was a Bell 525 Relentless that could fit twenty passengers. The other was an Agusta Westland 139 with a capacity of fourteen.

Count Delfino climbed out of the smaller one in a moss green corduroy jacket and khaki trousers, followed by Bill, his Antiquity Acquisitions Head, in a camouflage shirt and trousers tucked into spit-shined combat boots. Ten heavily armed troopers stepped out of the Bell 525 behind them. They were about three hundred metres away from where Eric's team watched their descent. Delfino gestured for his troopers to stay put while he walked towards the other group.

'Mr Roy,' Delfino smiled, 'I see you have managed to survive everything!'

'What the hell is going on?' Eric snarled.

'This is your rescue party; you should be thanking us.' He continued to smile.

'What do you mean?'

'We are here to kill that bastard Nassar and his stupid men and then give you a lift back to civilisation. But one small thing before that. My men will search you for whatever you've got back from the secret tomb.'

'What are you saying, Count?' Bill mumbled under his breath, visibly tense. 'Nassar is our man; he is working for us—you can't kill him and his men!'

'Of course I can! If they haven't been already killed in those explosions. My instructions were clear—"no explosives". And yet, look at that!' Delfino gestured towards the smouldering mountain. 'That bastard has blown up the Garden of Eden and the entire fortune that the tomb could have brought us, Bill, let alone all the plans I had in mind for the future!'

'What were your plans, Count? To extract more money from the Church? Or to sell Project Eden as an amusement park to billionaires?' Eric sneered.

'You are sharp,' Delfino remarked. 'Egoistic, but sharp.'

'Let me tell you why my interest in the tomb was so high. Ever since my encounter with Tessitori's work, I've read a lot and developed a series of hypotheses. If you're aware of the fourteen kings mentioned in the Bible, you would understand how big a deal it would be if one of their tombs were to be discovered today.'

'Yes, I understand.'

'Amraphel of Shinar is the first king mentioned.'

'Are we going to discuss all fourteen now?'

'I know you are not a man of patience, Mr Roy, but if you would only allow me to finish?' Delfino flashed him a knowing smile. 'The second king was Arioch of Ellasar. Researchers Aalders and Leupold both hypothesised that Ellasar could be identified with the city of Larsa on the lower Euphrates, since Ellasar and Larsa are phonetically similar, and it might be possible to find a link. But then I read more of Leupold's work and found something that left me spellbound.' Delfino widened his eyes in mock amazement. 'Leupold suggested,' he continued, 'that Arioch of the Bible was none other than Rim-Sin of Larsa. He acceded to the throne in 2098 BC, and according to Leupold, the expedition of Genesis 14 can be dated back to 2088 BC. Leupold also wrote that Rim-Sin was a great king who conquered the entire Mesopotamia and the Indus Valley...therein lies the connection, you see!'

'And you thought you'd find Rim-Sin's tomb and sell the story to the Vatican, positioning Ram Chandra, the lead deity of the world's largest non-Abrahamic religion, as a biblical king from the Middle East. You really believed this idea could help revive people's faith in Christianity?' Eric smirked.

'You are not a businessman, Mr Roy; you can't imagine how many times that idea could be sold, to how many institutes and organizations!'

'Count, shall we kill them now?' Bill was seething, even as Delfino continued to smile at Eric.

'I only make deals with winners, Bill, and it looks like they are the winners who lived to tell their tale. And you never know, I might decide to make an alliance with him someday!'

Eric stepped forward, looking up at a visibly infuriated Bill in his military fatigues. 'You look rather foolish, Bill. The English have a word for it—Popinjay…isn't that correct, Count?'

'You relentlessly impress me, Mr Roy.' Delfino burst into laughter.

'We saw Nassar flee, and while his hired forces lay buried under thousands of tonnes of debris at this moment,' Eric glanced at the ruins and shrugged, 'his brotherhood bastards are somewhere out there in the desert.' He looked around the wilderness, with the Zagros Mountains on his right and the desert stretching all the way to the horizon on his left. 'They will keep on threatening lives till the time Nassar is alive.'

'So, Mr Roy,' Delfino said, trying to bring some enthusiasm into his voice, 'it seems you are the one I'll be dealing with hereafter.'

'I don't understand.'

'This is still a big project for me! I need your knowledge and support to help me play the cards in favour of the Delfino Group.'

'What exactly do you mean?'

'I need you to help me with some fundamental questions—how can we build upon the link between Ram Chandra and Rim-Sin? How can we create a believable connection between Rim-Sin and Arioch and the Garden of Eden?'

'Or perhaps you could hop back into your helicopter with all your sinister-looking companions, especially that one in fatigues, and return where you came from.' Eric glanced coldly from Delfino to Bill, and back. 'But, if you really want help, I'd suggest adding a sensible knowledge organisation to the plethora of evil enterprises your group owns and inviting really talented people on board.'

'May I ask you to elaborate?' Delfino raised his eyebrows in a mock-excited expression.

'After you arrive in Udine, establish a non-profit organisation called "In the Name of History" foundation, to be headed by two of my friends here—Aurin Roy and Marina Martinez. Ms Jennifer Roberts and Dr Tracy Layard of the British Museum will be appointed as the deputy directors of Archives and Lost Languages respectively, and Dr Huntley as the technical director.'

Sensing Delfino's interest, Eric continued, 'The purpose of the organisation will be to develop innovative ideas for archiving and preserving knowledge and history and funding historical research and archaeological excavations. In contrast with your previous focus on labelling history with a price tag and trading in it, through this non-profit you will preserve history. However, should you choose not to establish this foundation, I will take all of the information I have on your antiquity-smuggling activities and disperse it through world media. Then perhaps you will come around to discuss things.' Eric paused to give Delfino time to ponder. 'If you acknowledge all the wrongs you've done in the past, Count, I'd suggest you accept this benign proposal.'

Delfino nodded thoughtfully. 'Maybe you're right. It'll definitely be a good business idea and an easy way to rope you in... With an archaeologist and academician like you on board and with the right kind of stories, the value of my ancient artefacts business will increase manifold. Let me see!' With that, he turned and began to walk towards the helicopter.

'No! You will say yes, and you will do it now!' a voice commanded from the back.

'Marina!' Eric cried, his mouth agape.

'And you will take all of us out of this place to Udine, along with the two injured people inside the cave,' she ordered.

♦

Delfino turned, with his eyebrows raised. 'Ah, I see...you're still the same unwavering girl.'

'I have done everything for you, Uncle,' Marina said pleadingly as tears formed in her eyes. 'I want you to listen to me this once.'

Delfino nodded with a smile. 'I will, Marina,' his tone mellowed. 'You are my only loving niece after all.'

'You better, because I have done everything you wanted me to do until now! You made me a thief. You made me a spy!' Marina's voice broke.

Without another word, Delfino waved the bodyguards towards the cave entrance. Minutes later, they came out carrying Dr Huntley and Suleiman on crude stretchers made with long rubbermats. Aurin looked at Eric and rolled his eyes. Eric kept a poker face and signalled him to get inside their ride. They walked up to Marina and followed Delfino and his men towards the helicopters. The team, along with their injured, climbed into the larger one after Delfino and the doors were slammed shut. The rotors began to whir, and within moments the Bell Relentless began its takeoff, its counter-rotating propellers sounding like a pair of industrial concrete mixers.

The sudden uproar and quivering motion caused the lump that had been choking Aurin's throat to break into a stream of tears. *There will be no Father Smit to see or talk to any more. Not today, not tomorrow—never. He is gone forever.*

The take-off was completed with a sudden lift of the nose. The mighty cliff above the Shanidar Cave danced like a yo-yo in front of Aurin until all he could see was the Prussian blue sky, and all he could feel was the sinking in his heart.

The pilot swung the helicopter around until he found the appropriate compass heading, then rammed down on the stick and gunned the throttles. Aurin was thrust back in his seat, and the copter was suddenly in motion, tearing through the sky a hundred feet above the ground. Eric, Aurin and Marina looked through the window at the thick cloud of smoke that engulfed the upper half of the cliff they had climbed a few hours ago. Their hearts throbbed along with the heavy sound from the big turbo shafts that blotted out everything, smudging recent and old memories in their minds.

EIGHTY-TWO

'His niece?' Eric sneered at Marina as he treated Suleiman's wound with a paste made from crushed leaves of the mythical plant they'd brought back.

Suleiman had been unconscious and still bleeding when Eric had first checked his pulse inside the helicopter. The bullet had left a deep wound in his shoulder. Eric applied a thick layer of the herbal paste on the wound and covered it with his handkerchief.

'A spy in the house of love!' Marina chuckled.

'That's cool!' Aurin said. 'An archaeologist who reads novels!'

'And a novel from the fifties, no less,' Marina smiled.

'After my father left me and my mother, Delfino was the man who helped us and took up the responsibility of my education. He is really not as bad as he seems!' she sighed. 'He needed someone with an academic background to help with his business, so I joined his group.'

'Why did you join Dr Huntley and Dr Hussein in the Nineveh excavation?' Eric asked.

'That was my plan,' Delfino said from his seat behind the pilot. 'When I heard Dr Hussein was up for a new excavation in Nimrud, I knew I had to plant someone on his team, because Nimrud corresponded with the coordinates of one of the locations Tessitori had noted. I had this hunch that something big might be unearthed if the excavation went well.'

'That's right…' Dr Huntley groaned in his makeshift bed on the floor of the chopper, 'that was exactly what I was trying to tell Eric when I met him at Kolkata airport—that something big might be unearthed soon…'

'You were right, Dr Huntley,' Eric nodded thoughtfully. 'We'll come back to that, but for now, too many things remain to be cleaned up!'

'I know what you mean,' Marina said. 'But I believe it's going to be a very nice evening in Udine, for all of us.'

'How very optimistic!' Aurin said.

'It beats the alternative, which is all that matters!'

'What alternative would that be?'

'Us being buried right now under tonnes of debris in the heavenly Garden of Eden.' She pointed a finger in the direction of the cliff they had just left behind. 'Dead to the world forever.'

EPILOGUE

Eric, Aurin and Dr Huntley stayed on for a week in Udine as Delfino's guests. The very first thing Eric did was send some samples of the plant, secured in an extremely sophisticated FedEx package, to Dr Naidu for testing, as Suleiman's wound showed signs of recovering within just three hours of applying the paste.

Within the first two days, the groundwork to establish In the Name of History, the foundation that Eric had suggested, was completed and the papers signed by three of the founding directors—Aurin, Marina and Dr Huntley. Dr Jennifer Roberts and Dr Tracy Layard both agreed to the proposition over a Skype conference and promised to finish the formalities in a month. The work of the foundation would start in another couple of months, and there was nothing much for the directors to do until then, so Marina went to see her mother in Barcelona.

The office of Cardinal Clemente, supported by Delfino Antiquities International, called a press meet in the Vatican to announce the discovery of the Garden of Eden. Eric Roy, Dr Muzahem Hussein, Marina Martinez, Aurin Roy, Father Gebrand Smit, Dr Peter Huntley and Mohammad Suleiman were felicitated as the pioneers of this unthinkable discovery. During the press meet, a ceremonial prayer was also offered for Dr Hussein and Father Smit. Suleiman could not be present at the felicitation, for he was off on a holiday with his family at an undisclosed location in Italy as guests of the Count of Udine. The good news was that he recovered in three days and his wound was almost completely healed by then. Delfino Antiquities International was mentioned as the sponsor of the mission, and Dr Tracy Layard, great-great-grand daughter of Austin Henry Layard, received mention for her path-breaking success at deciphering a spoken language that had been lost for four thousand years and for contributing thus to the success of the mission. The same day, the Pope inaugurated a photography exhibition in a prestigious Vatican gallery where large canvas prints of photographs taken during the expedition by Aurin Roy were on display. The Garden of Eden came alive in front of nine hundred selected guests and members of the media in the four-thousand-square-foot gallery, shimmering in the light of several crystal chandeliers.

The Vatican and Italian media, followed by the world media, published the story of the discovery with select video clips of the heavenly garden and the four rivers. Branded as the 'Discovery of the Millennium', the story created a huge stir and remained a major topic of discussion for people all over the world for some time.

In another seminar, the Pope announced the Vatican's plans to co-fund a series of geological, geophysical, botanical and zoological surveys, in association with some other foundations, of the newly discovered and already partially destroyed wonder of the world.

In his speech, the Pope talked about Francis Bacon's seventeenth-century interpretation of the Genesis, which wrongly promoted the subjugation of nature by mankind. His Holiness said, 'In his *Interpretation of Nature,* Bacon argued that control of nature was lost in the fall but could be regained through its conquest.' He added, 'Bacon used metaphors like "the image of nature is female, which is to be penetrated". This exploitation needs to be stopped, and the earth's resources need to be restored.' In a truly landmark gesture, he said, 'The Vatican wishes to take the first step towards that restoration and to fight climate change by commissioning more scientific research works and by documenting knowledge and relevant insights.'

◆

The festive season had dawned in India by the time they left Udine. Dr Huntley wanted to return to Trongsa, Bhutan, via Paro. Shaken by the events of the last few weeks and the grave losses they had suffered, Eric and Aurin couldn't think clearly about where to go or what the future held for them. This rather fantastical adventure had aroused a strange feeling of wanderlust in their minds, and deep inside, they both thought they would never find anything to satisfy it.

Eventually, Aurin decided to spend some time with Sarah and Jennifer at their Worcester house before flying to India. 'I'll get Jenny to sign the foundation documents as well.'

'The UK is not a bad idea, actually!' Eric said. 'I can tag along with you, if you don't mind, and stay with the Roberts sisters for a few days. I was anyway toying with the idea of paying a visit to Tracy to congratulate her for her momentous work in the field of language, discuss matters about the new foundation and above all, thank her.'

It was clear that neither of them wanted to go back home to Kolkata so soon. They would no longer be able to visit Father Smit at St John's Church in Chinsurah on weekends and spend time with him, talking about the best days of their lives spent on adventures together.

There were too many memories they had lived together, but in the end, not nearly enough to fill the emptiness in their hearts.

◆

Dr Huntley and the Roy siblings sat in the brand new glass-and-marble departure lounge of the Trieste–Friuli Veneza Giulia Airport, drinking complimentary coffee and waiting for their respective connecting flights to Paro and London.

Eric was rifling through his phone to keep his restless mind engaged. He came across a group photograph, taken a year back on the terrace of Dr Huntley's palatial house in Trongsa, Bhutan. 'It was such a sunny day...' He smiled. 'Good food, good people, good conversation—good times.' Father Smit smiled back at him from the centre of the picture. Eric grazed his fingers over Father Smit's face as he wept. 'I remember my promise, Father Smit,' he whispered.

Then he felt Aurin's gentle touch on his shoulder. 'I am sorry, Ric Da... I am really sorry about Father Smit.'

'So am I, Aurin.' Eric wiped his tears with the back of his hand.

'Temples fell, buildings crumbled, tombs were obliterated, and people were taken...' Dr Huntley said softly. 'Grieve not, my friend...be healed, for we are all flawed, we fall and we fail. Each one of us, whether with knowledge or without. We contribute to the suffering around us. If not with forethought, then by our pretence of innocence, our comfortable condemnation and our arrogance. When these frailties are relinquished, all becomes right in our thought and action. And therein lies every man's sacrifice and his salvation!' He sat breathing slowly for a while. Then he added, 'You need to find out what your salvation lies in, Eric... We all just need to find that one thing!'

Dr Huntley got up and walked towards the coffee kiosk.

'What now?' Aurin asked, looking at Eric.

Eric's eyes took on a distant look. 'I will keep my promise. I'll find out what secret Father Smit wanted to pass on to me, and then I'll hunt down Nassar and his brotherhood bastards and kill every last one of them.'

'Let's do it, Ric da... I am in!

AUTHOR'S NOTE

Disclaimer: Many of the book's crucial plotlines and twists are discussed in this section. Please do not read ahead if you haven't finished reading the book yet.

The idea of *Tomb of God* (*ToG*) first came to me in early 2014. I had just joined the BBC and was travelling with a colleague. We got into a discussion over the epics of the world and ended up comparing the Greek and Indian epic categories. After a good debate, we both agreed that these categories, and therefore the narrative forms that gave rise to them, must be brought together so that they may be reconsidered in light of their mutual illumination. I added that we definitely also needed to bring the Bible into the discussion.

Such comparisons of epics from different cultures could help in reformulating the more general philosophies that encompass them. This fresh comparative look could offer insights into the cross-cultural problem of bridging the human–divine divide on which narrative forms of this genre centred.

That was when the idea of discovering the Sanskrit epic Ramayana in the pages of history and writing a research-based thriller around it flashed in my mind. By the time our plane landed, I had started outlining my research plan.

I loved the concept but decided to reserve the idea for my second book since my first book, *The Job Charnock Riddle*, was almost ready. I knew developing the idea would require thorough research, which I couldn't undertake at the time.

On one of my paper presentation trips to the BBC headquarters in London, I wrote to the authorities of The British Museum and The British Library and stayed back in London after my presentation to complete my research for *ToG*. I paid innumerable visits to the museum and the library and made it through several sleepless days and nights before I could say I had enough material to finish my book.

During my days in London, I searched through volumes of ancient documents. I had already studied the architectural wonders of the Mesopotamian and pre-Harappan civilisations and done a comparative study of their scripts and pictograms. Access to the British Library, the British Museum and the research papers and books I found there on Sumerian and pre-Harappan scripts proved beyond fruitful, because I managed to unearth some documents that had never been issued to anyone. And then, by a life-changing twist, I got access to the BBC next-gen technology hub—the BBC Blue Room. These chance discoveries helped me expand my storyline beyond the plot I had originally developed.

Tomb of God would have been a six-hundred-page book, since I had enough research material to pull off that big a story. But my first critic, my wife, urged me to stop at the 450-page mark, and then my agent, Suhail Mathur of The Book Bakers, insisted on staying within the threshold of 100,000 words. I am thankful they did that, but the sad part of the whole affair is that some of my best findings could never make it to the shorter version. If a movie based on this book is made, I will try to get those parts included as bonus material for DVD release! As for the research and the archaeological facts contained in *ToG*, I personally attest to their accuracy.

Rim-Sin of the Sumerian King List resonates accurately with Ram Chandra of the Ramayana, as 'Sin' in ancient Sumerian meant the moon. His period of reign corresponds with the period of the Ramayana. Not only that, Rim-Sin's brother, Warad-Sin—a name that echoes Bharat Chandra—had ruled for twelve years prior to Rim-Sin, exactly as Ram Chandra's brother Bharat is described to have done in the *Dasrath Jataka*. Rim-Sin's father, Kudur Mabug, was from a place called Der, and scholars think this was actually Mohenjodaro. Some British scholars also argue that a river named Harayu in Herat, Afghanistan, was the Sarayu or Saraju of the Ramayana.

Details of the excavation of Queen Yaba's tomb is accurate. In fact a girl's corpse was discovered who didn't finish coiling the ribbon up her hand when she died.

Luigi Pio Tessitori was a real scholar and made a huge contribution to the discovery of a large part of our history. Historical details of all the ancient civilisations given in this book are entirely accurate (as are their exact locations). The ruins of Nimrud and Nineveh can still be seen today in northern Iraq. Shanidar Cave, where the prehistoric Neanderthal remains were discovered from the Zagros Mountains, can also be visited.

I hope my theories about deciphering a lost spoken language and deciphering the Indus scripts open up new ways of looking at decoding ancient languages and scripts. The mrutha sanjeevani discussion in the book was written in consultation with scholars, and the facts quoted from authentic sources.

The 'Across the Hindukush' journey chapters took me over seven months and two air journeys over the described route to write. The amount of research and satellite-mapping that went behind describing that journey was fanatical, all in the singular hope that the adventurer in each one of you feels part of the journey along with Aurin and Father Smit. I wish some of you who read *ToG* go on to visit some of the historical places I've described in the book to see them for yourselves.

If any of my readers wishes to learn more about the civilisations alluded to in the book, there are several non-fiction books that explore the period I've tried capturing in my story. I have included a reference list at the end of the book for those history enthusiasts.

A lot of sound, phonetics and linguistics are described in this book, for which I spent a huge amount of time with university professors, next-gen computer programmers and techies. The idea of writing and replaying sound in *ToG* was written in consultation with scientists.

And lastly, the details of hieroglyphics and other lesser-known

Egyptian forms of scripts are all accurate. The process of deciphering phonetic values of a 4000-year-old lost language as described in the book is absolutely logical and based on real research carried out by authentic sources. I hope some day this methodology is prototyped successfully.

A few of the friends who read the manuscript of *ToG* have asked me how I could blend fact with fiction so seamlessly in the book. I take that as a compliment, hinting that I have managed to do a good job of creating a believable environment inside my readers' minds. Honestly, my intention was to build a simple and logical bridge to connect the time, and places and the human–divine divide, and to do it subtly. Everything you read in *Tomb of God* has actually happened in my mind, and in my dreams, for five long years before it was translated to print.

For additional information about this novel and personal queries, please visit victorghoshe.com or write to vghoshe@gmail.com

REFERENCES

Avalos, Hector, *Illness and Health Care in the Ancient Near East: The Role of the Temple in Greece, Mesopotamia, and Israel* (Scholars Press, 1995).

Edwards, I.E.S., C.J. Gadd and N.G.L. Hammond (eds), *Cambridge Ancient History, vol. 1* (Cambridge University Press, 1971).

Hallo, William and William Kelly Simpson, *The Ancient Near East* (Harcourt, Brace, Jovanovich, 1971).

Joshi, Jagat Pati and Asko Parpola (eds), *Corpus of Indus Seals and Inscriptions, vols 1–3.1* (Suomalainen Tiedeakatemia, 1987, 1991, 2010).

Kramer, Samuel Noah, *The Sumerians, Their History, Culture and Character* (University of Chicago Press, 1963).

Lahiri, Nayanjot, *Finding Forgotten Cities* (Seagull Books, 2013).

Rao, S.R., *The Decipherment of the Indus Script* (Asia Publishing, 1982).

Richard, Meredith, *Driven Together: Historic First Crossing of Asia's New Highway to the West* (Mercury Books, 2008).

Sjöberg, Åke W. (ed.), *Sumerian Dictionary of the University Museum* (University of Pennsylvania, 1984).

Stiebing Jr., William H. and Susan H. Helft, *Ancient Near Eastern History and Culture* (Routledge, 2017).

Wheeler, M., *The Indus Civilization*, 3rd edition (Cambridge University Press, 1968).

ACKNOWLEDGEMENTS

My attempt at unravelling an enigma locked away for over four millennia would not have been possible without the help of a great many people from different parts of the world. The three years of research and investigation that preceded the writing of *Tomb of God* allowed me to meet experts in the fields of art, literature, history, physics, sound engineering, acoustics, linguistics, botany and cryptology, many of whom eventually became dear friends. Interestingly, several significant contributions came from absolutely unexpected sources. I wish to offer special thanks to each one of those wonderful people and mention some...

I start with the British Museum, the British Library and the Victoria & Albert Museum authorities. I specially thank Mr Hartwig Fischer, Director, British Museum, and Mr Roly Keating, Chief Executive, British Library, for the support they had extended to me for my long and odd hours of research in the Ancient Mesopotamia Gallery, Ancient Indus Gallery, and the Library Archives, and for the endless cups of free coffee.

I thank Shlomo Izre'el, Professor at the Department of Hebrew and Semitic Linguistics, Tel Aviv University, for his brilliant linguistic works on Ancient Sumeria and all his support. Thanks to the US Patent and Trademark Office for the sound writing-related artwork that is used in this book. Special thanks to Dawood Azami of the BBC Afghanistan office in the UK for detailed and insightful information about Hindukush and Afghanistan, which has infinitely enriched this book.

I am thankful to the BBC office at London for inviting me to spend time with the top-notch tech gurus in their futuristic facility named The Blue Room. My tour of that revolutionary facility and the discussions I had there helped me understand the mind-blowing possibilities held by futuristic technologies.

I am forever thankful to my family for their unfailing and tireless support. My wife Juthika and my sons, Shivank and Hrishaant, were my constant and only source of joy through the five years of rigorous work on *Tomb of God*. Having a Masters degree in Botany, Juthika helped me develop some of the technical sections of *ToG* as well. I thank my parents, my sister Monica and her family and my in-laws for their unconditional love. I thank my extended family, Beethika–Amitabh, Utpal–Geetali, Sujan–Shailey, Sam Mukherjee, Avik–Paulomi, Ranendra Goswami and Meghendra Banerjee, whose constant support through the ups and downs of my life has been indispensable.

My sincere thanks to the legendary actor Soumitra Chatterjee, for being part of the launch of my first historical fiction *The Job Charnock Riddle* (*TJCR*)—that turned out to be a remarkable success. I thank Sandeep Ray and Anik Dutta for their support. Special thanks to Shounak Ghoshal (unfortunately he is no longer with us) of *The Times of India*, who wrote fantastic reviews of *TJCR*, and to Gautam Jatia of Starmark. All of these people helped my first book reach out to its true audience, and I surely owe a part of its success to them.

Professionally, I'd like to thank my editors at Rupa Publications for appreciating the story of *Tomb of God* at the manuscript level and for believing that together we'll pull it off and make a fine addition to the Rupa arsenal. I thank my agent and friend Suhail Mathur of The Book Bakers for all his efforts to make this book better. Thanks are also due to my consulting editor Mahima Kohli for all her valuable inputs. Special thanks to my dear friends, Vish Dhamija, Kulpreet Yadav and Alaham Anil Kumar, for all their love.

Last but not the least, I'd like to thank the readers and fans of *TJCR*, librarians, booksellers and critics, who enjoyed my first novel and recommended it to others. Many of my readers wrote to me and showered immeasurable love—I remain thankful to them. At this stage of my career, I need all the love and encouragement I can get.

Since the publication of *TJCR* in January 2016, I have heard from so many of you, requesting me to write another book soon. Alas, I wish it was that easy. I love to write historical thrillers, but they take a huge amount of research even before I develop the plot—and you guys read too fast. But I promise to keep writing if you guys keep reading.

In the end, I hope you found *Tomb of God* was worth the wait.